PREFACE

Embers streaked across the grid-lined sky, dancing as their edges burned and leaving glowing amber trails in their wake. I watched as they cascaded, one by one, like snowflakes from a swollen cloud. But I knew better. Snowflakes were beautiful and innocent things. Their kisses were chill and playful—not like the embers that bit my tear-soaked cheeks, laying waste to the life I'd grown so fond of.

I'd been warned.

I didn't listen.

THE CHANNEL

STARLA MOORE

For information regarding permission, contact Starla Moore via email at starla@explorethechannel.com.

Published by Starla Moore in Beavercreek, Ohio.

Library of Congress Control Number: 2021921936

ISBN:

979-8-9851595-2-3 EBook

979-8-9851595-0-9 Paperback

979-8-9851595-1-6 Hardcover

 Created with Vellum

This book is dedicated to my wonderful Granny, who left Earth in August of 2020.

You would have hated all of the bad words, blood, and violence so I wrote CieCie's character just for you.

QUADRANT 5

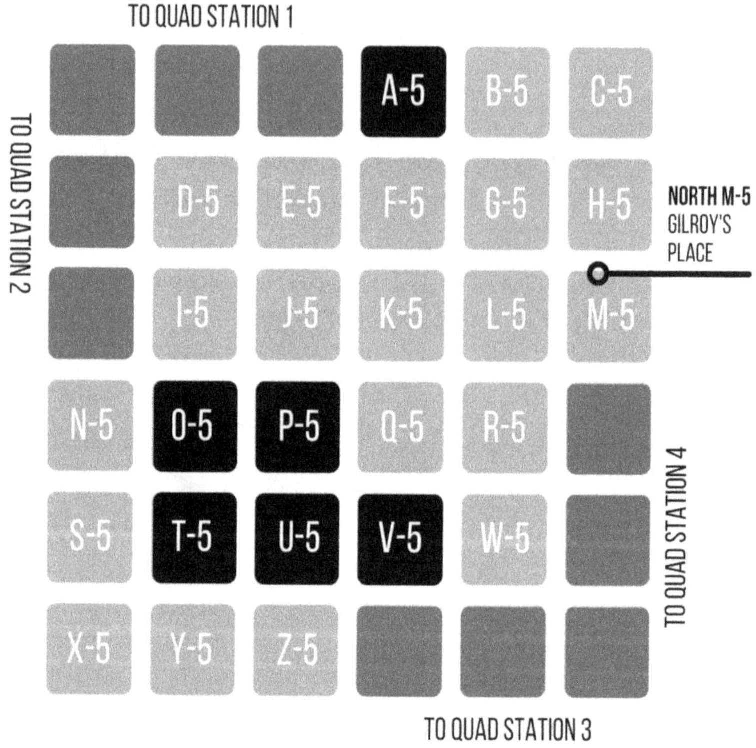

TO QUAD STATION 1

TO QUAD STATION 2

			A-5	B-5	C-5
	D-5	E-5	F-5	G-5	H-5
	I-5	J-5	K-5	L-5	M-5
N-5	O-5	P-5	Q-5	R-5	
S-5	T-5	U-5	V-5	W-5	
X-5	Y-5	Z-5			

NORTH M-5
GILROY'S
PLACE

TO QUAD STATION 4

TO QUAD STATION 3

- A-5: FIBER TO DIMENSION 14
- O-5: FIBER TO DIMENSION 15
- P-5: FIBER TO DIMENSION 18
- T-5: FIBER TO DIMENSION 16
- U-5: FIBER TO DIMENSION 17
- V-5: FIBER TO DIMENSION 19

 EDGE STATION

 STANDARD BUILDING

 DIMENSIONAL FIBER

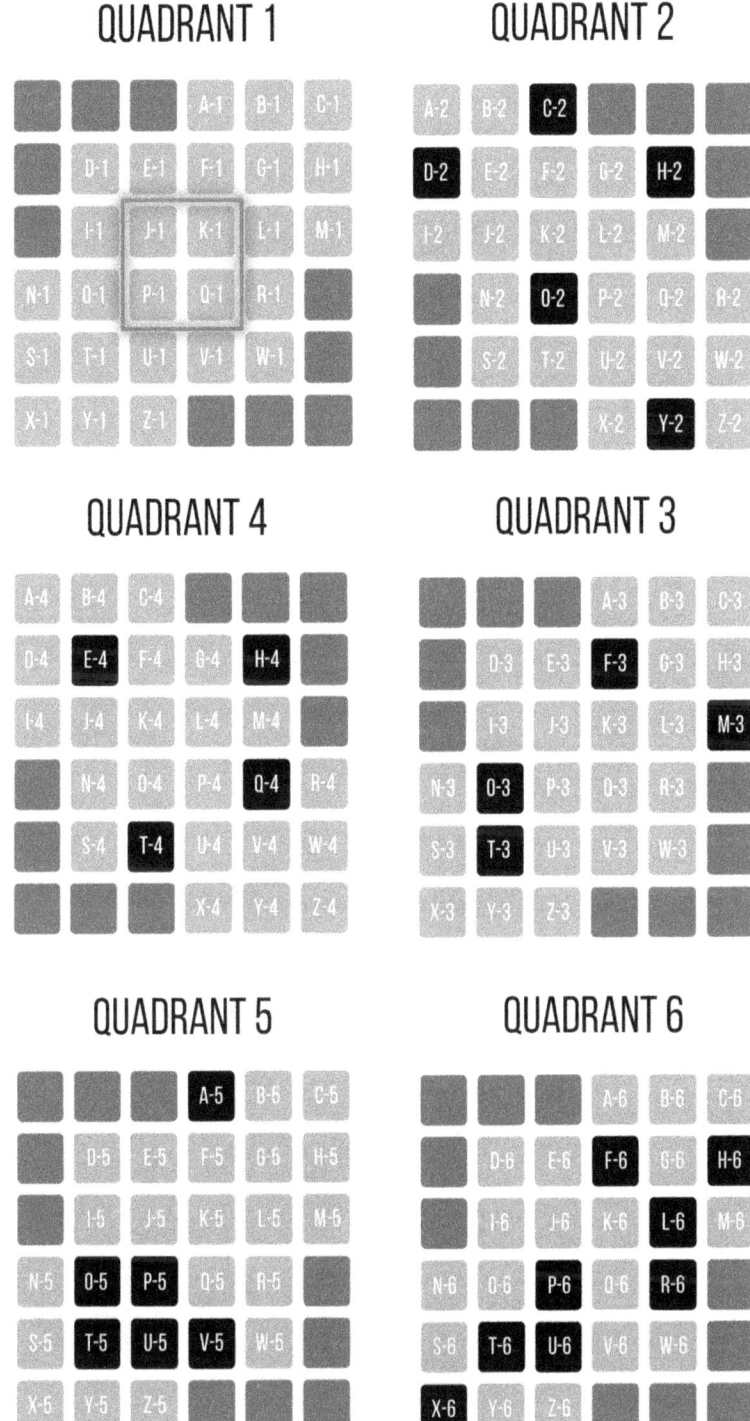

CONTENTS

1

THE OFFER

It was a sweltering late summer afternoon when I started packing my bags, anxiously awaiting the phone call that would bring me one step closer to escape. Not that someone like me had anything worthy of escaping from. *Escape* was a harsh word—or so it seemed at the time. This trip was more of a breather—a quick getaway to break up the weekly monotony I'd grown so complacent with.

It was the type of trip I'd daydreamed about ever since high school graduation. One from where sun-kissed social media blondes posted snapshots, posing in front of landmarks with fancy travel-sized lattes in hand. Granted, I'd be alone for this trip, and of course, there would be no one to take photos of me, even if I'd wanted that in the first place.

Don't ruin this. I tucked another shirt into my bag and shuddered a pace back from the gusting AC unit that hummed busily from my second-story apartment window. Who would have imagined—me, the queen of overthinking, ruining a moment of excitement and opportunity by tripping through the worst possible thoughts my stupid brain could generate?

Anyone who looked hard enough would see the evidence everywhere—paradoxically so because the evidence was nowhere. My apartment remained in a constant state of near-militant organization. Not a dust particle to be found on even the highest of my Ikea bookshelves or the lowest of thrifted end tables. Organization was my antidote for anxiety. I gravitated toward the controllables, especially now that my life was teetering on a razor's edge of uncertainty. At one time, I assumed it was just a "girl" thing, but the older I grew, the more I came to realize that my overactive mind was actually just a "me" thing.

Somewhere within my psyche, there existed a rational part of me. Everywhere else, there was *her*—the part of my brain that was wild and untamed, buzzing like a million bees who each whispered obscenities into my ear at the most inconvenient times. The hive was a more honest me. It was the part that brought the unthinkable to the forefront of my consciousness, even when my rational brain held a tight lead on my lips. Some things were better left unsaid—especially at work, where I felt more like a green polka-dotted alien than an employee. The grim reminder left me cramming socks into the side pouch of my luggage at double-speed.

Even after six months working as a secretary at Premier Edge Marketing, I still wasn't sure how I managed to land the job in the first place. I'd never been a believer of fate or wishes or magic, but if luck existed, it must have been on my side.

I was significantly underqualified, plunging headfirst into the only job that would accept my limited hours due to a crammed semester at Sacramento State. Even after receiving an interview request, my imposter syndrome was crippling. Walking through the glass-paneled doors of the beautiful historic building in downtown Sacramento reverted me into a small child, putting on oversized adult clothes and pretending to go to "big people" work.

I'm not sure what I expected that day. A stuffy office? Rows of gray walled cubicles? A musty waiting room with outdated magazines and orange '70s carpeting?

My intricate illusion melted away the very moment I stepped through those green-hued double doors. Expanding out in front of me lay a massive cathedral-style room, connected from floor to ceiling with white marble pillars. The floors were as intimidating as black ice, parted at the center by a long red carpet that met the tips of my quivering toes. At the end of the pathway towered a tall oak desk. Even vacant, it terrified me. Whoever usually occupied the position would have ample opportunity to examine guests before they ever stood in front of it. What an incredibly long and awkward walk of shame that could have been.

I should turn around. Pretend that I walked into the wrong building and quickly exit before anyone notices me.

Just as I pivoted to retreat, a thunderous voice called out.

"Vivian? Vivian Gilovich?"

I froze in place. *Too late now.*

A tall, olive-skinned man in a heather gray suit was rounding the corner of the room's far corridor.

I composed, swallowed, exhaled.

"Yes...uh...that's me?" The words spilled out as a question, and I silently cursed myself. *You're in over your head.* So much for creating a strong first impression.

"Vivian," the man greeted me again as he approached. "I'm so grateful that you were able to make it. My name is James."

He said the name expectantly as if it held a weight that I was meant to recognize. I scanned his broad face—stern but friendly with dark stubble dotting from his neck, all the way to his high leathery cheekbones. No, I didn't recognize this man at all. A rectangular glimmer reflecting on his chest caught my eye.

James C. Rivera, CEO
Premier Edge Marketing, CA Division

The freaking CEO of the company! My face flushed with heat as my gaze darted back to meet his now-narrowed eyes. *Crap!* Any good potential hire would have spent more time researching the company and its chain of command.

If I start running now, maybe I can make it back to my cab before it pulls away.

No. Damn it, no. I could do this.

"Mr. Rivera," I choked out, extending a trembling hand. "I'm so sorry. I was expecting—well—I guess I actually *wasn't* expecting—"

"No need to explain, Miss Gilovich," James chuckled as he took my hand with a confident grip. One, two, three hard shakes, and then he released.

Handshakes were not something I ever formally learned, having been raised by my mother. My dad wasn't around to teach me all the important "fatherly" life skills depicted in family-friendly sitcoms. I quickly cataloged the grip and the number of shakes in the back of my mind. *One, two, three, release.* No doubt, I'd be shaking a few more hands today. Especially if I somehow landed this job. Not that the war effort was going great so far.

"Normally, I don't greet our new talents," James continued, seemingly oblivious to my awkward gestures, "but unfortunately, we've found ourselves a bit short-staffed this season. Though hey, that's why you're here, right?"

The word "talents" caught me off guard. In my twenty-one years of life, I'd been called many things—talented was not one of them. I retained my carefully constructed smile as he chuckled again, so eager and so bold in his assumption that I'd soon blend right in with the marble pillars.

To my surprise, there was no interview to follow. No sitting awkwardly at his desk, being questioned about my work ethic, strengths and weaknesses, and responding with the very best kiss-ass answers I could vomit out, which honestly was a bit disappointing. Especially since I'd rehearsed my responses all morning.

"My biggest weakness? Well, sir, I'd say that I become very impatient when a project runs beyond its deadline. Any job worth doing is worth doing efficiently, that's what I always say!"

None of my meticulously prepared script was needed as James led me through the back corridor of the massive entry room and into an endless hall of propped oak doors that held long boardroom tables and solid wood desks. Every office was furnished with the stereotypical qualities of a television lawyer's office. Sharp-edged terracotta leather couches, dark-paneled wood grain walls, and reflective mirrored trays adorned with decanters of caramel-colored liquor that shimmered brightly in the morning light of the massive panoramic windows. The smell of brandy and old books loomed heavily in the air, which made the charming old building feel even more like it was plucked from a different era.

James introduced me to several men in freshly pressed suits and busty women in pencil skirts with glossy red lips as we toured the endless hall of doors. Everyone was absurdly polished—unnaturally even. I felt ridiculously underdressed in my paper-bag-waisted pants and frilled white button-up. Thankfully, if James had been disgruntled by my attire, he never showed it.

Instead, he explained the roles that were tied to each of the golden nameplates tacked to the left of every door. His tone mimicked that of a proud hunter, parading me past a wall of exotic taxidermy animal heads. There was Janie Lynn, Head of Accounting; Dennis Snyder, Marketing and Public Relations

Specialist; Brittany Keys, Junior Marketing Division; Heron Lawrence, who was apparently MIA, presumably out with the flu.

After a while, I stopped trying to memorize all the names and roles, convincing myself that these were things I'd surely nail down later on. Though I had to admit, James spoke of these individuals as if they were rare catches, hand-selected from the wilds of LinkedIn.

Why was he so intent on hiring an inexperienced undergraduate like me? Surely he'd seen that my resume stated I had no prior experience in marketing. Maybe he'd needed to fill some government quota that stated every company must have a certain ratio of barely-qualified employees. The thought was sobering, but I pushed it aside.

I gravitated toward a more palatable conclusion—maybe he thought I was pretty. A cheerful young face to have around the office and who would smile warmly when answering the phone or filing papers or bringing him coffee. For that conclusion, I couldn't truly be offended. With a mountain of textbooks tethered to my back like a lead weight, I didn't have room to be choosy. I could make this glass slipper fit.

After the tour concluded, I signed off on my NDA, submitted my background check, and was given a laminated photo ID badge, all on the same morning I'd first walked through the doors of Premier Edge Marketing. I couldn't believe it. Me, the queen of overthinking, had landed a job at one of the most prestigious marketing firms in Sacramento!

Thankfully, Mr. Rivera was patient with me during my first week, even through all my embarrassing questions and mistakes. Being a secretary in real life was surprisingly different than how movies depicted the role.

There was no filing of papers or warmly answering the phone only to put the caller on hold. No running to refill the coffee mugs of those in positions more important than mine. Most of my time was spent alone in my tiny office, stapling papers and banishing spam emails into oblivion. I wasn't permitted to explore the building or listen in on meetings. Occasionally, a door would slam as I passed through the hall, leaving me to wonder what secrets were being uttered within.

Working at Premier wasn't all bad, though. During my first week, I became very close with one co-worker in particular— Mr. Rivera's adopted son, Ryan Race. To be fair, the man made himself impossible to ignore. His handsome smile hung framed in gold on the vast wall of the firm's super-star players, having worked closely under his father for several years. Despite his high stature, Ryan was absurdly kind to me—or so it felt, since I was no more than the back-office secretary, and he was one of the leading influencers of the company.

In my first week working for the firm, Ryan popped into my stuffy makeshift office to bring me coffee. By week two, it was coffee and a blueberry bagel with cream cheese—plus a handful of office gossip that left us both giggling like children. On week three, he entered my office empty-handed and instead invited me to join him out on the street for lunch, where we discussed our life goals and the places we'd like to someday travel. This became our daily pattern, so comfortably predictable that I eventually stopped packing my own lunches.

As with everything that happened over the past six months, Ryan and I were no exception to the rule. We never formally declared that we were "dating," but it was obvious to everyone around the office that we were a unit.

Ryan was young and ambitious, the walls of his office decorated with degrees in business, marketing, and human resource management. And of course, he had a dashing face to go with the prestigious reputation. Blonde combed back hair, charming green eyes, and a smile that certainly aided him in his many decorated accomplishments. He was textbook perfect. My job was textbook perfect. It all seemed utterly criminal. How had I been so lucky over these last six months, and when would this insane streak of luck skid to a devastating halt?

A sudden buzz at my hip jarred me from my Ryan-Race-reverie.

Right. The phone call.

"Hello, Mr. Rivera," I answered, folding another shirt into a tight bundle as I held the phone between my cheek and shoulder.

"Vivian!" Mr. Rivera greeted. "I hope you're enjoying your day off."

"Oh, yes. Not so much a day off, though. I'm busy packing as we speak."

I stuffed the shirt into the edge of my overstuffed carry-on bag. This would be my first trip via air, and the idea of checking a bag was far too unappealing due to my knack of imagining the worst-case scenarios. I'd read too many gruesome horror stories of suitcases going on adventures separate from their owners and ending up in far-flung airports or never appearing again at all. I only owned a few nice outfits, and I wasn't willing to risk losing them.

"Ah, excited about the trip, I presume?"

My small adventure to Los Angeles wasn't scheduled until Friday morning, and it was currently only Monday night. I knew James would expect nothing less from me, though. My habitual overplanning occasionally had its perks.

"Just excited to get away for a while, I suppose. I've never been to LA."

Aside from the short trips to the ocean I'd taken with my mom when I was a child, I'd never been much for leaving the comforts of home. But this trip held so many new opportunities and new possibilities. A paid escape from the office would be good for my soul.

"Well, in that case, I have some good news," James continued. "I've got your tickets booked for 6:00 a.m. Friday. You'll be staying at Hotel Belair, where I've set you up with an executive suite."

I froze. The pair of jeans I'd been folding dropped to the floor as I took the phone from its wedged position on my shoulder.

"Oh, Mr. Rivera!" I sputtered. "You didn't need to do that!"

He ignored my interjection as if I hadn't spoken at all, though he playfully added, "Now, Vivian, generally we encourage our talent not to use company funds for extracurriculars. However, what you do after 8:00 p.m. is completely up to you. I hear the hotel pool has a bar right in the water! And Dennis once told me that they have the best cocktails in all of LA, if you can believe a word that man says."

My face flushed. I wasn't even sure if I had a bathing suit. If I did, it surely didn't fit me anymore. Not after six months of cafe lunches with Ryan.

"Mr. Rivera," I sighed. "You are so kind. Really, though, you didn't need to go through all this trouble. I would have been perfectly content with a room at the Red Roof."

"Nonsense," James snorted. "You're my newest star pupil, Miss Gilovich. This is just a taste of the travel opportunities to come. If all goes well with our client in LA, we may just need to book you onto our big trip to France this winter."

Oh, France! What I wouldn't give to travel abroad—to see the architecture, to taste the food, to experience the culture. *What did I do to deserve this?*

"That would be absolutely incredible, Mr. Rivera. I can't thank you enough. If there's anything at all I can do—"

"No, Vivian, you've done more in the last six months than I

ever could have asked of you. You're very important to us, and you become more important by the minute. This is the least I can do. And again, I'm so sorry that Ryan couldn't join you on your trip. Maybe next time."

His directness warmed my cheeks. This was not a subject I wanted to discuss, especially one-on-one over the phone. Dating coworkers was obviously against traditional workplace culture, and though we didn't flaunt our relationship, most people within the firm were aware that Ryan and I were seeing each other. But his own father? It seemed so wrong.

"It's no issue at all, sir," I rushed out the words, painting over my genuine hope of someday traveling with Ryan. "I'm excited to spend a bit of time on my own. Clear my headspace a bit, you know?"

Once again, James seemed to ignore my interjection.

"Well, Vivian, I hope you have a great night. You'll find everything you need for the trip on your desk first thing tomorrow morning. Look for a big yellow envelope."

"Thank you so much, Mr. Rivera, for everything."

Click. James never said goodbye.

After my bag was packed tight, I decided to call Ryan. He was ecstatic to hear the news of my booking arrangements, though I was positive that his father had likely clued him in earlier today. Mostly, I think he was just excited to hear my voice speak the words. I was fairly certain Ryan had it in his head that someday I'd climb the company ranks to stand beside him as one of the firm's all-stars. The big names at the firm. The most respected. *The somebodys.*

My expectations weren't nearly as high. Ryan had a big-wig father and several college degrees under his belt, as did everyone else whose 8x10 photos adorned the long hall of Premier. They had all worked very hard to be there. They deserved to be there. The thought of being an "all-star" seemed delusional for someone like me. Even after six months, I still felt like a heinous criminal who had been smuggled in on the bottom of someone's shoe.

And yet somehow, I was booked for a flight to LA to meet with a potential client who, I was told, would cause a chain reaction with the possibility of landing several more clients around the world. This wasn't "secretary work." I was being given a monumental opportunity. My stomach raged like a tide. So much pressure weighed on my shoulders. I had to get this right.

"This is cause for celebration, Viv!" Ryan said. "You're all packed? You have nothing important to do tonight?"

I glanced at the large vintage clock hanging above the TV in my tiny bedroom. It was only 5:00 p.m.

"Nope, nothing important on the agenda tonight."

I could sense his satisfaction radiate through the phone. "How would you feel about going to dinner? Somewhere nice," he added as if the word "nice" would increase the odds that I would agree. It worked.

"Yeah, hun, that sounds great. How nice are we talking, though? Should I adhere to any specific dress codes?"

When it came to Ryan, I was never sure. It wouldn't be the first time he didn't approve of my ripped-up jeans and oversized band tees. In fact, Ryan could be downright bossy when it came to fitting in with his fancy-pants crowd.

"Viv, when have you ever followed a dress code?"

"Okay, you got me there. So jeans and a tee shirt?"

"How about jeans and a dress shirt," he suggested. "But nice jeans, please. Not the ones that are barely held together at the knees. We wouldn't want anyone to get the wrong idea."

Ryan's judgment of my casual wear was the only real topic that we squabbled over and seldom in seriousness. Though it was always light-hearted, I could tell deep down that he wished

I'd dress more "ladylike." The primitive word made me shudder. A lady, I surely was not.

"Oh yes," I rolled my eyes, hoping he could hear the gesture. "We certainly wouldn't want the waiters to confuse me for a member of that grisly murderous tee-shirt-ripped-jeans-wearing-gang the news keeps headlining."

As I spoke the words, I danced snarkily to my closet in search of a "nicer-than-a-tee" shirt. I hoped he could hear the scritch of wire hangers sliding reluctantly over the rusty bar as I sifted through my wardrobe, compliant to his request.

"I wouldn't put it past you," he went along with the joke. "You are savagely dangerous."

"Oh, yes," I agreed intensely, removing a navy blue-button down shirt from the closet to examine it in the light. "As a recognized member of the tee-and-jeans-gang, murdering cotton-nibbling moth fiends is my life. How could you ever fall for such a street criminal?"

"Moths, huh?" he chuckled. "Well, I guess I was hoping I could set you straight. You know—a rags to riches story? From the foggy streets of Sacramento to the lavish life of Mrs. Race."

My heart stopped. *What the hell?* I lowered the metal hanger, gazing into the mirror that stood across my bedroom. *Mrs. Race?* Was that Ryan's way of dropping some sort of hint? I could see the blood drain from my cheeks.

"Viv?" Ryan prompted nervously. "You there?"

I composed myself, still watchful of the dark glimmer flicking within the chestnut abyss of my eyes.

"Viv?" His voice was more panicked this time.

"Yeah, I'm here. Sorry, I thought I saw a hole in the shirt I was planning to wear tonight. It was just a lint ball. No nibbling moths on my hit list...*for now.*"

I hoped Ryan had digested my clumsy cover-up. Marriage was not something I wanted to discuss, not even in the context of a joke. Everything was so perfect right now. With work, with Ryan, with life, with my future. I couldn't imagine complicating things between us.

"Okay," he responded, seemingly convinced. "I'm very glad. For the moth's sake, at least. Pick you up at seven then?"

"Sure thing."

"And hey, Viv? Maybe put on some eyeshadow or something. Nothing crazy. I just don't want you to feel out of place. The restaurant where we're going really is quite nice."

I groaned internally but held my tongue. "Yeah, no problem. I'll be ready."

"Perfect."

Click. Not saying goodbye must run in the family.

After wedging my phone back into the tight pocket of my jeans—the same jeans I planned to wear tonight along with the *hole-less* navy button-down, I glared at my reflection in the mirror and took a few paces forward. The color returned to my cheeks, and my eyes seemed less rabbit-in-headlights. Though the more I thought about Ryan's poorly aimed joke, the more the creases reappeared. I suddenly felt very old. Too old for only being twenty-one.

Mrs. Race? Mrs. Vivian Race? I mouthed the words, tasting each syllable on the tip of my tongue. No, I didn't like the sound of that at all. Unless he hadn't been serious?

Ryan had surely just been joking. *Right?* He would never propose such an idea in the form of a joke if he had been serious...*would he?* Roller coaster up, roller coaster down. My face bubbled with heat again.

Hypothetically, what if he had been serious? Had I offended him? The hive of my conscience was growing louder by the minute.

Ryan was a bit older than I was, and from the outside, he was the type of guy who appeared to "have it all." He owned his own condo, complete with a palm tree in the front yard. He drove a new black Mercedes with an expensive model name that I could never remember. He had a wealthy father and a great job where he was known and respected by everyone. The only element missing from his picture-perfect-puzzle was a loving Stepford-style wife. Did I really want to be the missing puzzle piece of someone else's hopes and dreams? And if the answer was yes, what would happen to all of my own hopes and dreams?

It wasn't a question I expected to answer anytime soon. *Was marriage something I wanted?* We hadn't even slept together yet. Nothing—up until now—caused me to think about a future together. In my mind, I was still much too young. Marriage was this faraway thing that adults did to lessen the blow of unexpected pregnancies.

The bees hummed louder as they waltzed between the letters of the word. *Pregnancy.* What if Ryan wanted to have children someday? After all, that's the next step after marriage, right? Hell, some couples say they'll never have kids and then end up having kids anyway. Was I cut out to be a mother? How would we both be able to maintain full-time jobs? No, of course not. That would be selfish. Motherhood would likely condemn me to the life of a housewife, endlessly dusting the framed symbols of Ryan's many accomplishments without contributing any of my own...

Stop!

I forced a cleansing breath into my quivering lungs. *Was I really self inducing a panic attack over a joke?* This was beyond ridiculous. Add another gemstone to my crown. Surely, the queen of overthinking earned it. Ryan was joking. 110% joking. In fact, he had probably forgotten all about it already.

Determined to put my mental bee hive to bed, I trailed my fingers down the line of shirt buttons, holding the wire hanger awkwardly between my chin and chest. After successfully popping each button from its hole, I shrugged on the navy top over the white band Paramore tee I was wearing—Ryan could deal with it—and refastened each of the buttons, three shy from the top. Nicer than a tee-shirt but not outside of my comfort zone and just dressy enough to keep Ryan's fancy-pants happy. My fingers flitted to my shoulder-length charcoal hair, and I tugged them hastily through the messy strands until they lay flat and cooperative.

Good enough. Those were words to live by.

I'd never been one to obsess over my appearance. Everything about me was selected on the basis of practicality. My short easy-to-manage hair. My comfortable wardrobe. My minimalist use of makeup, if I wore any at all, which was seldom. Not unless Ryan passively "suggested" it. There were many things that I really aimed high for in life, but maintaining any particular look or style wasn't one of them. My interests were more...academic. I was a *books-over-looks* type of girl.

When I was a child, my mother was never very strict. Now that I was older, I often wondered if this was due to the fact that she never needed to be. I was compliant with rules and punctual with schoolwork—every mother's dream.

Mom, on the other hand, was a breed all her own. She was a wildflower, who oftentimes played the role of the teenage delinquent rather than the responsible adult. It wasn't that Mom was a bad person or that she didn't take motherhood seriously. She was just...spontaneous. It was the only word I could really think of to describe her.

If I was a predictable spring breeze, she was a violent late summer hurricane. There was no consistency. Every decision she made was hair-trigger. Every emotion she felt was the strongest she'd *ever* felt. And she allowed those emotions to guide her like a ship left to the mercy of a raging storm.

It was for this reason that I didn't argue when Mom made the big announcement last year that she was moving to the midwest. "I'm just tired of living in shades of gold, Viv," she'd explained. "I'm ready for colors and seasons and snow."

It's strange how the metric distance had somehow dismantled what was once a very close bond between us. When she lived right around the corner, I constantly worried about whether or not she locked her doors or if she paid her electric bill. Now that she was over two thousand miles away in rural Indiana, she seldom crossed my mind. Maybe I was a bad daughter. Maybe this was just what being an adult felt like. Or maybe I should be making some effort to fix whatever had broken between us.

Guilt crashed over me without warning. I glanced at the clock again.

5:15 p.m.

Ryan wouldn't arrive for another hour and forty-five minutes. Since I was dressed and as ready as I would ever be— aside from the eyeshadow, which I contemplated not wearing anyway—I decided to call my mom. When was the last time I'd heard her voice? A week? A month?

I clicked the green "Call" button, making the quick decision to play it cool.

Ring. Ring. Ring.

After all, Mom hadn't called me either.

Ring. Ring. Ring.

She was just as capable of using a phone as I was.

Ring. Ring. Ring.

How had we grown so distant?

The deliberating was short-lived as a robotic voice spoke through the receiver, "We're sorry. The voice mailbox of—" Rustling sounds and static broke through the line seconds before my mother's sharp voice filled the delay. *"Hello. This is*

Missy Gilovich. I'm not available right now but if you leave your name and num—is not available. At the tone, please record your message. When you have finished recording, you may hang up or press one for more options."

A long low beep signaled the end of the recording. I couldn't help but smile.

"Hey, Mama, it's me. Got some pretty cool news from work today. Call me when you get a sec, okay? Love you. Bye."

Click. Unlike some people, I always said goodbye.

Well, now what? My bags were packed for LA. My laundry was completely caught up. I had no schoolwork to do. The apartment was squared away. I'd disposed of all food that would have spoiled during my trip, and I'd made it a point not to purchase produce that I couldn't eat before Friday.

Pressing "resume" on life when plans were on the horizon had always been a struggle. It's how my mind was hardwired. If I'd been settled in for the night, I would have no issue finding a book or movie or TV drama to occupy my time until bed. But the nagging pang of nearing obligation prevented the desire to start anything. If I was going to invest time into something like a book or movie, I wouldn't want to pause or put it down when Ryan arrived. The awareness of impending commitments made me incapable of relaxing.

So instead, I cranked up my favorite happy-song playlist and danced a rut in my beige apartment carpeting. Swaying to the beat of Emarosa's "Givin' Up," I straightened each of the plush hand towels that hung on the rack beside the bathroom sink, then rearranged all my cheap perfume bottles—first by size and then changed my mind and rearranged them by my personal favorites instead. That seemed more practical. While I was still in front of the bathroom mirror, I softly blotted the lids of my eyes with flesh-toned eyeshadow. *Take that, Ryan.*

After retreating from the bathroom, I finger-picked dark

fuzzies from my bedroom carpeting, which had undoubtedly fallen from the navy button-down I was wearing. That thought led me back to the floor-length mirror in my bedroom, where I twisted and turned to check for even more blue fuzzies that might fall off and litter the interior of Ryan's perfect black Mercedes. And since I was in front of the mirror, I combed through my hair once more, alternating indecisively between pulling it back or allowing it to lay flat.

Flat would be best, I decided. Ryan usually saw me with my hair pulled back for work. This would be something new, something fresh. Did men notice little changes in our hair? I always noticed when Ryan did anything new at all, even if that "new" thing was simply neglecting to shave his face. Every day added a new layer to his character. A new expensive watch, a new cologne, a new tussled direction to his feathery blonde hair.

What would flat hair say about me tonight? Was it bold and playful? Sexy? Daring? Or would it make my personality seem more flat than usual? Or maybe, just maybe, I was overthinking for the gazillionth time today, and Ryan wouldn't even notice my hairstyle or the blue fuzzies on my shirt or the order in which my perfumes were placed.

Relief flooded over me when I heard a knock at my door at 6:45 p.m. I'd been making an effort to build some semblance of order to my collection of tattered paperbacks, which lay in mounds across the floor. Hopefully, Ryan wouldn't mind the mess.

"You're early," I greeted as I swung the huge wooden door open.

Ryan looked perfect, as always. A form-fitting white collared shirt pulled against the long slender length of his narrow frame and tucked neatly into a pair of jet black jeans. His face was freshly shaven, and his hair was pushed back into intentional messy tufts. He could have been posing for a Ralph Lauren ad.

Maybe I really did under-dress. In my oversized blue button-down shirt and faded jeans, I looked like I should be posing for the local grocery store's advert in the Sunday paper.

"Yeah, sorry about that," Ryan said as he leaned casually on the door frame. "Traffic wasn't nearly as bad as I'd expected for a Monday night. Speaking of which, may I steal your bathroom for a second?"

Good thing I'd straightened the hand towels and rearranged my perfumes after all.

"You're totally fine," I said as I stepped aside to let him in. "Public restrooms are gross and stinky. My bathroom, on the other hand, smells like Coconut'colada Paradise and rainbows."

Ryan raised a single dark eyebrow with a smile.

"Aren't Pina Coladas already coconut flavored? The name Coconut'colada is kind of redundant, don't you think?"

I pointed my nose to the ceiling with a sarcastic snort. "Men just don't understand the complex layers of bathroom fragrances."

"You've clearly never been in a men's restroom in downtown Sacramento!" Ryan retorted, gripping his nose dramatically as he strode towards the bathroom.

Ryan and I rarely took anything too seriously when it came to our relationship. I guess that was why the mention of marriage had sent a shockwave to my core. We were just too comfortable and casual. We spoke the language of light sarcasm, never diving too far into the realms of more controversial topics like morals and values and futures. Nothing that could risk an argument or unveil a trait that either of us didn't like about each other. I wasn't sure how much Ryan would actually like me once he uncovered all of my OCDs— nail-biting, self-doubt, and the nasty habit I had of overinflating even the smallest of thoughts. I just wanted to maintain *this* for however long I could. Whatever *this* was.

It was a very short drive to Cordeiro's Steakhouse. The sun was low in the western sky, painting golden streaks of light over the black marble fountains that greeted us at the restaurant's long cobblestone entryway. Ryan extended a chivalrous hand, and we admired the fragrant orange chrysanthemums that lined the stone path as we strolled through the hot evening air. A man in a black suit propped open one of the wooden double doors, and Ryan released my hand so that I could enter first. Always a gentleman.

Over dinner and an expensive bottle of burgundy wine that Ryan had apparently pre-ordered when he'd placed the reservation, we discussed my upcoming trip to LA and the opportunities that this trip presented. If all went well, Ryan and I could be packing for France together in just five short months.

All these amazing experiences I'd dreamt of for so long, we could share them together. And at Christmas time! What could be more magical than a glistening scene of the Strasbourg Christmas Market, glittering under fresh snow and sparkling lights? Of course, I'd have to cancel the holiday plans I'd made with my mom in Indiana. She would understand, though. Especially if I mentioned my charming new boyfriend. I'd yet to tell her about Ryan.

With every sip of wine, my face grew warmer. A tingle buzzed through my lips like the wings of a cricket, and I pursed them tight as Ryan elegantly chattered about...*something*. I was losing track of my thoughts. Ryan propped his elbow on the tall oak table, swirling his wine glass in a small spiral motion as he laughed. *God, he was handsome.* I hadn't caught what he said, but I laughed along with him, blissfully aware of how silly I must look.

Why could *he* polish off three glasses of wine and still entertain without missing a beat? He was so dapper, so practiced in casual drinking. I'd barely made it a quarter of the way through my second glass, and my dimples burned with the smile I couldn't release. Surely he was aware that I'd sipped away my sobriety at least fifteen minutes ago.

As he spoke, I glanced at my pile of mashed potatoes. I was still smiling like a lunatic, but I didn't care. These were the best potatoes I'd ever had. When the waiter returned to the table, I'd request a box to take them home. They were the only thing left on my plate, but they could be a meal all on their—

"—think you should move in with me after the LA trip."

What? My fork clattered noisily against the ceramic plate, splashing steak sauce across the white linen tablecloth. *What just happened?* My gaze lifted slowly, and I focused on his face, attempting to assess his expression in my inebriated state. I was searching for a joke in his eyes, but he looked frustrated or maybe worried.

"Wait. What did you just say?"

"I said," he sighed, placing his glass delicately down onto the table and folding his arms neatly in front of his chest, "I think you should ditch that tiny apartment and move in with me after you return from LA. I don't like that place, Viv. I don't like the area. I don't like the neighbors. And I don't like leaving you there alone at night. I swear, Viv, when I was in your bathroom, I saw black mold around the window frame."

Why was this happening? Why now? Why tonight?

"Ryan..." I sighed, reigning back control of my mind. "I just...I don't think that's a good idea. Not yet at least. Trust me on this one, okay? My apartment is perfectly safe. I've lived there for years. And...you'd get sick of me if I was always around, taking up all of your free time."

A wave of ice rolled through my spine as I watched his

shoulders stiffen to tight peaks. "Or," he said with a cold calm that breezed his eyes away from my face, "maybe you're afraid that I'll take up all of *your* free time."

Yes, definitely upset. And very out of character. I'd never heard this acidic bite to his voice. It was a tone that made me feel very tiny, like a child who had been caught coloring on the walls, left staring shamefully at the artistic disaster they'd created. Maybe that's what this relationship was—an artistic disaster, sculpted from unrealistic expectations and wiped clean of realistic fears. *This was my fault.* I knew this conversation would happen someday or at least a conversation similar to it. Ryan would extend a vulnerable offer of his heart, and I would coldly swat it away.

"I swear, Ryan, that isn't the case. I know it's hard to believe, and it probably sounds cliché, but everything is going so great for us right now. I don't want to jinx it by rushing things, you know?"

My desperate plea for understanding hung in the air between us. I'd offer anything to lift this unpleasant pressure, engulfed in an unfamiliar environment and surrounded by the celebratory voices of couples enjoying their meals. The faint buzz in my head surfaced. *You don't belong here.*

Ryan lifted his gaze to meet mine. Several intense moments passed as he held me captive, squinting hard in thought. The silence was maddening. He broke his gaze with a slow shake of his head and smiled into the distance.

"You know what? You're right," he declared with a sudden composure to his tone. "We have a pretty good thing going on. Just know that my door is always open, Viv. Day or night. And," he hesitated for a moment to pick up his glass, "if you insist on staying in that walk-in closet that you call an apartment, you have to at least let me call mold control for you."

I rolled my eyes.

"I'm serious, Vivian," he insisted. "Black mold is no joke! Don't you know, it's what took out Brittany Murphy in 2009?"

It was clear that Ryan wasn't going to back down on this one, so I conceded to the lesser of the two presented evils. Cohabitate with Ryan permanently *or* allow someone to test the air quality in my apartment for deadly fungus.

"Fine," I agreed before tipping back my half full-glass and giving it the good old college chug. *I was done feeling things.*

2

KEEP IN YOUR POCKET

The subtle whisper of chill leathery air circulating through the black Mercedes was the only soundtrack as Ryan drove me home. His face remained impassive, illuminated by the soft teal of the dashboard. A million words swarmed my brain, but none were brave enough to escape into the open air. Instead, I sat with my hands folded in my lap and watched as the city lights streaked by.

We rolled up to my complex a little past 9:00 p.m. Though he'd voiced his fears about leaving me in my apartment at night, Ryan didn't offer to walk me inside nor did he get out of the car to hug me. Instead, he casually wished me a good night and handed me the black to-go box of potatoes that had been sitting in the back seat. Taking the leftovers from his hand made me ripple with a shame that I couldn't explain.

As I walked up the steps to my apartment doors, the Mercedes's engine was already humming away into the night. Normally, Ryan waited until I was safely behind the locked complex door to leave so that my back wasn't exposed to the dark street while I fumbled with my key card—not that anyone ever bothered me. It was the overall sudden lack of the gesture that crumpled my heart. Either Ryan thought I was safe enough without his vigilant eye, or he didn't care if a dark cloaked figure swallowed me up after his Mercedes turned the corner.

The card reader blinked green, and the click of the deadbolt unlocking broke through the silence of the foggy Sacramento street. I pushed the heavy door open with my hip, slinked inside through the narrow gap, and allowed the door to slam heavily behind me. It locked with another loud click.

My apartment complex was quiet and cozy with the main entrance officially locking for the night at 8:00 p.m. to those without a key card. There were no drunken college frat parties. No screaming children. No yappy dogs to bark through the night. In fact, if it wasn't for the occasional muted laughter through the walls or the thrum of an unevenly loaded washing machine above my head, I would have never noticed my neighbors at all. They were like ghosts—seldom heard and never seen. Which is exactly how I liked it.

My feet padded against the worn plush carpeting of the long second-story hallway, racing against the thoughts that still tugged my brain. I knew if I turned, I'd see nothing out of the ordinary. So why did I get the sense that my dark cloaked figure was following close behind? I certainly wasn't willing to be the fool who would spin around hoping to catch something that wasn't really there. *Add paranoia to my mental health bingo card.* I read each apartment number to distract myself.

203, 204, 205...

Was Ryan really upset tonight, or had the alcohol played a part in his flare of frustration towards me?

206, 207, 208...

What if tonight was a test? What if he was trying to take our relationship to the next stage? What if I'd failed?

209, 210, 211...

Was he still mad at me, even now as he drove home?

212, 213, 214...

Would he call me tomorrow to say that our relationship wasn't working out?

215, 216...

My body fell through the door of apartment 217 and spun to close it as quickly as if I'd actually been followed by the black-cloaked figure I'd imagined. The day started so great. Why shouldn't it end with slithering anxiety, a brain full of buzzing bees, and a stabbing pang of regret?

I'd told Ryan exactly how I felt tonight.

Why did it feel so wrong?

The next morning, I woke up with a splitting headache and a text from my mother. The bright glare of my phone screen only intensified the ice-pick that was splintering deep behind my eyes. I struggled to decipher the words on the screen.

> Droppd my phon in the rivr. Som buttons don't work anymor.
> I'll call you Friday whn I buy anothr 1

Only my mom could manage to drop her cell phone in a river. Then again, only my mom could get by using an ancient clamshell that still used buttons instead of a touch screen.

> It's fine, Mom.

Pain seared through my temples as I typed.

I have a business trip on Friday, though,
so I may not be able to answer. That's
the news I wanted to tell you about. Just
call when you can. Love you.

The moment my arms dropped back to my side, I felt the phone buzz in my hand again. Blinding light washed over my weary eyes just long enough to glance at her message.

Lov u 2

My arm collapsed.

Fifteen restless minutes passed before my final alarm sounded. Nothing could be more tortuous than getting ready for work on this day of all days. My brain hurt. My eyes hurt. My stomach hurt. And I still had three full work days until the LA trip.

After a reluctant stomp to the bathroom, I slammed the medicine cabinet door open and swallowed two aspirin with a paper cup of sink water. Food was the last thing on my mind, but the aspirin would just make me feel worse if I didn't eat. I dragged myself to the kitchen to hunt for last night's potatoes. Holding the little black box of leftovers brought back a familiar wave of frustration. What was Ryan doing this morning? Did his head hurt, too? Was he still mad? Maybe I should text him...

The acidic burn of aspirin releasing in my stomach raged violently, and I choked down two bites of potatoes to combat the churning. They weren't nearly as good as they'd been last night. *Jeez, I really had been drunk.* Maybe Ryan was feeling just as awful as I was.

Deciding how to approach this situation was harder than I imagined, but I knew that I only had two choices. I could either test the waters and attempt to get a sample of his mood through text, or I could wait until work and hope that seeing his face would be enough to alleviate my anxiety. There were only four days until my flight. I wanted to make the best of them. After all, if I was somehow able to win over our client and secure the France deal, all would surely be forgiven, and the undeserved daily attention from Ryan would be preserved. For once, maybe I'd even feel worthy of it. Not likely, but a girl could dream.

With that thought, I tucked my phone into my pocket, sealing my decision. I would talk to Ryan at work today, the same as I did every day, and life would sail smoothly back to normal. Maybe we could even go out for a *sober* lunch. The sentiment sounded very convincing, but my head throbbed too badly to persuade myself.

The short morning commute to the office was serene, giving my aspirin just enough time to kick in before my cab stopped in front of the green glass doors. An older couple waited patiently at the curb to take my place in the stuffy vehicle, and we exchanged quick "good mornings" before I turned and entered the historic marketing building.

Without speaking to anyone, I brisked methodically over the red carpet until it met the rear corridor and turned into my tiny office. It was one of the few rooms that was sparsely decorated since it served as a temporary space for those of lesser status in the company—*people like me.*

For the time being, my gray metal desk was more like a ceremonial altar, used as a method of sorting out the deserving from the undeserving. In time, I would be moved into one of the beautiful lavish studio rooms. Or so Ryan often told me. It was wishful thinking to me at this point. Though, the LA trip definitely had some promising opportunities attached to it. *As long as I didn't screw it up.*

Aside from my PC, a single manila envelope was the only

item on my desk. Sharpied across the front in black letters, it beckoned to me.

Gilovich, Vivian — LA

This was it. My escape. Packaged and ready for me to find. I wanted to open it right away and sift through everything James left for me, but my unease cried out in protest of unsettled business. *Find him.* I'd never truly be able to appreciate this moment with the looming uncertainty of Ryan and his mysterious mood still buzzing in my head.

I placed the large envelope back on my desk and turned toward the hallway. Maybe if I went to the coffee room, I'd conveniently bump into Ryan and suggest that we look through the itinerary together. A bit of time with him could be just enough to lift my spirits and ease the dark feeling that had been lingering since last night. Anything that might have the power to ward away the dark cloaked figure who followed me from the restaurant, insistently pulling at the strands of my sanity. My brain had no vacancy. No more room for extra passengers— especially dark-cloaked ones.

As I walked into the long hallway, the only smiling faces were those staring back at me from the many gold-framed portraits on the wall. Ryan's photo was the last one before I reached the coffee room. I forced my gaze away to avoid seeing my reflection in the glass that encased his white perfect smile. Instead, I stepped onto the white linoleum floor of the outdated break room and took quick deliberate strides toward the large counter of assorted coffee pots, fruit baskets, and bins of sugar and cream.

The room grew quiet at once. Several coworkers resided at the single table at the far end of the room. In unison, they closed the folders that lay in front of them, and their voices were reduced to inaudible whispers. I made my best effort to blend into the scenery, aware of the eyes that lingered on me. It might have been unnerving if it wasn't something that happened literally every day.

I quickly filled a paper coffee cup to the brim, tapped in two spoonfuls of sugar, and retreated from the break room without looking back. Maybe Ryan had gone straight to his office. Not a good sign, but at this point, I was determined to find him before my new black-cloaked nemesis could whisk me away from all rationality.

My pace grew more and more frantic as I made my way down the long hallway, sloshing the hot coffee with each stride. I could see Ryan's door in the distance, and unlike any other day, the sight of it wasn't warm and welcoming. It was sealed shut with no light spilling into the hall from the narrow gap underneath. Regardless, I stubbornly pushed forward until I stood in front of his golden nameplate.

"He isn't here today, Vivian," a familiar voice bellowed behind me as I lifted a hand to knock. I whirled around to face James, who stood with a briefcase in hand.

"Oh, hello, Mr. Rivera." I composed myself quickly. "Did... uh...did he say why?"

James relaxed his pose with a laugh and straightened his red satin tie.

"Oh, it's quite the controversy, Ms. Gilovich," he began, with a playful glimmer. "Word around the office is Ryan was out late last night with a lovely lady. He said something about a bottle of wine and a porterhouse. Would you happen to know what he meant?"

My cheeks flushed with embarrassment, but I felt a bit relieved by the news. Ryan was fine. Even more relieving was the confirmation that maybe the wine truly had been an influence in the acidic tone he'd used at the restaurant. And maybe, just maybe, he'd rushed off from my apartment because he wasn't feeling well.

How many glasses of wine had he polished off last night? Three? Four? And to think, he'd driven us both home in that state! I'd never seen Ryan drink more than one glass of alcohol with dinner.

James was waiting for me to speak, but all I could manage was an innocent shrug and a smile.

"Tisk, tisk," James shook his head. "I guess this is partially my fault. Bringing in a beautiful hire only to watch her woo my son."

Shit. My lips arranged into an uncomfortable smile, but my heart was growing audibly loud. He didn't look mad. In fact, he looked amused. *Why did I feel like some type of corporate-casual succubus?*

Before I could say anything more, James patted my narrow shoulder with two firm bursts that nearly drove my body through the carpet. "He'll be fine, Vivian."

I was grateful that he'd mistaken my discomfort as concern for Ryan.

"This isn't his first hangover-induced sick day. Anyway, I placed a folder on your desk this morning. You'll find everything you need for your trip inside, as well as a few extra things to thank you for jumping into the fire."

James lifted his briefcase awkwardly to glance at his watch.

"Oh, is it nine already?" he huffed, turning his body toward the corridor entry. "I apologize for running off, but unfortunately, I have a bit of business outside of the office this week. I'll try to catch up with you before your trip."

I smiled in response, still dwelling on the words "this isn't his first hangover-induced sick day." *What did that mean?*

"Thank you, Mr. Rivera. I'll go pop that envelope open right now."

James nodded in satisfaction and stalked off toward the main lobby.

I released the breath I'd been holding. *Crisis averted.* If Ryan and I were to stay together, we'd definitely need to talk about how to balance this work versus love relationship. For my sanity, at least.

When I arrived back in my office, I spilled the contents of the large envelope across my desk. There was a single plane ticket, a complimentary drink voucher for my flight, a blue company credit card, several pieces of paper with information about my hotel, and a map of LA. In the center of the map, a big red circle indicated the location where I'd be meeting our client. It appeared to be right next to the hotel or maybe even a part of the hotel itself.

James had made everything so easy. Not even someone like me could mess this up. For the first time since being assigned this trip, a small spark of confidence ignited. The questions that had boiled in my mind over the last few days were put to rest. All I needed to do was show up to the indicated destinations at the indicated times, all expenses paid by a fancy company credit card. My trip was on autopilot. *I could do this.*

As I gathered the assorted papers to tuck safely back into the envelope, I noticed one more item hidden beneath my pile. It looked like a flash drive but without the metal USB connector at the end. Instead, there was a strange metallic triangular plug. What kind of computer had a triangle-shaped port?

If I'd been traveling abroad, I might have assumed that it was specific to a different country. My mom once ordered a phone charger online without reading the description and was unable to use it because the plug was designed for European outlets. But this was unlike any plug I'd ever seen.

I turned the strange device over in my hand and noticed that a small black plastic label with white lettering had been adhered to the back.

Keep in your pocket!

Strange. This weird little memory card probably held important information for our client. Credit card details? Marketing blueprints? Everyone at the firm's social security number and name of their first pet? It looked innocent enough. Not a weapon or drugs or any type of threat to national security. I would ask Mr. Rivera about it later. *After the whole "I'm seducing your son" paranoia wore off, preferably.*

I had something very important to prove. Not just to Ryan and Mr. Rivera but to myself. *Confidence, Vivian, confidence.*

The remainder of my work week passed quickly, despite the fact that Ryan didn't make an appearance. I sent him several texts asking if he was okay, if he needed me to bring him anything, if he had seen a doctor.

But Ryan's replies were always short.

"Pretty sure I have food poisoning" was the longest response I received from him early on Wednesday morning. It must have been bad, judging by his uncharacteristic absence. I began to lose hope that we'd get to spend any time together before my trip to LA.

If I were like most girlfriends, maybe I would have thrown a fit or made a fuss. Any normal girlfriend would have driven to his home to demand answers, but this was part of the whole "not complicating things" rule. Keep it easy, keep it light. If Ryan wanted to talk to me, he'd tell me to come over. Or call me, at the very least.

Missing work was very unlike him, which was my only real glimmer of hope. People like Ryan didn't miss work due to upset feelings or damaged egos. If he felt well enough to stand on his own two feet, he would be in his office, maintaining his title of "all-star king of the jungle."

And yet, through all of my self-convincing, I still couldn't shake the feeling that I was missing something. I thought that I knew Ryan so well until our date, but maybe there were more colors to him than he'd shown over the last six months.

This isn't his first hangover-induced sick day.

By Thursday night, I had my single carry-on bag packed tight beside the door. My outfit for the flight was laid out on my dresser, and the strange flash drive was placed right on top of the pile.

Keep in your pocket!

The words rang out like bells in my mind. James had been in and out of the office all week and never seemed to have time to catch up with me. I thought about leaving a note on his desk, but I was beginning to get the feeling that this little device was something private. Maybe he wouldn't want his various assistants to know. I didn't want to be unprofessional, especially after the whole "wooing my son" comment.

Not a weapon, not cocaine, I reminded myself. *Something important, something too important for the messenger girl.*

I wished that Ryan would buck up and text me. He would tell me what the little device was, even if he wasn't supposed to. I bit my lip hard. I could coax him into telling me anything.

Maybe I could try texting him. After all, I hadn't bugged him a single time today, and my trip was in less than twelve hours. Plus, this was a work-related text. It was important —*maybe*, and Ryan would probably be eager to show off his knowledge of exclusive company secrets—*maybe*. Not to mention, it could be the kickstart that would get our normal happy-go-lucky banter revving again—*maybe.* For a man of his stature, Ryan was mysterious in his own way, but he was also relatively predictable. Men loved to show off their knowledge and know-how. Ryan was no exception.

Grabbing my phone, I snapped a quick photo of the device and attached it to a message.

> **Hey, hun—**

No. Not hun. Hun isn't businessy. I deleted the message and started again.

> *Hey, Ryan*

Better. Dip your toes. Test the water first.

> **Mr. Rivera put this thing in the envelope with my plane ticket. There's a tag that says I need to keep it in my pocket? Not sure what that means. Do you know what it is?**

The second my message cleared, a sequence of *dot, dot, dots* indicated that Ryan was typing his response. *Dot, dot, dot.* That was fast. *Dot, dot, dot.* Almost like he already had our chat open. *Dot, dot, dot.*

Finally, his reply appeared.

> Yes. Keep it in your pocket, Vivian. And for God's sake, delete that photo from your phone before you get us both in trouble!

Crap! I knew this thing was important. It probably had the client's credit card information or something else personally identifiable on it. Hopefully, I hadn't violated my NDA. I quickly clicked into my gallery, deleted the image, and clicked open my chat with Ryan again where I un-sent the message.

> No problem. Just deleted it. I assume I'm supposed to give this to our client? Mr. Rivera didn't specify.

Ryan started typing again.

> Just keep it in your pocket in the meantime and don't show it to anyone. The client will know what to do with it. Give it to him at the meeting. And please don't forget to smile. You can come off a bit abrasive sometimes.

Ah, I knew it. The flash drive held the blueprints to our secret marketing plan or something. I wasn't high enough in the company to know all the details, and that's understandable. I was still the new girl. My job was to pass along information, smile, nod, and be polite. I could do that.

My phone lit up with another message.

> Miss you.

A shock wave radiated through my body, and my fingertips tingled. This was the first time since Monday night that he'd said anything even remotely personal. *He missed me!* My heart sang out in sudden longing. I'd promised myself to remain professional. I'd promised myself that I wouldn't be reduced into a soupy puddle of emotions—but now I couldn't contain the words that my fingers danced to type.

> God, I miss you too Ryan. Like, really. You have no idea. My flight doesn't leave until 6 am. Do you want me to stop by to say goodbye tonight? I really reeeeeeally want to see you before I go. Sick or not. I could bring coffee. Or dinner maybe? Just let me know. I love you.

I bit my lip and watched the screen. This time, there were no *dot, dot, dots.* No notification that Ryan was replying. And there was no notification that my message had been seen.

Come on, Ryan!

I kicked back on my bed and stared at his previous message until dark clouds of drowsiness claimed my consciousness. Waiting for me behind closed eyelids was my familiar black cloaked figure, who once again tugged mercilessly at the strings of my sanity.

Morning came in the form of a shrill alarm clock screech. My phone was still clasped in my hand, and I was fully dressed from the night before. *Damn, I must have passed out. Poor Ryan!* Hopefully, he hadn't been waiting for me last night.

I tapped open our chat, but to my disappointment, there was no response waiting for me. My message from last night hadn't been read. He must have fallen asleep, too. At least he'd said he missed me. That was a start. The downside was that I'd neglected to plug my phone in before falling asleep, leaving me with only 3% battery. Just my luck. I'd have to find an outlet at the airport and text Ryan later.

Reluctantly, I pulled myself out of bed and changed into my travel clothes—a light oversized white tee shirt and one of the few pairs of jeans that I owned without holes in the knees. The thought of enduring a flight in business attire sounded absolutely miserable.

After double-checking my carry-on bag, taking out the trash, and locking all the windows, I took one last lap around the apartment and shoved all of my essentials into my pockets. Phone, house key, company credit card, ID, plane ticket, and the weird flash drive thingy, which I shoved as far down into my jeans pocket as I possibly could to ensure it wouldn't fall out.

Keep in your pocket!

Then I grabbed my bag and left my tiny apartment behind.

3

DARK PREMONITIONS

B y the time my cab pulled into terminal two, my phone had dwindled to a critical 2%. Even more frustrating, I was running late. Very late. Once inside, I had absolutely no time to charge my phone or grab breakfast as I'd originally planned. My confidence was beginning to wane. In its place, anxiety solidified. Everything was loud. Everything was foreign. Everyone seemed so angry.

Breathe. I could do this.

By 6:30 a.m., I'd made it safely onto my plane, and by 6:45 a.m., we were in the air. My stomach flip-flopped around like a goldfish. Every bump of turbulence left me gripping my cushioned armrest until my knuckles turned white. *Hadn't I just seen something about a plane crash in the news? Or was it a movie I'd watched?* I pushed the thoughts into the dark abyss where I stored all unpleasant things.

At last, our nail-biting ascension ended, and the plane slipped into a steady cruise. A beautiful blonde flight attendant appeared beside me with a cart full of snacks and tiny bottles of alcohol. *Breakfast is served.* She placed one of the little vodka bottles on my tray, along with a bag of salted pretzels. I'd have to remember to thank Mr. Rivera for the drink ticket he'd so graciously included.

Normally, I wasn't a day drinker, but this had to qualify as more of a sedative than a leisurely cocktail. Between Ryan-stress, travel-stress, and dying-in-a-plane-crash-stress, I was ready to find comfort just about anywhere—even if it was hiding at the bottom of a teeny tiny bottle.

The hour and a half flight passed by in a blur. *Thank you, Grey Goose.* By 8:15 a.m., the plane began to tremble as our landing gear touched down at the LAX. And by 8:30 a.m., I was hauling my bag through the noisy airport. As anticipated, a line of cabs waited along the exit terminal. I quickly chose the cleanest looking one, tossed my bag into the back, and collapsed beside it.

It was over. I'd survived.

"Where to?" the cab driver prompted, impatiently glancing over his shoulder.

"Um. Hotel Belair," I stammered.

The driver looked me over curiously for a moment, grunted, and edged the cab out and onto the crowded exit route. Onward bound.

LA was precisely as I'd pictured it. Golden sunbeams illuminated everything with a picturesque filter that made each palm tree, stucco-sided home, and rollerblading beach babe look like they were pulled directly from a travel magazine that you'd find in a doctor's office waiting room. I stared in wonder through the tinted windows and savored every sight, from street performers playing acoustic guitars to circles of teens passing hacky sacks gracefully between their heels.

Everything was washed in happiness here. I wished I could share this moment with Ryan. This seemed like a place where he belonged.

I tried to imagine his face illuminated in the golden filter of the LA sun. The way his blonde tufts of hair would toss and turn and how his white teeth would shine as he smiled. We could hold hands and explore the area, stopping occasionally to watch street performers, and admire the colorful art that sprawled across nearly every building.

The ache in my heart was an intrusive reminder that sent me reaching for the rectangular shape in my pocket. I pulled myself from the scene outside, blinking away a single tear that swelled in the corner of my eye.

For the last hour, I'd assumed my phone was dead, and that when I was able to plug it in, there would be a message waiting for me from Ryan. Surely, he read my last text when he woke up. Surely, he had replied by now. I tapped the screen on, and it lit up immediately. 1% battery and no new messages. My mood instantly soured. It was 9:00 a.m., which was normally when Ryan would be arriving at work, had he not been sick.

An idea popped into my head. Or more like a question that I wasn't entirely sure if I wanted the answer to. I only had 1% battery, but I needed to send this message now. If Ryan was at work today, I was going to find out. My fingers glided across the screen at lightning speed.

> Hey, Mr. Rivera. It's Vivian. I just wanted to let you know that I arrived in LA safely. Please let Ryan know when he's at his desk today. I don't want him to worry. Thanks!

The second I clicked "send," the message cleared. A few moments later, a response from James flashed onto the screen.

Sure thing. He just walked in so
I'll let him know. Good luck!

Then the phone buzzed sharply and died in my hand, along with my spirit. Ryan was at work, and judging by his message, James was oblivious to everything happening between us.

I blinked another hot tear away, just as the cab pulled up to the tropical paradise that was the Hotel Belair. But I couldn't appreciate the manicured palms that encircled the resort or the expensive luxury cars that lined the front drive or the handsome attendant who offered to take my bag as I made my way along the long sandstone walkway. My eyes remained focused straight down, too shattered to look or speak to anyone until I reached the white marble lobby. On a better day, I may have stopped to admire the massive fireplace in the center of the room, flickering white flames to the tempo of soft piano music. Not today.

When I made my way to the front desk with red puffy eyes and a brain full of buzzing bees, I acknowledged the new emotion that was blistering inside me—*resentment.*

I resented Ryan for making me feel this way. I resented his complete and utter lack of consideration for my feelings. I resented his inability to listen or make even the most meager effort to understand me, even when I put myself through intense social discomfort to stand beside him as an equal.

"How can we help you today?" chirped the desk attendant.

My mind was barely present.

"I have a reservation," I bleakly responded. "My name is Vivian Gilovich."

The woman seemed surprised that anyone could enter such

a beautiful place in such a sour mood, but she smiled warmly and asked for my ID.

As I pulled the Premier Marketing credit card and my driver's license from my pocket, something else slipped upward and out. Its silver triangular tip danced in the light just before it clattered noisily to the white marble floor.

Keep in your pocket! The words faced upward, glinting against the tile.

Before I had a chance to react, a hand appeared, plucking the flash drive from the ground. My gaze drifted over the length of the muscular tattooed forearm, which was attached to a black quarter-sleeve button-down shirt that hugged unnaturally tight to the man who stood before me. His shoulders were broad and rounded, the way a UFC fighter might have been built. Corded and vascular, his neck looked like several trees that had grown together to form one solid trunk, serving as a pedestal for his angular dark stubbled jaw. Even his raven hair was razor-sharp, diced into perfectly crisp angles.

Our gazes locked.

Black furrowed brows cast a dim shadow over two icy blue eyes that burned into me with a wild intensity that sent a thrill through my chest. His expression was unreadable. Not the expression you generally would expect to see when a stranger hands you something you've dropped in the middle of a five-star hotel lobby.

The desk attendant cleared her throat, snapping me from my trance.

"Thank you," I gulped and clumsily snatched the flash drive from the strange-looking man's hand. Completely unresponsive, his corded arm remained suspended in its outstretched position until I'd awkwardly tucked the flash drive back into my pocket and handed my ID to the attendant.

Casually, I glanced around the room with deliberate

disinterest, but I could still feel the man's gaze piercing through my spine. *What was this guy's problem?*

The attendant handed me a key card and pointed to the elevators located to the left of the desk. "Your room will be on the third floor and to the left, Ms. Gilovich. Enjoy your stay at Hotel Belair."

I picked up my bag and briskly walked toward the silver elevator doors. They immediately parted, as if waiting to aid me in my getaway. *Go, go, go!*

As I turned to push the third floor button, my gaze locked back on the man in the lobby. He hadn't moved an inch, which may have been comical if I hadn't been so unsettled by the sight of him. I willed the elevator doors to close just as those icy eyes slowly drifted from the floor and pierced directly into mine. *Go, go, go!*

Unblinking, expressionless, and hauntingly cold. It was as if a javelin had been thrown directly into my chest, pinning me against the elevator wall and holding me captive. My heart clawed itself into my throat. *GO, GO, GO!* Finally, the double doors slid closed, severing the man's glare.

I was released from the paralyzing hold immediately, and I stumbled against the wall to collect myself. Blood rushed back into my legs. Acutely aware of my surroundings once more, the air returned to my lungs.

What the hell just happened? Why had he stared at me like I'd committed some crime? And what was up with his appearance? Was he in a rock band? A freak show? A male stripper? Instinctively, I placed my hand over my pocket. The small outline of the flash drive was still there, pressed firmly against my leg.

When the elevator doors slid open, I sprinted into the hallway with my bag and key card in hand. A familiar anxiety crept at my heels—the black-cloaked figure of my nightmares who seemed ever-present anymore. If I were to turn around fast enough, maybe I'd catch it this time. Or maybe I'd see the strange man and his piercing blue eyes instead. Was he following me? My feet carried me past the long hallway of hotel doors and tacky framed paintings of gardens and cityscapes.

The line of numbered plaques led me to my room. Without glancing over my shoulder for fear of completely losing my nerve, I scanned the white keycard, opened the heavy wooden door, and darted inside. The moment it slammed shut, I twisted the deadbolt and latched the chain lock for good measure. *Safe at last...again.*

The room was dark and ice cold. My hands slid blindly over the textured wall to the left side of the door, then the right, until I found the switch. A glittering chandelier burst into a spray of dazzling light, casting rainbows in every direction. My breath caught in my throat. The panic in my chest loosened, and I dropped my bag at the door so that I could fully appreciate the sight of the executive suite.

What a room! Mr. Rivera would certainly be receiving a fruit basket of appreciation for these accommodations.

Twelve-foot-tall beveled ceilings connected navy curtains to flawless white marble floors. Not a single beam of LA sun escaped from the windows that hid behind the elaborate drapery. The central room was furnished with red velvet couches and spotless glass tables. Massive abstract black and white paintings lined each wall, and a beautiful ivory piano occupied the furthest corner of the room. Red and white rose sprays draped elegantly like fingers touching the keys. On the opposite wall was a massive stone fireplace, its mantle lined with more fresh roses. *How much had James paid for this room?*

The bedroom was equally as extravagant, if not more so. Directly in front of the king-size bed, a massive white chimney flue connected down from the ceiling. More vases with red roses lined the dressers, and the far side of the room opened into an expansive balcony that overlooked the LA hillside. Never had I seen anything more beautiful in my life.

I twirled around the room once and fell backward onto the bed of down blankets and puffy white pillows. It was still early, and my meeting with Mr. Rivera's client wasn't until tomorrow. After all the chaos and stress of the day, I allowed my muscles to relax against the soft sheets.

Ryan had been an absolute ass-hat, but that was just fine. *Whatever.* If he didn't care about me right now, why should I waste time or energy caring about him? He was the one stuck back in smoggy Sacramento, while I was here at the striking Hotel Belair.

And tonight, I'd go to the hotel restaurant to enjoy a five-star meal. Maybe afterward, I would stop by the pool bar that Mr. Rivera mentioned. Who knows? A handsome young lawyer or doctor might offer to buy me a drink. Maybe I'd say yes. My daydreams swirled as I tried to picture the scene in my mind. Everything flexed and faded until the image distorted wildly and the fog of sleep washed over my consciousness.

A handsome young bartender set a pink and white slurry of alcoholic slush in front of me. I smiled warmly at him. From my half-submerged barstool, the sounds of laughter and festive music filled the warm summer breeze. Crystal blue water lapped at my legs as I took a sip of the colorful drink in front of me. This was absolute paradise. The sun beamed through thick palm branches, leaving hot dappled spots across my cheeks, and I closed my eyes to take in all the sounds and smells.

By now, Ryan was probably stuck in the busy downtown Sacramento traffic, trying to commute home. The thought of his black Mercedes wedged bumper-to-bumper made me smile. *What a pity.* Meanwhile, I was relaxing at a bar. Not just a bar, but a bar in the middle of a pool in the middle of LA.

As I took a deep breath of the fragrant summer air, my eyelids darkened as if a cloud were passing overhead. Warmth was replaced with an unnatural chill. So much for my summer sunshine.

Annoyed by the turn in weather, I reluctantly opened my eyes—but to my horror, there was no cloud blocking my light. Instead, two icy eyes glared at me from beneath the veil of a black hooded cloak.

4

SUNSET BLVD

Gasping with the force of a hurricane, I flung my body from the nest of white fluffy pillows and spun around in manic twists. I was still in my hotel room. The sun had faded into a soft amber flame that bathed the rear balcony in warm light. *Shit!* The alarm clock on the nearby nightstand read 8:03 p.m. *No freaking way!* How had I slept eleven hours? I'd wasted my entire day! The pool would probably be closing soon!

My bag still lay beside the door where I'd dropped it. I fumbled across the room with dizzy legs and ripped the zipper open. Ryan was probably worried sick! He would definitely be home from work by now. I grabbed my phone charger and plugged it into a nearby outlet, then waited through the excruciating long start-up sequence. Finally, the screen lit up.

No new messages.

One missed call...from my mom.

And not a single thing from Ryan.

My blood boiled. My hands trembled. *Seriously?* Almost twenty-four hours had passed since he'd last messaged me. *And he'd had the audacity to say he missed me last night?* If I had died in a fiery plane crash on the way to LA, Ryan wouldn't be the wiser.

Oh, except he would because Mr. Rivera would have told him at work today, where Ryan was apparently too sick to go—unless I wasn't there, of course. Was he avoiding me? I had no doubt in my mind at this point. There was no other explanation.

Furiously, I clicked Ryan's name in my contacts, fully prepared to send him the nastiest of nasty texts, when my phone buzzed.

"Hello," I answered bitterly.

"Vivian?" the voice asked with a flare of alarm that only a mother's love could carry. "Are you okay? What's wrong?"

With my back to the wall, I slid to the floor in anguish and pulled my knees to my chest.

"I'm sorry, Mama. Nothing's wrong. Well...actually, a few things are wrong. But it's nothing you need to worry about. Just a bunch of stupid stuff." Tears threatened to spill over. I didn't want my mom to worry, but it was clear that she could hear the pain in my voice.

"Vivian, you sound like a mess," she soothed, "and more than you usually do. What's going on? Did you already leave for your trip?"

Right. It had been so long since my mom and I had spoken. She had no idea where I was. I'd only told her that I was going on a business trip in my last message. And she certainly didn't know about Ryan. Maybe it would be best to not even bring him up. The last thing I wanted to do was introduce my new love interest and discuss how he'd completely ghosted me this week.

But the more I heard her voice, the more I wanted to hear even more of it. Everything started to spill out. The date with Ryan. Him asking me to move in. The sudden lack of contact. My constant nightmares and anxiety.

"It sounds like you're under a lot of stress right now, Viv,"

Mom said with soothing concern. "I'm really glad that this Ryan guy has made you so happy...but men are weird, and it sounds to me like you hurt his ego."

I sighed in agreement. Sometimes, I forgot how similar Mom and I truly were, despite the fact that we lived opposite lifestyles. She continued.

"If I were you, I'd just focus on enjoying your trip. Live in the here and now. You said you two aren't formally dating, right?"

I thought about the question for a moment. Ryan had never referred to me as his "girlfriend," but we spent nearly every day together up until this week. It was as if I'd turned into some disregarded toy left sunbleached in the yard after I'd refused his offer to move in with him. It wasn't even like the refusal was a permanent thing. Maybe someday I would be ready...I just wasn't ready right now. Ryan had never really given me the chance to explain any of that, though.

"No," I replied sourly. "The words 'boyfriend' and 'girlfriend' have never been used, so I don't think so."

"So, have you two...you know?" She left the question open-ended, for both of our sakes.

"No, Mama. We haven't. It's all been very casual. You know, dinners and movies and stuff. Nothing serious. Not until he asked me to move in, at least."

"Well then," Mom paused for a moment. "I'm not telling you to give up hope, Vivian, but I wouldn't cheat myself out of a fun time in LA. Especially when this guy won't even take the time to message you back. You deserve to have fun, too, you know."

Deep down, I knew my mom was right—or maybe I was just vulnerable, and her erratic influence was rubbing off on me. I still couldn't shake the feeling that I was missing something.

With all my heart, I wanted to defend Ryan's character, but Ryan's actions didn't defend his own character. We'd gone days without contact, and it might have been even longer if not for the conversation about the flash drive. The first thing he told me was to delete the photo. Not just to delete the photo but to delete it "before you get us both in trouble."

Did Ryan only reply to my message to avoid becoming an accomplice to whatever company protocol I'd violated?

But why had he said he missed me? What purpose could it have served?

Mom continued, as if she'd read my thoughts.

"Honey, if this guy really missed you, he would show you that he did. You're a beautiful girl. And men say a lot of things, Vivian. Unfortunately, you have to decide for yourself which things are worth believing," she paused for a moment, as if a specific memory came to mind, "and which things are just decorative shackles to keep you accessible."

I was taken aback. Mom normally wasn't that...*profound?*

"Thanks, Mama," I sighed and stood up from the floor. "I think I'm going to take your advice and get out for a while. Maybe explore the area a bit."

"Good," she said with a *mom-knows-best* satisfaction. "Go have some fun for once. LA is a beautiful place. Just be safe. Don't do anything I wouldn't do."

I laughed at the irony. "That really doesn't set many hard barriers, Mama."

"Exactly!" she exclaimed enthusiastically, then continued with a touch of seriousness that I didn't hear often enough. "I love you, Vivian. Be careful."

"I will, Mama. I love you, too. Bye."

It was 8:30 p.m., and the sun would be setting soon. With newfound enthusiasm and a wicked determination, I ran to my bag and pulled out one of the nicer outfits I'd packed—a pair of black jeans and a skin-tight gray turtleneck that was always too hot to wear during the day. The sun would be setting soon, and I wasn't going to miss out on an opportunity to explore the LA nightlife. For the first time in my life, I was going to take my mother's advice.

It took me five minutes to slip on the new outfit, tug a brush through my tangle of dark hair, and fill my pockets with only the essentials—hotel keycard, credit card, ID, and my phone, which was now on 40% battery. *Good enough.* After lacing up the black boots I had packed for tomorrow's meeting, I stood in the mirror and gave myself a look-over. For once, I was more than just presentable. I looked pretty damn good. A spark of confidence ignited in me. *I was going out on the town!*

As I glided to the door, ready to take on the world, I noticed something glossy and rectangular lying on one of the glass tables beside my discarded jeans from earlier.

Keep in your pocket!

I didn't really need to take the flash drive with me, did I?

Keep in your pocket!

After all, tonight's outing was purely recreational.

Keep in your pocket!

I wouldn't possibly need to carry a company flash drive around LA with me.

Keep in your pocket!

What if something happened to it? It would be safer here.

Keep in your pocket!

Then again, Ryan had been pretty firm about keeping it with me until tomorrow.

Keep in your pocket!

"Okay, dammit!" I surrendered and quickly snatched the flash drive from the table, shoving it deep in the tight pocket of my jeans. No more mishaps.

I hurried through the door, down the hall, and into the

silver elevator. When I reached the ground level, the doors split apart to reveal a scene completely different from the one this morning.

Festive white twinkling lights lined the walls of the large white lobby, and a fire roared in the marble fireplace. Surrounding it were several formally dressed men and women, each clasping cocktails as they smiled and laughed. I wondered if they were all friends, or if they'd all just met here tonight by coincidence, each destined for their own separate journey but lucky enough to cross paths in the heart of LA. I longed to be one of them. To stand with a drink in my hand and feel included in a fancy social group. Or maybe I just wanted to belong to the same social class as Ryan and my fellow coworkers. If he were here, he'd undoubtedly be among them. Yes, he'd fit in seamlessly.

I pried myself from the festive scene and made my way to the front of the Hotel Belair. *Hanging out in the hotel lobby doesn't qualify for "exploring the town."* I needed to push through my comfort zone. For once in my life, I needed to explore without having a solid plan. I had no obligations tonight, and no one was around to tell me that I couldn't or to make me feel guilty for doing what I wanted to do.

Several cabs were parked at the front of the building. I hopped into the closest one, not caring whether or not it was the "nicest one" this time, and buckled my seatbelt. The tiny space was saturated with the bitter smell of patchouli.

"Where to?" the cab driver asked, his voice rich with an accent I couldn't recognize.

Where to? I guess I should have thought about that before I jumped in the cab.

"I'm new to the area," I blurted out, determined to sound confident. "Are there any strips around here? Like…with restaurants and bars?"

An incredulous look crossed the man's face.

"You mean the *Sunset Strip?*"

Oh. Duh. I should have known that.

"Yes! That's exactly the one I was thinking of," I lied.

The man nodded and turned forward but not before giving me a final disbelieving look in the rearview mirror. Then we were driving down the streets of LA in the final golden hues of the evening.

Sunset Boulevard crawled with life, even after the sun had completely fallen behind the LA hills. There were glowing record stores, fancy restaurants, expensive clothing outlets, and dozens of nightclubs outlined in pink neon lights. I had no idea where to begin, but I knew that if I stayed in the cab too long, I'd chicken out. I asked the driver to pull over as we approached one of the many neon club signs. There was a glowing martini glass on the front of the building and a marquee that read "The Basement."

The name made me nervous, but the line of expensive Ferraris and Aston Martins in front of the building helped to push me forward. I'd never been to a real club before. If this one was good enough for a Ferrari owner, it had to be nice inside, *right?*

A massive bouncer stood in front of the door, blocking the entrance with the span of his shoulders. His head was so shiny that it glowed pink from the light of the neon signs overhead in an almost perfect beam. I wasn't sure what to do. Was it like in the movies? Would he let me walk right in? Or did he need to rate me based on attractiveness before deciding if I was "hot" enough to enter? Maybe there was a guest list. Maybe pretty girls didn't need to be on a guest list. Was I a "pretty enough" girl?

Determined not to get turned away, I composed my very

best sexy expression and sashayed up to the massive bouncer. *Go-time.*

"Hell-o," I said with a flirtatious smile.

The man craned his neck to look down at me over his massive crossed arms. *Straight* down at me.

Oh god, I must look like a child.

"Hi, there!" he smiled back. The friendliness of his voice deceived his intimidating appearance.

We stared at each other, awkwardly smiling for several seconds. I could feel my face growing hotter with each blink.

"Nice night, isn't it?" he said.

My brow dropped. Was I missing a secret password or something?

"Yeah, it is," I replied, flipping my hair playfully. "I, uh—I'm new to the area so I was actually looking for somewhere to have a drink. You wouldn't happen to know anywhere, would you?"

I intended to end the sentence with a sexy wink, but it came out as more of a squint...and the corner of my mouth popped open at the same exact moment. I quickly played it off by jabbing my finger repeatedly in the direction of the door behind him. As I stood there awkwardly with one eye closed, my mouth open, and my finger hanging limply in the air, I realized that I probably wasn't getting into this bar.

The bald man stared down at me with an amused smile and shook his head with a laugh. "You over eighteen?"

"Yeah!" I answered in surprise and pulled out my ID. "I'm actually twenty-one."

He took the ID, turned it over a few times, and handed it back to me with a smile.

"I see a lot of underage kids with fake IDs come through here," he laughed, "and every single one of them has been a more convincing actor than you."

Blood rushed into my cheeks.

"No, I—I promise! It's a real ID! Hold on, I can pull up my insurance information on my phone for you to verify my identity..." I reached for my pocket, but the man exploded into laughter.

"Honey, that's the realest ID I've ever seen. I have no doubt in my mind that you are who you say you are. I just don't understand why you did all the..." He motioned his hand up and down over the span of my body. "...the hair flipping and what-not."

Embarrassed but with nothing left to lose, I admitted, "I thought this was one of those dress code type places. You know. The type where the bouncer hand-selects everyone who gets inside. To sort out the cool people."

The man doubled over, bursting into a peal of laughter that shook the sidewalk.

"And you—" he could barely manage the words, "you thought you'd increase your chances if you winked and pointed at the door?"

I opened my mouth to reply, but I had no words. Instead, I put my hands in the air and shrugged in defeat.

Still laughing, the bald man stepped aside and opened the red leather-padded door.

"Get in there, kid," he cackled, grabbing me by the shoulder and pushing me inside the loud club. "The name's Bruce," he called in after me, shouting over the music. "Come find me if you have any trouble. I'm working until three." The red door sealed shut, and I was consumed by the deafening vibration of bass.

It took a moment for my eyes to adjust to the dim light, which came from massive purple LED panels that covered every wall. The floors were a geometric labyrinth of glittering black hexagonal tiles and in the center of the room was a massive hexagon-shaped bar where several bartenders in silk vests distributed drinks. There were no chairs, aside from the barstools that lined the edges of the bar. Instead, every wall of the club was outlined in purple velvet couches. *Some basement!*

Women in sparkly sequined dresses danced and sloshed their drinks, and men in crisp dress shirts leaned against the bar to ogle over them. The main dance floor of the club was located to the rear of the building, but from where I currently stood, it just looked like a wall of wiggling shoulders and butts. A wave of nausea rolled through my gut. This atmosphere was completely foreign. An alien planet wouldn't have looked much different through my eyes.

For a moment, I considered going back outside to chat with Bruce. He seemed like a cool "dad-type" guy. We'd probably get along. But I decided I should at least give this whole club-thing my very best try before calling it quits. There had to be something to it, right? Most people my age talked very highly of nightclubs and dancing. I'd stick around long enough to have a drink and listen to some of the completely incomprehensible music before leaving to maybe check out one of the local restaurants.

Summoning my courage with a cleansing breath, I barreled ungracefully forward through the crowd, weaving between groups of wiggling butts and boobs and slick, sweaty skin. When I reached the hexagon in the middle of the room, I wedged my body against it and gripped onto the counter like a life raft. I knew my carefully illustrated sexy-face was long gone, and I was left gasping over the edge of the bar as if I'd just been pulled from the sea. *How the hell did girls my age do this?*

A bartender spotted me right away and mouthed what looked like the words "What will you have?" Maybe a drink would help to calm my nerves. Something sweet and tasty but nothing too strong. I definitely didn't want to get drunk and end up wedged in that dance floor butt-wall. The glowing array of bottles in the center of the hexagonal platform indicated that they could likely make anything I requested.

I thought for a moment, then opened my mouth to yell over the obnoxiously loud music—only, the moment I began, the music stopped just long enough for me to scream the words "STRAWBERRY MARGARITA" directly into the bartender's face. I clasped my hand over my mouth, absolutely mortified, just as the music loudly resumed. The bartender twisted a finger painfully into his ear a few times, turned, and began working on my drink.

Smooth. Off to a great start.

The second he placed my glass on the bar, I pulled out the company credit card and paid, declining a tab. I also left the poor guy a ten dollar tip to compensate for the hearing loss. With my tail tucked, I carefully carried my fish-bowl-sized pink goblet of slush to the nearest empty couch. I was overwhelmed and exhausted and ready to be anywhere but here. At least I could tell my mom that I'd tried. Mindlessly, I snapped a quick photo of my drink to send to her later, just to prove that I'd actually taken her advice. That would make her happy. She didn't need to know what an utter failure the night had been.

I took a sip of the sweet alcoholic slushy. It was good, but it reminded me of the last time I'd been drunk—which was, of course, with Ryan. What would he say if he knew I was here, alone at a nightclub in LA? He'd probably shame me for wearing jeans. And he'd certainly tell me how unsafe and irresponsible going out alone was. I ran through the argument we'd have in my head, and I thought of all the things I'd retort triumphantly at him. *Don't worry,* I'd say snarkily, *the big bald bouncer was looking out for me, which is more than I could say for you.*

I sipped my drink again, unable to conceal the snarky

smile that tore across my lips. In reality, I knew that I'd never be so bold in an actual argument. Nor would I think of such good comebacks. When it came to winning arguments in my own head, I was practically Johnnie Cochran. When it came to winning *real* arguments, I was more akin to a spaghetti-stained toddler who had been caught playing in the toilet water.

My intense line of thoughts was snapped like a rubber band. A sudden weight slammed on the couch beside me. The impact sloshed my margarita, and a chunk of pink slush landed on the toe of my boot. With daggers in my eyes, I glared at whoever had plopped down so carelessly.

It was a younger man, likely around my age. He wore a backward flatbill hat, and a gold chain dangled from his neck, contrasting over his plain black tee shirt. The moment our eyes met, he smiled at me with a bravado that nearly made me throw up in my mouth.

"Hey, baby!" he shouted, draping his arm lazily over the back of the couch behind me. The close proximity sent me scooting my butt all the way to the edge of the seat.

Oh god, I rolled my eyes, *here we go.* I pursed my lips together and waved slightly, while breaking eye contact so I could deliberately look around the room. Maybe if I ignored him, he'd move along to bug someone else.

"You from aroun' here?" He yelled the words directly at the side of my head.

Of course, it wouldn't be that easy. I hesitated for a moment to make it appear that I didn't realize he was talking to me. He continued to wait, staring directly at the lip I was gnawing on. *Damn.* I smiled a quick response.

"No. I'm here on business."

"Business?" Even over the music, his volume made me flinch. "What kinda business you into?" This guy didn't seem like the type to care about "business." Not a business that operates above ground, at least.

"Marketing," I answered with fake politeness. I was definitely missing Bruce.

"Marketing?" he repeated. The moisture from his sickly breath stuck to my earlobe. I nodded twice and looked aimlessly around the room again, desperately searching for an escape.

Maybe I could pretend one of these drunk girls was my sister. If I picked a super drunk one, she might even believe it herself. My gaze darted from person to person and from couch to couch, looking for any familiar face or anyone friendly enough to help me.

"What do you market?" the man persisted, leaning his body closer to me. The smell of hard liquor, cigarettes, and something skunky burned my nostrils.

I debated making a run for the door. But including the extravagant tip, my drink was over twenty dollars. Even if I had to chug the whole goblet, I intended to finish it, despite the fact that it had been paid for by Mr. Rivera's glossy blue credit card.

Hold your ground. Be strong. Bore him away.

"Anything I'm hired to market, I suppose," I responded thoughtlessly. It wouldn't have mattered if I'd given him a full run-down of the entire company. This guy was obliterated. Even sober, I don't think he could have kept up.

In a battle of fight or flight, I decided that flight was the most practical option. I scanned the line of couches directly across the room, searching for a vacant seat where I could flee and finish my drink. The crowd moved and parted to reveal small sections of the couches. Each time, they were occupied. *Was this hell?* If everyone was damned to swim in their own personal hell, this is *exactly* what mine would look like.

"Well, I'd hire you to market for me," the man slurred and

swayed. "My buddy and I wanna start a weed dispensary here in LA. You smoke weed, baby?"

I barely heard his words. I was focused on something across the room—something that I didn't want to believe I'd actually seen. The crowd collected into the area where my gaze now rested, and I waited intently for the bodies to sway enough to see the couch behind them. *It couldn't be. There was no way.* Two women laughed and tugged on each other's shirts, one of them grabbing the other by the arm. They both stumbled toward the bar. At that exact moment, I was locked into a familiar frosty glare, set below the shadow of a dark furrowed brow.

A jagged breath caught in my chest, just like it had in the elevator at the Hotel Belair. The man sat with massive tattooed arms crossed over his chest, legs sprawled casually, and eyes curiously locked on me. Directly on me. And just like at the Belair, I was frozen in place, held captive by his unnervingly frigid stare. *Why was he here?* Of all the bars in LA, why was the weirdo here?

Suddenly, the drunk guy snapped me from my hold and locked me into a different one. His hand wrapped tightly around my wrist, and he tugged me unwillingly to my feet.

"Come on, baby," he drooled and stumbled forward into me, then back without releasing his grip. I planted my legs to keep us both from tumbling to the floor. "Le's go outside where we can smoke."

In that instant, friendly Vivian was gone. No more. I tugged my arm hard toward my torso. "Don't touch me! Let go!"

The man put a second sweaty hand around my wrist. "No, no, no. Shhhh. I'm not gonna hurt you, baby. I just wanna show you somethin'."

I tugged my arm hard against my torso again, the pressure of his fingers bruising deep into my skin.

"You ARE hurting me!" I shouted, hoping someone would hear me over the thud of the bass. "Let go, man! I don't smoke!"

Thinking fast, I rolled my head completely backward. The entire scene behind me was now upside down. But the couch where the blue-eyed man sat was empty. As ice cold panic set in, my brain ran through hazy memories of self-defense moves I'd learned as a kid. With a deep breath and all the strength I could muster, I jammed a knee straight upward in an attempt to make contact with the man's groin. Somehow, he anticipated the move and pulled up his own knee to block mine.

"You're a piece of fuckin' work, you know that?" The man tugged my wrist so hard that he lifted my body off the ground, and I fell forward hard onto my knees. The impact stole the breath from my lungs and sent my drink crashing to the floor in an explosion of glass and slush. But no one around us noticed— or didn't care to notice.

Pain radiated through my wrist as the man tried to pull me to my feet again. "C'mon! Don't be such a bitch! Get up!"

My knees throbbed, and the claws of panic shredded my chest. As he tugged me upward, I reared back my head and filled my lungs, fully preparing to scream bloody murder until someone, anyone, came to help. But as I opened my mouth to let hell itself escape, a massive and ominous shadow crept over us both.

5

CAT HOUSE

"Ok, now you're starting to piss me off," a venomous voice hissed from behind, sending every hair on the back of my neck awry.

The man's tight grip around my sore wrist loosened, and I watched as his entire body lifted from the ground. Hot pulses of blood circulated back through my fingers, but I couldn't focus on anything other than the tattooed forearm that gripped the drunk man firmly by the throat.

"Le-me-go!" he gurgled, kicking his legs like a child being carried to bed.

The blue-eyed man stared at his catch, dark and expressionless. "I intend to."

A strangled scream split through the music. I watched in shock as the drunk man contorted through the air, followed by the loud clattering of his body making contact with metal bar tables.

Still frozen to the tile, I dared to glance up at the strange man who haunted my dreams. His gaze was locked in the direction of his human shot put, but he tilted his jaw down toward me.

"You okay?" he bellowed over the music.

Shakily, I pulled myself to my feet and dusted off the knees of my jeans.

"Yeah, I'm fine. What an asshole, *right?*"

The man tore his eyes from the wreckage where tables and the drunk guy were still piled in a heap. He examined my face curiously.

"Vivian, right?" I liked the way my name sounded on his husky voice, but how did he know? "From the Belair?" he continued.

"Oh. Yeah, that's me." He must have heard the desk attendant say my name when I checked in today. "And...you are?"

His shoulders noticeably stiffened. The drunk guy was still balled up in the corner, and no one else in the club seemed to be paying any attention to us. The man quickly surveyed the room, then answered. "Jacey Levitin."

"JC?" I asked. "What's that stand for?"

"No," he replied impatiently. "Jacey. *Jay-see.* Jacey." His expression twisted in frustration, and he tugged his earlobe uncomfortably. "Hey...You, uh...you wanna go somewhere else...to talk? It's too damn loud in here!"

Strange that he should be concerned with the noise since one typically goes to a club for the primary purpose of listening to the noise. Unless he had another purpose for being here. *Maybe he was waiting for a date? Maybe he'd been stood up?*

Aside from throwing a drunk man as effortlessly as a sack of potatoes, Jacey seemed harmless enough. Plus, he was staying at the same hotel as me. If all else failed, I had a cool tattooed bodyguard to walk me back. Apparently, I needed one because the night had turned into an utter shit show in between the space of one blink and the next.

"Sure," I responded with a nervous smile and followed Jacey through the red leather door.

Bruce was still leaning against the wall of "The Basement." His eyes narrowed and fixed on Jacey, as if he were trying to decide if I was being kidnapped by this strange looking man. I smiled warmly at him and waved goodbye. His posture relaxed, and he waved in return.

"Friend of yours?" Jacey inquired over his shoulder. I followed his fast steps.

"No," I breathed heavily, trying to keep up. "I think he was just looking out for me."

Jacey grunted but kept his swift pace down the brightly lit strip. Neon lights splashed beams of color into the dark edges of his raven hair, and groups of people turned to eye him suspiciously as we passed. At least I wasn't the only one who thought he looked out of place.

"Where are we going?" I asked, after walking two blocks from the club.

Jacey stopped and turned toward me. His face was puzzled. *Was I not supposed to follow him?*

His blue eyes darted from left to right, then fell on me. My heart pounded under the weight of his heavy gaze.

"You hungry?"

What a strange question. My stomach growled furiously. *What a well-timed question.*

"Yeah, actually, I am. I'm running on a bag of pretzels and alcohol."

Without warning, Jacey stalked down the street again. Both hands in the pockets of his jeans, his shoulders pushed up level with his ears, as if he was shivering away a cold breeze.

Was there something seriously wrong with this guy? Not that I wasn't socially awkward, but compared to Jacey, I was the queen of pizzazz.

"I know a place," Jacey muttered over his shoulder, "if you want to go."

An open-ended offer. He didn't look at me as he spoke, and his voice was distant as if he didn't really care if I followed or not. The way his eyes darted around was reminiscent of my own anxious tendencies—ever watchful of the dark cloaked figure that always seemed to evade me. The dream from earlier popped into my head—haunting eyes leering from under a dark hood. I shook it away.

"Yeah, I'm starving," I answered. "Is it far from here?"

"No, not too far." Clearly, a man of few words.

I continued after Jacey at what was a sprint for my short legs, examining him from behind. He wasn't an overly tall guy. I guessed that he stood around 5'8. But he was stocky and built. Every article of clothing he wore appeared as if it had been painted on his body. The tailoring was amazing and likely very expensive. His dark jeans gripped his tree-trunk-sized legs and cinched in the middle to bite into a solid thickset muscular waist.

He was still wearing the black quarter sleeve button-down shirt from this morning, but in the dim light of the LA strip, I was able to pick out new details. Rather than a standard business cut, Jacey's shirt consisted of sharp individually sewn panels that mimicked the cut of a military uniform. It hugged and contoured over his rounded shoulders, surely designed to accentuate his muscular figure. I didn't blame him. If I had a beach body like his, I'd never wear sleeves.

How had such an attractive guy ended up so incredibly awkward? I craved to know more.

Under the neon glow of the city lights, I searched for clues within the tattoos that covered his exposed forearms. The intricate designs were all black. Most were sharp in areas, intertwined like the workings of a machine. In other areas, though, the designs crept and twisted like vines. I wondered how high up his arms the strange tattoos climbed. Only his forearms were visible, but it appeared that the strange black ink covered more than just his visible skin.

"Cool tattoos," I mused.

Jacey shot a quick glance back at me but didn't respond.

Yes, definitely a man of few words.

After what seemed like a mile walking, we slowed our pace. The buildings on this section of the strip were brightly lit, and cheerful music hung thick in the air. Strange choice for the man who looked like a death metal guitarist.

Jacey motioned his hand toward a small cafe on the approaching corner. There was a pink cartoon cat on the sign overhead and brightly colored bubble letters that read "K-Sing: Cat K-Pop Cafe."

"Uhhh." I froze in place. *Was this his idea of a joke?*

Jacey looked at the glowing sign, looked back at me, and shrugged. I didn't move.

Sighing, Jacey turned back toward the cafe with his hands still in his pockets and pushed inside. My eyes bugged out of my head when the door opened, and a stream of bubbly Korean lyrics spilled into the night air. The sound cut off after the glass door closed behind Jacey, and I was left standing alone on the sidewalk.

This guy was absolutely nuts!

I shifted my weight from my left hip to my right, waiting to call his bluff. *Any moment now,* I thought, *he'll come back out laughing. Any moment.*

In the distance, I heard the shattering of broken glass. *Crap.* The silhouettes of several men approached, stumbling every which way. *Come on, Jacey.* The men were still a block from where I currently stood, but their loud voices were thick with intoxication.

"Ok, fine!" I spat in anguish and pushed my way into the

cafe. I'd rather endure Korean pop music than more drunken lunatics any day.

Bright colorful bubble lights hung from the ceiling, and the entire cafe was packed shoulder to shoulder with singing guests. From a stage in the corner of the room, a man's voice cracked painfully high as he read lyrics from a large teleprompter. I covered my ears and pushed through the jumble of gyrating bodies, scanning the crowd for the one big body that didn't match.

A hand caught my shoulder. I wheeled around to find Jacey, his stone face expressionless as he pointed to a doorway in the back of the room. We moved together through the crowd that parted like the red sea when they saw Jacey's massive form —clearly not their typical patron.

At last, we reached the door. There was a small wooden sign above the entry that read "Cat House." *Where was he taking me?* The only cat houses I'd heard of were the kind that contained naked women. Or at least, that's what I had seen in movies.

Nervously, I followed Jacey inside. As the door sealed behind us, the sound of boisterous K-pop stopped and was replaced by soft muted mews. I couldn't stop the puzzled expression that creased my face, and Jacey coaxed me into the room with the wave of his hand before I actually believed what I was seeing.

All around us were the lithe bodies of furry little cats.

An orange tabby eagerly bounded to my feet, weaving his body through my boots as he rubbed his cheeks all over my legs. As I bent to pet him, a deep rumble erupted from his chest. When I glanced at Jacey, he was standing beside a large tree-shaped perch, scratching the chin of a poofy white kitten. *Absolutely unbelievable!*

I gave the orange tabby a quick pat on the rump, stood, and

walked over to Jacey. He didn't look up from the white kitten he was scratching, but a slight smile crossed his face.

"Not what you were expecting?" Amusement danced in his blue eyes.

I chuckled in embarrassment and kicked my toes together. "Not quite."

"I like animals," Jacey explained, running his fingers over the length of the kitten's body, all the way to its tail. "They're always exactly what you expect them to be."

Maybe I'd been all wrong about Jacey. Sure, he was socially awkward, covered in tattoos, and was strong enough to toss a full-grown man into the air like a football. But this...this was far from anything I'd expected.

I was still smiling, too shocked to speak, when a petite waitress appeared beside us, holding two menus. I ordered a ham sandwich and a "cat-uccino."

"Black coffee," Jacey said, declining the menu without looking away from the white kitten.

Of course, the tough guy orders a black coffee.

"You're not hungry?" I pressed, as the waitress skipped away cheerfully.

"No," he answered. "Not a fan of the food here."

I narrowed my eyes in suspicion. *Was my sandwich going to come with a side of hairball?*

Jacey noted my panic and threw a quick smile in my direction. "I mean the food in LA. Not specifically the food *here*-here."

"So, you're not from around *here*-here?" Finally, a chance to get to know the mysterious blue-eyed man.

Jacey turned from the white kitten, but a troubled expression now stained his face. He moved to one of the few tables that weren't occupied by lounging cats and plopped heavily into a small cafe chair. Its legs groaned under the weight.

"No," he answered, crossing his thick arms over his chest.

A gray tomcat pushed its face between my boots, begging for my attention. "Excuse me, sir," I whispered, stepping over its body and sitting in the chair across from Jacey. So, he wasn't local to the area, despite the fact that he knew about this hole-in-the-wall cat cafe. Very curious.

The waitress reappeared, placing my sandwich and our two coffees on the round table between us. A cat-shaped puff of frothy latte foam jiggled on top of my cappuccino. I was always amazed by latte art, but this was almost too realistic to drink.

Jacey peered over the table at my cup, then looked to the waitress, who was already walking away.

"Excuse me," he called after her.

She turned back with a flirtatious flutter of her long lashes. I couldn't help but hold back a snicker as I took a bite of my sandwich.

"Can you do that to mine?" Jacey motioned to my jiggling foam cat with his hand.

I nearly choked on my mouthful of food. The waitress searched his expression for sarcasm, but he continued to stare up at her with intent sincerity.

The waitress picked up his black coffee with a smile and bounded back behind the counter where the sound of clanging spoons erupted. I stared back at Jacey, trying to find the joke in his eyes, but he just shrugged.

Moments later, the waitress reappeared with Jacey's black coffee topped with its own jiggly latte foam cat. After she'd skipped back to the kitchen, he turned the mug so that the cat was facing him and stared at it thoughtfully for a moment. His gaze drifted up, and his eyes locked onto mine. A devious grin crossed his lips. I couldn't help but burst into laughter.

"You are absolutely unbelievable," I snickered, pushing a spoon into the head of my latte cat and stirring it into foamy oblivion. Jacey made no move to do the same. He just continued to rotate between staring at me, surveying the room, and admiring his foam cat—arms crossed over his chest.

A soft vibration radiated through my pocket. I lifted my hips from the cafe chair and extracted my phone. My heart sank at once when I saw the name on the screen. It was Ryan. *Why now?*

"Who is it?" Jacey leaned his body over the table, trying to eye the screen.

"It's no one," I sighed in frustration before rejecting the call and placing the phone on the table beside my plate. "I mean, I guess he *was* someone a few days ago. But as of recently, he's turned into a bit of a no one."

Jacey's brow dropped into a straight line, still staring intensely at the black screen. Maybe he was worried that some crazy boyfriend was out searching for me. It gave an explanation for his erratic eye darting earlier. *No, that's silly.* There's no possible way he could have known that I had a boyfriend.

"Don't worry about it," I assured him. "Really, it's fine. He lives in Sacramento anyway. Not to mention, he's like...a shrimp compared to you. You could probably kick his ass with your eyes closed." Ryan was taller than Jacey by at least a few inches, but he was built like a bean pole. I used to like that about him. Sitting next to this very attractive and beefy cat-loving man, I wasn't so sure.

Jacey continued to sit motionless, staring at the phone as if willing it to ring again. "Sacramento?"

"Yeah, that's where I'm from. And Ryan, well, he's lived there all his life." I took a quick sip of my coffee. Jacey seemed content to listen, so I continued. "We met at work. He's...my boss's son.

"Over the last six months, we've kind of been seeing each other. I know you're not supposed to do that...date coworkers." I bit my lip, unsure of whether or not Jacey even wanted to hear this. Talking to him was better than talking to no one, and I was too frustrated to cork the bottle. "But now, I don't know. Over the last week, he's just kind of ghosted me. Up until now, he hasn't called at all."

Jacey seemed impassive. He listened intently, never taking his eyes off the phone.

A heartbeat later, it began vibrating across the table. *Of course.* Jacey craned his neck at the same moment my hand reached forward, his eyes glowing with interest. I didn't need to check the screen to know it was Ryan.

"Go ahead," Jacey mused.

I bit my lip nervously, then clicked to accept the call. "Hello?"

"Where are you, Vivian?" Ryan's voice was cold and unsettling. The sterility reminded me of the night at the restaurant.

"Nice to talk to you, too," I retorted, ripping my gaze from Jacey and twisting my body sideways in my chair so that I faced away from the table.

Meanwhile, Jacey poked at his latte cat with a spoon. He scooped up the little smiling foam face, extending it to the floor where a few meowing cats gathered. Each crowded around the spoon to lick at the frothy foam.

"Vivian," Ryan breathed desperately. "Where the hell are you?"

My face radiated with heat as my sanity boiled over. *How dare he!*

"Where am I? Where AM I?" I hissed, sending several

cats bolting nervously away from the table. "Ryan, I've been trying to contact you for days. You haven't called. You haven't texted me. You didn't even go into work until today, fully aware that I wouldn't be there. What the hell is your problem?"

The line went silent. If not for the stagnant sound of Ryan's ragged breath, I would have assumed he had hung up.

After several excruciating moments, he spoke. "Tell me where you are."

"I'm in LA," I ground my teeth. "With a new friend."

Jacey looked up, still catering to his crowd of furry fans.

"Where in LA?" Ryan demanded.

His overbearing tone made my stomach churn. This wasn't the Ryan I'd grown to know, and I couldn't help but wonder if he was drunk. Or maybe the Ryan I thought I knew wasn't the "real Ryan" at all. Maybe the real Ryan was this domineering jerk, who only cared about me when he thought it would benefit his ego.

Jacey craned his head to the side, clearly listening for my reply. *This was immature. So immature.* This wasn't how adults behaved. And I certainly wasn't making a good impression on my new friend.

"Look," I composed myself, glancing over at Jacey. This time, he was staring intently at me. Our eyes remained locked as I spoke. "I'm going to get off the phone and enjoy the rest of my night. Tomorrow, I'm going to meet with James's client, get on my plane, and come home. Until then, I think you should spend some time thinking about whether or not you value our relationship, if that's even what this is."

I was proud of that response. Normally, I didn't stick up for myself. It felt good. Cleansing even. Ryan needed to know that I wasn't the type of girl who would tolerate the domineering attitude. The line went silent for a moment, and I pulled the phone away from my face to see if the call was still connected. It was.

When Ryan spoke again, his voice was nothing more than a whisper, and he mouthed each word with excruciatingly slow acidity that chilled my blood to a halt. "You're already with the client, Vivian."

6

DOWN THE RABBIT HOLE

E verything moved in a flash. One moment, I was holding my phone. The next moment, Jacey was plunging across the table, ripping it from my fingers. He crashed onto the floor, sending cats screeching in every direction.

"FUCK OFF!" he screamed before hanging up the phone and throwing it into the adjacent wall. It shattered into a hundred glimmering shards, sending cats screeching and skidding wildly across the tile floor.

"Where's the rheotron?!" Jacey wheeled around, jumped to his knees, and grabbed me by the shoulders so that his face was only inches from mine. I opened my mouth in shock. No sound came out.

"The rheotron, Vivian! Did you leave it at the Belair?"

The what? I had no idea what the hell Jacey was talking about. Or what had just happened, or why my phone was scattered into shards on the floor behind us. I shook my head, trying to express confusion through my stone cold panic.

Jacey's eyes overflowed with desperation when, like the strike of a match, light appeared within the depths of his dilated pupils, and he muttered the words, "Keep in your pocket."

With a quick plunge of his arm around my torso, he lifted my body off the cafe chair and shoved two fingers into the pocket of my jeans.

Mortified, I found my voice. "Woah, Jacey! What the hell are you—"

One by one, he tossed out my ID, the company credit card, and my hotel key, sending them soaring across the room. Last, he pulled out the black flash drive. Turning it over in his hand, he glared at the device furiously for a moment, then shot his icy eyes to me.

"We have to get out of here. Close your eyes." Muscles taut, he pulled me to his body.

"Wait! What are you—"

In a blinding flash of blue light, the room around us warped into a long cylindrical beam. My face seared with heat, and a hysterical scream erupted from my throat as my body smashed into Jacey's ribs.

Burning! I was burning alive! I felt like a spider being pulled through the hose of a vacuum—only this hose was scorching hot and made entirely of a light so bright that even with my eyes closed, my retinas were on fire.

This is it. I'm dying. I'm going to die, and I'll never even know why or how.

We plummeted into an endless spin. Contorted and twisted, my limbs vanished into dust, then burned as they reformed in all the wrong places. My body arranged and rearranged, scattering into millions of tiny particles, then coming back together in a powerful collision as my head hit the ground.

Everything snapped into darkness. There was no more blue light and no more burn. I was dead or maybe in the process of dying. I wasn't sure which, but I was just glad that the twisting was over.

So, this was the end. It was different than I'd imagined. Quieter. At peace with the final act of fading away, I allowed my limbs to relax, and I released my mind into the sea of blackness. A single fish, swimming from the shore of my consciousness and into a place of quiet serenity. Free and peaceful.

"Vivian," a voice broke through the dark, disturbing the still waters of my dreams in a ripple of light.

I nestled my head drowsily into the hard ground below me, not quite ready to be alive again.

"Vivian, wake up. We have to move."

Who was that? Who was speaking to me?

The ripples of my endless sea lit up with the memory of today. Ryan, Jacey, the phone call, the flash drive, the blinding beam of light...

Reluctantly, I opened my eyes.

Jacey was on his knees hovering above my body. He searched my face for signs of life. Relief pulled at the corners of his brows when I blinked.

"Good. You're awake," he announced stoically. "We need to get off the street."

A million questions flooded into my mind, but none emerged from my lips. I was too fixated on Jacey, who looked very different from the man I'd shared coffee with at the cat cafe only moments ago.

The panels of his black button-down shirt had disjoined, forming multiple solid black plates. A dark tattered cloth encompassed his neck like a scarf, and his shoes—once, leather oxfords—were now black quarter calved boots. I shook my head in dismay. This was all a part of some delusional *Alice-in-Wonderland-esc* hallucination. *What a strange way to die.* Clearly I'd watched too many science fiction movies. Any minute, it would all fade away, and I would return to my dark void of serenity.

"Vivian," Jacey said again. His voice grew desperate. "I literally have no time to explain. If you can't stand up, I'll have to carry you. But if you stay here, you're going to die."

Well, that's just great. I'm already dying. Is it possible to die after you've already died?

With all the strength I had left in my body, I pushed myself upright and looked around. The scene in front of me only intensified my initial conclusion. I had to be dead.

The city around us was washed in neon light, reflecting bright auroras from the wet stone pavement where my hands were still planted. Heat radiated from the concrete as if it had baked under the summer sun, but the area was cast under a veil of blackness, and the sky above was blanketed in an unnerving starless crimson.

Tall black buildings surrounded us, but they were unlike anything I'd ever seen. They must have been at least ten stories high, and each were exactly the same size, height, and shape, all placed an equal distance apart. They looked like identical sharp-edged cubes, evenly spaced with just enough room for roads and alleyways to run between them. Bright fluorescent light lined every building, casting a halo of deep purple, pink, and blue over everything in their wake. Jacey's eyes seemed to glow under the neon pallet of the alien cityscape.

"Where are we?" I finally managed to choke. My throat burned as if it had been singed with a hot iron.

Jacey offered me an outstretched hand, which I reluctantly took. He pulled me to my feet and quickly surveyed the area. Once he was sure we were alone, he cast his glowing blue eyes back over me.

"This is The Channel."

7

THE CHANNEL

The words held no meaning to me. Like the bizarre cityscape around us, I couldn't comprehend enough to build conclusions or answers. Where once my neurons sparked and fired on overdrive, my mind was now completely drained of any tangible memories or thoughts that could define the surreal environment. There was no reference point. I'd never seen anything like this before. It was as if my eyes had been clouded through the distorted lens of a funhouse mirror.

Jacey grew noticeably impatient.

"Let me put this into terms you can understand," he hastily whispered in a voice that oozed of disgust. I flinched. "You can't be seen here. And I can't be seen with you. So we can either start moving, or we can both die. Your call."

The sudden bite in his tone snapped me into reality. I was alive—yet somehow, I was no longer in LA. A chill crept up my spine as the cold wave of realization gust over me. I had so many questions, but only one escaped my lips.

"Where do we go?" My voice was no more than a whimper.

Jacey grabbed my wrist, still sore from the bar, and we sped down one of the shadowed angular alleys. Our boots clashed noisily against the wet pavement, sending a spray of water glinting in shades of pink and blue with every step. Masked in shadow, we passed several stacks of large metal containers. From them spilled wires, pipes, and other unrecognizable metal chunks. In the distance, I could hear deep voices, laughter, and the hum of machinery. *What was this place?*

After a few minutes, Jacey slowed, and we fell into a more steady stride. I wasn't yet sure if it was safe to speak, but I had too many questions to stay silent any longer.

"Are you going to tell me what the hell is going on?"

Jacey spun on me so quickly that my body fell against the wall and into the shadow of the building we'd been trailing. With his face only an inch from mine, I could feel the emotions boil from his skin. His face was contorted with rage, uncertainty, and straining desperation that caused his dark brows to crease in the center of his forehead. Like a cornered animal, I couldn't predict his next move. My heart raced.

Jacey's eyes dropped from mine and craned his neck to survey the area around us. When his gaze locked back on me, the anger was gone, replaced with a cold stoic detachment.

"Starting now," he whispered gruffly, "I need you to assume that everything you know about your world is wrong."

"Yeah, that's real original, Jacey!" I exclaimed. "Which science fiction movie did you rip that line—"

With a snap, Jacey clasped a massive hand over my mouth.

"Shhhhhh!" he hissed in my ear. "At any given moment, there could be over a hundred eyes on us!"

Was he kidding? I wanted to cry out. To scream and curse and shove this deranged man away from me. But what good would any of that do? I didn't even know where I was. A single tear brimmed over my eyelid and fell onto Jacey's finger. He pulled his hand from my face, inspected the droplet, then wiped his hand with the black cloth from his neck.

"Look, I know I owe you an explanation," he stated, the

wrath fading from his eyes, "and I'll give you one. I promise I will, okay? But right now, we need to get you to a safe location so I can figure out how the hell to fix this. How to get you back home."

I sniffled again and nodded. My mind was a haze, void of thoughts or conclusions or answers. But "home" was a word I could understand. I wasn't sure where I was, but I knew that I wanted to be home. I grabbed onto the word with both hands.

Jacey pressed his back against the wall beside me and extended his forearm out in front of him as if examining a watch. I lifted my head curiously, just in time to see the black edge of one of his many tattoos ripple and rise from his skin. Where ink once covered, a solid rectangular mechanism boiled outwards from his wrist. Without warning, Jacey's face was illuminated with a dull green glow.

"What the hell is—"

Jacey silenced me with a wave of his hand. Seconds later, a hiss erupted from the green glowing screen of the strange device, and a staticky male voice buzzed around us.

"Hey, Jacey! Where have you been, man? You back from the Earth re-eval?"

Jacey flinched at the fizz of volume.

"Dane!" His face lowered as he hissed into the device. "Damn it, you were right. I ran into trouble. I need you to meet me in the alley west of J-5."

"Damn right, you're in trouble!" the voice replied playfully. "Gilroy and CieCie are all up in arms about the credits you owe them. I sure hope you brought back a souvenir tee shirt or a shot glass or something because they're pissed."

Jacey rolled his eyes and groaned, slamming his head against the wall behind him several times before raising his arm back to his face. "Dane, please."

The static ceased for a moment, and the voice continued. "Oh shit, Jace. You're serious? What kind of trouble?"

"I'll explain when you get here," Jacey answered. "Just do me a favor, okay? Come alone. If Gilroy catches wind of this, I'll never hear the end of it."

"Yeah, yeah. I'm on my way. But hey...you seriously owe me one. This is the second time this week I've covered for you. People are going to start thinking I'm still under The Five."

"I highly doubt that," Jacey replied.

Within seconds, the green glow from his arm faded. *Apparently, they didn't say goodbye here either.* I watched unblinking as the rectangular device sank into the surface of Jacey's forearm, rippling and transposing back into the unusual tattoo. *What had I just witnessed?* I was certain of what I'd seen —but it simply wasn't possible.

Jacey continued to stare at the design. "This makes things a bit easier," he said dryly. "For jumping, I mean."

His tired eyes met mine again, but I had no words. Nothing made sense from the moment I'd arrived in this strange city, if that's even what it was. Jacey could clearly read my confusion.

"Channel jumping. It's the process we use to move across dimensions."

"People move across dimensions?" I choked in astonishment. Is that what the blinding light had been? We were on a different dimension? Panic surged through my core.

"Well, not everyone. Just Channel Jumpers, like myself."

More incomprehensible gibberish. Nothing Jacey said made a lick of sense. Channel jumping? Dimensions? It made so little sense that I couldn't even formulate a decent question that would help me to understand it, and Jacey didn't seem intent on making sure I understood anyway. He rested his head back against the wall and closed his eyes.

For several moments, everything was quiet. I'd almost

convinced myself that we were back in LA, stowed away behind a building. Maybe I'd been drugged, or maybe I was drunk. Maybe we were just sitting innocently, waiting for a cab to take us back to the Hotel Belair.

The illusion quickly melted away when I allowed my gaze to wander around the strange black alley. Overhead, the sky rippled in an unnatural dark crimson, blotched with lighter gradient spots but still dark enough to cast the entire area in blackness. The harder I stared, the more I noticed what appeared to be gridlines across the expanse of space. They were a hue lighter in shade, and each intersected at equal points, creating thousands of tiny squares.

This couldn't be Earth. The pavement was wet as if it had been raining. But there was no sky, no clouds, nowhere for rain to fall from.

I wished I could see more. The buildings on either side of us made it impossible to view farther than what was directly overhead.

"Are we in space?" It didn't look like space. Not that I'd ever been to space—but I knew enough about space to know that there should at least be stars.

"More like *a space*," Jacey answered idly. That explanation didn't satisfy me.

"Obviously, it's a space," I pressed, turning to Jacey, who was still propped against the building with his eyes closed. "Everything exists in a space. I just...Look, I'm sorry if I'm being difficult. I just really need to know what's going on and when I can expect to be home. My mom has probably been calling me by now, and I'm sure it's getting late."

Jacey's head didn't move, but he crooked one eye open to shoot me a quick sideways glance. "More like *if* you can expect to be home," he corrected.

My brain felt like it could explode at any moment,

screaming questions in the chorus of a thousand furious bees. *Was he serious? He couldn't possibly be serious!* If we got here— wherever *here* was—there must be an equally fast way to get back home. Before I could question him further, the smack of fast footsteps sent me pressing my body back against the wall.

Shit! Someone was coming. It was dark in the shadow of the massive building, but if the footsteps got any closer, I was positive that whoever was creating them would see me. And what would happen then? Jacey said we'd both die if we were seen which meant—*oh, god!*

Jacey grew alert at once, straightening his posture so that the thick armored plates on his shoulders made him appear twice his size. Was this all a part of some sort of intergalactic space military? It might explain the edgy futuristic haircut and the techy wrist implant. *Then again, what did I know?*

The sound of boots on wet pavement advanced, growing louder and louder by the second. I peered around Jacey, whose body almost shielded mine entirely. From my hiding place, I could see the slender silhouette of what appeared to be a man approaching. He was taller than Jacey but narrower.

"What'd you go and do now?" the man called out brightly.

His playful voice matched the one from Jacey's strange wrist device. Relief flooded audibly from my lungs. This must be who we were waiting for, the man Jacey referred to as Dane. Relaxing his posture at the sound of the familiar voice, Jacey stepped forward, revealing my position in the shadows.

Dane froze in place, mouth agape. "Woah, what the hell, Jace!"

Jacey's eyes bulged, and he threw up both hands.

"I know, I know!" he sputtered. "I fucked up. I really fucked up."

Dane eyed him suspiciously, then looked back at me. "So, what? Did you knock her up or something?"

"No!" he shouted, disregarding his own volume. "Why the hell would she be pregnant?" Jacey froze in place. He glanced over his shoulder to shoot me a quick questioning look that sent my cheeks ablaze.

"What the fuck, Jacey?!" I seethed.

"Yeah!" Dane yelled from in front of us. "What the fuck, Jacey?"

Jacey's head moved from me to Dane and back again, as if our words were a plinking ping pong ball.

"No one is pregnant!" Jacey stated, arms outstretched to silence both of us.

Dane leaned back on his heels. Several moments passed before he spoke again.

"So wait. Why did you bring her here?"

"I didn't mean to bring her here," Jacey groaned. "This was my eval partner. Or she was supposed to be. I don't fucking know anymore. She doesn't have a clue. Total civilian."

Dane eyed me again, less suspiciously this time.

"You two aren't like...?" He made a finger-in-hole gesture.

"No, Dane," Jacey sighed. "I literally just met her. Look, I'll explain everything when we get back to Gilroy's place, okay? Until then, can you please just help me get her there? Unseen, preferably. I'm not in the mood to kill anyone today."

That final remark should have shocked me, but I was still watching Dane. He was a lot younger than Jacey. Tall, slender, with a face that was still full of youth, I guessed that he must be in his early 20s. He wore a snug black leather jacket that crowned high at his waist and a pair of tight jeans that made his legs look like two perfectly parallel lines. His feathered tawny hair glowed pink in the far-away neon light that gleamed from the mouth of the alley.

"Alright," Dane announced. He shrugged off his jacket and

held it out to Jacey, who snatched it away and extended it to me.

"Put this on," Jacey instructed.

I eyed the jacket hesitantly, took it from his hand, and slipped my arms through the still-warm sleeves. It lay heavy on my shoulders, and it smelled like sawdust and motor oil. Dane watched with an approving smile as Jacey pushed past us and started down the alley.

"We don't really dress in the typical Earth-attire here at The Channel," Dane said, stepping forward to stand at my side.

Even as distraught as I was, I noticed that he was ridiculously handsome. He had the type of face you'd expect to see in a teen heartthrob melodrama, and his eyes glowed with a welcoming enthusiasm. As we set off down the alley, Dane kept a close stride while Jacey led the way.

"I don't suppose you've ever been off Earth dimension?"

Jacey shot a disapproving glance over his shoulder, but Dane didn't seem to care.

"No," I answered timidly. "Honestly, I have no idea where I am or what the hell is going on. One minute, Jacey and I were drinking cat-uccinos. The next minute, there was a bright flash of light."

"Cat-uccinos?" His smile crept ten miles wide.

The cockiness of the question ignited something inside of me. Was I blushing? Jacey's quickened steps were my saving grace, and I angled my head low to hide the smolder of my cheeks. *Keep it together.*

The neon glow intensified as we neared the mouth of the alley. In the distance, I could see the wider street ahead and the buildings that formed its edges. Was everything diced into perfect squares here? The buildings, the sky, the roads, and the alleys all connected at perfectly ninety-degree intersection points.

Jacey was the first to reach the head of the alley. He looked sharply in both directions, then signaled for us to follow as he turned left onto the larger cross street. As I stepped into the glare of the fluorescent-lined buildings, my jaw dropped to the pavement.

The city was a light show, and the road seemed to never end in either direction. While every building was identical in shape, size, and depth, each was unique in its own display of colorful beams and lighted signs. The wet pavement only intensified the array, creating a reflection of neon auroras that boldly contrasted against our long shadows.

We passed what appeared to be a hotel or maybe an apartment complex, adorned at the top with a massive humming purple sign that read "Vacancy." On the opposite side of the street, I picked out a few buildings that could have been shops or maybe restaurants, but the symbols on their pink and blue signs were foreign to me. Steam billowed from street vents, briefly capturing light before they dissipated. Every few paces, man-high heaps of scrap and mechanical debris spilled from alleyways and out onto the main path we followed.

I kept close to the wall, occasionally stepping around humid steam vents as I trudged further into the unknown. Dane matched my slower pace step for step as we followed Jacey.

"If you see anyone, just play it cool and keep your head down. We'll get you somewhere safe...Hey, I just realized. I don't know your name."

He certainly was more talkative than Jacey. Normally, I wasn't a big talker, but it was nice to indulge in a bit of conversation after the night I'd had.

"It's Vivian," I replied, glancing at Dane.

Now that we were out of the darkness of the alley, I could see his face more clearly. His eyes glimmered in a brilliant emerald shade that reflected under the fluorescent ambiance. His light skin was untouched by the creases of age or stress, and he walked with a confident spring in his step.

"Well, Vivian," Dane continued as we ambled after Jacey, "knowing Jace, he probably hasn't explained much yet. The big goon."

Jacey's shoulders stiffened in front of us. I expected him to turn around, but he continued walking.

"Don't pay too much mind to him. We were in training together so I've endured my fair share of his nonsense. You're actually lucky I'm here! Would you believe that I'm originally from Earth dimension, too?"

"I'm sorry," I interrupted. "I'm actually not sure what you mean by Earth dimension."

A huge smile crossed Dane's face. "Damn girl, you really don't know?"

I shrugged in limp defeat under the weight of the heavy leather jacket. Was I the only person not in on some sick joke?

Dane's expression grew dark and mischievous, and his teeth gleamed in pale neon highlights. "You aren't on Earth anymore, Vivian."

"Yeah, I kind of figured that. The sky on Earth doesn't look like a big red waffle."

"Sweetie, you don't know the half of it," Dane bumped me playfully with his shoulder. "The Channel basically is just a damn big waffle."

"I'm still not following." Why was everything such a guessing game?

"Alright," Dane began thoughtfully. "Think of The Channel like a heart. We're currently standing on the central hub of all unified dimensions. And instead of blood, this heart pumps resources, baby."

"Resources?" I echoed.

Dane laughed, clearly amused by my ignorance. He was enjoying this way too much, but at least he was willing to explain more than Jacey. Not just willing. He was as giddy as a child.

"Yeah! Like gaseous elements, heat, water...the essentials for life. And not just Earth life. We support quite a few dimensions. I can't remember how many—"

"Twenty-six," Jacey turned abruptly to face Dane, his eyes smoldering. "The Channel supports twenty-six unified dimensions, governed by the Federation of The Five. A Federation that I proudly serve, and a Federation for which I would gladly die. A Federation that would rightfully track me down, hang me by my ankles, and extract every bone from my body with a dull butterknife if it were ever discovered that I brought a run-of-the-mill Earth civilian to The Channel. So, if you two are done blubbering, I'd like to keep moving. Quietly."

With a swift pivot on his heels, Jacey continued marching down the road, shoulders bristling. Dane nudged my shoulder with a smile and nodded me forward, his expression condescending to Jacey's tone. He seemed totally unphased, but he complied regardless and continued the journey in silence.

I'd been given plenty to process in the meantime. The buzz of my mental beehive was amplified with this new stack of unanswered questions. The Channel was separate from Earth...but it was somehow connected to Earth, along with other dimensions. But Earth was a planet, not a dimension, right? Unless there were different versions of Earth?

With every bit of new information, a million more questions sprouted like weeds. I instinctively touched my pocket where my phone should have been as if the internet would have answers. A pang of realization festered. *Everything was gone. I was gone. Ryan was gone.* What had happened after he called me? Did he know this strange place existed?

Dane nudged me again, raising a finger to silently point toward something in the distance. A small group of people stood on the opposite side of the street. Two women and a man were outlined in turquoise light that streamed behind them from the corner of one of the large square buildings.

My heart pounded heavily in my chest. Jacey fell back to cut the distance between himself and Dane and me. As we approached the group, I faintly picked out their voices. The man was speaking, though I couldn't understand what he was saying. His voice was clipped and unfriendly.

"Keep your head down, Vivian," Dane whispered encouragingly. "Just a couple of street goers. They won't bother us."

Jacey positioned his body pointedly in front of mine, and I buried my head into the collar of Dane's jacket to hide my face. *Would a group of strangers really be able to pick me out, just based on my face or my clothing?*

As we passed, one of the women raised her head to watch us. From the corner of my eye, I could see that her expression was sharp and unwelcoming. She wore a white tank top, but her thin feminine shoulders were armored in large black pauldrons, and her forearms were covered in twisted tattoos. The other man and woman continued speaking to each other in hushed voices. They seemed unconcerned with our group. After a moment, the third woman turned back to her friends, and the beat in my chest steadied again.

"Nobody's gonna fuck around with us," Dane whispered to me once we'd cleared a safe distance from the three street goers.

"Not when we've got Jacey with us. Jumpers are like The Channel's personal secret service organization."

That explained the heavy armor. Though, from the looks of it, everyone here seemed to wear some form of bodily protection. Even after removing his jacket, Dane's upper body was covered in a hard paneled navy outer shirt. It reminded me of something a motorcyclist might wear to prevent road rash.

"Not to sound rude," I whispered, "but if Jacey is so scary to these people, why do we need you here?"

This time, it was Jacey who snickered.

Dane ignored him. "Groups look a bit less conspicuous," he explained. "Jumpers are usually seen alone. But seeing one of The Channel elites walking around with a pretty girl in Earth garb? Now that might raise a few heads. Think of me as your handsome escort."

"Oh, please," Jacey grumbled through his teeth.

The street ahead darkened. Though the buildings each still held the same shape, the bright colorful lights grew fewer and fewer, and the air became stagnant. After several minutes of walking, Jacey looked over his shoulder. "We're almost to North M-5. Was Gilroy home when you left?"

"Nope," Dane answered.

"And CieCie?"

Dane shrugged apologetically. From Jacey's tone, it didn't seem like his friends would be very welcoming of an outsider. My stomach churned at the thought of more confrontation.

Jacey rolled his eyes and continued walking until we reached one of the large dark buildings that made up the corridors of the city. Its front consisted of a massive set of double warehouse roll-tops. To the left, there was a single rusty metal door, illuminated by a flickering yellow bulb. I held my breath as we approached the building. Dane threw me an encouraging glance, stepping back so I could stand between Jacey and himself.

Jacey placed a hand on the silver doorknob but stopped abruptly and turned to me before twisting it. "When we get in here, I want you to let Dane and I do the talking. Not a word from you, understand? Our group isn't used to unexpected company. And if CieCie comes out, for the love of fuck, don't talk to her about your clothes."

My teeth sank into my bottom lip as I nodded. It seemed that my Earth clothes would be a problem. A lump formed in my throat, and I swallowed hard as Jacey twisted the knob and stepped inside. A hand clasped my back. I jumped in surprise, only to twist and find Dane smiling. With his hand still on the small of my back, he gently guided me inside, closing the door behind us with a loud *click*.

8

GILROY'S PLACE

There were no words to describe the space around me. It was dirty yet clean. Dingy yet beautiful. Cluttered yet intentional. The building had obviously been used as a warehouse at one time but not anymore. Only traces of its former life remained—a rusted fire escape that connected to an iron catwalk overhead, white paint-chipped brick walls, and dented stone floors.

The huge industrial space had been converted into a home. Massive and open, the lower level consisted of a living space, complete with two battered leather couches, a dusty corded rug, and a small metal shipping container repurposed into a coffee table. The walls were lined with similar metal boxes, most overflowing with wild tangles of wire and machine parts.

Overhead, the catwalk broke off into three square rooms, their walls made entirely of glass. But what stood out the very most was the amount of greenery. Vines and ferns draped from large pots that were bolted to tall ceiling beams, forming leafy curtains that shielded several of the glass walled rooms. Two large trees grew from jagged holes broken into the concrete floors. This was the first time since arriving at The Channel that I'd seen greenery. Not just greenery but familiar greenery. Earthly greenery.

Dane rocketed over the back of one of the dilapidated brown couches and landed on the cushion with a creak. Throwing his feet on the table, he lounged back and rolled his head to look at us.

"Come sit with me, Viv. Make yourself at home."

His attitude certainly was much more carefree than Jacey's. I smiled weakly and moved across the room to sit beside him. The couch bowed with a threatening creak that announced it could collapse in the center at any moment. Dane draped his arm around my shoulder and gave me a shake. The unexpected contact was startling. I wasn't used to being touched. Aside from quick hugs, even Ryan seldom touched me.

"You just let Jacey do his thing. He'll get everything sorted, don't you worry. Then we'll work on getting you back to Earth." Through the words, Dane's eyes danced with a spark that made me believe he didn't really want me to leave right away. Judging by his initial reaction, they must not see outsiders very often.

I smiled weakly, unsure of how to respond. The world around me had just been turned upside down. Yet I was grateful that Dane joined us. It was hard to be anxious around someone so charming. Touched by white fluorescent light that brought new detail to his face, my cheeks flushed at the sight of his smile as it pulled tightly over perfect cheekbones.

"Dane? S'that you?" a rough voice echoed from the back of the warehouse. The tone was sharp like whiskey, cut with a metallic southern drawl.

Jacey quickly moved beside us.

"It's me, Gilroy," he called out, glaring at Dane. Anger seethed between his brows.

Apparently, Dane had been wrong. This "Gilroy" was

home after all. My chest constricted into a familiar bind, and I took my bottom lip between my teeth.

"Jacey? Ya'll back already?" The voice sounded closer this time.

"Shit," Jacey spat under his breath. "Keep her here please. I'll go talk to him."

Jacey sprinted toward the back of the warehouse. The noisy thud of his boots on the concrete floor grew quiet after a few seconds. Dane and I were alone. I decided to seize this opportunity while I could.

"Would now be an okay time to ask what's going on?" I whispered. "I'm so tired of waiting for an explanation." Jacey promised me that as soon as we were off the street, he would explain everything. We were off the street, and Dane was way more enthusiastic with his explanations than Jacey. Not to mention, I was pretty sure I could melt Dane like butter in my hands, if necessary.

"Damn, girl, I don't even know where to start!" he replied, though I could tell by his cocky grin that he planned to tell me everything.

"How about The Channel?" I suggested impatiently. "What is it? A planet? A city? Are we in space?" The pressure to retrieve answers quickly ticked on, like pulling slippery fish from a barrel. I may not have the chance when Jacey returned. Thankfully, Dane seemed more than willing to meet my demands.

He sat thoughtfully for a moment, then an idea sparked in his eyes. With a swift flick, he unhinged the cargo container in front of us. As if loaded on springs, it snapped open with a dusty thump. Dane swatted away a few drifting dust particles and coughed. I leaned forward a few inches to get a better look inside. To my disappointment, the box was full of more scrap metal, wires, and what appeared to be computer parts. They rattled and scraped as Dane sifted through the junk.

"I know it's in here some—Got it!"

Retracting his hand, I realized that he was holding a plastic toy Rubik's cube. The colored blocks were all mixed up and disorganized, as if the last person who played with it gave up and chucked it into the box.

Dane slammed the lid closed and turned to me.

"Ok," he started, holding the cube out for me to see. "Imagine this is The Channel."

"A cube?" I cut in.

"Lots of things in nature are perfect cubes. Is it any weirder than your sphere-shaped Earth?"

I couldn't argue with that logic. "I guess not."

"Exactly!" Dane continued excitedly. "And like I said before, The Channel is the central heart of all unified dimensions. Twenty-something of them."

He glanced around as if he expected Jacey to appear and admonish him again for not remembering the exact number. I remembered though. Jacey said there were twenty-six dimensions, but I still didn't know what that meant.

"The Channel is run by a sort of government. We call them The Five because there are five chairmen who dictate the whole thing. And Channel Jumpers, like Jacey, work directly under those bastards."

Jumpers—that was the term Jacey used in the alley. He seemed pretty dedicated to his job, if that's what it was.

"You don't like the government?" I assessed.

"It's not that I don't like 'em," Dane replied. "I actually worked for them for a while. They're just corrupt, as most governments are. A lot of faceless cowards who hide behind their Jumpers. Folks like Jacey worship them like gods, but not even Jacey has ever met any of them in person. Anyway, these five chairmen basically make all the decisions for The Channel."

"And what do they do, exactly?"

"They manage imports and exports," he said. "Dimensions are unified into The Channel based on the resources they can feed into The Channel. It's an 'I scratch your back, if you scratch mine' deal. In turn, we feed those dimensions resources they lack. But—and here's the fucky part—if that dimension ever becomes unuseful to The Channel, it gets torn away. Literally."

I struggled to follow the massive brain dump of information, but I knew our time was running out. I could always reflect on each element later. I continued panning for gold.

"What do you mean by *torn away?*"

Dane tossed the cube above our heads and snatched it out of the air gracefully. None of this sounded absurd to him.

"Well, you know how a heart pumps blood through the body?"

I nodded.

"Well, The Channel has a similar system. For each of the dimensions unified under The Channel, there's a sort of artery that plugs into The Channel's central core. Like a big power cable. We call them fibers. And through those fibers, a constant flow of resources move to and from The Channel. It's like...the ultimate subway system."

He pointed to a few squares on the cube, as if indicating where some of these fibers were located on a map.

"And The Five," I concluded, "they stop resources from moving through this subway system if the dimension doesn't have anything useful to offer?"

"For the most part." Dane leaned his face closer to mine, his eyes smoldering. "As a part of The Channel, these dimensions are under our secret protection. We look out for them and make sure they always have the resources they need. Folks like Jacey. But, if your dimension is deemed a liability—"

Dane made a scissor snipping motion to the side of the cube. His hands were barely hovering over my knees. The proximity sent a shudder through my spine.

"The Channel halts its exchange of resources. Can you guess what resources Earth receives from The Channel?" The flames in his eyes flickered wildly. My cheeks flushed with heat. He didn't wait for my response. "Nothing too important," he whispered, leaning even closer. "Just oxygen."

He winked and fell back against the couch cushion, all intensity gone as he twisted and turned the Rubik's cube methodically, not concerned with actually solving it.

"But how do you—"

I had no time to finish. Jacey's footsteps returned, followed closely by a second set.

"Here comes trouble," Dane whispered sarcastically.

Jacey was the first to round the corner from the back of the warehouse. His expression was unreadable, but he remained fixated on me as he closed the distance. Behind him, another figure followed at a slower pace. He walked with a wobble, and his feet shuffled heavily with every step. A long brown coat hung from his shoulders. Underneath, his frame seemed broad, like an old weather-worn tree. As he approached, I noticed a whisper-thin curtain of peppered hair peeking from under a strange misshapen cowboy hat with bug-eyed goggles on its crown. When his gaze landed on me, his black peppered mustache twitched.

Jacey gestured for me to join him in front of the couches where the man called Gilroy waited. His eyes were narrow with age but even more so with scrutiny. He looked me up and down like a sun-baked cowboy assessing a calf, then looked back to Jacey.

"Boy, I swear," he spat, his accent sharp like rattlesnake venom, "if brains were leather, yo'uldn't have enough to saddle a Junebug."

Jacey's eyes submissively dropped to the floor. He made no effort to move, no effort to speak. I was suddenly very uncomfortable. As I suspected, there would be no welcome committee for me.

Gilroy must have seen the silence as a clear opportunity to continue. "So dumb. So got'dang dumb, you couldn' pour piss outta boot with the instructions wrote on the fuckin' heel."

I heard Dane catch his own laughter behind me with a snort. Jacey winced. I turned just in time to catch Dane clasping his hands over his mouth.

"And you!" Gilroy shouted so loud that the concrete floor trembled. "You reckon somethin's funny now, do ya? Yer just as much a partta this mess as Jacey so git that shit-eattin' grin off yer face!"

Dane jumped to his feet. The Rubik's cube clattered noisily to the floor. "Hey, don't loop me into this!" he shouted. "I'm not the one that brought her here! Since when is it a crime to help a friend?"

Gilroy crossed his arms over his chest as if he was about to administer punishment to a disobedient child. I would have rather been out on the streets than in this room.

"Y'all don't know dip-shit from apple butter, do yah? You done fucked up, boys. Bothaya. Bringin' another civi to The Channel."

Another? I wasn't the first? There was no time to ponder this new information before Gilroy pointed a long crooked finger in Jacey's face.

"Y'all are 'bout to reckon wit a shit storm, an I ain't 'bout to be the one to wipe yer asses. So why'on't yah both pack up yer shit 'n go 'caus I'm done wit'cha."

His words seethed with finality. Several stagnant moments passed. I held my breath, too frightened of the whimper that might escape if I relaxed.

"Gilroy." It was Jacey who spoke. His voice was rich with sincerity. "How long have you known me? How many times have I pulled you out of the radar of The Five, even when I knew the gamble could cost me everything? I didn't ask for this, but I am asking for help. And I'd only ask if I truly needed it."

Gilroy's eyes burned into Jacey's for several tense seconds. He took a deep breath. "Well, bless yer pea-pickin' lil' heart," he hissed. My heart dropped. "Yer sweet talkin' might work on Dane an CieCie, but it ain't workin' on me. We gots enough mouths to feed round 'ere without y'all brinin' in more got'damn catawampus!"

It was insane how quickly my perception of Jacey and Dane changed. Both stood like disappointed children who had been told they couldn't keep the neighborhood stray dog. I expected these armored heroes to fight back or beg at the very least. Both just stood with their heads hung low, unwilling to look at me.

Now what would we do? Without a place for Jacey to map out a plan, I'd be back on the streets. I still wasn't entirely sure what that would mean for me, but judging by Jacey's and Dane's defeated expressions, I could assess that the outcome wouldn't be good.

Just as it seemed all hope had been washed away, a bright and musical voice called from the catwalk over our heads. "Oh, yoooo-hoooo! I see you, boys! And who's that with you?"

The petite figure danced so quickly across the catwalk and down the stairs that I could barely see her. At first, I thought I was looking at a child, but as she skipped to us, I realized that she must be closer to my age, though her clothing wasn't the least bit indicative. She wore a long white shirt with hearts and yellow smiley faces that draped to her knees, which met with a pair of long pink socks. Her hair was long, messy, and blonde, setting a golden frame to her small childlike face and bright blue eyes. Aside from the huge pair of goggles that hung around her neck, she looked...normal. Like a girl I might have passed in the halls at school.

"O-M-G!" she squealed in excitement. "Another girl! No. Way. And look at you! Look at your shirt! And those jeans! Where's this one from?" She looked excitedly to Jacey.

"Earth dimension," he replied, shooting a long questioning glance in Gilroy's direction. He was still fuming.

"Earth? Like, the one with Elvis and the GAP?"

What a weird question. Her eyes glittered expectantly as she waited for my response.

"Uh, yeah. We have both of those things. Or, we did. Elvis sort of...died. A while ago..." I trailed off as the girl's face clouded with dread.

"Oh, no!" she gasped. "Elvis died? When? Who killed him?"

"N-no one killed him. He—"

"CieCie," Gilroy interrupted, "why'on't you go on back upstairs. Us here men 'r 'avin us a private conversation."

His tone was stern but fatherly. I wondered if CieCie was his daughter. Or maybe her childlike demeanor just made it hard for Gilroy to use the same rattlesnake venom tongue that he used when speaking to Dane and Jacey. CieCie didn't seem to understand that I was the focal point of their "manly" conversation. She grabbed my hand tightly and tugged me toward the stairs.

"Well, we'll leave you men to it then!" she called brightly behind her. By the time anyone was able to react, we were on the stairs. Jacey stepped forward like he wanted to chase after us, and Gilroy's leathery face looked paler than linen strung out to dry. But it was too late. CieCie was pulling me up the stairs, across the creaky metal catwalk, and into one of the glass-walled rooms overlooking the warehouse.

In between the curtain of ferns that decorated the walls of the room, I could see that Dane and Jacey were already receiving another verbal lashing from Gilroy down below. I couldn't hear what he was saying, but the metal floor of the glass room vibrated with the bass of his roars. The sight made me relieved that I'd been pulled away. One more moment of their raging testosterone, I might have combusted on the spot.

CieCie was completely unphased by the commotion. She tugged my arm before using her thin hands to push me backward. Startled, I landed with a bounce onto a bed completely covered in fuzzy pastel plush animals. By the time I pushed my body upright, CieCie had turned away and was digging in one of the large shipping crates that lined the glass walls of her room. It was unreal how quickly this girl moved. She tossed several articles of clothing out on the floor behind her before turning back to me with a bundle in her arms.

"Treasures," she whispered with pride.

Falling to her knees on the floor in front of me, CieCie flattened out the shirts. One was a well-worn Elvis tour shirt, faded with pieces of the printing chipped away. Another was a massive men's GAP tee shirt, each letter embroidered in a different colored thread. The last was a promotional shirt, advertising a $2.99 Christmas special for a carwash called "Bubba's" in Lafayette, Louisiana.

"Jacey brings them to me when he visits Earth," she explained. "I don't know a lot about the other dimensions, but I like to learn. And Earth has the most interesting designs. We don't have pictures like these on our clothing." She caressed her hand over the faded prints. "Do you know anything about these two?" she asked, pointing toward the carwash and GAP tees. I wasn't quite sure what she was asking.

"You mean, where they come from or—"

"Yes! Tell me everything!"

I half-heartedly glanced through the ferns to the warehouse floor below. Jacey seemed to be pleading with Gilroy. His hands motioned wildly as if he were playing out tonight's happenings. Dane was standing nearby, chewing his nails. The odds weren't looking great. Anxiety crawled up my spine like the prickling legs of a spider. I forced myself to look away from the scene.

"Well," I refocused, unsure of how to explain the shirts in a way CieCie would understand, "the GAP is a brand name. And GAP stores only sell GAP clothes. It would be like if I made clothes, I might call my brand 'Vivian,' and I could open a store that only sells Vivian clothes."

CieCie's eyes looked as if they could shoot rainbow beams at any moment. "So, your name is Vivian! Does that mean you *know* GAP?"

I smiled for the first time since we'd arrived at Gilroy's place. What a sweet girl she was. I found it surprisingly easy to talk to her, allowing myself to throw a towel over the elephant in the room for the time being.

"No, I don't think GAP is named after anyone. Lots of brands are named after people, but some have random names."

"Random names..." CieCie repeated, studying each of the shirts.

"And this one?" she pointed to the carwash design. The print displayed a shiny gray muscle car parked in front of a decorated Christmas tree. This one would be harder to explain, but I was grateful for the distraction. Even with my limited marketing background, I hated the idea of promotional clothing, especially for one-time events. What a waste. Anyone but CieCie would have turned this hideous shirt into a dust cloth. How to explain...

"Do you have advertisements on The Channel?"

CieCie looked puzzled.

"Like, pictures or people who try to persuade you to buy things?" I pressed.

"Buy things?" she echoed.

Okay, I guess they don't have commercial advertising.

"Where do people on The Channel get new things, like clothes? Do you have stores?"

"Oh! Oh, yes!" CieCie's eyes ignited again. "We have markets where we make trades. And there's also Mercantile dimension. But we have to use our credits for that. Jacey owes me six credits so he's been making it up by helping me grow my shirt collection."

So they had a form of currency on The Channel. That was good to know. Maybe I could learn just as much from CieCie as she was learning from me.

"Okay, so this shirt was made by a business that wants you to spend your credits with them. And to do that, they give these shirts to a bunch of people to wear. So, everyone who sees those people will know that Bubba's Car Wash wants them to visit their store."

CieCie smiled, but she didn't seem to fully understand. Did they have cars on The Channel? I expected her to ask what a carwash was, but instead, she traced her fingers over the shirt, pausing on a decorated Christmas tree in the foreground of the image.

"And do all the trees on Earth look like this one?" she asked in wonder.

It was silly to assume that The Channel celebrated

Christmas or any Earth holidays, for that matter. Especially religious holidays. I chuckled at the irony.

"No, we only do that once a year. It's a sort of party we have on Earth that most people celebrate. And some of us decorate a tree to put gifts under."

CieCie's hands shot to her mouth, and her eyes grew into massive glittering pools. "I'd very much like to have a tree party, Vivian." she whispered.

How had someone as innocently wide-eyed as CieCie come to live on The Channel? Everyone I'd encountered so far seemed as rough-edged as the cube they lived on. And it seemed like everyone was tied back to the government—The Five, as Dane called them—in some way.

"Can I ask you something?"

CieCie's face perked up. "Of course!" she chirped.

"How'd you end up here? On The Channel, I mean."

Just as CieCie opened her mouth, someone tapped on the doorframe.

"Knock, knock," Dane announced. He strolled in the room, ballerina-twirled around, and fell backward onto the bed of pastel animals. A few squeaked in protest, and several shot into the air. His black pants and navy armored shirt looked ridiculous next to the pink kittens and teddy bears. CieCie grabbed a purple bunny and tossed it over Dane's face. He groaned a playful sigh but didn't move.

"We were having girl time!" CieCie protested, tossing another stuffed animal. This one knocked the first just enough to expose his jaw. He was smiling. The pressure released from my chest all at once. Surely, a smile meant good news.

"Did you guys talk to Gilroy?" I whispered urgently, lifting the animal from Dane's face. He peeked one eye open, then closed it. The smile never left his lips. I dropped the stuffed animal back onto his face.

Meanwhile, CieCie was gathering an armful of plushies from the foot of the bed. She hovered over Dane's head for a moment, winked at me, and dropped the entire pile. His arms flailed, fighting away the monsoon of colorful fluff. It was the opening attack of an unexpected war.

In a fury of pastel colors, Dane wildly launched stuffed animals across the room. A pink bear soared overhead, whirling past my head before bouncing against the glass wall with a plunk. CieCie squealed as a yellow bunny thumped against the back of her head before falling to her feet.

"Oh, headshot!" Dane called victoriously.

So that's the game?

Thinking fast, I grabbed a pillow that was slumped over in the corner of the room and held it out like a shield to guard my face. CieCie crouched behind one of the shipping crates at the far side of the room. Over and over again, stuffed animals smacked loudly against our shields. Dane kneeled with spread legs on the mattress, launching ammunition in even intervals as he cackled like a sugar-high child.

"Catch this!" CieCie taunted. In a flash of orange fluff, a huge cat-shaped pillow soared through the air before thumping directly into Dane's torso.

"OOOF!" The force sent him sprawling backward onto the bed.

Seeing my chance open before me, I dove forward onto the bed and planted myself squarely on his chest, pinning his arms at his sides.

"Oh, really Vivian?" he smiled with a viper's curl to his lips. "I think I like this view."

"How about this view instead?" I smiled back with mock innocence. Then I smacked him repeatedly in the face with my pillow shield. "I'm only going to ask once. Did. You. Talk. To. Gilroy?"

Giggling like a child, he tossed his head from side to side in an attempt to escape my feather bludgeoning, but CieCie was already at my side.

"We could tickle him," she suggested, her voice sweet but sinful.

Dane squirmed under my thighs. "No, no, no!" he gasped breathlessly. "I'll talk! I'll talk!"

I dropped the pillow onto his face and rolled off the side of the bed, landing on my feet. Dane sat up, still eyeing CieCie suspiciously. I sensed a brother-sister bond between them that only furthered my confusion. How were these absurdly different people related? As much as I wanted CieCie to answer my questions about her existence here on The Channel, I knew that the answers I sought from Dane were far more critical right now.

"I told you, Vivian," he smiled as he fingered through his messy hair, "Jacey took care of everything. He always does. Well—that's a lie. He usually does. Most of the time. He did today." His tone was absolute. Did that mean I could stay? Gilroy didn't seem like the kind of guy to be easily persuaded.

"It didn't exactly look like the two of you were winning the argument last I checked," I pointed out.

CieCie responded with another eruption of childlike giggles. "Don't worry, Vivian," she laughed, collapsing on the floor in front of the bed. "Gilroy is just a big fuzzy wuzzy teddy bear. He'd never really kick Dane and Jacey out. Who would make dinner?"

Dane rolled his eyes and chucked another stuffed animal in CieCie's direction. It missed its target, sliding across the floor until it collided with a pair of black boots in the doorframe. *Shit.* How long had Jacey been standing there?

"Gilroy wants to talk to us." He bent to pick up the stuffed animal at his feet and looked at CieCie who was still sitting on the floor. "Did I give you this one?" he asked, tossing the pink ball of fluff to her.

She caught it with both arms and hugged it to her body. "You gave me all of them, silly!" she giggled.

Jacey was responsible for all these toys? I looked around at the pastel piles of plushies that were still strewn around the room. There were at least a hundred of them! Add another layer to Mr. Tough Guy's character. I was getting whiplash from the constant perceptive shifts.

Dane sprang from the bed and stretched before strolling to the door. "Guess I better get cooking then," he remarked as he nudged past Jacey.

So Dane was the cook of the clubhouse? As hungry as I was and as much as I liked Dane, I was irrationally unnerved. Jacey said at the cat cafe that he didn't like the food in LA. Maybe what he really meant was that he didn't like the food on Earth. The crease in my brow must have given way to the whirlwind of new concerns spinning in my head.

"Food here is better than your Earth garbage," Jacey assured me.

"Oh yes!" CieCie agreed, "And Dane's food is yummy! Just wait and see!"

Nestled in the lower level of the warehouse, a tiny kitchen occupied the far left corner. It was complete with a high-top table, built from scraps of wood and mismatched pipes. I quickly noticed that the table had no chairs.

Dane was dancing to the tune of a deep bassy beat from the counter to the stove in a rhythmic pattern. Over his shoulder, I caught a glimpse of the stovetop—it was unlike anything I'd ever seen before. The surface was made from a glossy black glass that radiated a spiral of blue dancing light within its depths.

Before I had the opportunity to investigate the strange kitchen further, Gilroy appeared from the rear warehouse door. His room must be located in the far corner, I assessed. I still wasn't sure where Jacey and Dane slept, assuming that everyone lived together here in this strange warehouse.

"I'm hungry 'nuff to eat the northern end of a southbound pole-cat. What you over there cookin', boy?" Gilroy stalked to the table, slamming down a large mug full of mysterious sloshy liquid.

Jacey leaned against the high-top, staring sightlessly at the woodgrain. He didn't seem to notice Gilroy at all.

"Sorry, Gilroy," Dane called over his shoulder. "We're actually having the southern end of a northbound pole-cat tonight."

I was positive that he was kidding, but my stomach churned regardless.

"Vivian?" Jacey called without looking up. I'd kept my distance, unsure of whether or not I was welcome at the table, with the static of tension still buzzing in the air. CieCie had skipped off, promising Dane that she'd be back in time for dinner. I wished she had stayed.

Nervously, I took a spot next to Jacey. Gilroy's eyes analyzed my every move with cold calculation, but he didn't speak.

"I'd prefer to do this before CieCie get's back so Dane, you're gonna have to listen up," Jacey started.

The music rolled to a barely audible volume, and Dane angled his head slightly but continued his dance around the kitchen as he worked. Gilroy took a long swig out of his mug and nodded for Jacey to begin.

"Tonight, I narrowly avoided an attempt against my life, as well as Vivian's life," Jacey announced.

My throat tightened into a knot. *What? That couldn't be possible!* "What do you mean?" I exploded. "Who?"

Who could possibly want to kill me? And why? My mind raced to everyone I'd encountered in LA. The cab drivers, the front desk attendant at the hotel, Bruce the bouncer, the bartender, the drunk man that Jacey roughed up, the woman from the cat-cafe, and Ryan who called me just before my life changed forever...

You're already with the client, Vivian.

9
THE COLLAPSE

Jacey placed something black in the center of the table. In my jumbled mental state, instinct willed me to reach out and grab it. It was mine, after all. I was supposed to have it. But reality quickly smashed into me with the force of an eighteen wheeler as I read the distinct white lettering under the fluorescent warehouse light.

Keep in your pocket!

My heart pounded in my ears. Yes, it was mine—but there was something very, very wrong about that fact. I remembered the way Jacey leaped over the table at the cafe, how he screamed at Ryan before smashing my phone, and how he ripped the device from my pocket. *What was this thing?*

Jacey turned to me with intensity burning in his eyes. I searched their blue depths for answers, pleading for the explanation I'd waited all night for. Within them, I only found ice.

"Do you know what this device is, Vivian?"

I turned from the table, away from Jacey, from Gilroy, from Dane, shaking my head in an attempt to process what was happening. *No, this thing wasn't mine. I knew nothing about it. I didn't want it anymore. I wanted it far, far away from me.*

"I...I thought I did!" I choked. "James...I mean, my boss gave it to me. I was on a business trip! It was for our client...but Ryan said you were...I mean, I thought it was a memory card or...or..."

The words spilled in a jumble. Panic was replaced with a familiar frustration that prevented my thoughts from forming into sentences—like a dream, where you open your mouth to scream, but nothing comes out. *Did they think I did this? That I was somehow responsible for everything that happened tonight?* I wanted to explain. I needed to explain! But for some reason, an explosion of sobs was all I could force from my lips.

Jacey placed a massive hand on my shoulder and spun me back around to face the table. Dane was standing close by with eyes overflowing with concern. His sincerity only made me more frustrated. I didn't want them to see me cry. I just wanted to know why I was crying. *Why did this happen? Why was I here?* I wanted to go home. Mom would be worried by now.

It was Gilroy's voice that broke through my beehive of frenzied thoughts. "This here ain't no memory stick, girly. It's a rheotron. And a fuckered up one at that."

Tears streamed down my face as I frantically turned to him for answers. It was the first time I'd directly engaged with him, but all past hesitation was gone.

"Please," I pleaded, gripping the edge of the table until my knuckles burned white, "tell me everything. I need to know why I'm here...and I need to know how to get home."

Gilroy's narrowed eyes burned into me. With a twitch of his peppered mustache, he reached out and grabbed the device from the table. Jacey continued to stare at the wood grain where the device had been. Dane was now standing behind me, close enough that I could feel his body heat against my back. We each waited intently for Gilroy to speak.

He took a long swig from his mug and slammed it hard on the table.

"Welp, I guess we're gonna have to start from the top. Otherwise, ain't none of this gonna make a lick 'o sense."

I nodded. More information was good.

"Alright then, Viv'yan. The Channel, well...It's a sort of inaccessible anomaly, closely guarded by thems who serve under our central gove'ment—folks like Jacey. There's no way t'find us. No way t'detect us."

I leaned anxiously against the table.

"Under this gove'ment are twenty-six unified dimensions, each directly plugged to The Channel by what we call fibers. Our fibers exchange resources t'all twenty-six of the unified dimensions, most'a who are oblivious to our presence. In order to travel t'these dimensions and t'move resources discreetly, we need to be able to travel 'cross dimensions unseen. And there are only two ways t'do this—directly through a dimension's fiber...or, with one o' these," Gilroy held up the device. "A rheotron."

I recalled what Dane said earlier about fibers. He'd mentioned that The Channel was like a heart, and the fibers were like the arteries that pumped resources. He didn't mention that they could be used to travel to other dimensions.

"So, I just need to walk through a fiber, and that will take me home?" I pressed eagerly.

Gilroy smiled slightly but shook his head.

"It's not that easy," Jacey cut in. His voice was deep with strain as if every word carried a painful weight. "Fibers aren't like freeways, Vivian. They are dangerous, even for me. And the fiber that leads to Earth...it's one of the worst. Pirating, raiding, kidnapping—you name it. I only travel to Earth when I'm assigned a job, and we use rheotrons, when possible."

"Think of them as international waters," Dane added,

sliding beside me. "They aren't totally void of rules, but they are void of morals. You have to consider that every dimension has its own definition of morality, which makes policing them impossible. Earth is a perfect example of this. Every one of Earth's countries follows a different moral code. Fibers are more like...immoral playgrounds."

I was grateful that Dane spoke to me in terms I could understand. In this confusing universe, he helped to paint clarity. I couldn't have imagined going through this with tight-jawed Gilroy and Jacey.

"What about the rheotron?"

The new word tasted foreign and unnatural on my tongue. I didn't feel like I should know its name, let alone speak it. *Why did I have this thing? Why didn't Ryan tell me when he...*

A rolling wave of pins and needles crept up my spine. Ryan's text from the night before slammed unbidden into my mind like a car crash. The impact of the mental collision took my breath away. I gripped the table for support. Everything around me seemed to dematerialize in that instant—the warehouse, Gilroy, Jacey, Dane. Each faded into blackness. The only image in my head was the screen.

Keep it in your pocket! And for God's sake, delete that photo from your phone before you get us both in trouble.

He knew.

"It's bugged, Vivian," Jacey's defeated voice pulled me from the darkness. "The rheotron your boss gave you is bugged. He expected you to give it to me, and he likely expected you to be next to me when I plugged it into my Central Connect. The second it detonates, anyone within a hundred-foot radius of the blast will be sucked in. And as of right now, we have no idea where it leads."

"I gotta few theories," Gilroy added, "but ain't a one of 'em good."

"Right after you got in the elevator at the Belair, I called Dane and let him know there was a random civilian walking around with a piece of Channel-issued government equipment."

"And I told him to follow you," Dane added.

"I had no intention of actually talking to you. I'd planned to keep my distance and watch. Try to figure out what your intentions were, but you just did normal shit. Honestly, I had no idea what to think when I followed you to that bar." His mouth curled into a scowl. "Then that drunk fucker started pawing at you, and my plan went all to hell. I figured I'd get you somewhere quiet to talk, but when your asshole boyfriend called, I knew something was up."

Ryan? What did he have to do with this? There was so much to process. The sentences were like individual puzzle pieces, but none of them held enough information to explain the full picture.

"So...wait. You must have used a rheotron to get us back to The Channel tonight, right? It was a click, a zap, and boom— we were here. Can't you just zap me home?"

"Vivian, these things are complicated pieces of machinery. The Channel only revolutionized this technology a few years ago. The rheotron I used to jump back to The Channel is strictly a return device for emergency situations. It's a standard Channel-issued piece of equipment. We can't use it to get to another dimension. Only back from one if shit hits the fan. The fact that I pulled you from a dimension with me was risky enough. They aren't designed for multiple travelers. You just happened to be small enough that the rheotron I carry was able to pull the weight of us both."

Dane shot Jacey a sharp glance that I didn't have the time or will to comprehend. My knees were trembling like brittle twigs, threatening to snap at any moment. I knew that every second brought me closer to answers that I wasn't ready to hear. It was all stacking and building, leaning and swaying toward the final conclusion that I was positive would collapse my heart. But if the strain killed me, at least I'd die knowing. At least I wouldn't be blind as I had been for the last six months. I wasn't sure if I could bear the answers, but uncovering the truth was all I had left.

I forced the words through my teeth. "Who orchestrated this?" I needed to know where to direct this surge of hatred that ripped me away from home.

An image of my mother collected in my mind. She stood in my empty apartment, sobbing as she packed my belongings into boxes. Lost without a trace. Another missing person, assumed dead by baffled investigators. How long would it take for my mom to realize something was wrong? How long would it take her to fly to Sacramento, only to find my apartment clean and empty? Had she called my phone already tonight, wondering if I'd made it back to my hotel safe?

Dane placed a hand on my shoulder, but I stiffened under its warmth. I didn't want comfort. Not now. Not after all this. The truth was coming, heavy and merciless, threatening to collapse my chest in an instant. And I wanted to grasp the full weight of the truth.

"Gilroy traced a name back to the bugged rheotron. It was checked out of a government armory last week," Jacey said hesitantly. "We aren't sure of the details. Just the last name of the person who signed it out."

"Who?" I demanded, shrugging Dane's hand from my shoulder.

Jacey pursed his lips, turning his whole body to face me. I braced for impact.

"The name the armory gave us was J.C. Rivera."

I was wrong. My heart didn't collapse—it completely

imploded. An inferno unlike anything I'd ever experienced overcame me. I slammed my fist so hard into the wood table that my knuckles split at their seams. "That ASSHOLE!"

Dane jumped in surprise, but Jacey and Gilroy remained motionless.

So, Mr. Rivera was a part of this? Did he know? Did he know what would happen? Did he plan for me to die tonight? Or was that the whole point? The puzzle pieces began to connect, illustrating a six-month-long story that now made too much sense.

Mr. Rivera never thought I was special the day he hired me. He just needed a sheep to sacrifice. Someone who wouldn't ask questions. Someone stupid. Someone who would comply. Someone disposable. It could have been me or anyone else who walked into his office that fateful day. *Did that mean Ryan was in on it, too?*

Blood trickled down my hand, and I flexed my fingers as they began to stick together. Dane took my forearm and gently pulled me toward the sink, but I jerked away.

"And what about Ryan?" I demanded pointedly at Jacey. Surely, Ryan couldn't have been playing a role in this for the last six months.

Jacey watched my blood-soaked fist as he spoke.

"He somehow knew you were with me. That we'd found each other a day earlier than their little scheme intended. Once their plan started to go awry, the asshole probably tried to jump in and intervene." He shrugged, raking his hand through his hair. "I assume he only called to see if you were still alive."

This was too much. What exactly was the plan? To send the stupid new girl off on a suicide mission? For what reason? Why the hell did they want to kill Jacey so badly?

There were still too many missing pieces in the puzzle. I needed to know more, but my head was growing hazy with overload. I painfully flexed my fingers again, grasping the hollow air in an effort to collect my shattered reality. Until I fully understood what was going on, I had to hold myself together. I had to know where the truth ended and the lies began.

Was my job at Premier real? Was there really a Premier Edge Marketing firm? Were the people—my friends and coworkers—real?

Every fragment of my sanity was fleeting. The entire infrastructure of my life was a lie. Everything I knew. Everything I'd worked for. All was shattered into a broken mirror of insignificance that reflected back my expression of sheer blind stupidity. I was running at the edge of a landslide. My feet were sliding ever closer to the mouth of blackness. Would I ever know how snared I was in their trap? Would I ever know the full extent of their deception?

The impact announced its arrival with devastating blackness. My legs buckled as the room blurred around me. The last thing I remembered was Dane's panicked expression as he lunged to catch me. Everything slipped into darkness.

"Vivian, it's time to wake up."

I blinked my groggy eyes, adjusting to the bright light that streamed through the large bedroom window. This couldn't be real. Yes, I was fairly certain that I was dreaming—but everything was so familiar, so vivid.

Dust particles danced within sunbeam ribbons, and the sweet smell of cinnamon and cloves filled my senses. A gnarled tree swayed outside, decorated in a thousand memories of climbing and falling and climbing again. Its skeletal branches were encased in ice and flurries drifted to settle against the corners of the window pane.

But wait. Wasn't I forgetting something? Yes, I was sure there was something I was supposed to be—

"Vivian!" the voice called again warmly. *Mom?*

I lowered my feet to the cold wood floor and stumbled out of my room. This couldn't be real. It couldn't be...And yet, everything was just how I remembered it. Family photos hung in the hall, the faces of long-dead loved ones smiling at me as I passed by.

"Vivian, hurry up, sleepy head!"

My steps grew frantic. "Mom?" Left, then right. The hallway began to sway. I braced myself with a hand to each wall, scaling through a silver screen of memories.

New school shoes squeaking over freshly polished floors.

Toy cars racing and crashing against oak baseboards.

Socks slipping and sliding in makeshift ballet twirls.

When I reached the living room, my knees quaked.

Mom.

Mom was there, sitting on the floor in a yellow sunbeam. Beside her, a brightly lit Christmas tree glistened with sparkling white lights and a trove of handmade ornaments I'd made her as a child.

"Merry Christmas, Vivian!" she beamed.

Was it Christmas already? It couldn't be. And this—my childhood home—hadn't it burned down years ago?

Just as I stepped forward, a hand grasped my shoulder. Its connected wrist was encased under a black sleeve. My body went rigid, and a chill raced up my spine as a velvety voice caressed my ear.

"Every mask grows heavy."

"Vivian!"

A broken scream escaped my throat. Someone had me! Hands—there were hands on me! My limbs flailed in a wild tangle, but I couldn't move.

"Vivian, wake up! You're dreaming. It's okay!"

My eyes shot open, and I sucked a cold breath into my lungs. Dull light streamed between the thick ferns of the glass paneled room. A white blanket was wrapped around my body, soaked and sticky with sweat.

Dane's cool fingers pushed a tangle of damp hair from my cheek and tucked it behind my ear. My heart slowed to a dull ache.

"Where am I?"

"My room," Dane answered apologetically. "I figured it'd be better than the kitchen floor. You need to eat something, Viv. You're as pale as death."

Realization settled in. I must have fainted after my panic attack in the kitchen. My chest still ached, caging my heart's empty thrum. I didn't want to exist. I didn't want to be here. Food was the least of my growing list of concerns. And sleep clearly wasn't an escape from the overwhelming combination of emotions. I was sure that if I closed my eyes, the dark-cloaked figure would still be there waiting for me.

"CieCie is pretty worried about you."

Dane gestured to a neatly stacked pile of clothes on the foot of the bed—her treasured Bubba's Car Wash shirt and a pair of black silk shorts. I sat up, my tight sweater and jeans rubbing wet and uncomfortable on my skin.

"Sorry about your sheets."

Dane smiled. "Hey, don't you worry about that," he spoke

softly. "Sweat washes out. I'm significantly more worried about you right now. Why don't you go to the bathroom and change? I'll replace the sheets and heat some dinner for you."

His kindness was uncomfortably overwhelming. I wanted to dive headfirst into it, to embrace it. But I was afraid. Everyone I cared about was out to get me, and I was positive it was due to my own naivety. What if Dane was just another deception? What if this was just more fabricated kindness, designed to torment me, the stupid gullible girl?

As if in response to my blistering thoughts, Dane pulled back the blanket and took my hand. I winced as a biting pain shot through my knuckles. They were bandaged, but blood completely soaked through the cloth and left streaks of red all over my shirt, jeans, and Dane's white sheets.

He rubbed a soothing thumb over my sore knuckles. "Sweat washes out—but blood doesn't. Let's get this taken care of, too."

Dane pointed me toward the bathroom, which was located at the far end of the iron catwalk. The warehouse was dim, and my feet ached as I shakily hobbled by CieCie's dark glass cube. I held her bundle of clothes tight to my body. *She'd been worried.* For some reason, a pang of guilt surged through me.

When I reached the small industrial style bathroom, I stumbled out of my sticky wet clothes. There was a single shower stall in the corner of the room, but I was in no mood to figure out how it worked. With trembling hands, I ran cold handfuls of sink water over my arms, legs, and face. I unwrapped the bandages from my fingers and rinsed the dried streaks of blood from my hands and wrists.

The water stung more than I anticipated, but my dry throat ached for the cold. Cupping my hands together, I filled my palms with water and took a long deep swig. Shock ripped through my body. I immediately spit the mouthful of water back into the metal sink and stood, gasping. It was saltwater.

Another reminder that I wasn't on Earth anymore. I wondered if saltwater was one of the resources The Channel pulled from another dimension.

Frustrated, I gathered my bundle of wet clothes and bandages and retreated barefoot back to Dane's room. He was tucking new sheets into the corner of the bed when I arrived.

"Woah," he gasped. "Your eyes! Your eyes are so red! What did you do?"

My throat still burned like fire. "The water," I choked. "It's salty."

"Oh, shit! Yeah, I should have warned you. We have separate taps for freshwater and saltwater here," Dane said sympathetically, pulling a cup of water from the side of the bed.

I stumbled across the room and took it from him greedily. Within seconds, it was empty. I collapsed onto the cool blankets, exhausted with existing.

Dane took my hand again and sat on the floor beside the bed, this time inspecting the splits in each of my knuckles. His fingers were cool and careful, dancing expertly between each of the joints in my fingers as he wrapped them with fresh gauze.

"I know how you feel, believe it or not. This was all pretty shocking to me, too. When I arrived at The Channel, I mean." His eyes never left my hands, but he smiled warmly as he worked. "I was eighteen. Fresh out of high school and oh, so naive. I genuinely thought I was a badass until reality struck me down and spit me out here. It was my dad who wanted me to join the military. This isn't quite what I had in mind, though." His smile faded. "A few guys in suits pulled me aside one night after they saw me leaving my recruiter's office in Seattle. They said they had a better job offer for me, and I took the bait."

"So wait," I cut in, sitting up. Dane kept my hand in his,

though he was finished wrapping my bandage. I made no effort to pull away.

"You mean, The Channel recruited you right from Earth? How does that work?"

"Normally, it doesn't," Dane smiled admittedly, "but like I said, I had the constitution of a tortoise. I thought I was signing up for some secret-service-type job. Like, they hand-picked me or something. You know. On account of my overall badassness."

He winked, but there was a tight strain in his voice. *Was he like me? Deceived into believing he was more important than he actually was? Lied to?* My heart ached. Maybe we had more in common than I'd initially believed. *Maybe Dane was safe.*

"Then I met Jacey, and things got a bit better," Dane continued. "He helped me throughout my training. Like the big ox of a brother I never had. I mean, I had a brother on Earth. But he was a drunk. You know how that goes." He rolled his eyes. "Jacey, he just...always took the Jumper-thing too seriously, ya know? I couldn't handle the pressure after a few years. Never knowing the face or the purpose behind the commands. Watching dimensions die at our hands. I couldn't be a part of it anymore."

There was something on his face that I couldn't explain, but the strain of new emotions brought light creases to his forehead.

"So you left?" I pressed.

Dane reached to the floor where he'd placed the empty cup and picked up a bowl. It was filled to the brim with a strange orange soup that smelled like nothing I'd ever experienced before. My stomach growled.

"I'll keep telling my story, Vivian, but you need to eat. Jacey will kick my ass if you don't."

I eyed the bowl suspiciously.

"It's curry," he answered.

That seemed too...*normal*. I raised an eyebrow. "I don't believe you."

"No, really!" he laughed. "Curry is pretty much all we eat on The Channel. It's convenient and quick to prepare. Every unified dimension has a manner of ingredients that make some variant of the recipe possible, though the quality varies drastically." He winked. "Trust me. Mine is the best."

I was still suspicious, but I took the curryl anyway. There was no spoon, so I tipped the bowl to my lips and sipped. *Maybe The Channel didn't have spoons.* I was pleasantly surprised by the curry, nonetheless. It reminded me of the comforting bowls of tomato soup my mom would bring to my bedside when I was sick. I kept sipping as Dane continued.

"To answer your question, yes. I left The Five. You can really only gain access to The Channel if you join the central government, but once you're in, you don't have to serve indefinitely. After a few years of service, you can opt out and take on a more subtle role. Gilroy served for thirty-something years before buying this warehouse and became a Central Connect mechanic."

"Jacey mentioned something about the rheotron plugging into his Central Connect, but I'm not sure what that is." I hated to interrupt him, but I needed to understand as much as I possibly could about this strange world. Especially if I was going to be stuck here for a while.

Dane thought for a moment, then began rolling up the sleeves of his dark blue shirt. I realized at once that I had only seen his arms hidden beneath sleeves. How different they looked from what I'd imagined. His forearms were vascular and corded, completely covered in tattoos, similar to Jacey's but faded. Instead of a deep contrasting black, they bled into a smudged blue-gray that looked not at all indicative of his young age.

"Central Connect is our primary line of communication with The Channel. It's like social media—but also like a bank account, I guess. Intrusive, I know. We all have to have one, and they are linked directly to a CC device that we have to carry with us. Creepy, right? It gets weirder.

"High government officials tend to use retinal implants, but common folk have to carry a physical device with them. Most opt for glasses, but there are also pocket-sized projector versions. Jumpers are luckier than most. They have access to these cool tattoos, but they stop working after your service concludes. I'd show you, but..." He trailed off, as if he was saddened by his faded tattoos and any glory or honor that once came with them.

They'd been rendered useless designs and were not at all pretty. More like slashes ripping into the canvas of an expensive oil painting. The more I saw of Dane, the more I felt like he resembled artwork, even with the faded tattoos. It was a shame that they no longer worked. Curiosity itched me for a better look at one. I recalled the way Jacey's tattoo transformed into a raised green glowing screen and how he used it to speak to Dane.

"I actually saw Jacey's earlier today. I just...couldn't believe what I was seeing."

Dane admired the twisting black lines on his forearms. I tried to hide my own admiration as well but not for the tattoos. Wearing sleeves should have been a criminal offense for this boy.

"Yeah, they're really something when they are functional. Once Channel Technology learned how to engineer cybernetic tattoos, The Five started inking us from head to toe. Weapons, computers, tracking units, you name it. My CC may be obsolete, but my weapons system functions just fine."

Cybernetics? How was that possible? My mind wandered

full circle as I thought about what other tattoos he might be hiding...and where?

Dane appeared to be amused by my bewildered expression. "Different dimension," he reminded me.

Everything here was different yet so similar to the world I was familiar with. I wondered what the other dimensions were like. Were there strange alien lifeforms? Or were they just slightly different parallels to the world I was used to?

"So have you been to any other dimensions? Other than Earth?" I asked as casually as if I were inquiring about a road trip. My stomach gurgled. Dane pointed to my bowl of curry with a cocky grin, a bargained exchange before he'd continue. I took a sip.

Satisfied with the response, he answered.

"Technically, all dimensions unified by The Channel are 'Earth' or the planet itself, at least. Your version of Earth is dimension six. But all of the unified dimensions are tied to your round planet, if that makes sense."

"It really doesn't," I laughed. Not that anything made much sense to me.

"I like to think of every dimension as a page," Dane offered, "and your planet is the book. The title of 'Earth' just happens to be the sixth page. And The Channel only selects the very best pages to unify."

So, Earth was just one of the lucky pages. I wondered how that happened.

Dane took the bowl from my hands and placed it on the floor. I hadn't even noticed that it was empty. Now that I no longer had anything to hold, my hands were confused and unsure.

"To answer your question," Dane propped his elbows on my bare knees and looked up at me from underneath his raven feather lashes, "I've been to most of them. The ones that have a high enough oxygen-based atmosphere, at least. Not all twenty-something of them are human habitable."

Normally, that response would have been intriguing. I had so many questions about the other dimensions. We could have explored a thousand avenues and filled hours with conversation. But this foreign physical contact was so intoxicating that I barely heard his answer.

His emerald eyes locked into mine so intensely that I had to break away. My hands balled together uncomfortably in my lap, fighting an invisible urge to let them roam. To rake them through his messy hair or run my fingertips roughly over the budding stubble of his cheeks. I was so hollow and alone and confused, but more than that. I was furiously and utterly starved.

I'd spent the last six months doing my best to be good to Ryan, to respect him, as well as his wishes—right down to how I spoke and how I dressed. To maintain a look, an attitude, a posture that never felt my own. Like a marionette manned by a narcissistic puppeteer. To fit in enough to be wanted, even at the expense of my own comfort. And now, here was Dane, who barely knew me—but who, despite that, was washing the blood from my hands and comforting me.

Was his heart racing, too? Was it need that lingered in his eyes, or was he just showing sympathy to a wounded bird?

No. My mind was spiraling in a toxic direction. I was hurting, and any cravings that plagued me at that moment stemmed from my own shock and confusion. My behavior was pathetic. Dane continued to look at me, but I made a conscious effort to remain still.

"Twenty-six," I blurted.

He blinked in confusion, like I had snapped him from his own reverie. As much as I wished I could, I was sure that I'd never know what he'd been thinking about. That was probably for the best.

"Jacey said there were twenty-six dimensions," I continued, hastily trying to smother the embers I'd previously been fanning. "And you say that most of them are habitable? That must be fascinating. What are those like?"

Invisible strings in my chest pulled tight, then snapped as Dane took his elbows from my knees and stretched. I didn't want him to move. *Selfish, selfish.* I could feel the heat of our conversation beginning to fizzle out, along with the bitter knowledge that I'd soon plummet into solidarity.

Dane yawned and stood from the floor, collecting the bowl and cup he'd brought from the kitchen.

Don't go. I tried to keep the disappointment from making an appearance on my face.

"The other dimensions? Totally brutal," he answered warmly but obviously ready to close our discussion. "Almost as brutal as Jace will be when he finds out I kept you awake. Why don't you try to get some sleep? We have a busy day ahead of us."

Before I had a chance to protest, Dane slipped through the door, and I was alone in the glass room. Dim orange light streamed over the contours of the white blanket, reminding me that *alone* was the last place I wanted to be. As exhausted as my mind was, I knew sleep would be impossible.

The night before, I'd slept eight hours waiting for Ryan—the name smoldered red as I thought it—to message me back and another eleven hours when I reached my hotel room in LA. And judging by the stillness of the warehouse, I'd probably slept for several hours after my episode in the kitchen. But with everyone asleep, what could I do?

Reluctantly, I cocooned myself into the new blanket Dane left for me and tried to close my eyes, but the protesting twitch in my lids always tugged them back open. I allowed them a few minutes to wander. Maybe then, they would cooperate.

The glass walls of Dane's room were covered in long draping ferns that offered more privacy, making it darker than CieCie's room had been. A clothing rack in the corner was filled with strange black, brown, and navy jackets, each covered in armored plates.

Unlike Jacey's clothing, these plates were more styled, as if intended to be discreet, maybe even fashionable. They suited Dane's slender frame. I replayed my first glimpse of him approaching in the alley tonight. Each time, I pictured him in a different jacket. He was graceful, sleek, and predatory in an almost hypnotizing way.

This led me to wonder if Jacey's armor was intentionally designed to look sharp, broad, and intimidating. It would make sense for his line of work. Especially if he was tasked with visiting different dimensions or traveling through fibers. Apparently, those were very dangerous. But Jacey seemed quite dangerous, too.

He intimidated me, and I'm sure this was no secret to him. I still had no idea what he was physically capable of. With one arm, he'd effortlessly tossed the drunk man at the bar like a rag doll. Even then, I'd sensed that he was holding back. The drunk man was a nuisance, but he wasn't armed. Had there been a reason to kill him and risk making a scene, I was sure Jacey was more than capable of doing so. Not that anyone at the bar would have stood against him. Even the bouncer appeared startled as he watched us leave. It was easy to assume that Jacey was intimidating by design.

Not to mention, Jacey was significantly bigger than Dane, though Dane was taller. Naturally, this would make Jacey appear more intimidating—but it was really their faces that set them apart. Dane was wide-eyed and full of youthful enthusiasm, while Jacey's face could have been chiseled from stone.

What had he seen during his time here? Dane said he'd only worked for the government for a few years before growing tired of it. What was Jacey's reason for staying? Where did he come from, and what made him so passionate about working for The Channel?

My mind continued to spin in circles, building a catalog of questions, each one nudging me further and further past the point of return. There was no possible way I could sleep tonight, if "night" was a concept here. From what I could tell, the sky was a confined sea of red gridlines—"an inaccessible anomaly," as Gilroy put it. Just a single thread, woven into the reality of the unknown.

After tossing and turning for several more minutes, I decided I'd had enough with my brain. Building up courage, I crawled out of bed and made my way out onto the catwalk. For the first time since arriving, I was able to truly survey the warehouse uninterrupted. Maybe it was better to focus on what I could see, rather than stressing about the unknown. There had to be answers hidden here.

I started with the most curious element of the room. The two trees that grew from the lower levels were ten or maybe fifteen feet tall, their branches brushing the edges of the iron walkway with large pointed leaves. Like so many of the familiar things I'd seen at The Channel, they were out of place. Their roots pushed up cracked slabs of the concrete floor, fighting to make enough room to survive. How long before they reached the ceiling, and when they did, what would happen to them? For lack of an answer, I moved on to scan the next-most curious element of the room.

Across the catwalk gaped a large half-circle-shaped window. Its upper panes were streaked with dull purple and blue light from the distant faux auroras. Beyond it, a sea of crimson sky filled the remainder of the window. I took a step forward before noticing that its lower pane was propped open slightly.

Maybe I'd be able to get a better view of the city. My bare feet burned cold as I tip-toed across the iron catwalk and toward the crimson glow of the outside world. As I approached, I began to make out a hushed voice.

Startled, I stopped. *Who was out there? Was it Dane?* Whoever it was, they were sitting right outside the window. Their black silhouette was hunched over as they murmured to themself. Definitely too broad to be Dane.

Cautiously, I crept forward. With every inch, the words became clearer—but still, they lacked meaning.

"I don't care about your hunches. Without solid evidence, there's nothing I can do right now."

The voice was deep and familiar—*Jacey.* But who was he talking to? Was he using his Central Connect device? Listening in on his call was definitely rude, but I wasn't ready to interrupt him yet. What evidence was he talking about? Was this about Ryan and the rheotron? I didn't hear a voice respond, but Jacey continued anyway.

"You know I can't do that. Having her here is bad enough. I can't risk exposing you."

My heart raced so loudly that I expected Jacey to hear it. Sneaking up on him probably wasn't a good idea. I didn't understand the conversation he was having, but I could tell that it wasn't intended for additional ears. If I turned and fled, Jacey would likely hear my retreat. My best bet was to reveal myself. I'd pretend I just arrived, and maybe Jacey would explain more about his secret conversation. If he didn't, I'd make it a point to ask him at a later time.

I took a few noisy steps forward and yawned. "Jacey?" I called out in my most convincing groggy voice. "Is that you?"

He didn't seem startled. It was almost as if he knew I'd been there all along. Without turning, he quickly shoved something in the pocket of his armored jacket.

"You should be in bed, Vivian. Or did Dane's childish flirting give you nightmares?"

His voice was bitter, but I was getting used to the acidity. I peered out the window to find where Jacey had been sitting—a narrow ledge that directly overlooked the alley where we'd first arrived at the warehouse. In the distance, the buildings glowed in brilliant colors, casting aurora-like splashes into the smoggy haze above the city.

As I'd guessed before, the warehouse was isolated in its own dark corner, surrounded by identical cube-shaped buildings that were left unlit. The view was beautiful in its own terrifying way. Like the black depths of the ocean floor. I carefully sat on the narrow ledge beside Jacey, draping my bare legs over the side of the building.

"Dane has actually been a big help," I admitted. Without Dane, I would have spent the night bleeding, soaked in sweat, and with an empty stomach. I didn't want to admit to myself that his nurturing was the only thing that held me together tonight. He made my once-vacant soul less empty.

"It doesn't matter anyway," Jacey shot back coldly. "We're leaving tomorrow."

Leaving? I studied his expression for several moments, waiting for him to explain. His eyes were empty blue voids, staring lifelessly across the expanse of geometric shapes. *Why was he like this?*

After several excruciating silent moments, I asked, "Going where?"

"To get you new clothes and some light equipment," he

answered, gesturing toward my exposed legs. "I don't know how long you're going to be here. It could be a while. Gilroy is doing all he can, but we don't have a lot of spare parts right now, and building a two-way rheotron is risky business. I'm confident he can do it—more than confident actually—but in the meantime, we need to keep a low profile. You can't exactly wear CieCie's pajamas out on the streets. Especially if..." He trailed off.

"If what?" I pressed.

"If something were to happen, Vivian. We may need to travel to several dimensions to gather the parts Gilroy will need. I can't tote you around, totally unprotected."

"And what about Dane? Is he coming, too?" I dared to ask.

Jacey turned to me, his frosted eyes blazing.

Immediately, I regretted the question, but I wasn't able to reel it back in after it escaped my lips. A familiar chill crawled up my spine as I braced for his venom.

"Why would Dane need to come?" he growled.

"Well," I started, trying to sound reasonable, "wouldn't it be better to bring him along? I mean, I know he isn't a Jumper anymore. But doesn't he still have military training? Surely, it would be better to bring him along, right?"

I'd hoped that my rational explanation would satisfy him. In reality, I didn't know if my anxiety could handle a solo expedition with Jacey. He was utterly annoyed with my presence, that much was clear. I was a nuisance that put his job at risk, and he wanted to be rid of me as quickly as possible. Which was just fine with me. I needed to get home. But for as long as I was here—or away from home at least, I would prefer to have Dane around, too. For my sanity.

"Don't be an idiot, Vivian," Jacey shot coldly. My heart sank. "Dane is too distracted by you to be of any use. He'll end up dead with his tongue hanging out."

I no longer tried to hide my disappointment. The conversation was growing uncomfortable, reflective of what tomorrow would be like. I didn't want to go with Jacey.

"Dane said that you traveling with me alone might be suspicious, though. Isn't that why he joined us on the street tonight?"

Jacey's shoulders stiffened, but he didn't respond. After a few moments, he pushed his fingers into his temples and breathed.

Was this it? Was he giving in? My heart thrummed heavier with hope.

Jacey turned to me. Through narrowed, ice-cold eyes, he scowled with a menacing intensity that burned straight through to my core. Instinct and fear willed my body to shrivel. The panic in my expression seemed to only make him angrier, so I was surprised when he spoke that his voice was deathly calm.

"Dragging you around is going to be enough of a burden." Staring deliberately into my eyes, he added, "Your existence right now is a burden."

He held my gaze, ensuring that I suffered the full weight of the intent behind them. *I was a burden.* He wanted me to know that my existence burdened him.

It wasn't anything new to me, I realized. My chest pooled over with despair, but as I allowed it to overflow, the sadness heated and boiled into a new emotion. My busted fingers flexed, and my scabbed knuckles split with a sharp pop from under their bandage. I was never in control—*of anything.* I hadn't been on Earth, with Ryan, or since I'd been here. I was always someone's tool or someone's burden. There was no middle ground for me.

I wanted to swing my fists at Jacey's stupid face like I had with the kitchen table. I'd probably break my hand on his thick skull in the process, but it would be worth it. My face grew hot, and tears brimmed over, burning as they rolled down my cheeks. Jacey's expression did not change, even as his pupils shifted to follow a tear as it rolled down my nose. It tickled uncomfortably, but I didn't dare whisk it away.

Without warning, Jacey stood and ducked back through the window. His feet thumped as they landed on the catwalk. "Go to bed, Vivian," he whispered coldly over his shoulder before turning away.

I remained motionless, trembling in an overwhelming monsoon as his footsteps grew quieter. My resolve was boiling over, constricting my throat with ache. *Not yet.* I wouldn't allow myself to combust until I was sure he was gone.

The screams of my silent storm swarmed, assaulting my mind like frenzied wasps and making it impossible to form a single rational thought. Silent tears continued to cascade, one by one splashing hot onto my bare thighs. My knees trembled wildly, filled with the aberrant desire to launch my body through the open window.

After several painful moments, I permitted the pot to boil over. Diffusive sobs escaped my throat, and I rested my head against the cold window frame in defeat. *How much could a human endure in a single night before their heart gave out?* My chest ached with such intensity that I wrapped my arms around myself. If I released my hold, I was sure I'd shatter into pieces.

Burden. I repeated the word in my mind. *Even in a totally different dimension, I was someone's burden.* Another agonizing sob ripped through me. I allowed the anguish to burn, like the deep crawl of a match set to paper. If I could defuse this bomb now, I might be able to stay composed tomorrow. When I'd be alone...*with him.*

My mind raced erratically, ricocheting from one bad thought to the next. Mr. Rivera used me. *Used me.* Ryan allowed me to be served as a sacrifice. *He didn't care about me.*

He said only what was necessary to keep me around, just until I'd served my purpose—*to die*. I was supposed to die today. I shouldn't be breathing. I shouldn't be their burden. And I didn't even know why. What was the purpose of it all? Even if I made it back home, what was there to go home to? Who could I trust?

My strained gasps were dizzying, and my lips tingled. I could sense myself slipping away, the path my mind so often traveled when panic consumed me. Maybe I'd pass out again. Maybe I'd fall from the ledge. I pictured it—twisting and contorting in the air until I reached the street below. At least I wouldn't be a burden anymore. *No.* I couldn't do that to Dane or poor innocent CieCie.

"Vivian?"

I whipped my head around, relaxing at once. Dane stood with his arms outstretched toward me cautiously. His expression was heavy with panic. I wiped a tear from my face, trying to cover the shame of my episode, but the creases in Dane's forehead told me that I hadn't hidden a thing.

"What are you doing out there?" he demanded, wrapping an arm around my torso and pulling my body effortlessly back through the window.

I welcomed the warmth of his grip, suddenly aware of how cold my skin was. My legs quivered weakly, and I lurched forward the moment my feet touched the catwalk. He placed his hands on my shoulders to steady me. *Why was he so kind?* From the moment he met me, Dane had been nothing but kind. He had no reason to be—he just was.

Magnetic force tugged me forward. *Fuck my rationality.* I collapsed into his chest and whimpered in full surrender to the wild crumbling of my sanity. I didn't care what he thought. Maybe I was crazy and unstable. That was fine. There was no way I could endure this pain on my own. I'd stop breathing. I was certain. He could think of me as a stupid hysterical girl, as long as he stayed.

His muscles were stiff and rigid as I gripped onto the foreign contours of his body. I waited, anticipating the pressure of his hands pushing against me. Any minute, he would untangle my arms and send me back to bed. His body eased, and to my surprise, Dane gripped me tightly into his chest.

"Damn it. I'm sorry. I knew I shouldn't have left you alone."

"I know this sounds stupid," I sputtered, "but please don't go."

Dane's arms swallowed me up, caving in the painful walls around my chest. He didn't let go, even as he walked me back to his room. As we lowered together into the soft nest of his bed, I allowed myself to tremble, unashamed of the consuming pain that teetered me over the edge of sanity.

The dark cloaked figure was replaced with warm arms that encased my wild heart. The scent of cedar and motor oil drowned me, and I allowed myself to drown. Tears continued to flow. With each sob, he gripped me tighter—and I welcomed the pressure, along with the cadence of his heart racing against my ear. He would help me make it through the night, and I didn't care what that meant for tomorrow. I didn't care what Jacey thought. I would survive.

10

SUSPICIONS

The hum of machinery and muffled voices from the warehouse floor slowly eased me into consciousness. CieCie and Gilroy were speaking somewhere below. My eyes crept open, bleary and tear swollen. *Was Jacey awake yet?*

Despite being an adult who could make my own decisions, I didn't really want him to find me in Dane's bed. An asshole like Jacey wouldn't understand that nothing physical happened. I just...needed to not be alone.

No, not just needed. I absolutely couldn't have fathomed the idea of being alone. The comfort Dane gave me was more intense than anything I'd ever shared with Ryan, which I knew was pretty pathetic since I'd cried myself to sleep last night. But this synchrony of waking up beside someone was completely foreign. I could feel every breath Dane took, every movement he made, every rustle and stir.

Still, an unexplainable darkness lingered. Like I'd done something wrong, even though I knew that I hadn't. Was I feeling guilty because of Ryan? *No. Absolutely not.* I wouldn't allow it. The man lied to me about cross-dimensional travel and groomed me for some freak-show sacrifice. It all sounded way too absurd to be real. I hadn't come to terms with it all myself.

And I still had no idea where the lies began and the truth ended.

One thing I knew for certain, though. He and I were never real. Maybe he, himself, was never real—or the version of him I thought that I cared about. A fabricated character, designed for the sole purpose of manipulating me into this trap. I would not allow this toxic line of thinking. Not for him. I would embrace this situation. If anything, I deserved to be cared for, even if it was just a surrender to pity.

Dane's arm hung heavily over my back, pinning me to the bed as he snored. My body was warm and tired, but I rolled toward him anyway. He snorted loudly, then blinked awake, clearly as unaccustomed to this as I was.

"Oh, hey," he smiled warmly. His voice was a mixture of milk and honey and everything purely designed to make a girl blush. My heart raced. I was positive that I looked like an old cat left out in the rain. The puffy red eyes and messy hair should have been enough to frighten anyone away. But at the moment, I didn't care, and it didn't seem like Dane did either as he outstretched a heavy arm and pushed a strand of hair behind my ear.

His smile held no expectations, no judgment. Ryan always forced me to be perfect, but right now, I didn't need to be perfect. In fact, the longer I laid with Dane, the more I realized that I'd never felt more unapologetically and imperfectly myself. Unfortunately, the drowsy bliss was cut short.

Loud boots were stamping toward us, and I didn't have to look up to know Jacey was approaching. There was no time to undo our nest. I quickly scooted my body away from Dane, hoping to make it appear that we'd just bunked together rather than cozied up. *That was normal, right?* I was willing to do anything to keep Jacey's loud mouth quiet.

Dane seemed to have other ideas. He wrapped an arm

around my torso and greedily pulled me back to him from under the blanket. Not knowing what to do, I allowed him to drag my body even closer than it had been previously.

Was he purposely trying to piss Jacey off?

The smirk on his face confirmed my suspicion. It was too late to react, though. Jacey was standing in the doorway, arms crossed over his chest.

"Thought you were sleeping on the couch."

His tone was cold and emotionless but not as angry as I'd anticipated.

Dane rolled onto his back and stretched. "Yeah, well," he smirked, "my bed is warmer."

They glared at each other, like two snakes poised to strike. I wasn't willing to wait around for the outcome of their inevitable squabble. Instead, I pulled away from Dane's grip and hopped to my feet. I hadn't done anything wrong. If anyone should be ashamed, it should be Jacey. After all, he was the one hosting mysterious late-night window discussions, which I had yet to confront him about.

Narrow blue eyes followed me around the room as I gathered my pile of sweaty clothes and my boots from the night before. For once, I ignored the icy daggers he shot into my back. Dane was still in bed, lips upturned, and his arms kicked back behind his head.

I gathered my clothes and tried to squeeze through the door without acknowledging Jacey at all, but he caught my shoulder hard in his hand. I grit my teeth, anticipating an argument. From the corner of my eye, I could see that Dane was beginning to bristle.

"Don't put those back on," Jacey said quietly, not meeting my gaze. Dane's shoulders relaxed. "Go to CieCie's room and borrow an outfit from her."

He released my shoulder, and I continued past him without

looking back. By the time I'd reached CieCie's room, Dane and Jacey's barking voices were sending vibrations through the warehouse.

"I don't know about this, CieCie," I muttered. The reflection in CieCie's floor-length vanity mirror may as well have belonged to a stranger. "You must have something else that will fit me. Anything at all. What about the Elvis shirt?"

"No!" CieCie wailed. "If Elvis is dead, it means he won't be making any more of his shirts! Where will I ever find another one, Vivian? *Where?*"

I was too exhausted to explain or argue. Instead, I closed my eyes, tipped my head to the ceiling, and took a few deep breaths. When I opened them, CieCie was standing beside me.

"The thing is, Vivian, you look just like everyone else here at The Channel. Which is what you want, right? This may look weird to you, but I pinky promise, you're going to blend right in!"

A look of doubt crossed the face of my strange reflection. She was me, yet she looked so foreign. Her hair was a dark tangled mess, barely touching the white collar of the too-tight white paneled button-up that visibly constricted her breathing. She crossed her legs one direction, then the other, veiled by a tan pleated skirt that looked like the perverted uniform of a 70's Catholic convent. But I knew she was me because only my eyes could look so hideously red and puffy.

CieCie re-wrapped my bandage, laced my boots for me so I wouldn't split my knuckles *again*, and brushed my tangled rats' nest of hair. I declined, through all her pleading, when she asked to add braids and ribbons, but I reluctantly promised to let her play with my hair again when—or if—I returned to

Gilroy's place. I was dressed and as ready as I'd ever be for wherever the day would take Jacey and I.

Just Jacey and I, I sulked bitterly.

By the time I made my way downstairs, everyone had gathered in the kitchen. Dane was at the counter, hastily chopping what appeared to be a basketball-sized radish, while Gilroy leaned against the tall wood table, sipping from his large mug. I didn't look at Jacey long enough to figure out what he was doing, though CieCie seemed very interested in whatever it was and excitedly bound to his side at the table.

Like last night, I was out of place. Everyone appeared to have a pattern that they followed, a family routine that they instinctively kept to. Not knowing what to do with myself, I decided to join Dane. There was something about a man who could cook that intrigued a selfish part of me. Maybe I could chop something or at least watch as he chopped whatever he was chopping. I'd help any way I could, as long as I didn't have to stand at the table with Jacey.

"Hey, Viv. How are you feel—oh, HELL—" Dane sputtered when he glanced up at me, and the large knife he'd been using clattered noisily to the floor.

"I'm sorry. I didn't mean to startle you. Here, let me grab that," I offered.

"No!" Dane stopped me with an outstretched hand, repeating more calmly, "No. It's fine. You're fine. I'm good. You just—damn. You startled me. You look...really nice, Vivian."

Oh, right. The skirt. My cheeks flushed with red hot embarrassment.

Suddenly, Jacey's words from the night before made sense.

Dane is too distracted by you to be of any use. He'll end up dead with his tongue hanging out.

As much as I didn't want to admit it, maybe Jacey was right about not bringing Dane along—not that I was willing to concede. Alone time with jerk-face-Jacey was the last thing I wanted. But I also didn't want to see anyone get hurt. Especially Dane. I was beginning to grow...attached to him, for lack of a better word. I preferred him alive.

At the risk of causing an unwanted amputation, I reluctantly turned back to the table and took a place next to CieCie. She was preoccupied with Jacey. Maybe I could just enjoy a few minutes of silence. Each of them was taking turns tinkering and prodding a strange square device. Colorful wires flayed out of its open side like octopus tentacles on a circuit board. At first, I assumed Jacey must have been directing CieCie's hands, but I was quick to realize the opposite.

"Now just snip this wire here," CieCie said. The tan goggles she'd worn around her neck yesterday were strapped tightly to her face, causing her hair to bunch in messy plumes around her ears. Paired with an oversized pastel green sweater, she looked like an adorable little bug.

"Here? Right here?"

"Yep! That one. Next, you're going to connect the red wire to the blue wire."

"Red wire to blue wire. Got it."

"And after you've finished that, you're going—NO! Not that one!"

A sudden pop snapped between them.

"OW, FUCK!"

Jacey leaped back from the table. The device billowed a constant stream of black smoke, and the smell of burning rubber tainted the air.

"Jacey, you dumb-dumb. Don't you know your colors?" CieCie scolded, grabbing the device from the table. Her lips turned down at the corners as she examined the scorched circuit board. With a frustrated sigh, she chucked it across the room and directly into an iron bin of scrap, which sat at an impressive distance away. It clattered loudly into the can.

Jacey gripped his hand between his legs, cursing under his breath.

"The boy don't know 'is colors, don't ya know," Gilroy chuckled. Jacey glanced up sourly, but Gilroy only puckered his bottom lip out in response. "Aw, what's wrong, Jacey? More confused than'a fart inna fan factory?"

For the first time since last night, I smiled. Gilroy shot a quick wink in my direction.

"CieCie, why'on't ya brew us some quinic?" he offered with a laugh, clunking down his empty mug. "You drink quinic, 'on't ya?"

"Qui-what?" I had never heard of it.

"Qui-nic," CieCie clarified, skipping to the counter beside Dane. He handed her a tan burlap bag, and she swiftly tipped its contents into a large welded silver kettle.

"Oh, shoot," Gilroy apologized. "You'll have'ta forgive me, Viv'yan. We aren't used to havin' civi-folks round here. Quinic's like...dammit now, I can't remember the word. Hey, *dumb-fuck!* What'd they call quinic on Earth?"

I wasn't sure which "dumb-fuck" he was asking. In fact, it seemed like he was waiting to see which of the boys would respond first. Dane froze in place as if considering whether or not his dignity was worth sacrificing.

"Coffee?" Jacey offered after a moment.

Gilroy's eyes lit up with amusement, and he shot me another wink. I winked back, struggling to contain my laughter.

"Yeah, coffee! That's it!" Gilroy exclaimed. "You drink coffee on Earth?"

Vivid memories of the cat cafe from the night before struck like lightning in my brain. I quickly pushed the image aside.

"Yes, almost every day," I replied. "But I assume the coffee here is a bit different, right?"

"You bet your ass it is!" Dane shouted from over his shoulder.

"Dane!" CieCie squealed. She smacked him on the arm with a thump. "Language! There are ladies present!"

With an exaggerated gasp, Dane grabbed two mugs from the counter and held them to his eyes like binoculars. "Ladies? Hot damn! Where are they?" he whistled as he pretended to survey the room.

CieCie snatched the mugs from his hands, smiled sweetly, and stomped hard onto Dane's foot.

"Sorry, kiddo," he smiled at her, crossing his arms over his chest. "That stopped working when I started wearing the steel-toed boots."

Frustrated that she'd lost the game, CieCie carried four mismatched mugs to the table, then returned for the kettle.

"Now listen, Vivian. This stuff may taste yucky to you. I have to drink mine with sugar," CieCie warned, filling Gilroy's large mug first. It must have held at least half of the kettle.

"Bah, swogtrottle. Got'sta' at least try it straight! Sugar'll just muddle the flavor."

CieCie filled a smaller white mug and placed it in front of me. It looked like an average cup of coffee. Even the mug itself seemed to be from Earth, unless other dimensions had mugs, too. That thought on its own could sprout a few dozen new questions. I decided it wasn't worth the effort to ask.

Dane and Jacey both eagerly awaited my reaction. CieCie bounced up and down with excitement. I clasped the warm mug between my hands and brought it to my lips, trying not to inhale before tasting it. As the warm liquid washed over my tongue, I thought that it tasted very similar to stale black coffee —until the complexity of the flavor truly registered. It tasted like licking a nine-volt battery, cooling the burn with lemon juice, swished with a handful of copper pennies.

Jacey must have read my panicked expression. He ran to the scrap bin and slid it across the floor and to the table in one screeching motion.

I immediately spit the mouthful out. "Thank you," I gasped.

By that time, everyone was laughing.

"I tried to tell you!" CieCie chided playfully as she plinked several white sugar cubes into my mug.

The quinic was better with sugar, though I was pretty sure the sugar was the only thing I actually enjoyed about it. Dane brought us each a large bowl of pea-green curry, and Jacey began organizing the day's plan as we sipped from our bowls.

"Getting Vivian some appropriate gear is my first priority. Returning her to Earth is going to take a while. So in the meantime, she's going to need to dress for protection. That means we'll have to travel to Mercantile dimension. I've decided that Vivian and I will go alone today." Jacey added the last bit very quickly.

Dane opened his mouth to protest, but Jacey stopped him with an outstretched hand.

"Jumpers don't travel in packs," he explained sternly, "and bringing an extra body to a unified dimension would only raise unnecessary suspicion. Traveling with Vivian is already a huge risk. You can follow us as far as the Edge Station. Then, Vivian and I will cross from Quad Station Two and immediately head to the port at M-2."

"In Earth speak, please?" I butted in. If I was going anywhere, I wanted to at least understand where and why. If anything, it would help me blend in, rather than staring around like a tourist on vacation.

As usual, Dane was the one to offer an explanation.

"Remember how I said that The Channel is like a big cube? Well, Edge Stations are the edges of the cube that connect each of the six sides. They're kind of like a revolving door...but also kind of like a staircase. You can walk through them, and they'll spin you to the neighboring side of the cube. For context, we're on the fifth quadrant of the cube in the M sector. The Port you'll be traveling to is M-2, which is on the second quadrant, in the closest sector to the Edge Station. You won't have far to go once you reach Quadrant Two. Getting to the Edge Station will be the longest part of the trip, aside from..."

Dane hesitated.

"Aside from what?" I pressed.

"Aside from your trip through the fiber." His voice was dry.

So we were traveling through a fiber. One of the "immoral playgrounds" he'd warned me about the night before. The blood in my lips chilled, and I tapped my foot nervously.

Jacey straightened up and reclaimed the stage. "Spare us the dramatics, Dane. The fiber to Mercantile dimension is probably the safest of the twenty-six dimensional doors." He looked back to me, clearly trying to extinguish my distress. "The Mercantile fiber is used for daily trade. No one traveling through it has time for scuffles."

Dane seemed unconvinced. I wasn't sure who to believe.

"I still think I should come along," Dane grumbled.

Before Jacey could argue, a shrill ring chimed from across the table. Gilroy reached into his pocket, pulling out a small black cube with a glossy eye like a camera lens.

"'Bout damn time," he said, tapping the box. The ringing ceased, and its lens sputtered a stream of green light, illuminating a perfect square space on the table in front of it. With a hard stamp of his index finger, Gilroy activated the screen.

"CC message," Jacey explained.

This must be one of the Central Connect devices Dane mentioned.

Gilroy studied the projected screen for several moments, then looked back to the three of us.

"Been workin' with a few'a the good folks from Central Intelligence this mornin'. They're thinkin' they may have'a lead on this Rivera fella."

I swallowed hard. Was this it? Would I finally understand how Mr. Rivera was connected to The Channel? And what about Ryan? Over the last few hours, I'd considered multiple theories, but nothing seemed plausible.

In the back of my mind, I hoped that it was all a big misunderstanding. That Mr. Rivera had simply been tangled with the wrong people, and somehow he'd been obligated to The Channel. Didn't CEOs get stuck in bad business dealings all the time? And maybe Ryan was simply caught in the crosshairs. The notion was comforting, but there were too many holes for it to be believable.

"Viv'yan, what all'd you know 'bout this Mr. Rivera?" Gilroy inquired. Everyone turned to me, their eyes alight with curiosity.

"Well," I started, "I've always really liked Mr. Rivera. Six months ago, he hired me for an open secretary position at his marketing firm. The thing is, on Earth, normally it can take a few weeks before you're actually hired for a job that you apply for. But Mr. Rivera hired me on the spot. I always thought it was odd how quickly things had moved. My best guess was that he saw potential in me. He was always very kind, almost like a father figure."

Dane shifted uneasily. A part of me hated seeing him so worried, yet the greater part of me was flattered by the undeserved attention.

Gilroy sat back in his chair thoughtfully. "The cards just

ain't linin' up. This Rivera fella hired you an sent'ya off a few months later wit'a untraced Central Gov'ment issued rheotron that'd been bugger'd all ta hell. First, I wanna know who inna'hell—on Earth of all places—was smart enough'ta bugger it." He pulled the rheotron from his pocket.

The sight of it made me shiver in revulsion.

"I been workin' on rheotrons since the day they were issued, and I ain't seen nothin' like the work that's been done on this'un," he continued. "Second, I wanna know who this Mr. Rivera fella is to us. How's he connected to The Channel an whose he workin' for? And lastly, I wanna know why inna'hell anyone would put so much effort inna targeting someone like Jacey? Just a regular ol' Jumper?"

"There's also the matter of Rivera's son, Vivian's boyfriend," Jacey added.

"Ex-boyfriend," I corrected bitterly.

"Fine. Ex-boyfriend. Anyway, this Ryan guy knew that Vivian was with me when we were on Earth. She was instructed by Mr. Rivera to meet with a client in LA the following day, but we ended up bumping into each other earlier than they'd anticipated."

Dane spoke up. "How did that happen exactly? Jacey only mentioned that you were in possession of a rheotron. He didn't say how he found out about it."

I blushed. "That was my fault," I explained. "Jacey and I were staying at the same hotel. While I was checking in at the front desk, the rheotron fell out of my pocket. Jacey was the one who picked it up."

"And you're lucky I did," Jacey said. "Seeing that rheotron led me to follow you to the bar. No one from The Channel would have been careless enough to drop such a valuable piece of equipment for all the world to see. I knew you had no idea what you were carrying. If not for your clumsiness, we might both be dead."

I paused to consider that for a moment.

"You're very lucky, Vivian," Dane pointed out. Though his words were warm, they gave me no comfort. We had a pile of insignificant occurrences and facts in front of us, but none of them seemed to connect. A question surfaced in my mind.

"Jacey, what exactly were you doing on Earth to begin with? I mean, if the Central Government sent you, don't you find it a bit odd that Mr. Rivera knew enough to book us at the same hotel? And if we were intended to meet together the following day—today—where exactly were we supposed to meet? What was your mission?"

Jacey stiffened, as if reluctant to answer.

CieCie, who had been quiet up until now, whispered, "You haven't told her?"

My face flushed. *What hadn't he told me?* My gaze shifted from Dane to CieCie to Jacey, but no one would look up from the table.

Jacey swallowed hard. "I was tasked with performing an Earth re-evaluation. My mission log stated that I'd meet with someone from our resource committee at the Belair lobby, where we would discuss your dimension's progress."

His expression was tight with remorse as he continued. "The Channel has toyed with the idea of disconnecting Earth's fiber for several years. We run eval after eval, hoping to see some behavioral shift in your people," he paused, exchanging a knowing glance with Gilroy.

Disconnecting Earth's fiber? But that would mean...

"Unfortunately, the primary resources we retrieve from Earth have become so contaminated over the years, we're benefitting very little from their unity. Your saltwater supply is so tainted that we can only use around twenty percent of the water we import. For the amount of oxygen we have to offer in exchange, we are wasting more resources than we're gaining."

My knees buckled, too brittle to support my weight under the cinderblock pressure now resting in my chest. I leaned against the table and allowed the words to fall into place. If the oxygen on Earth was mainly supplied by The Channel, disconnecting the fiber would be the end of my dimension. Everything would slowly die, leaving the Earth as an empty shell. Every tree, every blade of grass, every animal and insect, every man, woman, and child. The end of my life and everyone I knew. The end of my mother.

"If y'all are done yappin' for now," Gilroy's voice snapped me from my crisis, "I have a bitta' intel that may be of interest to ya." He pointed to the green projected screen on the table.

I'd forgotten about the Central Connect message. Jacey and Dane both leaned forward eagerly.

"My friends at Central Intelligence took'a look in'ta Jacey's gov'ment file. I wanted to know exactly who drafted up that mission. Turns out, they have no record 'o him ever bein' tasked with an Earth re-eval this week."

"No way!" Jacey rushed to Gilroy's side of the table and leaned over the screen. Disbelief crossed his face as he read the projected message out loud.

"Based on our current intelligence, Channel Jumper Jacey Levitin of Sector J is currently on standby and has no outstanding assignments."

He looked back to Gilroy, who offered a confirming shrug in response.

"So, what does this mean?" Jacey urged.

Gilroy tapped the device again, and the screen vanished. "It means, dumb-fuck, that the message ya got last week about yer special eval-mission wasn't actually from yer buddies at the central gov'ment. Somebody on the inside was workin' wit the enemy an' sent you off to get killed."

This news should have frightened me. An unknown force was manipulating a cross-dimensional government in order to kill Jacey, as well as myself. A sane person would have been horrified. Instead, I was only relieved that my dimension was safe—at least, for the time being.

"And I can almost betcha," Gilroy went on, "that if this Mr. Rivera has someone smart enough to bugger a gov'ment rheotron, they're prolly smart enough to hack a simple gov'ment communication system as well. We can't be certain, but it's the best lead we got."

I realized that CieCie was staring at me. "Vivian?" she asked.

"Yeah?"

"I don't want to bring up bad memories or anything, so I truly apologize for asking...but I'd like to know a bit more about your boyfriend, Ryan."

"Ex-boyfriend," I corrected.

"Yes," she smiled apologetically. "Ex-boyfriend. I'd like to learn a little bit more about him so that Gilroy and I might do some research on our own while you and Jacey are away at Mercantile dimension. Were you and Ryan together long? And why exactly did you break up?"

Again, Dane shifted uncomfortably beside me. I wished that I could spare him from having to hear all these details. I liked Dane a lot, and I was fairly certain that he was crazy about me. My past love interest was the last thing he'd want to hear about.

Then again, it wasn't like Ryan and I had a passionate heart-throb relationship. We hadn't even slept together. Not in the figurative or literal sense. The more I thought about it, the more I realized that Ryan and I didn't have a whole lot of anything outside of work and eating. Work was his entire life. I now understood why, though I wasn't sure what his work consisted of or its purpose. All I was certain of was that Mr. Rivera was behind it.

"Ryan was Mr. Rivera's pride and joy," I explained bitterly. "So, of course, when he took interest in me, I was star-struck. We started seeing each other the same week I landed the job, and we spent nearly every day together after that." I paused.

Saying the words out loud made me realize how utterly absurd they sounded. I paved the road to my own naivety with every syllable. "We never acted like a traditional couple. Even after six months. A lot of that was my fault. In fact, Ryan asked me to move in with him just a few days before I left for LA. I turned him down, though."

"Why?" Dane asked.

I was caught off guard by the question. Was he trying to further the research efforts, or was his question of personal interest? *Poor Dane.*

"I guess I just didn't see any reason to rush things. At the time, I was happy with how things were between us. But when I told him that I didn't want to move in with him, he...changed."

I glanced at Dane. His green eyes seemed troubled, as if he was trying to put all these confusing puzzle pieces together while his fingers thrummed rhythmically against the table.

"After I turned down his offer," I continued, "Ryan stopped coming to work, almost like he was purposely avoiding me. He said he was sick, but I don't know. Something seemed off about the whole thing. He also didn't answer any of my text messages. Well, actually—he did answer one."

I pointed to the rheotron that Gilroy placed in the center of the table.

"I took a photo of the rheotron and sent it to Ryan a few days after Mr. Rivera left it for me. He'd placed it on my desk in an envelope, along with my plane tickets, but he didn't include any explanation. At the time, I wasn't sure what it was, and I never got a chance to ask Mr. Rivera about it. So the night before I left for LA, I sent a photo of it to Ryan, hoping he could explain. The response he sent was very troubling."

I closed my eyes and pictured the glowing phone screen in my hands.

"He told me to keep the device in my pocket until I met with our client, and he told me to delete the photo from my phone. He seemed mad. He said to do it before I got us both in trouble. Big emphasis on the word *both*. I found it very odd at the time, but I did as he said. Honestly, I'd just assumed I violated some company policy. It was all very innocent."

"Did he tell ya anything else 'bout it?" Gilroy asked.

"No," I admitted, wishing I had more information to give. "But he did say something strange right afterward. Or at least, it seemed strange to me at the time, given the context of the situation."

"What did he say?" Dane pressed.

"Well, after avoiding me for nearly a week and immediately after telling me to delete the photo, he said he missed me. When I replied to him, he didn't respond."

"And you didn't hear from him again until the call at the Cat Cafe?" Jacey assessed.

"Correct."

"Cat cafe?" Dane echoed with a mocking grin.

I shot him a swift glance, and the smile faded as quickly as it came. No need for the inevitable squabble. Especially now.

There was so much to digest. Every time we uncovered a new bit of information, ten more questions appeared. How was Mr. Rivera, a simple businessman from Earth, connected to The Channel? More importantly, why would a simple businessman on Earth carry out an assassination attempt on someone like Jacey? And how was Ryan tied to these occurrences?

After the table was cleared, we said our goodbyes to CieCie and Gilroy, who promised to continue with their research in our absence. Dane was to join us for the first leg of our journey and then return to Gilroy's place to help with their search.

We set off on foot, following the same straight path we'd traveled the night before. Though I was certain it was morning on The Channel, the dark crimson sky was unchanged. The only thing that differed from last night was the number of people who occupied the streets. Dozens of eyes lingered on us as we passed, every gaze pricking a straight path into my skin. At any moment, someone could recognize that I didn't belong.

"You're going to be just fine, Viv," Dane encouraged. "You look just like everyone else here. Better, in fact."

CieCie's uncomfortable outfit didn't help me to feel any less out of place. As we passed the first large group of people, I swallowed hard and tried to fake a confident stride. Head high, one boot in front of the other. I was hyper-aware of how my feet moved, how my heels made contact with the pavement. *Was I still walking normally?*

The group didn't appear to be concerned with our passing. Several spoke in rough voices, and others lingered on the outskirts of the crowd.

Much like the group we passed from the night before, they dressed in mismatched armored pieces. Rather than full jackets like Dane's and Jacey's, most of the street-goers only had fragments of protective plating, all of which were dented, scuffed and damaged.

A man in a black paneled vest eyed Jacey suspiciously as we passed, but he quickly dismissed us and turned back to his conversation.

"What's up with the dingy armor?" I whispered once I was sure we were out of earshot.

"Ex-Jumpers," Dane replied. "There aren't a lot of non-government jobs on The Channel, so once you've broken off from the government, credits can be a little hard to come by. And new gear isn't cheap. If you wreck your service gear, you're kinda stuck with the scraps."

"Your gear doesn't look wrecked," I pointed out. It was even more immaculate than Jacey's.

Dane smiled proudly and raked his fingers through his hair. "That's because Daddy takes care of his gear."

Jacey stopped abruptly with a pivot on the heel of his boot like a soldier called to attention. His eyes were blazing blue flames.

I braced myself.

"First of all," he growled, "your armor might look a little less pristine if you actually put yourself in danger every once in a while. And second, if anyone is *Daddy* around here, it's me." With another sharp pivot, he turned and continued walking again.

Dane and I stared at each other dumbfounded for several moments before both of us exploded into a chorus of laughter. By the time we collected ourselves, we had to sprint to catch back up with Jacey, who had stopped a few yards ahead.

At first, I thought he was waiting for us. But once we reached his side, I realized he was examining a sign that hung beside the building's open overhead door. Its letters were illuminated by the purple fluorescent light that skirted the edges of the building: "J-5 North General Supply"

"Just a quick detour," Jacey said, stepping forward. "You two wait out here." Without another word, he disappeared through the dark doorway.

Supplies? What kind of supplies could Jacey possibly need?

"What's he up to?" I turned to Dane, but the expression on his face froze me.

His brows were pulled heavily, creasing his forehead into hard lines that I'd never seen before. The childlike glimmer in his green eyes darkened under the cavern of his brow, shielding away the pink fluorescence that illuminated half of his face. Without warning, he grabbed both of my arms and pulled my body startlingly close to his.

I gasped at the sudden jolt. A few rugged-looking men glanced in our direction as they passed but didn't slow their pace. The implications of this disturbed me a bit more than I was willing to admit, but I knew Dane's intention wasn't to hurt me.

"What are you doing?" I whispered sharply.

He held me at a forearms distance, eyes searching mine desperately under the pale glow.

"I don't like this, Vivian," he whispered. "I don't like that he's taking you. I mean...I don't like that he's leaving me here and taking you away. He shouldn't be alone with you. He more than proved that last night."

"So demand to come with us!" I pleaded. I didn't want to be away from Dane any more than he wanted to be away from me. He was my life preserver in the storm. There had to be a way.

Dane shook his head bitterly in response. "He isn't going to listen. He literally never listens. Look, Viv...just do me a favor, okay? Stay on guard, please? You're smart. Way smarter than I think he knows. I can see it in you."

Dane glanced quickly in the direction of the supply store before continuing. "Jacey has been acting a bit...off lately. I don't know what it is, but over the last few months—it's just weird. He hasn't been himself. You don't know him like I do,

Vivian. There's something going on, and I'm not sure what. Even Gilroy and CieCie see it."

My mind focused on the memory of Jacey's back, silhouetted by the dull light of the neon cityscape as he whispered from the window ledge. I wanted to tell Dane about the secret conversation I'd listened in on last night. About how Jacey told the other person that he wouldn't risk "exposing them," whatever that meant.

Dane's eyes clawed at mine, but I wasn't quite ready to reveal this dark secret. I wanted the opportunity to speak to Jacey alone first. We had a long day ahead of us. With enough time, I was certain I could pull the veil of secrecy enough to discover whatever it was that Jacey was hiding.

"Hey, it'll be okay," I smiled, failing to make my voice match the confidence of the words.

Dane frowned.

"He's probably pretty stressed right now, you know?" I offered. "It's not every day that you find out your name is on someone's hit list. And me being here certainly doesn't help matters."

For a brief second, a look of annoyance crossed Dane's face. Before I could analyze it further, he quickly rearranged his expression and relaxed his grip on my arms.

Almost inaudibly and without breaking eye contact, he whispered, "Please be safe. I don't think my heart can endure any more loss."

11

EDGE OF THE WORLD

E lectric currents vibrated through my arms as Dane released them. His words left behind a tight quiver in my chest. *What did he mean by "more loss?"*

A heartbeat later, Jacey appeared through the darkened doorway of the supply store. His face grew alert when he spotted us.

"What? What happened?"

Dane composed himself at once, all traces of his suspicion washed away.

"All good, boss. Just standing around wondering what the hell you're buying in there." Smooth, deceptive, his voice held no note of its previous edge, and he stared at Jacey with his casual posture.

It was like a switch had been flipped. So easily, Dane was able to mask his true thoughts and suspicions. Night and day. Somehow, I envied him for it, the way a timid rabbit might envy the more cunning fox. *A damn handsome cunning fox.*

Jacey seemed convinced.

"Here, Vivian." He held out a small black bundle.

"What is it?" I took the item from his hand and turned it

over. It was heavy and thick, made from a sort of black leather. A horizontal harness connected to two metal rungs at its top.

"It's a waist bag," he answered, gesturing to my skirt. "You'll need something to, uh...tote CieCie's clothes back home after we get you geared up at Mercantile dimension."

Heat flushed my cheeks. *This was the reason for our detour?* Surely, I could have just carried the thin articles of clothing back by hand.

I wasn't sure what to say or how to arrange my face. Accepting gifts was not my strong suit, even as a child. My natural reactions were seldom gracious, and I never knew how to show the right amount of appreciation.

To make matters worse, the bag seemed nice. Not that I had any frame of reference for Channel fashion, but on Earth, it's something I would have considered very nice, even if it wasn't my style. A "thank you" was the appropriate response to the gesture, but guilt was the silent voice that echoed in my mind. *Was Jacey being kind? Maybe even apologetic for his behavior last night? And this was how I'd chosen to react?*

"Here, let me help you with that," Dane offered. He grabbed the bag from my hands and looped his arms around my waist. Touching me was completely effortless for him.

God, he's so smooth. My heart pounded like a bird trying to flail its way out of a cage. I stood helpless in his snare as he fastened the buckle over my hips.

When I glanced at Jacey, his eyes dropped to his boots, and he tapped his foot impatiently against the pavement.

"All set," Dane remarked, taking a step back from me.

I let out a long breath, realizing I'd been holding it the entire time. The bag hung heavily, flattening the pleating of my skirt tight against my thigh. I couldn't have imagined carrying the clothes in my hands to be any less cumbersome, but my mind darted back to Jacey—or more so the possibility that he'd made some attempt to be considerate, that he'd thought he was helping me.

"Thanks," I murmured. He didn't look up, but I still wanted him to understand that I appreciated the gesture. Especially since we had an entire day ahead of us. If this was an apology, it was probably best to accept it and move on so we could both focus on the mission at hand. Jacey opened his mouth but was cut short.

"Hey, no problem, Viv!" It was Dane who responded.

Just as I began to object, Jacey started down the street again, head buried in its usual position between his shoulders. Dane nudged me forward with a smile. There was nothing I could do but follow in my default state of frustration.

We navigated through the geometric city silently for some time. Buildings grew brighter and with the light came more strangely dressed people. Like nocturnal creatures crawling from dark crevices, the streets had come to life.

Roll-top doors revealed curbside bars that rang out with clanging glasses and slurry voices. A woman in a stained apron reached out to Dane from a restaurant window, offering him a sample of curry in a small cup. He declined with a charismatic smile. A man's face appeared in the dark of an ally as we passed, illuminated by the flame of a lighter as he ignited a cigarette.

With every step, I slipped further and further from the path of reality. Alice and her Wonderland adventures were laughable in comparison.

A roar erupted from behind us, and I turned just in time to see what looked like a group of motorcycles blast through the darkness. Instead of black rubber, the bikes sped forward on glowing neon tires. The gust they created as they passed brought my hair to life, and I sputtered to blow a messy strand from my lips.

"Show offs!" Dane shouted, cupping his hands to amplify his voice.

Jacey quickly turned and shot him a disapproving glare, but it was too late. From the alcove of a building several paces ahead, a slender figure slinked from the darkness. As Jacey turned back to the street in front of us, his shoulders winged out like a cobra flaring its hood. Someone had recognized them.

Dane grabbed my hand hastily and tugged my body against his.

"What are you doing?" I whispered frantically.

"Shhhh. Trouble. Just roll with it."

I looked back to the dark figure, nervously measuring the distance between him and Jacey. Both stopped in their tracks, roughly ten feet from each other. The man was tall and broad-shouldered with a long tangle of tawny hair pulled back at his nape. Through the pink-hued ambiance, a string of glowing tattoos trailed the broad girth of his stubbled neck, and dipped into the flare of his collar. These were different from the central connect tattoos.

A chill quivered through my body as I realized that they must be one of the cybernetic weapons Dane mentioned. Like Jacey, the man wore an impressive armor-plated trench coat. Long and black, its tail grazed the wet pavement as he crossed his arms over his chest.

"Jacey Levetin. It's been a while since I've seen your face."

Though his voice was friendly, I could sense thick electric tension building in the air. Dane's hands grew cold and clammy between my fingers, and his muscles coiled tight. Definitely not a friend.

"And who is that behind you?" The man leaned slightly

and nodded a stiff chin toward Dane and I. An uncomfortable lump formed in my throat as our eyes met.

This was it. I'd been discovered. My heart accelerated into a frantic rhythm that hummed through my earlobes. Dane tugged my body closer so that my feet were nearly on top of his.

"'Bout time to get your eyes checked, eh, Rhett?" Dane called out. "Vision not what it used to be? I'm offended by your lack of observance. I'd recognize that pretty little ponytail of yours anywhere." Through Dane's antagonizing, I could sense the stretch in his nerves. He swallowed hard, giving evidence of his wavering confidence.

Rhett chuckled darkly before taking a single step forward. Jacey aggressively matched the movement, putting only a few feet between them.

"Dane Caufelt," Rhett mused. "Always one for jokes. Here, I've got one you might like. What do you get when you mix a spindly armed burnout with a roid-raged rent-a-cop?"

With fists balled, Jacey lurched another step forward. His body vibrated in anticipation, which Rhett acknowledged with another sharp cocky grin before his leering gaze rested back on me.

"And what about the girl?" he hissed. The breath caught in my chest.

Dane's grip around my body tightened. "Must be a shock to you, seeing one in person for the first time. Don't be nervous, Rhett. With pretty hair like yours, it's probably no different than looking in the mirror."

My skin prickled with each testosterone-fueled insult. Every instinct told me to be strong, and maybe that would have been the right thing to do on Earth. But here, I was completely out of my element.

Rhett was growing visibly impatient with their game. His jaw tightened stiffly, and he dropped his hands to rest within his pockets, a move that made Jacey grow rigid. I scanned the man's body intently but couldn't see anything beneath the dark cavern of his jacket.

"We're just passing through," Jacey growled. His eyes remained locked on the pockets where Rhett's hands had disappeared.

Rhett noted the direction of the icy gaze. He casually pulled his hands from his pockets and assumed a less threatening pose, arms back over his chest.

"Well, I certainly wouldn't want to keep you. Why don't you see to it then?"

Shoulders still flared in breadth, Jacey stalked forward. Rhett made no effort to move from our path, forcing Jacey to sidestep around him. Dane wrapped a tight arm around my shoulders and guided me forward. Every step sent a quiver through my chest.

Rhett's head remained low as we drew near, but the dagger-edged smile never left his lips. His words were nearly inaudible, shooting a wave of instant revulsion through my spine as we passed. "Pretty thing. Come find me when you get bored of these infants."

Dane locked his jaw but offered no retort. Instead, he craned his neck and planted a possessive hard kiss on top of my head, pausing just long enough to ensure Rhett saw the gesture. From behind, I could hear Rhett's amused breathy chuckles fade into the distance.

We continued on for several moments. My teeth gnawed mercilessly on my bottom lip. Occasionally, I would shoot a sparing glance behind us, searching for signs of pursuit. But the street was barren, and the brightly lit haze grew dimmer and dimmer. After we'd gained a safe distance from the more populated section of the city, my heart resumed its predictable beat.

"What the hell was all that about?" I whispered.

Jacey fell back so that we moved in a tighter knot. The streets were darker ahead, and fewer people gathered, making conversation more comfortable.

With an apologetic shake, Dane released his death grip on my shoulders. "Sorry about that, Viv."

Before I could respond, Jacey whirled around in a blinding streak. I jumped in surprise as he grabbed Dane's jacket by the collar and dragged his slender body forward in a vicious motion. Though Dane was the taller of the two, Jacey managed to pull their eyes level. My heart sputtered back into an anxious flutter.

"Do you think before you speak? Or do you just open your mouth and BAM, stupidity gurgles out?"

Dane's shock quickly twisted into a snarl. With both hands, he shoved hard into Jacey's chest. "Let go of me, asshole! If you had something to say, you should have fucking opened your own big dumb mouth. But you didn't. As usual, you stood around and waited for me to handle your bullshit."

Dane turned his head and spat on the pavement before continuing. "If you haven't noticed already, I'm not a god damn Jumper anymore. And if you've got some beef with Rhett or whoever else it is that wants to fucking kill you, that's cool. But do me a solid and leave me out of it. And for fucks sake, leave her out of it, too." Dane pointed a finger aggressively in my direction.

Feral rage radiated from Jacey for several tense moments. Dane remained deathly silent. Neither of them so much as blinked.

I alternated my gaze desperately from Dane to Jacey, unsure of how to break apart their weird animalistic eye contact. *Stupid moronic boys.* This was not the place for their childish squabbling. We were wasting time. I could feel it—the sense that I was missed. By now, someone back home had surely noticed my absence.

A picture of my mom's face flashed in my mind—her velvet cheeks filled with blood, and her eyes streaming as she listened to the ghostly signal of my voicemail. She would have called my phone last night. I was sure of it. Soon, she would realize I hadn't made it back to the hotel. I knew deep down that mom would continue calling. Even if it were concluded that I'd died or been abducted or simply ran away, she would never stop calling. She would never give up her search for me.

Yes, we were wasting too much time. With a deep breath, I stepped forward and grabbed the paneled sleeve of Jacey's jacket. He snapped a cold glare in my direction but didn't release his grip on Dane.

"Let. Him. Go."

A spark danced briefly in Jacey's pupils. If I hadn't known better, I may have mistaken it for amusement. He studied me for several moments. With a deep exhale, Jacey's knuckles loosened around the leather of Dane's jacket, and he took a step backward.

"Look," I said, before either of them could speak, "I know this is stressful for you guys, okay? I get it. But for just one moment—for just one single moment—could you both pull yourselves together and start behaving like adults?"

Neither answered, both too stubborn to reconcile. But after several tense seconds, Jacey nodded, and Dane relaxed his posture. It was as good as I was going to get so I moved on to more important questions.

"Who was that guy anyway?"

"Rhett is a senior Jumper, enlisted around the same time Dane and I did," Jacey answered. So Rhett and Jacey were both senior Jumpers. That would explain the intricate armored jacket and the grisly neck tattoo. But not the begrudging attitude.

"Why does he have it out for you?"

We began our trek again, this time at a slower and more deliberate pace. Though the tension had lifted, I could still sense an uncomfortable presence within Dane, who ambled at my side with his head low.

"Like we told you before, Jumper's work alone," Jacey reminded. "We don't get along. We don't travel together. We don't associate. And usually, when we bump into each other, which happens pretty frequently, it ends up in a fight. And one less Jumper."

"That doesn't sound very—" I measured my words carefully, "—efficient. For the whole organized cross-dimensional society thing."

"What do you mean?"

"I don't know," I admitted. "I guess I was expecting something a little less primal?"

Jacey's laugh carried into the hollow street ahead. I waited for some attempt at defense, but he didn't continue.

"So what about you and Dane?" I asked. I hoped this wouldn't resurrect the tension. Dane lifted his head as if he were just as eager to hear Jacey's explanation.

"Dane isn't a Jumper," Jacey answered matter-of-factly.

This response didn't appear to satisfy Dane, who exhaled an impatient huff. Jacey could dodge my questions all he wanted, but I wasn't giving up.

"I'm not asking if Dane is a Jumper. I'm asking how you guys met. Which on Earth is a fairly common question that doesn't typically require an intensive amount of time to answer."

"You'd be surprised," Jacey grunted, speeding his pace

enough to establish that he was no longer a part of the conversation.

Unbelievable. I looked at Dane incredulously but instantly realized that his body was only a hollow vessel. I wasn't sure that he'd been listening. With eyes trained ahead, pupils unmoving as though not focused on anything tangible, he was clearly lost in his own head. It was a mask that I knew better than most—disassociation. My heart longed to save him from this internal riptide.

"You good?" I whispered with a playful nudge to his shoulder.

Dane blinked.

"Yeah!" he said with a sudden brightness. "Yeah, I'm great. How about you? Are you nervous about visiting a totally new dimension?"

The reaction shouldn't have been off-putting, but I knew better than to believe its glossy exterior. Aversion. Dane was troubled by Jacey's outburst. Like a light switch, he once again pivoted his demeanor, just as he'd done after confronting me at the supply store. The shifty fox. I knew there was more he wanted to say or maybe there was just more that I wanted to hear him say, but I decided to wait. At least until Jacey and I returned from Mercantile dimension, and everyone had time to cool down.

"I probably should be," I answered, "but to be honest, my frame of reference is so small that I'm not entirely sure what to be nervous about. Can't be any worse than here, right?"

"Nah, you're gonna be fine."

His voice was thick with glossy enthusiasm, a two-way mirror that I couldn't see the other side of. The shoulders of his jacket were still misshapen and twisted from where Jacey's hands gripped them. *Poor Dane.* He didn't deserve to be at the butt-end of Jacey's attitude.

The echo of his warning cycled over and over through my mind. *Jacey has been acting a bit...off lately.* What was Jacey hiding behind all of the rage?

I decided not to bother Dane with any additional questions during the last quarter of our journey. Lights grew brighter, captured within the thick haze as we approached a more active part of the city. I was a little more confident within the alien crowds. Very few people took notice of our passing, and those who did spent more time looking at Jacey rather than Dane or I.

Being ignored was a natural feeling. Back at Premier before my life was flipped upside down, I could coast beside Ryan all day and still be rendered into the wallpaper by most. Ryan was the headline while I was the fine print, easily missed. A chameleon. For once, the natural camouflage was a beneficial adaptation.

Several sharp buildings ahead, the street opened, and the horizon touched the crimson sky as abruptly as a razorblade. This must be it—the edge. What would it be like on the other side? Would gravity work the same way, like someone standing on the North versus the South pole? Surely I'd be able to feel the abruptness of the transition with no natural curvature or miles between axis points.

The buildings around us cast long shadows across the pavement, a thin amber glow indicating the end of Quadrant Five. Several paces ahead, a rectangular opening dipped into the ground, like the entrance to a subway station. Above it glowed a flickering blue sign: "To Quad Station 2"

As we approached, I realized that the light only touched the first few stairs before they vanished into blackness.

"Well, here we are," Jacey declared. He lifted his tattooed forearm horizontally in front of his chest. A wave of nausea rushed through me as the black designs of his skin began to waver and bubble into a boiling eruption of solid matter. The wrist device emerged like a submarine breaching the ocean surface, held tight to the bone with taught spindles of stretched skin.

Seeing the emergence up close wasn't as magical as I'd interpreted it in the dark alley. No, magic wasn't the word for this. Magic would have implied that this was instantaneous or that there was some lack of physical sacrifice. An action of magic wouldn't have resulted in such a grotesque mutilation of flesh and bone, a violent manifestation of man-made functionality.

Dane shifted uncomfortably from one foot to the other, pulling my attention from the macabre technology. Our time together had dwindled to its final moments. Biting my lip, I glanced at Jacey. He was busily fidgeting with the screen of his Central Connect. It appeared that I had a few minutes to spare.

When I turned back to Dane, his shoulders were hung low, and the childish spark in his green eyes was dull.

"Well, I guess this is it. Wish us luck." I said with an encouraging smile.

Too seriously, he murmured, "I do wish you luck, Vivian. I truly do." Then his arms were around me, gripping my face hard against the cold panels of his jacket. My muscles tensed instinctively, but the sweet oaky scent wafting from his body willed them to relax.

For a moment, the world vanished under my feet. Nose in my hair, I felt him inhale deeply. "When I woke up yesterday morning, I had no idea you existed. Now look at me, Vivian. I'm at the edge of the world saying goodbye, and my heart hurts. This fucking sucks." His muffled words wove through my hair, sending a thrill through my core.

"I'll be okay," I whispered. "I've made it this far."

"Remember what I said," he mouthed, barely audible over the hum of the city. He arched his spine back and tilted his head playfully. This was the Dane I'd grown used to over the last two days. The light of the blue neon sign reflected like glistening jade in his eyes, and I longed to stare into them for just a little longer than our time would allow.

"Hurry back." It wasn't a request. It was a plea.

"I promise."

12

DIMENSION TWENTY-SEVEN

My chest hurt too much, and my heart sang too loudly. I watched with reluctant ache as Dane was swallowed into the long shadows of the hazy city. If I'd ever known affection before this moment, I'd known it all wrong.

No, this was different. This emotion was a foreign object, nestled into the fibers of my heart, as foreign as The Channel itself. As foreign as the neon ambiance, the strange armored clothing, and cybernetic tattoos. Never before had I experienced the lingering phantom of an embrace that could never last long enough.

Only an hour ago, I would have denied it, but when I watched Dane disappear between the haunting buildings, it was like witnessing a piece of myself burn away. A small ember of my soul, searing into nothing.

"It's time to go." Jacey's voice shattered my reverie. By the time I'd torn my gaze from the city, he had already stepped into the mouth of the stairwell. I closed my eyes and took a deep cleansing breath, then followed after him.

Inside the stairwell, the air was cool and smelled of damp stagnance and stone. My hands trailed flat against the walls, feeling my way through the abyss of blackness. Several times, my feet lost their rhythmic flow, and I stumbled into Jacey's back. He barely seemed to notice and only helped to steady me when I cried out after completely missing a step.

Was this damn thing endless? I had yet to see any trace of light to indicate an exit. *How long had we been climbing?* My muscles burned sore and heavy, the way they did after an hour on the stair stepper machine at the gym. Climbing, climbing, climbing.

But wait...

That couldn't be right. Hadn't we been going down the stairs?

Gingerly, I lifted a foot, feeling for the next step. My boot made contact faster than my brain anticipated, and I rocked forward, falling hard into Jacey's back for the fourth time.

"Ooof."

The stairs had changed from descending to ascending, and I wasn't sure how or at precisely what moment it happened. My legs were limp noodles as my mind struggled to predict what the ground below me would feel like—or what it was supposed to feel like.

"How is this possible?" I gasped, using Jacey, who was higher up than me to balance myself.

"If I was smart enough to understand that, do you think I'd be here right now?" I could hear the smile on his lips, and I quickly released his shoulders.

He started again, but his pace was slower. "Don't analyze too hard, Vivian. You'll drive yourself mad. The Channel defies a majority of your Earth physics. Molecular structures are different here...or something like that. Hell if I know. I just take everything at face value and roll with the punches."

Before I could question further, a soft purple glow silhouetted Jacey's broad frame. I craned my neck to find its source. Ahead, the stairs were bathed in hazy beams, streaming from the rectangular opening of the tunnel. We'd made it.

I remained on the fourth step, cloaked just beneath the veil of darkness as Jacey stepped up onto the surface. He surveyed the area and gestured for me to follow.

"Welcome to Quadrant Two."

Gravity didn't sway my feet unevenly as I'd expected. From what I could tell, the sharp-edged buildings, wet reflective pavement, and colorful ghostly haze were identical to Quadrant Five.

Along the street ahead, a rainbow of glowing bikes leaned in parked positions, their riders gathered at the first set of square buildings. One of the riders watched our approach with interest, her face hidden beneath the visor of a glossy white helmet. Atop its smooth crest were two glowing teal cat ears.

Jacey brisked past the group without a sparing glance, even as more of the riders lifted their heads. I kept my chin high and my stride even. Jacey's relaxed posture was evidence enough that the area was safe. Despite the fact that I wanted to punch him in the face nearly every time I looked at him, I knew I was safe at his side.

At the far side of the building was an open roll-top door, outlined in a thin blue glow. "That's our fiber," Jacey said.

Not quite what I expected. "It just looks like a garage door," I questioned, glancing at Jacey.

He grinned knowingly and opened his mouth but closed it again. To my surprise, he extended his broad arm and placed a single finger under my chin, angling my jaw to the sky. A gasp caught in my throat.

"That," he corrected matter-of-factly, "is our fiber."

Jutting from the flat rooftop of the building was a massive translucent pipe as wide as a twelve-lane highway. Its surface shimmered like a hologram, buzzing occasionally with a glitching static fizz. I squinted hard, trying to locate its end. For as far as I could see, the pipe continued straight up into the crimson grid of sky. There was no end. It *was*, then it *was not*.

"See those veins?" Jacey pointed to the far side of the pipe.

Running along its wavering surface were a tangle of thin wire-like strands. From my position on the ground, I could only imagine how wide they really were. Next to the massive fiber, they looked like threads.

"That's how we transfer resources to and from The Channel. We have twenty-six of these ports across the six Channel quadrants, and each of those ports can have up to four veins, depending on what we're importing or exporting."

Jacey had mentioned these fibers back at Gilroy's place, but I never imagined them to look like this. They were unfathomably gigantic, at least double the girth of the largest buildings in Sacramento.

"What gets imported and exported from Mercantile dimension?" I asked in awe.

"They are a fully industrious society," Jacey explained, "so we remove a lot of the toxins that would otherwise harm their civilization. Carbon dioxide, sulfur dioxide, nitrogen oxides, and mercury compounds. Basically, just the chemical overflow and noxious smog caused by the constant burning of production fuel."

That explanation accounted for all four of the twisting veins.

"So they don't import anything from The Channel?"

Jacey chucked. "I'd say our generous removal of their deadly emissions is enough of a gift. It helps to keep our societies tight, which makes organized trading possible. Most of the items you see on The Channel were brought from Mercantile dimension."

That explained a lot. "And they know you guys exist? I was

under the impression that The Channel was like...top-secret digs."

"Not all dimensions are equipped to handle the reality of what is. Especially when, what *is*, often *is not*—and what *is not* often isn't a concept that can be understood by less civilized dimensions."

Less civilized? I remained fixed on the long tunnel in the sky. "I don't understand."

"Exactly," he said, "which is why Earth isn't a dimension we can openly organize with. We have connections with a few select scientists and one or two of your wealthy elites. Aside from that, causing that much societal disruption would be more chaotic than it's worth. We give Earth supplementary oxygen, and in return, they give us saltwater. We're a fly on the wall. Intervening with the natural order of your world is unnecessary and dangerous."

When I tore my focus from the sky, Jacey was already stepping through the roll-top doorway. "Wait for me!" I sprinted after him.

No way was I allowing our conversation to end now. Blessed with good luck, I'd struck gold after panning for two days. Jacey was in a better mood, and for once, I was getting answers. I'd keep panning the stream until I was wealthy with the knowledge I longed for. Or until Jacey told me to fuck off. And even then, I'd probably try a few more times.

Beyond the entryway of the building expanded a long hallway, illuminated overhead by zigzagging turquoise fluorescent filaments. The air was butter-thick with blue haze, nearly masking the open doorway of a dimly lit elevator. Jacey ushered me inside with a smile I couldn't understand.

"What?" I asked.

He shook his head. "Your face."

What was wrong with my face? I quickly lifted my hands, rubbing them frantically from forehead to chin.

"No," Jacey laughed, as the double doors slid shut. "I was thinking of the elevator at the Belair. When you looked back at me in the lobby. I thought for sure you were going to piss yourself."

My hands fell from my cheeks. "Of course you thought it was funny," I grumbled. "You weren't the one being petrified. You do realize that I thought you wanted to kill me, right? Like, legit follow me to my hotel room and murder me? Big serial killer vibes, Jacey."

The elevator shuddered underfoot, and the lights flickered in dim succession. Jacey turned dramatically slow to face me. His features sharpened as long shadows cast down from his raven hair, allowing only a sliver of light to slice across the ice of his irises. For some reason, I shriveled under his menacing glare. *How was he able to do that?*

"I'd apologize," he grinned viciously, "but being scary is kind of what I was trained to do. You didn't seem to be bothered by my scariness at the nightclub when that hyena was attempting to drag you off like a piece of meat."

Memories of that night flashed like the shutter of a camera lens. I shivered, ignoring the amused shadows that had crept into Jacey's eyes.

"That was different," I retorted, though I agreed. In this light, Jacey was terrifying. I forced a shuddering breath.

"Even so," Jacey said as the silver doors reopened, "you'll soon be very grateful for my big serial killer vibes."

If I'd had the time, I would have snapped back. But the new sight in front of us stole away all budding thoughts in my mind before they could blossom into sentences. Another strange anomaly.

Jacey extended his hand. I didn't question the sudden

uncharacteristic chivalry. Instead, I placed my palm in his and allowed him to lead me out of the elevator and into the massive landing. By some magic or science—I wasn't entirely sure which—we stood before a massive round passage. No, not massive. The Statue of Liberty was massive. The Eiffel tower was massive. This...this was something entirely in its own class of gigantic.

The tunnel we'd seen strewn vertically into the sky was now laid out straight in front of us, connected to the wall of the building we'd just exited. *No, not the wall.* It would have been the roof. *Oh, this was too confusing.* Was gravity different on The Channel, or had I gone mad?

"How—" I started to ask, but Jacey's tug on my arm clipped the question from my lips.

"Stop overanalyzing." It was a demand.

Oh good, more mood swings. I bit my lip and allowed him to tug me forward. Apparently, I'd need to continue my overanalyzing in silence.

I realized that we were in a narrower, more platformed section of the fiber. Like a subway station, a solid line of barriers divided the space, allowing entrance into the wider-bellied tunnel ahead. Twelve giant half-circle archways broke in even intervals across the wall. In front of each arch, several people in varying degrees of armour lined up in front of them, waiting to pass through to the other side.

From the open mouths of the arches, bright luminous beams of light streamed into the darker landing. It was the brightest light I'd seen since we had arrived at The Channel, almost like...sunlight? No, it couldn't be. I would have seen the light from outside.

Questions burned on my tongue, but I didn't dare to ask Jacey yet. He seemed too deep in concentration as he tugged me along the platform.

My bandaged hand started to ache, crumpled in his fist like a wadded paper ball. I tried to straighten my fingers as we approached one of the large arches, but his coarse knuckles were unyielding.

"Hey," I nipped at him once we'd stopped in front of the arch. "I may need this hand again someday. Would you mind letting up with the death grip?"

He looked at me quizzically then opened his fingers, releasing my caged hand. It was white and pricked with the pain of a million pins and needles. I flexed my knuckles, forcing hot blood back through my fingertips. When I looked back at Jacey, he was still staring at me.

"What?" I snapped. He didn't respond.

"What?" My voice grew louder.

He blinked. "Hmmm."

Was he seriously making fun of me? I couldn't hold my temper any longer. "You know, you're not as scary as you think," I flustered. "In fact, I find you to be quite stubborn." Jacey blinked again in...*what? Surprise?* I crossed my arms over my chest, hoping for any reaction at all. I didn't even care if it was anger.

The corners of his lips twitched in a mocking movement. "Hmmm."

I threw my hands up in defeat. "Oh. My. God. Jacey. Would you please stop with the grunts and start talking like a normal human being?"

He held my gaze for several unrelenting seconds. Then his blue eyes broke, and his lips parted away into the biggest wolfish grin I'd ever seen on his face.

What was this? I was overwhelmed by the tidal wave of nonsensical Jacey-mood-swings.

"You know," he said, " your face turns pink when you're mad."

A searing heat burned across my cheeks.

"Like a little ladybug," he added playfully.

Oh, that's it! Using both hands and all my strength, I shoved Jacey hard in the chest. He didn't so much as sway. Gazing at me with amusement dancing in his eyes, I realized that I'd never seen him this way. Not even at the cat cafe, before the *awfulness*.

"Jacey, I really don't understand you."

The smile on his lips evaporated before my eyes until his mouth was once again nothing more than a straight line. "Our turn," he noted, nodding toward the landing behind me.

Hot to cold. This man was going to give me an aneurysm. I glanced around the large landing. The other people who gathered in front of the nearby archways had all passed through, leaving Jacey and I alone on the platform. With a *hmph*, I turned on my heels and brushed past him.

The arch ahead cast a long U-shaped shadow over the black landing where we stood. As I approached, I began to understand where the backlight came from. The tunnel head wasn't just lit. It was made entirely of light.

The walls of the fiber wavered and shimmered in translucent white auroras, bright as the sun and illuminating the entire expansive tunnel. My mouth popped open as I stepped through the arch, utterly small and insignificant in comparison to the bizarre scene around me.

The fiber was a giant tube-shaped terrarium. It was its own self-contained biome, where blades of grass shone green and vibrant in the light, occasionally interrupted by a tree or bushel of shrubbery that dotted the tunnel. A foot trodden path worn through the center, paralleled with the wheel tracks of a recent passing vehicle.

Jacey stepped beside me, and for the first time, I truly saw the details of his face under bright ambient light that allowed no place for secrets. Deep scars that marred his cheeks and forehead were now intensified. Purple half-moons hung deep and cavernous under his eyes, and his eyelids were painted in tired shades of lavender.

He stood with his eyes closed, hands behind his head and inhaled deeply. Deep within the fibers of my heart, a new pity bloomed for him. I'd never noticed how tired he looked until now.

Tearing my gaze from his scarred face, I took a deep breath. The air tasted thinner and crisp, free of the smog and motor oil smells that made up the atmosphere of The Channel. It was the first breath of fresh air I'd taken since we'd left Earth.

"Little piece of faux paradise," Jacey mused. He opened his eyes and guided me forward with a wave.

I was too awestruck to ask questions, but Jacey humored me with information as we made our way over the manicured green terrain.

"The Channel tries to keep these spaces maintained to avoid trouble. I guess The Five assumed that if they kept the spaces pretty, travelers would be less likely to murder each other between dimensions." His tone was unconvincing.

"Does it work? I mean, the grass and the trees and stuff? Does it help to keep the peace?"

The purse of Jacey's lips told me that it did not. "A few trees and some grass isn't enough to stop raids and pirating."

Raids? I glanced around nervously. Nearby, a man in a long trench coat lay kicked back under the shade of a tree. He seemed to be asleep, veiled by the wide brim of a brown floppy hat.

"You don't need to worry about this fiber, though," Jacey said, noting my anxious gaze. "Nothing bad happens here. We're in Mercantile dimension territory. They help to maintain the area, the rich bastards. The other twenty-five dimensions, though...that's a whole other story. All the foo-foo nature garbage isn't enough to keep bad people from doing bad things. Most of the other fibers have already been thoroughly pillaged and vandalized. A few aren't even lit anymore, and their trees have either died or been stolen."

"Stolen?"

"Uprooted. Chopped up. Used for firewood, tools, and who-knows-what-else."

A thought popped into my head, and I shot a suspicious glance at Jacey.

He smiled, knowing exactly where my mind led me. "No, Vivian, I didn't steal the trees at Gilroy's place."

"Where did they come from?" I asked. It was a question I'd been holding since last night, right before I found Jacey on the window ledge.

I still needed to ask him who he had been talking to. *Later.* After I'd warmed the water a bit more. Ever since Dane left, Jacey had been unusually talkative, and I wasn't willing to jinx the sudden generosity of information.

Oblivious to my inner turmoil, Jacey smiled, keeping his eyes on the road ahead. "I planted those trees for CieCie after we..."

I glanced at him in time to catch a painful expression crease through Jacey's brow. Obviously, there was an uncomfortable memory attached to the trees. "After you what?" I prompted gently.

Jacey shook his head as if dismissing a bad thought. "It's a long story."

"Well, how long is this fiber?" *Don't leave me hanging now!*

For several long moments, we walked in silence. The only ambiance came from the soft padding of our feet over the tightly manicured grass. Though the fiber looked green and earthy, the lack of wind added an alien stillness to the atmosphere, a reminder that I was not home. The trees did not sway, and their leaves did not rustle. Through the beauty, there was an eerie calm that surrounded us.

I realized that we must be deep in the fiber. The subtle hum from The Channel had faded away. Just as my teeth took hold of my lip in resignation, giving up on my question, Jacey answered.

"I planted the trees for CieCie after we brought her home. After The Five exiled her dimension." His voice was dark and confessing.

A sudden wave of cold nausea crept through my body. *What?*

"The Five exiled her dimension?" I exclaimed in dismay. "How? Why?"

He shook his head again. The discomfort on his face was as bold as his scars, but after several excruciating moments, he continued.

"It was one year after I'd finished my training. Me and a few other Jumpers had been tasked with performing a final sweep of a dying world, dimension twenty-seven."

It all became clear. The way he snapped when Dane didn't remember the number of unified dimensions now held a new meaning. Jacey remembered because he was there when the twenty-seventh dimension was severed. It was there, stained across his skin like a blistering brand. *What had this man seen?*

"It was all fucked. The whole damn planet," he went on. "Dimension twenty-seven was supposed to help supplement the saltwater supplies we normally collected from Earth. But they were so transfixed on intrinsic issues. Religious wars and unnecessary violence, far beyond even those we monitor on your dimension.

"By the time I was sent in to salvage resources, it was too late. The entire dimension was decimated. We'd been told that multiple bombs had been dropped before our arrival, but nothing can prepare you for...that. The dead outnumbered the living, and the living who were left weren't worth saving. Most of them, anyway."

His eyes became glassy as he continued, his voice strained and tight. "I was out scouting through the ruins when I found them. A woman and a man—or *most* of a man. There really wasn't much left of him. And the woman was in bad shape. With her dying breath, she told me she'd hidden her two daughters in the cellar of her home before the bombs fell. She didn't ask me to save her. I think she was at peace with death. She just asked me to go to the house and find her daughters.

"On my way there, I spotted another Jumper, stumbling through the wreckage. He'd always been a piss poor scouter. A total waste of government resources, in my opinion. But when I mentioned the girls, he was suddenly full of fire."

"Dane?" I whispered. Jacey nodded. So, I'd been wrong. *Dane was there, too.* This must have been why he was so bitter toward the government. It wasn't that he didn't care. He had been on the front lines with Jacey from the start.

"We busted in the cellar doors and found the girls huddled in the corner, completely covered in blood. CieCie wasn't afraid at all, the little monster. The moment she saw me, she ran and jumped in my arms. It's like she knew we were there to take them away. Mia on the other hand...she didn't move when her sister did. She was tiny, starving, and already fading.

"Dane scooped her up just as the echeloning of fire teams carpeted the town. It was the first time either of us traveled with a rheotron, and neither of us even knew if the girls would be transported with us. But somehow, it worked."

I was so absorbed in the story that I blinked in confusion when Jacey stopped speaking. The end of the tunnel loomed in the distance. It looked just like the first port with twelve arches expanding across a long barrier. The sight wasn't as welcoming as I'd anticipated, making me wish that the fiber had been longer. I needed to hear the rest of the story.

"And then? What happened to Mia?"

Jacey buried his head between his shoulders. His mouth was hidden behind the black scarf that encircled his neck. Only his eyes drifted to me, tired and telling. I knew the answer before he spoke.

"She didn't make it," he whispered. "I've never told Dane this, but I don't think her soul left that cellar. CieCie was so young at the time. I just wanted her to believe her sister made it out. And Dane...I wanted him to believe that his sacrifice meant something. That he'd helped to bring that little girl some peace in her final moments."

My throat constricted, and a single tear rolled down my face. I reached to blot it away before Jacey noticed, but he was already extending his arm out to me. In his hand was the black scarf. I took it from him and blotted my eyes. He'd stopped walking, allowing me a moment to collect myself. After a few cleansing breaths, I held the scarf back out to him.

"No, keep it. Not that I hope you'll cry again, but if you do, you might need it." His eyes shone with a liquid sympathy I'd never seen before.

Everything made sense now. His brotherly relationship with Dane, his tenderness toward CieCie, and CieCie's perpetual childlike demeanor. Even Dane's bitterness toward the government made sense. They weren't just friends. They were a family.

One final question festered. I considered saving it, but Jacey was finally being open with me. I wasn't sure when I'd have this opportunity again.

"What happened to Mia? Her...body, I mean." The words

seemed heavy and out of place once I said them, but a bittersweet smile turned his lips.

He glanced at me, eyes glowing in the bright light of the fiber. "That's why we planted the trees, as a memorial to Mia. A place where we knew her ashes would be safe."

I was very grateful for Jacey's scarf. Another hot tear rolled down my face as I recalled CieCie's excitement when she asked if we could have a tree party. She must have been thinking of her sister. I vowed to find a way to give her that party when we returned. It was the least I could do for the sweet girl whose age was frozen in time.

"You ready to cross?" Jacey asked. His voice was lighter and more at ease as if a weight had been lifted.

How long had he been carrying those memories on his shoulders? I smiled, grateful that he'd chosen to confide in me. Maybe traveling alone with Jacey wouldn't be so bad after all.

"Yeah," I grinned at him, wrapping his black scarf around my neck. "Let's go clothes shopping."

13

MERCANTILE DIMENSION

"Can I ask one more thing?"

We'd reached the fiber's twelve-lane port. This was my last chance before we crossed into a completely new dimension, where all thoughts would undoubtedly be consumed by the unknown.

A sudden thrill shivered through my body. *A new dimension!*

"Shoot," Jacey answered coolly. I thought carefully for a moment. Even in his lightened mood, questioning Jacey was still akin to defusing a bomb.

"You said that The Channel imported saltwater from dimension twenty-seven."

Abruptly, Jacey paused in front of one of the large archways and looked at me in confusion.

Touchy subject. I knew it would be. At risk of being interrupted, I quickly continued.

"And you also said that saltwater is the primary resource that's imported from Earth. Why? What does The Channel need all of that salt for?"

His shoulders noticeably relaxed. It was quite apparent that he didn't want to discuss the logistics of dimension twenty-seven any further. He must have been grateful for the shift in direction. Not that I didn't have plenty more questions about CieCie's homeworld, but I could always ask Dane to fill in the blanks later.

Dane. What was he doing at this very moment? Probably helping Gilroy and CieCie with their investigation. Would he be at the warehouse waiting for me when we returned? Would he be excited to see me?

"Thermoelectric power plant cooling." The answer came so quickly that I barely understood the words.

"Excuse me?"

With a cocky grin, he repeated, "Thermoelectric power plant cooling." The words were matter-of-fact.

Was I supposed to know what that meant? I pursed my lips and shrugged.

Jacey's expression morphed before my eyes. "The Channel isn't a big magical resource spewing cube, Vivian. You think it just generates life to other worlds on its own?"

No. Maybe? Hell if I knew. I really hadn't considered the nuts and bolts of it all.

"It's a resource management system and a power plant," Jacey explained. "Just on a...cross-dimensional level."

A power plant? The explanation was fascinating, but it didn't answer my question. "What's that have to do with salt water?"

Jacey crossed his arms, looking more like his usual grumpy self. "Do you not understand how a thermoelectric power plant works?"

"Ummm...no?" Why did he always talk to me like a child? And why would I know how *thermo-molecular-whose-a-whats-its* work?

Jacey tipped his head back in exasperation. "For fucks sake," he groaned. "So, in as few words as possible, The

Channel's internal core is a boiler. You understand what a boiler is, right?"

I couldn't control my eyes as they rolled to the back of my head. "Yes, Jacey," I sighed, wishing that I'd saved the question for Dane. His explanations were far less chastising.

"Then you know that boilers turn water into steam, right? That steam moves through the central core to a subsector of turbines, and those turbines power six generators, one for each side of The Channel. Those generators power the fibers. That's how we transport resources." He took a deep breath as if he'd just run a mile.

"And you need saltwater...why?" I dared to ask.

He slapped his hand over his face, fingers sprawled over his cheeks like spider legs. Through his middle and index finger, he stared at me the way one might stare at a child who asked "why is the sky blue?"

"Because it's conductive, Vivian," his exasperated voice muffled through his palm. "God, what are they teaching you on Earth?"

"I'm sorry," I murmured. "You can't get mad at me for trying to understand, Jacey. This is all completely new to me. I was an office secretary, for God's sake. Not a damn scientist."

After a moment, his muscles visibly relaxed. He slid his hand up his face to rake his fingers through his hair. "I know, I know. Look, I'm sorry, okay? I've never been a good teacher. Or a good talker. If you haven't noticed, I tend to keep to myself. You can't blame me either. It's how Jumpers are wired."

"So, what you're saying is that you can't be held accountable for your actions. That the behavior is totally excusable, and I should just get used to it?" My voice was growing more bitter by the second. I *could* and I *would* blame him. His excuses were weightless.

Jacey's answering grin caught me off guard. "Exactly. See, now you're getting it."

The unwanted smile that spread across my lips infuriated me. Jacey infuriated me. His constant mood swings infuriated me. So, why had we both broken into laughter? It was like all the tension melted away under the bright ambiance of the fiber.

We were at a crossroad where everything that had become familiar over the last hour would soon be gone, and I'd be left with more questions. Would this ever get easier? Or was the timeline here destined to always be mercurial, shifting my emotions from one extreme to the next like a ball rolling through a tabletop labyrinth?

"You ready to go?" Jacey's focus strayed toward the archway.

Wordlessly, I nodded, and we started toward the port once again. Past the massive arch was a long, black stone landing, and at its end were twelve ominous elevator shafts. They were dark and unwelcoming. Unlike the clean silver elevator we'd taken back on The Channel, these were ancient-looking and encased in a layer of amber rust. Their sidewalls were exposed to the open air, made up by a waist-high panel of oxidized grating.

"Uhhh, are these safe?" I murmured nervously as we approached one of the open doors. As if on cue, a thin sliver of rust fell from somewhere above and onto the scuffed elevator floor.

Jacey smiled deviously. "Nope. Let's go."

He waved me inside first.

Here goes nothing.

As my feet touched the platform, the elevator trembled and swayed underfoot. "Woah!" I gasped, grabbing the flakey grating to support myself. A waffle pattern of gritty orange residue stained my palm.

Jacey stepped inside next. In response, the box quivered down several inches, strained under his weight.

We're gonna die, we're gonna die, we're gonna die.

The ping of a small bell rang out, and a single oxidized door screeched painfully until the elevator was closed. I looked at Jacey questioningly.

With a sharp raise of his eyebrows, he punched a solitary red button next to the door.

For a moment, all was quiet. Did this elevator work? Did any of them? Did Jacey push the right button? He must have. There was only one. I listened hard for the sound of movement in the neighboring shafts. None of the other elevators seemed to be moving either.

Jacey opened his mouth to speak but was cut off by the subtle creak of metal somewhere above our heads. Lips still parted, he frowned at me in silent question—*Did you hear that, too?*—just before the floor dropped from under our feet.

Caught in a violent free-fall, we were suspended in air, trapped within the rusty box. "Oh, fuck!" I screamed, snaking my fingers through the grate of the elevator wall.

Jacey had both arms extended, bracing himself dead center on the elevator floor like a stocky version of the Vitruvian Man. My skirt fluttered wildly, and my hair danced around my face, gripping my lips in tendrils. The elevator was gaining speed, clattering against the walls of the shaft with a deafening roar of metal on brick.

Like a dog meeting the end of its leash, we snapped to an abrupt halt. The impact sent my body slamming against the ceiling of the metal box, then back down, where I landed squarely on top of Jacey. We both tumbled hard to the wooden floor with a thump.

"Oooooouch," I groaned, rubbing my head where it had smacked against the ceiling.

Jacey's solid body was sprawled out under me. His chest heaved heavily against my face, and his eyes were wide with shock.

Dazed, I scanned the elevator floor until they rested on something small and silver, just outside of my peripheral vision. *A bottle cap?*

His hand reached across the floor and snatched it. He shifted underneath me to tuck it in his pocket. I could barely register what was happening. I couldn't move. My legs were still trembling as adrenaline coursed through my recovering body.

"Hmmm. This one must have been broken," Jacey murmured.

I lifted my head from his chest incredulously. "You think?" I shouted.

Cautiously, he pushed my body off his chest and stood stiffly to his feet. I stayed on the ground. *The sweet, sweet solid ground.* With a groan, Jacey stretched and shook his head as if he'd just woken from a pleasant nap. My heart hadn't caught up with us yet. It was still pounding somewhere up above our heads.

"Ready to go?" Jacey asked.

We nearly died not even a minute ago! How could he be so collective?

"No," I gasped, closing my eyes. "I think I'll just stay down here."

Jacey kicked my boot. I opened my eyes to find him hovering over me. The ghost of a smile creased the corners of his lips. "Okaaaay, but I'm pretty sure you're going to want to see this."

His stormy gaze fixed back through the grates to whatever waited beyond. *Damn my curiosity!*

By the time I'd pulled myself to my knees, the screech of

metal on metal pierced the silence, and the elevator door painfully slid open. I cinched my eyes shut as an uncomfortable frisson sent goosebumps down my spine. After a moment, the sound stopped. Slowly, I reopened my eyes.

Jacey offered me his hand, but I couldn't tear my gaze away from the alien world that lay in front of us, even as he hoisted me to my feet. My trembling boots carried me out of the elevator and onto a cobblestone street where I spun in slow circles with my face to the sky.

Jacey smirked his typical cocky grin as he moved to stand beside me. "Welcome to Mercantile dimension."

Hundreds of half-timbered buildings in shades of burnished copper and brass were stacked ten stories high, their pitched tops partially masked by thick plumes of gray. In the distance, towering smokestacks billowed out steam that hung in the air like a wool blanket. To the right, a dusty steam engine chugged along a suspended railway that snaked between buildings, its cars swaying from side to side. My mind couldn't decide if I'd stepped into the past or the future.

I spotted a man extending an oil torch toward a black iron street post. He was dressed in a seventeenth-century style waistcoat and black oil-splattered breeches. When the lantern overhead ignited, a burst of orange flames illuminated two copper goggle lenses that shifted quickly in our direction. I stiffened as he cocked his head curiously. The strange man pulled the torch back from the post and continued down the street, where more lamps were waiting to be lit.

"Watch out!"

Jacey grabbed my arm and tugged me hard. I called out in shock just as a large wagon raced across the cobblestone where I'd been standing. As it passed, it sent a wave of freezing cold mud crashing against my legs.

"Watch where you're going, fuck nugget!" Jacey boomed, but the wagon was already almost out of sight.

CieCie's skirt hung drenched from my hips, and the pleating was completely saturated in spatters of mud. *Damn it. Did The Channel have stain remover?* Hopefully, CieCie wasn't too attached to this outfit.

My brow fell as Jacey's hand unexpectedly clasped my face. My lips puckered like a fish between the pressure of his thumb and index finger as he tilted my head from one side to the other. "Are you okay?"

"Yeah," I gasped, pulling away. "Second heart attack in the last five minutes. I'm good. No need for...whatever you're doing."

I stood with my hand clasped over my chest. *Sensory overload.* So much was crashing down at once. It made me long for the quiet comfort of standing around the table at Gilroy's place.

"You sure you're okay?" Jacey's voice was stained with concern. *How un-Jacey of him.*

"Yes," I assured him. "This is just a lot. *A lot a lot.* I'm okay. Just need to let my brain catch up."

Jacey frowned, clearly unconvinced, but he remained silent.

After a few deep breaths, my legs felt steady enough to carry me again. "Okay, let's go. I can't believe I'm saying this, but I think I preferred walking through the fiber. This...this is not what I was expecting."

We started off down the cobblestone strip in the direction that the wagon had sped off. Jacey remained close, keeping his body between me and the road this time. Somewhere ahead, a wail broke through the hiss of steam and humming of engines. Then another and another. I looked to Jacey for answers. *Were those people screaming?* His impassive expression was alarming, but I continued alongside him, determined to not make another spectacle of myself.

After a while, the street ahead opened into a large plaza. Its perimeter was lined with more wooden steam-powered wagons. They shivered and sputtered plumes of smoke, creating a deafening mechanical cacophony. Somewhere beside us, a man's voice hawked over the sound.

"Mugs! I've got mugs here! Coffee mugs, quinic mugs, beer mugs, tea mugs. Big mugs, small mugs, mugs for bugs even. You there, sir!" the man cajoled, waving toward Jacey. "When's the last time you called your mother? When's her birthday? Don't tell me you've forgotten to buy her a gift!"

Jacey turned a threatening gaze on the man.

"Unless you've got an urn back there, no," he growled.

Oh no. Embarrassment for the merchant flooded over me at once. To my surprise, he continued smiling, his teeth barely visible through his curly, red mustache.

"Well then, sir, I have just the thing for you!" The vendor reached under the table and produced a decorative stein, topped with a polished silver lid. "This handy Mothers-day-out mug is perfect for toting dear mommy around the town square without spilling her in your hair! Take her to the park! Take her on a date! Just don't take her for a drink, or you'll be pissing gray!"

I clapped my hands over my mouth.

In a flash of black leather, Jacey rounded the booth of colorful mugs and saucers. "You little shit!" he boomed. Several cups teetered over the edge and crashed to the ground as the vendor leaped over the table and darted down the plaza with Jacey racing noisily on his heels. "Get your puffy-pants wearing ass back here, you little..." His voice quickly faded as they both vanished into the crowd.

So much for not making a spectacle. I briefly considered

following them but decided against it. That crazy little man was pretty fast. Jacey would be back soon, likely empty-handed. I reached down and picked up the only mug that hadn't shattered. It was crisp and flawless. Definitely not handmade, I noted. I placed it back on the table and observed some of the other dishes that were displayed. All were crisp and perfectly manufactured as if they'd been created in a modern factory on Earth. *How strange.*

Turning from the table, I gazed around the plaza where a dozen more boisterous street vendors were hawking their wares to men in overcoats and women in plumed corseted dresses. There were kettles and blankets, bicycles and truck tires, souvenir tee shirts, and stuffed toys. *Very strange indeed.* No two items appeared to be of the same era.

I glanced nervously to the place in the crowd where Jacey had vanished. Still no sign of him or the mug vendor. What would Jacey do if he actually caught the poor bastard? I didn't want to consider the answer to that. Instead, I tentatively followed the perimeter of the plaza until it led me to the next wagon, not straying far enough that Jacey wouldn't be able to spot me when he returned.

Piles of clothing were stacked in colorful bundles across the booth. On the back of the table, I spotted several armored jackets and a heap of dented pauldrons. *Bingo.* Just as I reached my bandaged fingers out to touch them, a busty woman leaned adroitly forward, using her breasts to block my hand. Embarrassment flooded over me, and I immediately retracted.

"Your boyfriend is weak north of his ears, ain't he?"

Was she talking to me? I locked eyes with the woman, trying to keep my gaze anywhere but her overflowing corset. Her warm brown cheeks were framed in long black beaded tresses that trailed the length of her curvy frame.

A fiery bronze glow was captured in her high cheekbones

as she smiled with mischief alight in her eyes. "Can't say I blame him," she said, tapping a long red fingernail to her chin. "Todd's been chucking corn kernels down my blouse all week. 'Bout time someone gave him some exercise." As I struggled to find my voice, her red rose petal lips twitched ever-so-slightly.

"He's not my boyfriend," I choked.

She held my gaze for only a second before her eyes rolled dramatically, and her body followed the motion. Like a too-full glass, her corset brimmed over with the movement.

"Sweet girl, are you truly so simple?"

Was she being serious? I opened my mouth, but no sound came out.

The woman fanned her lashes and shook her head.

"Baby, baby, baby. Look, see. I know a thing or two about men. Trust me. When you've got a chest like mine, your intuition evolves sharper. I make a fortune in this plaza selling dingy ol' clothes to dingy ol' men. Call it marketing expertise."

As she said the words, she sloshed her chest from one side to the other. My cheeks burned hotter than the lampposts that surrounded us as I forced my eyes to stay on her face.

"And that man...before he went running after Todd at least...that brawny man was eyeballing you like a pigeon on a pastry. I know that look. I see that same look almost every day. He's into you, baby doll. Those baby blues don't lie."

An embarrassingly loud snort burst through my nose. *She thought Jacey liked me?* The idea was so delusional that I could barely process it. The woman cocked her chin questioningly as laughter erupted from my throat.

"I'm sorry," I giggled, bracing against the table as the woman crossed her arms. "I don't know what you think you saw," I continued, "but Jacey is more of a...a bodyguard. Or an escort. What I mean to say is, we're just together. Traveling together." I flustered through the tight pull of the absurd smile that refused to leave.

With every word, the woman's sharp eyebrows inclined a bit more. "Uh-huh. Okay, baby. Well, I know what I think I saw because I saw it. But I'll let up. Since coins speak louder than advice from a nosey ol' woman, what can I do you for today?"

Relieved that the inquisition was over, I redirected my attention to the pile of armored jackets that lay buried beneath the heap. They were dusty and faded, and some were marred with deep gashes. I wished Jacey would hurry. I had no idea what I was looking for.

"Well, baby, what'll it be?" the woman prompted.

"Protection. I need protection. Bodily protection," I hastily clarified. How much was I allowed to say? Jacey didn't exactly brief me on the "not-to-dos" before our arrival. I shot another anxious glance over my shoulder. *What was taking him so long?* When I turned back to the woman, her arms were splayed wide on her hips, and her brows were angled in dagger-sharp peaks. *Did I say something wrong?*

"Protection, you said? Wai-wai-wait. Did that boy hurt you?" Her gaze fixed on my bandaged hand, and fury danced in her raised cheeks.

"Oh, no!" I gasped. "Jacey didn't do this. I did. I uh—punched a table. Long story."

Her red lips flared after a moment. My response seemed to bemuse her, but I was eager to avoid the subject.

"Jacey looks like a hardass but don't let him fool you. I don't think he could actually hurt anyone. He's a bit of a softie," I added.

A hand landed hard on my shoulder. I shrieked like a lunatic just before Jacey stepped beside me with a deranged smile set across his face.

"I kicked that scrawny little fuck's ass all the way to the edge of town!" he announced, shaking me proudly.

My mouth fell open. *What timing!* When I glanced back at the woman, her expression melted into amusement once more as she devoured Jacey.

"Took you long enough," I hissed, snaking away from his hand. "You could have at least left me with a shopping list!"

"Damn, Vivian, I'm sorry. That little guy was fast as hell. Plus," he added, "I had to stop and clean my boot on the way back."

Clean his boot? Why would he need to—

"After I pulled it out of his ass, I mean."

Oh. My. God. Was this man void of shame? My cheeks were on fire, and I was acutely aware of the woman, who was snickering behind the table.

"Pigeon on a pastry," she mouthed with an innocent pop of her red lips.

Her voice caught Jacey's attention, and his eyes grew wide when they met the brim of her overfilled corset. A fly in a trap. The woman tossed a sweet doe-eyed grin in his direction and fluttered her long lashes. Though I respected her insanely efficient marketing tactics, this was getting too awkward. Without thinking, I hastily reached across the table and yanked one of the armored jackets from the bottom of the pile.

"We're here for protection, right? Let's get to it then. Will this work?" I held the black leather jacket to my chest.

Jacey didn't move. There was a tight strain in his jaw, like some weird and magical force was holding his eyes just below the woman's face.

"Jacey!" I shouted.

With a jolt, his eyes whipped away like he'd just been snapped from a trance. It took him a moment to register what

I'd asked. As I stood holding the jacket impatiently to my chest, Jacey's brows shot up in a mischievous smile.

"You're sure you want that one?" the woman behind the table cut in.

Now what? I looked at the jacket in my hands. Was it ripped? *Wait...No!* I threw it down at once and covered my face with my hands. A perfectly rounded W-shaped pattern had been cut into the chest, like a puzzle cube waiting to be completed with just the right-sized breasts. Both Jacey and the woman were laughing hysterically.

"Come on. Lighten up, Vivian," Jacey nudged me. "The sooner we get this done, the sooner we can get back home."

I soured at the word. *Home.* His home, yes—but not my home. My home was quiet, comfortable, and predictable. You didn't need armored jackets or cybernetic weapons to survive there. *Had mom tried to call me yet?* This thought was my undoing. My chest ached with the bitter reminder that something within me had fractured. Until I heard mom's voice again, a piece of me would always remain broken.

"Just get what we need, Jacey. I'm ready to leave." The unrelenting anxiety was taking its toll. Like trudging through deep snow, fatigue was setting in.

Sleep sounded nice. Soft blankets. Silence. Darkness. Warm arms. *Would I be in Dane's bed again tonight? Would he be there, too?* My cheeks grew unexpectedly warm. *Shit. Don't think of that now.*

The merchant woman offered several different jackets from her collection. Most were excessively worn and damaged beyond functionality. After Jacey's latest rejection—a hideously oversized brown leather monstrosity that hung all the way past my knees—the woman became visibly desperate.

"I just know I have more jackets hiding 'round here!" she

shouted to us from the bed of her wagon. Her voice was growing frantic. "Don't ya'll go running 'til I find 'em!"

It was clear that she wasn't going to allow us to leave until we'd purchased something.

Jacey and I spent the time staring silently into the plaza. People-watching was my guilty pleasure back home. I could spend hours just sitting in crowded coffee shops or bookstores, observing how people moved and interacted. The way they walked, talked, stumbled, or scratched unmentionable places when they thought no one was looking. It was humorously humbling at times and soddening at others.

From across the cobblestone plaza, I watched as a tanned man in a crisply starched cap bent low to kiss the lips of a soft dove-skinned woman from under her parasol. She spun it in her fingers, and her cheeks blushed as pink as her lace lined dress. It was reassuring to see that some things were the same, no matter what dimension you came from. The sight thawed my heart. They stood across the plaza, gazing at each other with love radiating between them. A perfect romantic painting. The man took her hand, gently kissed it, and led her to one of the many merchant wagons.

"Get a room," Jacey groaned. I glared at him in disbelief. His hand was deftly flipping something in the air and catching it.

God, he could be so insolent! Unable to contain my fury, I rammed his shoulder hard with mine, causing him to almost drop the small item in his hand.

"Watch it!" he gasped.

Laying open-side up in his palm, I recognized the silver bottle cap from the elevator. Inside was an image, a tiny black silhouette of what I could only guess was a dog or maybe a wolf. Before I could get a good look, he closed his fingers around the cap and slipped it back into his pocket. His eyes were locked on me, narrow and sinister. I knew this look. It was the same arctic glare he'd pinned on me in the elevator at the Belair.

What the hell was his problem now?

"Fooooound it!" wailed a voice from the wagon.

Jacey's gaze released me, and I was left in my usual scattered state of confusion. Another question left unanswered. But of all the mysteries I'd collected on my pallet over the last two days, I decided that the mystery of the bottle cap wasn't worth solving right now. Knowing Jacey, it was probably some freaky death trophy he'd pulled from a body. I still found it hard to believe that Mr. Brawny-Weirdo was a trained combat soldier. *Weren't soldiers more controlled than this?* His temper was just too hair-trigger.

"Found it, found it, found it!" the merchant woman exclaimed triumphantly when she reappeared. A gray heap of leather was folded over her arm. "See? I told you I'd find something! Mama Venus always comes through."

I briefly glanced back to Jacey, whose eyes were once again locked just south of her chin. Yes, Venus seemed like a fitting name for the witty woman who trapped men like flies. I had to give her credit where credit was due. She had one hell of a marketing campaign packed into that corset, and she knew exactly how to persuade her shoppers.

To my surprise, the gray leather jacket that she unfolded was absolutely immaculate. Tapered at the waist, it was similar to some of the armor from Dane's collection. Venus held it up and motioned excitedly for me to try it on. As I slipped my arms through the sleeves, I was wrapped in a secure hug that reminded me of my weighted blanket back home. The gray leather fit perfectly. It was as if it had been tailored just for me.

Black flexible side panels gave the jacket extra mobility, making movement effortless, despite its relatively heavy weight. Vertical armored panels on the back of the jacket met with ribbed leather shoulder pieces, and the inside was plush and quilted with a black fur lining. This was the one. I looked to Jacey with a hopeful grin, our previous confrontation long forgotten.

He nodded approvingly. "That'll work for the outer layer," he said, tapping his finger to his bottom lip. "Now we need a base layer."

Venus clapped her hands victoriously and jumped headfirst back into the wagon to search.

14

ELECTRIC DANCE

I was a new human. A stranger, redesigned with only a few obscure pieces of my former self. My legs looked longer, leaner, and stronger, sheathed within a pair of ribbed black moto-style jeans. Jacey had said the legs were reinforced with "ultra-high-molecular-weight polyethylene." I had no idea what that meant, but I did know that my legs looked damn good. Especially paired with the gray leather jacket, Jacey's black scarf, and my new white kevlar-fiber-woven tee shirt. Venus screeched like a banshee when she found it for me.

The clothing technology that evolved from Mercantile dimension was mind-blowing. It made me feel even more bitter about Earth politics and advancements.

We could have been a part of this. We could have lived in a world that openly organized and traded with cross-dimensional societies. Societies who progressed so far technologically that they abandoned petty war entirely. We could, as a planet, be a part of this widely advanced cross-dimensional world—but I knew I'd never see it in my lifetime. If only the typical Earth citizen could see it. If only they could be made to understand how the primitive politics of our planet were actually holding the entire dimension hostage, never able to expand outward. There was so much more.

"Beer, Vivian?" Jacey asked. I glanced at him suspiciously, his lip twitched with a wisp of amusement. "It's surprisingly similar to Earth beer," he assured me.

Why was his smile so infectious?

"Like your fucked up version of coffee?"

He laughed at the memory. "No, nothing like quinic. The beer here is alright. A bit of a pissy aftertaste, but what beer doesn't have a pissy aftertaste?"

"You're not really selling it," I smirked.

"Says the marketing girl," he said, slamming a frothy mug in front of me. I'd never liked beer, but seeing the mug—cold and dripping with beads of condensation, I found myself reaching for it.

We were seated across from each other, our table placed under the belly of a massive zeppelin that hung from the ceiling. The pub was dark and cozy, tucked into the back of one of the many brick buildings that lined the merchant's plaza. An ambient jazzy beat fizzled from bronze radio horns at each corner of the room. The walls were decorated in a messy collage of machine pieces, cranks, gears, plane parts, and cannons.

I studied the impressive collection of strange artifacts as I sipped from the tall mug. To my surprise, it tasted like beer. Not good beer...but beer, nonetheless. Though I didn't particularly like the bitterness, it tasted like home. Hot summer evenings, grilling hot dogs and toasting marshmallows with Mom.

Mom.

I blinked with the speed of a camera shutter, wishing away the thoughts of her. *Not here. Not now.* But it was too late. She was an echo, ricocheting from every corner of my consciousness.

Surely, she knew I was missing by now. Panic wouldn't have set in yet. Not until she made the police report. They'd likely want her to travel to Sacramento first to check my apartment. She would dig through my things and find absolutely nothing, and this is when she would begin to truly panic.

The police would likely search the LA area. Maybe a camera somewhere in LA caught Jacey and me walking together down the Sunset strip. My kidnapper and ideal suspect with his frightening face and tattoos. The local news stations would have their work cut out for them, requesting the public to keep an eye out for my 5'8 oaf of a captor. Mom would watch the footage, cursing the burly villain who stole me away. Then she would shift the blame to herself for ever encouraging me to go out on my own.

"Hey. Yoo-hoo, Vivian," Jacey said, snapping his fingers. I blinked. "As interesting as that wall of trash may be, I'd like to order some food. You hungry?" Jacey was staring across the table at me, completely unaware of my hypothetical thunderstorm.

What was wrong with me? We were supposed to be having a good time. I needed to pull myself together. This was the reward for our efforts before we started our long trek home, and unlike me, Jacey was completely at ease.

His body was sprawled back in his chair, and his legs were spread wide and lazy. If he didn't make me so furious ninety-nine percent of the time, I might have even thought he looked handsome. This new veil of calm was very flattering on him. Contagious even. I allowed myself to release the tension from my shoulders and took another sip from my mug.

"I actually am hungry," I replied, "but I don't know what food this dimension has."

Jacey leaned over the wooden table, eyes darting from side to side as he scanned the parchment menu in front of us. As he did, the thick cords of his neck bunched in a tight plunge that vanished into the depths of his collar.

I wondered what he hid underneath all those layers. The man was an absolute monster with the type of body that Greek sculptors would have given their life savings to chisel into marble. I didn't notice I'd been gawking until his eyes drifted to mine for a millisecond before dropping back to the menu.

Shit! My head dropped between my shoulders, and I hid my twitching lips beneath the folds of my scarf. No wonder Jacey always buried himself in this thing.

Maybe that's why he seemed so at ease now. Without his scarf, I could read the missing pieces of body language. The relaxed cords of his neck, the subtle slack of his stubbled jaw, the twitch in the corners of his mouth as he read. Not quite a smile but definitely not a frown.

"Well," he announced, looking up, "we've got one hell of a walk back. And it isn't every day that I get to visit Mercantile dimension. So I'm pigging. You ready for prembalts, capperloin, and hambing?"

"Uh, I don't know...to be honest with you."

Jacey's eyes narrowed, and he breathed for a moment before splitting into his wolfish grin. "You're just going to have to trust me, I guess."

The charmingly rough texture of his voice caused me to burrow back into the scarf.

Oh, shit. I did trust him.

Dane was mistaken about Jacey's motives. Sure, he'd been an asshole—but clearly he was stressed and justifiably so. Someone was trying to murder him. Murder both of us. With so much at stake, the pressure would put anyone on edge. Now that I had the appropriate equipment, things would be easier for him. For all of us. We just needed to figure out how to get me back home.

I wasn't sure of much anymore, but damn—I was absolutely certain that capperloin was the single most wonderful thing I'd ever tasted. Between the two of us, Jacey and I polished off two giant platters of mysterious meats, breads, and cheeses. I had no idea what any of it was—nor was I brave enough to ask, but my faith in Jacey paid off. The boy knew food. Maybe not how to cook it, but he definitely knew how to eat it. I'd have to remember that.

As we started toward home, I was very grateful for the black waist bag that now held CieCie's muddy skirt and white button-down shirt. My belly was full, and my muscles ached. With a long walk ahead of us, I was happy to let my arms hang and swing freely at my sides as we strolled along the cobblestone strip. A trail of oil lanterns illuminated the ground in bright circles of orange light, contributing to the warm monochrome pallet of the impending dusk. A question popped into my mind.

"Is the sun the same here?"

"Same sun. Same galaxy. Same planet," Jacey answered. "Humans are the only differing factor between most dimensions. The many paths humans have taken is what sets each dimension apart. A decision made by a single man could be the altering factor that tips the axis."

"And if there were no humans?" I dared to ask.

"There are plenty of dimensions that don't have humans," Jacey replied. "And they are all nearly identical."

I looked at him, puzzled. The warm lamplight reflected from his skin and cast long shadows under his brow. He was much more intimidating in the low light. No wonder he thrived so well on The Channel. The dark was his element.

"Humans are the differing factor," he repeated. "Without humans, the world moves in a singular, parallel direction, no matter what the dimension. The world has its own will to live, and since the world will outlast any human lifeform, the future of all dimensions is much the same."

"And what about the dimensions that lack oxygen?" I recalled the conversation I'd had with Dane when we first arrived at Gilroy's place.

"Very few dimensions completely lack oxygen. As long as there's green shit growing from the dirt, there's oxygen. Sometimes just not enough for humans to survive. But in time, life always returns. Sprouts turn to forests, and the planet heals itself. Biologically speaking, humans are the worst possible thing that could happen to a planet. Planets without humans rarely fail."

"That's a bummer," I mused.

Jacey shrugged. "It is what it is," he said simply.

We were approaching the long brick wall that housed our exit—the rusted elevator shafts.

Crap. I'd forgotten about those. My head still ached from the initial trip. No way was I stepping foot on another tetanus-inducing metal death trap. As we approached, I noticed a stocky woman leaning against the wall in between two of the open elevators.

"Pigeon and Pastry!" she called out.

"Venus!" I smiled. "What are you doing here?"

She bounced and bobbed over to us enthusiastically, then captured me in a backbreaking hug. "Market closes at sundown. I wanted to see y'all off. And remind you not to take the elevators. Unless you want a concussion for dessert." Her voice was warm and cheeky as she squeezed me against her chest.

"There's another way up?" Jacey asked.

Venus released her hold, and I desperately recovered the air that had been gushed from my lungs.

"See, that's what I love about you Channel folk. Well-funded but dull-minded. Every merchant's dream," she smiled innocently and fluttered her long eyelashes before pointing to the farthest door in the row of elevators. "Last door on your left leads to a staircase. The elevators have been decommissioned for years. Most of y'all Channel folks know that, though, so we stopped sending up door guides to direct the traffic."

Oh, thank god. I breathed a sigh of relief.

"Well, that fucking figures," Jacey sniffed. I could tell he was relieved and probably felt a little silly for not knowing about the stairs in the first place.

We each gave Venus a quick farewell hug and promised to visit the next time we returned to Mercantile dimension. Deep down, I knew that I probably wouldn't be returning. But I couldn't bring myself to tell her that. It wasn't like I could explain that I'd been dragged to The Channel illegally and was breaking multiple cross-dimensional laws.

Soon, this nightmare would all be over. I'd be on my way back home. Back to my apartment, my mom, my life. Or most of it anyway. The parts that were safe and predictable. It was hard to imagine what my world would be like when I returned.

Obviously, I'd have no job and no boyfriend. That was a given. But what about Ryan and Mr. Rivera? Both of them knew where I lived. Would they come looking for me? Would they want to finish what they started? I could always move to Indiana to be with my mother. Yes, that seemed like the most logical solution. But if they were able to use Channel technology, they would probably be able to track my location and that could put my mom at risk.

Jacey and I were noisily thudding up the zigzagging stairwell when a single, chilling realization struck me. *Nowhere would be safe.* Not until we discovered what Mr. Rivera and Ryan planned and not until they were stopped. My pace increased, and my boots grew loud and impatient.

"Slow down, Vivian. We're not racing the sun here. Light in the fiber comes from the walls."

Jacey had misplaced my point of concern, but I didn't feel like sharing my fears with him. I decided on a different line of questioning to hopefully put my mind at ease.

"Do you think Dane, Gilroy, and CieCie found anything?"

"Nothing important," he said, holding up his wrist. The twisting Central Connect tattoo was partially exposed, peeking from under the roll of his sleeve.

Right. If they'd found anything, they would have called him. My heart withered at the edges.

"It'll all work out," Jacey said, stepping onto the black platform of the fiber's landing. He held his hand out to me. "After all, hanging out with us isn't all that bad, is it?"

No, it wasn't bad. It wasn't bad at all. But being worlds away from my mother with no way to tell her that I was okay? That was unbearable.

Surrendering to the gloom, I gingerly extended my hand to Jacey. To my surprise, he grabbed it gently and laced his fingers between mine, pulling me along the black platform toward the twelve archways.

"I'm sorry I've been such a dick, Vivian. I'm going to start trying to be a better friend to you."

The declaration shook me. It was solid, sturdy. A pledge. I looked at him, waiting for him to say something more. But he continued walking, dragging me along after him with his eyes focused ahead. I decided to let it go.

We passed through an arch toward the center of the barrier. The fiber's familiar light once again washed over us. I liked it here. The way the air smelled and the texture of the grass under my boots. For as long as I kept my eyes off of the walls of the tunnel, it felt normal. Earthly.

Jacey broke his hand from mine, and we continued walking, our strides languid and calm. The atmosphere between us evolved so much over the course of our journey.

Jacey folded his arms behind his head as he strolled. "So, do you have any interesting questions for me?"

Was he actually asking me to ask questions? My alarm bells chimed on overdrive. "Uh. Yeah. Tons actually." It seemed too good to be true. *Was this a trap?*

Jacey raised his brow. "Let's hear them then. We've got a long and boring walk ahead of us."

The hive was activated as a million questions buzzed and swarmed through my head. *Where to begin?* One voice seemed to vibrate louder than the others, but I ignored it. No hard questions yet. Start with something simple.

"Okay. Here's one. If Dane is from Earth, and CieCie is from dimension twenty-seven, where did you come from?" This is one that had been bugging me all day.

Jacey seemed amused by the direction of my first inquiry. "Don't dig too far, Vivian. What you'll find is far, far less interesting than you're imagining."

I expected him to dodge the question, but a moment later, he ran a hand through his raven hair and answered.

"Honestly, I don't know which dimension I came from. A smuggler brought me to The Channel as a very small child. All I remember was a black hooded jacket and a woman's hands as she gave me to Gilroy. She told Gilroy that my mother had died, or at least, that's what Gilroy has always told me. He had no idea who the woman was, and he didn't ask her. He just took me and raised me until I was old enough to start training." His voice was nonchalant.

I was grateful that the subject didn't seem to bother him. No parents, no recollection of his home, nothing to feel bitter about.

"Is that why you're so dedicated to your job?"

He thought for a moment, and his brow creased slightly, then released. "I'm dedicated to my job because it's the honorable thing to do, Vivian."

Okay, that answer seemed simple enough. I scrambled to think of another question. "How old are you?"

He looked at me quizzically again, and I tensed. *Was that the wrong thing to ask?*

"Why? How old do you think I am?"

He inclined his brow with interest as I studied his face. Dark circles around the eyes. Gentle creasing at the corners of his lips. A sharp angular jaw.

"Hmmm. I'm guessing thirty."

Jacey's knowing grin was indication that I'd hit close to the mark.

"Twenty-nine actually. You were pretty close. Anything else you'd like to know?"

Get comfortable, Jacey. I'd been packing away questions for two days, and the floodgates were open.

"Does it rain on The Channel?" I decided to start at the top. This was one of the very first things I'd wondered since my arrival.

"No," he answered. "Can't really have rain without clouds."

Instinctively, my gaze shot to the domed tunnel overhead.

It was bright and shimmering, just as it had been on the first journey through.

"The pavement. It was wet when we first arrived at The Channel. I remember it being the first thing I noticed when I woke up in that alley, but I couldn't figure out why."

A look of understanding crossed Jacey's face. "Oh, right. That'd be the condensation from the thermoelectric cooling process. It's also why The Channel looks perpetually foggy. Our boilers can get pretty steamy. Like your own little slice of foggy Sacramento." He nudged me playfully as we passed a line of lush green trees.

I didn't want to think about home at that moment, though, so I quickly came up with another question. "What are the other dimensions like?"

His head cocked to the side. "All twenty-six of them?" he asked, surprised.

It seemed like a reasonable question to me, but I revised it for the sake of saving time. I had plenty more that I wanted to ask.

"Tell me about five of them. We can save the others for later." Not that I thought he was keeping track, but I didn't want to use up all of our time. There was still the matter of his secret window conversation to address.

"I already know Earth is dimension six. Dane told me."

He nodded. "And you also already know Mercantile dimension. Dimension five. They are one of the oldest unified dimensions, and one of the few that we openly trade with. I used to go there a lot with Gilroy before I began Jumper training. Today was the first time I've visited in several years." His smile touched all the way to his eyes. "It was a good trip. I don't get to eat like that often."

He patted his stomach, and we both laughed in mutual appreciation. It was the most I'd eaten in over a week.

"I'm glad you took me," I admitted.

The smile didn't leave his face as he continued. "Dimension two is a wild one. Not a place you'll find any travel brochures for. The timeline there took a weird direction around sixty-six-million years ago when a massive asteroid narrowly missed the planet."

"If it missed the planet, how was the timeline affected?"

"Because, it was *supposed* to hit the planet," he explained. "That asteroid was an essential part of your planet's timeline. It was responsible for the mass extinction of the dinosaurs and for kickstarting a new stage of life. Without that asteroid, mammals remained at the bottom of the food chain, and other life just continued evolving and growing. Reptiles grew larger brains, then hands, then they lost their scales. Some took on a human-like bipedal form but at insane sizes due to the oxygen-rich atmosphere. It's fucking terrifying, Vivian, trust me. There's a reason we call it Colossus dimension."

Wow. What our scientists wouldn't give to know about this. My morbid curiosity took hold. "Does anyone from The Channel go there?"

"Only for the purpose of re-evaluation. The uh...big fuckers have quite the taste for us."

Shock churned my gut. "Oh."

Jacey must have sensed my discomfort. He continued, his tone lighter. "Dimension two definitely has its benefits, though. In fact, that's where we source all of the oxygen that we export, including the supply we filter to Earth."

We'd reached the halfway point of the tunnel. In the distance, twelve black arches dotted across the long barrier. I still had so many questions.

"That's two dimensions. Three more to go." My voice was enthusiastic, but deep down, a small surge of panic flickered. What if his mood shifted once we were back in the dark void of

The Channel? Time was running out, and the most important question was still sealed behind my lips.

"Right. Well, there's dimension one. Unfortunately, it's uninhabitable, but we keep the port open. Some of their atmosphere and life has taken refuge in the fiber, which is what we source."

I was eager to get through the final dimensions, but I conceded to my curiosity. "What made the dimension uninhabitable?"

Jacey smiled, almost apologetically. "The sun burned out."

"What?" I gasped in shock.

"Yeah, it was slow going for a few years. I knew there was something fucky with their sun. It just kept getting dimmer and dimmer. We caught word that the whole thing had burned out, and that was a whole shit show on its own. We only had a few days to get as many people to The Channel as possible before the whole damn planet froze over."

Jacey must have noticed the stress that creased my forehead. "Don't worry, Vivian. It's the only time we've seen it happen. Pretty sure your dimension will be fine." His tone was reassuring, and I let out the breath I'd been holding.

"So, what happened to the planet?"

"Oh, it's still there. It's cold, but it's there, floating around without an anchor point. All of the planets probably are. Can't really have a solar system without a sun, so who knows where they've all drifted off to."

I shook my head in amazement. This was unreal.

"So, what's in dimension one's fiber that's so valuable?"

Jacey smiled, and as he did, he rolled up his sleeve. The twisted tattoo on his arm looked even more unnatural under the bright light.

"A lot of strange evolution took place after dimension one's collapse. Our fibers literally work like fiber optic wires.

Without light from the sun, the entire fiber went black. And that caused all these strange mutations. We'd assumed that when photosynthesis could no longer take place, the plants would all just die off. Instead, new plants started popping up. Glowing plants. It was truly bizarre. Bioluminescent mushrooms and strange shrubby-type things. Since the plants couldn't rely on sunlight, they created their own. The place is fucking beautiful."

I'd never heard Jacey use the word "beautiful." Even if it had been preambled by "fucking," hearing his voice form the word made me smile.

"Then we discovered that the mushrooms could be used to produce ink. I don't know how they do it, but somehow our government was able to turn those glowing little toadstools into these." He held up his arm, and the grotesque transformation began. Skin bubbled and boiled, and a glowing green screen breached the surface, like a submarine emerging from the sea. His skin was pulled so tight around the sharp edges of the device that I found myself biting my lip.

"Does that hurt?" I whispered.

Jacey looked bewildered. "Hurt? Uh...I mean, it definitely doesn't tickle, if that's what you're asking. We get used to it."

We'd stopped walking. Jacey was standing awkwardly, fumbling with the green glowing screen. He lowered his wrist, and I watched as the device submerged itself. For a moment, the design of his tattoo continued to glow in steady intervals of light. After a few more seconds, it dimmed, and all was normal again.

"So. Ink...from glowing mushrooms. Interesting."

The smile returned. "I think so. It was one of the biggest advancements of Channel society. Was that enough dimension exploring, or do you want to hear more?"

"I want to hear more," I assured him. Two more dimension

overviews, then I'd ask about his window conversation. There was still plenty of fiber left to walk through. We started off again.

"Well, we've covered one, two, five, and six. So I guess I can fill in three and four." He looked up, smiling again. "Dimension three is another cool place to visit. It's a lot like Mercantile dimension. Totally Channel friendly and aware of our presence. Their planet is almost entirely covered in water."

"What caused that?" I asked, knowing there had to be another crazy alternation in the timeline. Jacey's nod told me that I was correct.

"As a society, they evolved insanely fast. Too fast. Their accelerated industrial era caused a dramatic increase in the planet's temperature. Unfortunately, their solution to the heat issue ended up causing an even bigger problem."

"Which was?"

"They invented refrigerants."

"Refrigerants like refrigerators?"

He shook his head. "Refrigerants like air conditioners and insulation. And yes, refrigerators, too, though I'm sure any of those items on their own wouldn't have been an issue. It was the absolute industrial boom of these advancements that finally did the ozone in.

"Earth dimension was smart enough to minimize the use of chlorofluorocarbon in refrigerants when they realized how dangerous it was. Dimension three didn't get the memo fast enough. By the time they realized that their ozone layer was being broken down to dangerous levels, it was too late. All of their ice and mountain glaciers melted, leaving a majority of the planet covered in water."

"I thought you said their dimension was fun to visit," I pointed out. A planet covered in water didn't sound like much fun unless you had a boat.

"Oh, it is!" Jacey said. "They adapted. With the lack of solid surface area, they were forced to build up. It's really quite ingenious. Entire cities carved into mountains with massive bridges connecting them. And with all that water, boats are the standard mode of transportation. It's a sea dog's paradise."

What a strange path my world could have taken. One little mistake could have changed everything. *A decision made by a single man could be the altering factor that tips the axis.*

"And dimension four?" I asked, eagerly. The twelve little archways in the distance were becoming bigger and bigger by the minute. My teeth took hold of my bottom lip as Jacey explained.

"The dimension of Scholars. Number four is reserved for the brainiacs and brainiacs in training. Nutty bastards are what they are. Every once in a while, The Channel will recognize that one of their recruits is too smart for their own good. So rather than wasting all that potential on a grunt-work job, they send them to dimension four to harness those skills. They're basically a private council that works for The Five and shapes how we interact with the other dimensions." His voice was laced in repugnance. "Every major scientific breakthrough comes from dimension four. They have no war. No religion. Nothing but happy foo-foo brainiac bullshit. It's a fucking snore-fest."

"You seem a little bitter," I pointed out.

He frowned. "Not bitter. I was destined to be a Jumper. Everything about me makes me the perfect weapon for The Channel. If I had to sit around and read books all day, I'd probably throw myself off a cliff."

His mood had gone stale and just in time for my final question. The one I'd been dwelling on all day. The one I'd been too afraid to ask. My time was up. The arches ahead were growing in size. *Now or never.*

"I have one more question." As I said it, my feet stopped. Jacey continued for several steps before he realized I was no longer beside him. He turned abruptly, and the space between us solidified with uncomfortable tension.

"Spill it." His eyes narrowed.

Could he tell what I was going to ask? *No. He couldn't possibly know.* I swallowed hard.

"Last night...when I came to the window, I thought I heard you talking to someone."

Cautiously, I braced myself for anger. His expression was clouding by the nanosecond.

"I wasn't," he stated flatly.

"But I heard you."

"What did you hear?" His voice cut sharp as he stiffened.

I was once again a child, small and vulnerable under his penetrating gaze. But I couldn't back down. Not after we'd come this far. I needed to crack the code.

"You said something about evidence. And you said you couldn't risk exposing them. Exposing who? Who was it, Jacey?" My voice was even and calm, but I knew my expression was betraying me. Jacey could see my fear.

He leaned on his hip, rooted to the ground where he stood. *What was he hiding?* Cautiously, I took a step toward him. He craned his jaw upward in response and filled his lungs so that his chest was wide and threatening.

"Jacey, just tell me. Please," I pleaded. "Are you hiding something from Gilroy? From Dane and CieCie?"

His frown deepened as I recited each of their names. *Oh, shit!* Was Dane right after all? Was Jacey really hiding something sinister?

I took another step forward.

Jacey's lips drew back at the corner of his mouth in warning. "Would you shut up?" he growled.

What? My throat tightened in a fearful bind that sent waves of nausea ripping through my stomach. Jacey was angry. *Really angry.*

"I'm sorry, Jacey. I just—"

"Not you!" he shouted, turning abruptly to face me. The blood in my veins buzzed with adrenaline as his body sprawled into a threateningly wide stance. Was he having a mental breakdown? A psychotic episode?

"Not now, not now, not now!" His guttural scream sent me sprawling backward. The rage in his eyes was unrecognizable from anything I'd ever witnessed before. He was feral. An animal, cornered and dangerous.

"Jacey, you're scaring me." My own voice was no more than a quivering whisper.

For a moment, we stood in complete silence, our eyes locked together like predator and prey. I wanted to say more, but the words wouldn't form. My skin pricked with cold sweat.

"You should be afraid," he rasped.

Shock radiated through my body. As I opened my mouth to speak, Jacey's expression morphed unexpectedly from rage to panic as they fixated behind me. I pivoted on my heel just before something solid and cold smashed against my cheek.

Pain. Pain seared through my jaw like lightning. The grass raced toward me, and I hit the ground with a sickening thump. More searing pain...and flashes. Camera flashes. It was like everything existed in blinding momentary flashes of clarity.

Jacey was standing over my body. His face was contorted into a scream that I couldn't hear. *Who was he screaming at?* Flashes. Confusing, mind-consuming flashes. *Who was he screaming at?* I turned my head weakly. Several feet away stood a man in a long brown coat. He wore a wide, floppy brimmed hat that shadowed his eyes.

I'd seen him before. *Where had I seen him before?* Flashes.

Enveloping, earth-shattering flashes. *Shit.* The sleeping man! It was the sleeping man from our first trip through the fiber.

Clarity crystalized as my pupils reclaimed their focus. The man was holding something. No, not holding. His arm was a *part* of something, long and cruel and bittersharp. I was paralyzed in horror as its glowing blue edge swung toward my face again.

Closing my eyes, I waited for impact. But it never came. Instead, Jacey's arm locked around my torso, then it was gone, and I was tumbling through the air. Another sickening thump. I lifted my head weakly from the grass where I'd landed.

"I hope the cheap shot was worth it," Jacey snarled viciously. Ready to strike, he was several feet away, poised in front of our attacker with his body flared like a cobra. "Because now, I'm going to paint the grass with you."

The man's darkened eyes quickly darted in my direction with torn interest. Jacey caught the movement and thrust forward a step.

"Don't fucking look at her!" he hissed. "I'm right fucking here."

His voice was seductive, an invitation that the attacker accepted as his glare refocused in Jacey's direction. *Was he...enjoying this?* The breath caught in my throat as Jacey's lips upturned into a deranged smile.

In a violent blur of black and brown, the two men came together in a vicious assault. The sound of metal clashing against metal rang with their impact. I couldn't understand what I was seeing from my dazed position on the ground. Fighting the dull ache in my skull, I forced my head upright, squinting through the sea of still grass. The raging beat in my chest went cold.

Jacey's tattoos were unsheathed from their sleeves. The twisting designs that once covered his arms were now wild glowing blue tendrils, jutting from his body like vines that snaked around the shaft of a wicked polearm. Its pronged blade fizzled and sputtered with an electric current that licked the surrounding air. I realized with horror that Jacey's forearm and the weapon were physically grown together, directly connected through a glowing blue spider web of veins that rooted into his wrist.

There was little time to understand what I was seeing. Our attacker was plunging forward again, swinging his own polearm high overhead. But Jacey was faster. As he spun to counter the attacker's overhead blow, the polearm responded in a fluid arc of blue light that ripped through the air. His movements were effortless, and a vicious smile spread across his face as the shaft of his weapon halted the rivaling blade with a clang.

"You sure as fuck better kill me." Jacey's menacing low chuckle momentarily stilled the attacker's weapon. "Because if you don't, your life is forfeit." He lunged with raw primal power, sending a musical echo of clashing metal through the fiber.

Fear seized my spine as I watched the sickening display of blades and limbs and lethal fire that radiated from Jacey.

The attacker angled his body low, his own polearm moving in an even and flowing series of thrusts. Jacey's boots skirted across the grass, gracefully dodging every jab. Frustration was building across the man's face. His movements were becoming more jagged—more aggressive. His nervous eyes shot to me in an instant. They were wary, all signs of confidence lost. He knew he'd underestimated Jacey, and by the way his brows pinched when they met mine, he knew that I *knew* as well.

Jacey saw the moment of hesitation and seized the opportunity with a graceful leap. His boot touched down on the shaft of the attacker's polearm, driving its barbed blade deep into the grass. In a flash, tendrils of blue glowing sinew snapped from the man's arm like taut rubber bands as Jacey stomped the long shaft of the weapon. And then there was blood. So much blood. It flowed like ribbons from the man's exposed bones as the shaft of his weapon was torn from his body with a disgusting rip.

Bile rose in my throat. My eyes burned, unblinking and disbelieving as Jacey took three threatening steps toward the man.

"Fuck you! Shit, shit, shit! My arm!" the attacker cried out. His voice writhed with pain as he stared down at the weapon that now lay bloody at his feet. The surrounding grass was spattered with red droplets that contrasted grotesquely under the bright light of the fiber.

Was Jacey going to kill him? Panic shivered through my spine. The man attacked us first. He wanted to kill us, to kill me...but something within my core pleaded for me to call out. To beg for mercy on behalf of the pitiful man.

Jacey leaned back casually on his heels. A morbid teasing grin spread across his cheeks as he reached into his pocket. *For what? A weapon?* The man watched in terror, gripping his flayed arm tightly between his legs in an attempt to salvage his blood.

"What are you doing?" he screamed in agitation. Head still angled threateningly low, Jacey glazed over with feral rage. He retracted his hand and opened his palm to reveal a small silver bottle cap. A long black wisp flowed forcefully from Jacey's palm.

"Feeding my nightmare."

15

DAXX

The blackness seized the space around Jacey, spiraling in several fast circles until it collected in a single dark cloud at his side. Horror willed me to run. To scream. To race through the archways and put distance between myself and the hideous scene. But I couldn't move. My muscles were locked, damning me to watch the nightmare unfold.

From the black cloud, a long animal leg stepped forward, then another, and another. The smoke shaped itself into an elongated, wispy canine form. Its legs were lengthy and thin like a cheetah. Its face was narrow and pointed like a wolf. Dark tendrils danced from its body, and as its maw drew open, a gasp of terror was the only sound that escaped from my paralyzed body.

"Vell, vhat do ve have here." The voice was a low breathy hiss, slipping through a mouth that sliced across the length of its entire head. With a morbid Cheshire grin, a long pink tongue skimmed over parallel rows of white dagger teeth.

I couldn't breathe. I couldn't blink. My gaze was fixed on our attacker, who looked like a sniveling child in the wake of this monster that had manifested beside Jacey. The man's lips quivered, moist with long strings of mucus that poured from his nostrils.

"Please," he pleaded in wet gasps. With bloody hands clasped together in prayer, he now ignored the strands of flesh that dangled grotesquely from his arm. "Please, sir, please no. Please take my credits. Take everything I have. Just take your dog and go."

"Doooog?" the creature rasped. Like a ribbon caught in the wind, it shot around the man in a smokey spiral until its form materialized again directly behind him. The man's eyes brimmed with tears as he forced them closed. With a deep hiss, the creature's gruesome maw eased over his shoulder, and its tongue lolled out.

"I've been called demon. Devil. Monster. Voule beast, yesss. But never dog."

"Ple-he-he-heeeease," the man cried out, bubbling snot from his nostrils.

With its hollow eyes longing and hopeful, the creature looked to Jacey, who stood with his arms crossed over his chest.

My stomach rolled violently. *Jacey...is this what you've been hiding?* I knew he was dangerous, that he was trained to fight and to kill but not like this. Never like this. He'd said his job was honorable. There was nothing honorable about this.

The man was still whispering a stream of breathy prayers into the crevice of his clasped hands. He was pitiful, completely disarmed, and begging for mercy.

Please Jacey, I willed him silently. *Please.*

Dread rolled through me as Jacey nodded approvingly at the creature.

No!

In a rush of adrenaline, shock, or maybe just blatant stupidity, I leaped from my position in the grass and raced forward. "No!" I screamed desperately as the ground slipped under my boots. "No!"

Jacey turned and intercepted my body with his massive arms. I kicked and flailed, pushing violently against him.

"Don't kill him!" I wailed. "Please, Jacey, don't kill him!" Tears morphed my vision into a wet lens of amplified light and colors—green, red, and a menacing cloud of black. My face was crushed into Jacey's warm chest as he squeezed me.

"Vivian," he whispered into my hair. "You have to calm down."

The soft caressing of his voice was revolting. *He was a monster! An absolute monster!* My hands continued to push weakly into the leather of his jacket as I sobbed.

"Vriend ov your'sss?"

The unexpected hiss sent my spine stiff. Still wrapped in the solid cords of Jacey's arms, I dared to turn my head in the direction of the sound. Large and milky, the creature's pupiless eye strained wide, as if trying to rip through the depths of my soul.

"Knock it off with the dramatics, Daxx. You've got her scared shitless."

The creature gasped, craning its neck in a gesture that looked like offense.

"Any dramatics I vlourish are only those I have devoured vrom you." Its voice was smooth, a mocking hiss.

To my surprise, Jacey eased my body down his chest until my feet touched the blood spattered grass. His arms loosened, but he continued to hold my forearms tightly as he studied my face.

The tears that brimmed my eyelids fell in unison, and my vision was clear enough to return his gaze. I expected to see a monster. A killer. The violent man who I'd watched dance in a battle of blades, just moments ago. But within the depths of his blue irises, I only saw Jacey. Concerned, brutish, asshole, pigeon-on-a-pastry Jacey.

"Vivian." His voice was apprehensive. "Listen to me. This is Daxx. He's uhhh...well, he's kind of a part of me."

"The very bessst part ov you," the creature hissed in my ear.

"Damn it, Daxx, would you quit fucking scaring her? I just got her breathing again!"

"As you vish," the creature rasped, and its long wispy body slithered out of view.

I looked at Jacey in desperation.

He shook his head as if he'd just sent away a misbehaved child. "You'll get used to him. Unfortunately."

I couldn't believe what I was hearing. This thing—this morbid nightmarish thing—was somehow a part of Jacey? I was terrified, mortified, but mostly, I was furious.

"Jacey, tell me what's going on this instant. And spare me all your 'dancing-around-the-truth' bullshit because honestly, I nearly fucking booked it to Gilroy's."

His face crinkled in confusion.

"Oh, and none of your volatile attitude either!" I added. "I am so damn close to snapping, and I can't handle your mood swings."

Reluctance flickered in his brow.

"Vivian. Just listen, okay? The mood swings...I know how bad they are. I know. You think I want to be this way? I've lived through some shit. Some fucked up, absolute *shit-show* shit. Not a day goes by that I'm not angry about it. I'm absolutely fucking mental, Vivian. But Daxx...Daxx helps me to control it. He was *built* to help me control it."

"What do you mean?" I demanded.

"This creature is the physical manifestation of all my fears, my anxiety, *my rage*." He emphasized the words by pulling my hand over his heart. The air caught in my lungs as my fingers splayed out over his chest. Our eyes, only inches apart, locked in a cold tangle.

"Anger, anxiety, aggression...Daxx feeds on those negative emotions. He takes those burdens from me and uses them to manifest into a physical being. Not just a being but a weapon. All the emotions he collects are stored, available to me whenever I deem it necessary. Then he detonates. He was a fucked up Channel experiment that I was tasked with terminating two years ago. But I just couldn't, Vivian. I needed him."

"So, that's who you were talking to?" I snapped. "All of this bitterness and secrecy? All...all because you were hiding some fucking anger-eating *pet*?"

The black cloud appeared beside my face in an instant.

"Mmmm," the creature rasped through endless teeth. "The vear in this one. A banquet of voreboding."

"Daxx!" Jacey boomed.

The creature lingered, a long wisp of smoke with an equally long smile. "Viviaaan, yesss. I much enjoy thisss onesss company."

With a flicker of his hand, Jacey chased away the smoke as if it were a cloud of gnats. The creature cackled wickedly as it dispersed. Jacey rolled his eyes in response. He fixed his attention back to me.

"Look. I'm sorry I didn't tell you about him earlier. I'm not even supposed to have him. I reported his termination...and if Dane, CieCie, or *God-forbid* Gilroy were to ever find out, they'd lose their shit. I need him though, Vivian. You have to understand. Without him, with everything I've been through, everything I've seen...I would've off'ed myself.

"I'm fucked up, Vivian. But Daxx gnaws at the anxiety that consumes me until it's bearable. He makes me a tolerable human. Not just for me but for them. It's what his kind was created to do. To help Jumpers eliminate emotions that could jeopardize their missions."

My jaw was clenched stubbornly. He was pleading. Bargaining. Begging for my understanding and for my vow of silence. This was an emotion that I knew. I was still mad as hell, and a million-and-one more questions whirled violently behind my lips. But I relaxed the tension in my shoulders and took a deep breath.

"Okay."

"Okay?" he questioned.

"Okay, I won't tell anyone. And I'll try to understand. But Jacey, you have a lot more explaining to do."

Still grasping me at forearms length, he blew out a slow breath. His face calmed, and the creases in his brow released. "Thank you."

Gratitude. A new emotion I'd never seen him express before. The dangerous monster melted before my eyes, and at that moment, I wanted nothing more than to reach out and wrap my arms around him. The thought brought a warm flush to my cheeks, and I shyly dropped my gaze to the ground before he noticed.

Spatters of red still stained the grass beneath my feet. A gruesome reminder of what had happened here today. The blood had already dried into a sticky matting, and the sea of green was parted slightly where the attacker's polearm had previously been.

Wait. Alarm struck down like lightning. *Where was the polearm?* It had been there a moment ago.

My gaze shot to Jacey in confusion, but his face mirrored my own. An abrupt whoosh whistled past my head. I turned on my heel just in time to watch helplessly as the muddy barbed blade sank deep into Jacey's outstretched forearm. His face twisted in agony. At the opposite end, the man grasped the shaft of the weapon with a victorious smile.

"Daxx!" Jacey screamed. The black mass of nightmares manifested beside us in an instant. Its mouth stretched menacingly wide in anticipation. "Rip him the fuck apart!" Jacey's militant command tore through his clenched teeth.

Eyes wide and eager, Daxx shot forward. The air was filled with the grotesque sounds of skin ripping, bones crunching, and the last agonized gurgle of wet lungs being crushed between long wicked jaws.

I couldn't look. I couldn't watch. Jacey slowly sank to his knees, gripping the long shaft of the weapon. It was buried deep within his tattoos, tangled between the cybernetic roots and human veins.

Tuning out the violent sounds behind me, I knelt beside him. "What do I do? Oh god, Jacey, how do I help?" I cried. He was losing blood at an alarming rate, and we had nothing to stop its flow.

Fuck! This was all my fault! I should have let Jacey kill the bastard when he was down. My trembling hands raced along his bloody skin, but I didn't know where to put them.

His teeth ground together as the air hissed through his lungs. "Ball up your scarf," he groaned. "Ball it up. Put it in my mouth."

I followed his instructions without question, ripping the scarf from my neck and pushing it into his face. He bit down on the black fabric and closed his eyes, then took a jagged breath and jerked the shaft of the polearm. It ripped free of his muscle with a sickening snap, shredding everything on its way out. My stomach twisted, threatening to heave up the meal we'd just eaten. A muffled scream ripped through the fabric of the scarf, and tears brimmed his lashes.

Oh, Jacey. My big, stupid asshole, Jacey. What have I done? I didn't know how to help.

He rocked back and forth in pain, tossing the bloody polearm to the ground and gripping his shredded arm at the elbow. He spit the scarf into his lap and hissed a sharp command. "Get it. Tie it. Here. Hard."

A tourniquet, right. I followed his pained orders, pulling the black fabric tightly, just before the crease of his elbow.

"Daxx!" Jacey yelled.

The wolfish creature materialized beside me in an instant. Blood dripped from its mouth, but I was too focused on Jacey for the sight to affect me. A hard thump rocked me backward as Jacey tipped over into my lap. His chest was heaving, and his eyes cranked tightly shut. I couldn't stop my own panicked tears from falling onto his chest, leaving dark spatters on the hard plate of his jacket.

"Daxx," he rasped. "Stay with Vivian. Until I recover. Stay. With. Viv..."

"Jacey!" I screamed. His eyes rolled back, white and pupiless, and his breathing grew quiet. "Jacey, no, no, no!" My hands grasped his face, and the tension in his jaws relaxed under my touch. His skin was warm and rough, budded with a sharp shadow of stubble. But his chest was still rising and falling in ragged bursts.

"He's been through vorse," Daxx hissed.

The grass shifted as the creature sat beside me. The feather-soft brush of his long wispy tail made me jump as it wrapped around my back. My shoulders bristled. I wanted to wave it away or blow it away like a puff of smoke.

My heart constricted, and a long defeated sob escaped my lips. Jacey's breathing became even but shallow. We were stranded. Alone in the fiber with no way to call for help. And

Jacey was injured. How long would it take for a random Channel-goer to pass by? What if they weren't friendly?

"What now?" I whispered hopelessly.

"You're asking meeee?" Daxx asked in astonishment.

I looked into his milky eyes. The smoky black body was nearly solid, towering over me like a terrifying shadow.

"I guess I am," I confessed.

Daxx flicked his tail over my back once more in a soft movement that made me shudder. "Vell. Jacey ssseems to vind the best answers in hisss moments ov clarity." His milky eyes lowered to mine. "Shall I give you...clarity?" he hissed.

I had no idea what he meant. This beast, this monster, who just ripped a man to bits—*this was my best hope?* Jacey told me that Daxx was a part of him. My gaze flitted to Jacey, whose lips parted softly as breath flowed through his chest.

"I...I guess so." I swallowed hard. "Yes, do whatever you need to do. Just...help me to get him home. Help me to take him back to Gilroy's place."

Daxx closed his eyes and lowered his head. "As the lady vishes," he hissed, lifting his long ribbonlike tail again. It flickered in a smoky dark haze, then the soft feathery texture rested over my shoulders, and a shiver pulsed through my spine.

My mind, the endless buzzing hive, grew still. I was no longer in the sea of green. No, I was in a quiet place. All vibrations calmed, and the deafening hive was now a low, orderly whisper. Like bees traveling in a synchronized line. No more agitation. No more uncertainty. The air that filled my lungs was a sterilized cold wash that raced through my body and eased the swelling in my head.

Jacey stirred in my lap, nestled safely with me in this expansive quiet space of white. And suddenly, the answer was there. *Clarity.* I blinked.

We were in the fiber once again. I grabbed Jacey's injured limb and pulled it over his chest. It was firm and heavy, protesting against my pull, but I held it tight. "I need to access his Central Connect device," I murmured. Daxx's tail lifted from my back, and I watched as the black cloud trailed and solidified in front of me. "This is the wrist it normally comes out of. Do you know how to access it?"

My body tensed as Daxx lowered his head and sniffed the mangled tattoos. "It isss beyond my ability."

Frustrated, I pulled Jacey's wrist higher on his chest and slowly prodded my fingers over the few twisting black designs that were unharmed and uncovered by the scarf. The muscle underneath was firm but not solid. My heart sank. Of course, the screen didn't simply exist within his body. It must be formed of his conscious will. *Now what?*

A glimmer of silver at Jacey's side captured my attention. The bottlecap. I picked it from the tangle of blood-smattered grass and turned it over in my fingers. Inscribed inside the lid was the wispy black wolfish silhouette. "What is this?"

"A sssummoning device," the creature's voice hissed quietly. "The object to vich my sssoul isss bound."

Great. Another micro mystery weapon, like the rheotron I was forced to carry. Hastily, I shoved the cap into the tight pocket of my jeans as the words "Keep in your pocket" rang mockingly through my mind. *No.* I couldn't allow myself to surrender control like that again. If this monstrous creature was tied to Jacey, it was safe. Safe to me, at least. Jacey would have warned me if it wasn't.

"Sssomeone isss coming." The abrupt hiss was barely audible, growing smaller with each syllable.

I glanced to where Daxx had been sitting, but he was nowhere to be seen. *Who was coming?* Panic surged through me.

"Daxx?" I whispered. No response. "Daxx, where are you?"

"Just passing through, eh?" The familiar voice called every hair on my body to attention. "Looks like you two ran into some trouble. Where's your scrawny fuck boyfriend?"

Shit, shit, shit.

Hesitantly, I turned. Rhett stood only a few feet away, his body tall and rigid and a menacing grin spread across his face. *Where the hell was Daxx?* Jacey stirred in my lap, then stilled again.

"Quite a lot of blood here for such a small hole," Rhett said, stepping forward with his eyes on Jacey's injured arm.

Shit! The attacker's body! I turned to Daxx's scene of execution, but to my surprise, there was no body. No pieces. No bone. Had Daxx...eaten the man? The whole man? I didn't have time to think about this.

Summoning all my courage, I rearranged my face and turned back to Rhett. "Are you going to just stand there, or are you going to help?" I demanded.

Rhett's eyebrows shot up in surprise, but his smile grew wider. "A little bossy now, aren't we, little lady?" he chuckled darkly. "Why would you assume that I, of all people, would want to help you and lieutenant meatball?"

Rage boiled in my veins. Abandoning my own safety, I crafted a threat. After all, he had no idea who I was. Who I really was. And so, I would be exactly who I needed to be, just like Dane had been. The sly fox.

"Because if you don't," I threatened calmly, "I'll unleash hell on your Central Connect system."

"Oh please, do tell. What are you going on about?" His posture was smooth, but as the words flowed from his lips, Rhett's body swayed ever so slightly. I was gaining traction.

"You have no idea who I am, do you?"

The smile dropped from his lips at once.

Yes. His confidence was waning. I continued before his mind could catch up. "Gilroy will certainly be displeased to hear about this...encounter." A worm on a hook.

He scowled. "Who are you to that old tinkerer?"

Yes, he took the bait.

"Old tinkerer?" I laughed, rolling my eyes. "I think you know that Gilroy is far from just a tinkerer. Though, you must not know *too* much about him..." My sentence trailed off as I stared with illustrated innocence.

"What do you mean?" Rhett demanded. He was growing wary.

I may have a chance.

"Well, if you *really* knew Gilroy, you'd also know that he has a granddaughter. A granddaughter who he has trained quite well, if I do say so myself."

Rhett's lip twitched, a smile forming at the corners.

Crap. I held his gaze intently, grasping at the threads of the lie I stitched.

"Gilroy would never commit such treason as to sacrifice the integrity of a Jumper."

The statement was a brick wall. The checkmate. Unless...

I allowed my smile to spread dramatically wide. Then, I snapped it away instantly. Coldly. Rhett's eyes widened.

"Well," I growled, "I'm not Gilroy. And I couldn't give two shits about your integrity."

For several excruciating moments, Rhett loomed over us without releasing my gaze. From my lap, I felt a low groan rumble in Jacey's chest. Then he was still again.

"Fine," Rhett snapped.

It took every ounce of my effort to fight away the victorious smile that dared to creep across my face.

"But the old man fucking owes me for this. I'll let them know where you are, but after that, I'm out."

He held his wrist at chest level, causing his sleeve to fall to his elbow. Underneath, a twisted tangle of black tattoos outlined in glowing blue contours started to bubble and transform. I looked back to Jacey as Rhett booted up his Central Connect device.

I could breathe again, truly breathe. After so much uncertainty, we were going home. *My temporary home.*

Jacey's lips puffed heavily. The blood that dripped from the gash in his arm was beginning to cake and dry.

"Your boyfriend has been alerted," Rhett growled.

When I lifted my head, he was retreating toward the archway that led back to The Channel, his long coat sweeping the grass.

"Thank you," I called after him.

The words caught him like a lasso, and his feet froze in their place.

"We don't thank strangers here, Vivian."

The roguish tone sputtered my heart to a stop. *I hadn't told him my name.*

"Best not do or say things that some might find...obscure." Then he was gone, swallowed by the shadows of the twelve black arches.

16

PROJECT KATHARIZO

It took Gilroy and one additional passerby to lift Jacey into the rusty transport wagon. To my disappointment, Dane stayed back at the warehouse with CieCie, so I was left dozing beside my injured partner in crime as we were toted back to M-5.

The day was growing fuzzy, like a distant memory that eludes your consciousness the more you try to grasp it. Revelations about CieCie's homeworld, our trip to Mercantile dimension, the battle in the fiber, and the grotesque creature that I carried in my pocket.

Instinctively, I dropped my hand. Pressing through my jeans was a smooth round outline. Another anomaly. I sighed.

Fatigue crept its cold claws over my eyelids. Yes, it had been a long day indeed. Resting my hand over the reassuring rise and fall of Jacey's chest, I closed my eyes and allowed myself to fall into a mercifully dreamless drift.

"She's in there? Is she hurt?"

"No, son, I reckon she's just a lil' tuckered out onna count of

all she went through. Gotta be a shock onner system."

"I'm telling you, Gilroy. I knew this was going to happen. I fucking called it this morning, remember? I told him how dangerous it was. But no, jackass Jacey had to go and play hero again. Now the asshole's nearly lost his favorite arm, and we're all left to clean up the mess."

"Now, Dane, I know yer mad. But honestly, son, that ain't no way to talk 'bout yer friend. That boy's walkin 'round more nervous n'a long-tailed cat inna room full'a rockin' chairs. Everybody makes mistakes under pressure."

"Yeah. Well. Lately, Gilroy, it seems like Jacey has been making a lot of them. And every time he does, it seems like I'm the one who gets stuck with the fallout."

"Dane...look, son. I know this last year has been rough on ya. It's been pretty damn rough on all of us."

"Gilroy. Stop. Stop trying to sympathize. Stop trying to tell me the singsong story about how everything is going to be okay because we both fucking know that it's not. I'm doing my best, okay? Given the circumstances, I am truly, truly doing the very best while holding the shit-smeared cards I've been handed. You can't ask any more from me than that."

"Well, son, what's yer plan then? 'Cause, either way, times gonna keep on tickin', and the longer we piss 'n moan 'n stand around lickin our gumps, the longer it's gonna take us to figure out who's behind all this fuckery."

"And then what? When we find out who's behind it, what happens then?"

"Welp...I reckon we'll do as we always do. We figure it out when we get there."

"Hey."

The back of a cool hand against my cheek sent me blinking into consciousness. I was flat on my back. Glass walls. Vined plants. Soft light.

"Hmmmm," I groaned into the familiar puffy white blanket. Gentle fingers tucked a strand of hair behind my ear.

"I let you sleep as long as I could," Dane whispered, his voice like silk on my restless soul, "but I figured you'd want to know what we found while you were away."

What they found? My body shot forward.

"Woah! Hey, calm down, Viv. It's okay. We have time," Dane soothed.

He'd been sitting on the edge of the bed but was now sprawled out on his side, one arm rested diagonally across my knees. The weight was grounding. I leaned back on my elbows and relaxed my sore muscles again. After so much chaos, we were finally back...

"Where's Jacey?" I asked. Had he made it back home alright? And what was it that Dane and Gilroy had been talking about earlier? The ghost of their conversation slipped between my fingertips the harder I tried to gather it.

"We got him into his room. The asshole didn't even wake up until we had him up the damn stairs. He's rough, but Gilroy says he'll be okay."

The sharp bite of Dane's voice dissipated my clouded memory. *That's right.* He'd been mad at Jacey for not letting him come with us today. How different things would have been if Dane had been beside us. The man in the fiber may not have even attacked if there had been three opponents.

"You were right," I whispered.

Dane cocked his head to the side. "I probably was. But about what specifically?"

His voice was like cool water on a burn. Up until this point, I hadn't realized how much I missed this boy. But now, seeing him here, sprawled out so casually across my body as if the spot was reserved for him...*damn. Just, damn.*

"About today. You should have been there. None of this would have happened if you'd been with us." My throat constricted with an uncomfortable dry tug. The nightmares of the day crawled under my skin, visions I'd never forget, and more blood than I'd ever seen before.

Dane seemed to sense the darkness that crept over me. Drawing his arm forward, he hooked his index finger under the seam of my sleeve and traced soft lines down my arm. His green eyes were fixed aimlessly on the blanket. I leaned into his touch, craving the comforting contact.

What was going on in his head? Was he still mad at Jacey? Was I? This mess truly was all his fault, and though I knew that, I couldn't bring myself to place all of the blame on him. Everything I learned today, I'd only learned because Jacey and I went to Mercantile dimension alone. After seeing him bloody and broken, curled in my lap in a defenseless pile, I couldn't force myself to be mad at him.

"I should have been there," Dane agreed, lifting his gaze to mine.

My chest quivered. There was a dark intensity there, written so clearly on his face that I didn't bother to reclaim the breath that escaped my lungs.

"Next time, I will be. Fuck what Jacey thinks."

Dane drew to his knees, his body weight pressing into either side of the blanket that enveloped me. My heart raced, surging warm bursts through my locked limbs. I watched my own confusion reflected back in his predatory eyes.

Is this what I wanted? Whatever this was? The hive swarmed, each voice sounding their threatening protests in my ears. *You barely know him. You just met him. He's a stranger. You'll never see him again when you return home.*

Dane rocked slowly forward, eyes wide in a silent question. The responsive parting of my lips was his undoing. "Fuck what Jacey thinks."

His mouth crushed desperately onto mine. Lightning crashed straight into my heart. The bees were all struck dead at once, cascading around us like tiny embers, sending the space around us into a silent blaze. Every question, every fear, every ounce of uncertainty was stilled in time as I ripped my arms free from the binds of his weight and tangled my fingers into his wild hair.

I did want this. I wanted it so badly. With my white flag held high, I surrendered to the wildfire that raced through my veins. His lips became forceful in their exploration, possessive and heavy with an undefinable need. Just as I began to fall overboard, he released me. I sucked in a long jagged breath.

"I'm not letting you out of my sight again," he whispered, leaning his forehead against mine.

I was spinning violently, at odds with all the foreign emotions that I'd only ever read about in books. Everything made sense. This was all new. What I'd had with Ryan wasn't real. A still puddle against a raging hurricane. My inexperience with love was his perfect camouflage. He'd defined a new normal, while shaping me into a compliant cover for his mysterious dark deeds. And I still didn't know why.

The bees hummed softly again, rising from the ashes in tiny puffs of smoke. "What happens now?" I whispered.

I could feel the tight tug of Dane's smile against my skin. He pulled back to look at me, with a dazzling glimmer like the sun captured in emeralds. "Now, we go downstairs and try to pretend we're not crazy about each other."

With a sharp wink, Dane jumped to his feet and extended an arm to me. I pulled the blankets from my legs and took his hand, following him out of the room.

How could I be normal? Act normal? Walk normal? His fingers fit so perfectly between mine, as if they were always meant to be woven there. I wasn't sure what these feelings represented to me, but they shook me more than anything I'd ever known, even through their innocence. *Was this what falling for someone was supposed to feel like?*

CieCie was seated on one of the brown dilapidated couches when we reached the warehouse floor. Colorful books and magazines lay scattered across the makeshift coffee table, their pages worn and sunbleached. Some were spread open to reveal sales pages of wrapping paper, snowflake crafts, and holiday recipes.

"CieCie has been researching Christmas," Dane mused.

CieCie's gaze shot up. "Vivian!" she squealed, leaping to her feet. "You won't believe it! I found Christmas books! In the trash! Tree decorating, gift wrapping, cookies, horn-deer, fat red man...we're going to have the best tree party ever!" Gripping a *Home and Garden* magazine to her chest, she gazed up thoughtfully at the nearest tree that swelled from the warehouse floor. "I'm not sure how we'll get the little rainbow tree lights, but I'm determined to figure it out. You'll help, won't you?"

"Of course," I smiled. She wanted to do this for her sister. For Mia. Of course, I'd help.

Dane took my hand. "Let's go to the table. Gilroy will want to brief you on yesterday's findings."

"Yesterday's?"

"Yes," Dane nodded with a smile. "Yesterday's. You and Jacey didn't get back until late last night. I told you that I let you sleep as long as I could. It's the next day."

The third day. Day three away from home. The search parties would most definitely be looking for me. Mom would be in a full-blown panic.

"What's wrong?" Dane asked.

I didn't realize that I'd been gnawing my lip. The concern in his voice swept me into guilt. I knew he wouldn't want to think about me leaving. Especially not now, after these...*feelings* had been established between us.

A small part of me didn't want to go either. I wanted to know more about Dane. I wanted time with him. I wanted to learn more about the world outside of *my world*. But the greater part of me, the mechanical and rational part of me that I hated, knew that I needed to get back home. Maybe I could plan visits with Dane. He said he was from Earth. Surely, he could come to see me. *Right?*

"Nothing." The lie was firm. Whatever was going on between Dane and I was a pleasant escape. And it seemed that he needed it just as much as I did. I wasn't ready to ruin it. Not yet. Not until I had to.

"I don't believe you," he whispered, low enough that CieCie couldn't hear.

The vibration on my ear sent a spider-legged shiver down my neck. But to my relief, he didn't press further. Instead, he pulled me toward the kitchen area. *Back to business.* Gilroy appeared from his usual doorway at the back of the warehouse just as we reached the high-top table.

"Well, well, well. There's sleepin' beauty. And Viv'yan, too," he smirked.

Dane rolled his eyes as he leaned casually against the table. "She's ready to hear what we found."

"I'll make quinic!" CieCie chirped from behind us, dancing toward the counter.

One step closer to answers. My fingers thrummed impatiently against the wood grain as we waited. One step closer to revelations that I wasn't sure I wanted to hear. One step closer to the truth of why I was here.

When we each had a full mug in front of us, Gilroy began. "Project Katharízo. Do them words mean anything to you, Viv'yan?"

CieCie, who had been plinking sugar cubes into my mug, paused to watch my face.

"No," I replied. "I have no idea what you're talking about. I mean, we had a ton of marketing projects at Premier, but I never paid much attention to what they were called."

With a final plink, CieCie dropped the last sugar cube into my mug before moving to the vacant side of the table.

Dane and I exchanged an anxious glance. *What was this all about?*

Clearing his throat, Gilroy continued. "And that's just the problem. See, we don'know any more than them two words. *Project Katharízo.* Somehow, that code name is tied to this whole debacle wit Mr. Rivera. CieCie an I spent all night researchin', but the most we could find was the Earth definition of the word."

"Katharízo," CieCie whispered. "On Earth, it's the Greek word for cleanse."

"Cleanse?" I repeated. "Cleanse what?"

Gilroy shrugged. "We was hopin' you'd know," he admitted.

Dane shook his head, leaning hard against the table on both palms. "I don't know, Gilroy. To me, this all sounds pretty far-fetched. I mean, where did you even pull this data anyway?" His voice was cut with skepticism.

Gilroy's brows shot up in surprise. "My sources are my own," he grumbled defensively.

As much as I wanted to back Dane up on this, the news from Gilroy was all we had to work with. It wasn't much, but it was something.

"That's all you found?"

"Yep. That's all we found."

"You'll keep researching?" I pressed.

Gilroy nodded. "Of course. Hell, we ain't got nothin' better to do 'round here these days. Aside from nursing Mr. Lugnuts back to health."

I'd nearly forgotten about poor Jacey. "How is he?"

Gilroy took a quick swig from his mug. "That's sorta the next thing I needed to talk to ya'll about. Jacey'll be fine, don't you worry 'bout that. But his Central Connect system, well, that's another story. Whole thing's fuckered all'ta hell. I can rewire the device, no problem. But we're gonna need to get an arms merchant in here to ink it all back together. An that won't come cheap."

"And we're fucking broke," Dane murmured.

Tight lines creased his forehead, marring his sweet boyish face. The stress was beginning to take a toll on him, too. I wanted to slide my hand over his to make some form of contact with his skin. But I knew that would be impossible until we were alone.

"Yep. We're broke," Gilroy nodded, "but we may be able to work somethin' else out."

Dane's glare locked sternly with Gilroy's. "No."

"Now, Dane. Jus' listen for a sec—"

"No."

"Damn it ta hell, Dane. Would you please just—"

"NO!" His palms slammed against the table. "I'm not fucking taking her out there again! You see what happened the first time? And that was with Jacey! If I got hurt out there, we'd be fucked. Totally fucked."

"What are you guys talking about?" I demanded.

Dane's eyes didn't leave Gilroy's as he spoke. "He wants us to go to the dimension one fiber."

Dimension one? My mind raced through each of the dimensions Jacey told me about. Five was Mercantile, four was either the water dimension or the brainiac dimension, and three was whichever four wasn't. Two was the giant people-eater dimension. That only left one option.

"The arms merchant will trade repairs for bioluminescent ink," I concluded.

"Yes," he answered warily.

"Jacey told me everything," I explained. "About what happened to dimension one and why The Channel left the fiber intact. About the mushrooms."

"Awesome. Was that before or after he nearly got you killed?" His voice was thick with resentment.

"Dane!"

"Well, damn it, Vivian!" he growled, throwing his arms up. "I'm pissed, okay? He takes you out of here without me, puts you at risk, almost gets himself killed. And now...now I'm supposed to take you back out there and do it all over again to save him?"

"Yes," I stated flatly. "Because you care about him. And because we need him to get better so he can help us."

Dane turned to face me, ignoring Gilroy and CieCie's baffled expressions.

"I care about *you*." He enunciated each word as if they cloaked a million more that he wanted to say.

"And I care about *both of you*," I retorted.

Our words hung suspended between us for several moments. Dane turned and leaned heavily back on the table. His expression was once again strained with lines of defeat. He was worried about me. This was only natural. I wished I could tell him that we'd be safe. My hand slipped down to my pocket where the small circular lump pushed tight against the denim. If only I could tell him about Daxx.

"We'll leave tomorrow after you've rested more," he growled, clearly unhappy.

Relief flooded over me. "Thank you."

My fingers moved from my pocket, and I knotted them together at my waist, over and over again in nervous tangles that loosened the bandages around my knuckles. With a sigh, Dane took my hand and began unraveling the bandage.

"I'll get her another wrap," CieCie chirped, jumping up from the table. She and Gilroy had been so quiet that I'd forgotten they were in the room.

"No need," Dane said, pulling the final loop from my hand. My knuckles were sore, each one outlined in a purple water coloring of bruises. But the four splits had fully scabbed over. "We need to let it breathe."

I flinched as his thumb brushed over the four scabs. If these little cuts hurt, I couldn't imagine the pain Jacey was in. If we were leaving tomorrow, I'd need to talk to him soon. *Alone.*

"Are you hungry?" Dane asked, his voice soft once again.

"Yes," I lied.

"Okay," Dane smiled, releasing my hand. "I'll start on dinner then. CieCie, do you want to help?"

In an instant, she was standing at the counter. "Oh, yes!" she squealed.

Good. That would keep them busy for a few minutes. I decided to make my escape. "If you guys don't mind, I'm going to go up and check on Jacey."

"Last cube on the right, just before the bathroom," Gilroy nodded toward the catwalk above our heads. Jacey's room was the closest to the kitchen, directly above our heads.

"Thanks," I murmured, making my way across the warehouse floor and toward the stairs.

As I passed the shipping container where CieCie had left her stash of holiday magazines, I caught a glimpse of several bookmarked pages. Curious, I stopped to see what she had been reading. One contained recipes for gingerbread cookies and ideas for decorating gingerbread men. The other was an old dog-eared magazine from the 70's, outlining how to make popcorn garland. Smiling, I placed the old magazine back on the pile and started up the creaky metal staircase.

"Knock, knock," I called shyly.

Jacey was sprawled out on a bare mattress. His glass box was sparsely decorated, unlike Dane and CieCie's rooms. Its walls were free of vines, and the only item aside from the too-small bed was a clothing rack that leaned unevenly in the corner.

"I'm awake," he croaked. Sweat gathered in beads across his forehead, and sharp shadows seemed to cling to the sloping features of his bare chest. It was the first time I'd seen his skin exposed, which was streaked with blood and glistening with sweat. My heart ached as I watched a harsh breath catch in his chest, then rasp out with an audible hiss.

"May I come in?"

"Said I was awake, didn't I?"

Even in this weakened heap, the iciness of his raspy voice intimidated me. Head low, I stepped into his room and took a seat at the foot of his bed.

"Dane is making dinner," I said shyly, trying to start with an easy opener. This was becoming my go-to method with Jacey. Start with light conversations before working my way into more pressing topics.

"Not hungry," he grumbled.

I quickly pivoted to another direction.

"Daxx said you'd been through worse than this. After you passed out, I mean."

Silence. *What had I done now?* Gingerly, I coaxed my gaze to Jacey's face. His expression was puzzled but not mad. It was a start.

"Do you want him back?" I asked, reaching for the little round imprint in my jeans.

"No," Jacey stopped me. "You'll be safer with him. Dane can't protect you tomorrow. Daxx can."

"How did you know that we're leaving tomorrow?"

"Bionic ears," he scoffed.

"You heard us?"

"Of course, I heard you. I hear everything. The kitchen is right below my room."

A single bead of sweat cascaded down his forehead, outlining the dark caverns of his brow. Dane hadn't been shy in his criticism when we were downstairs. And Jacey heard all of it.

"I'm sorry," I whispered.

"For?"

"For everything."

"Don't be sorry," he scolded. "Not when you can't think of anything to be sorry for. None of this was your fault. You have no reason to apologize. It's stupid."

"I'm sorr—" His glare froze the words in my throat. "Nevermind."

Around Jacey, perpetual shame was becoming my default state of existence. I never knew what to say. A small child, always making mistakes and being scolded but never truly understanding why. When I glanced at him, his eyes were closed, and the strain of his face loosened. If only there were a way to chase away his discomfort.

An unbidden vision surfaced—his head resting unconsciously in my lap, and the gentle puff of his lips. He was *my Jacey* yesterday in the fiber. Protecting him had been my number one priority. Now laying here in this weakened pile of sweat, he was again the ice cold stranger from the Belair lobby. I wanted *my Jacey* back. The one with the wolfish smile, who teased me until we were both doubled over in frustrated laughter.

"This is who you are without Daxx," I guessed.

His eyes squinted open.

Crap, did I wake him?

He watched me for several silent moments before answering. "This is who I am. Daxx just...makes me more tolerable."

Tolerable. The word sank like a lead weight in my stomach. What a way to think of yourself. Just tolerable.

My chest tightened as I turned the words over and over again. He was more than just tolerable. In fact, there were times during our journey that I genuinely enjoyed his company. But there was no in-between with Jacey. No neutral mood. He was either a cloudless sky or a raging storm, constantly teetering from one extreme to the other. The whole charade had to be tiring for him. It certainly was tiring for me.

"So tomorrow. If something happens, I mean. I just take out the bottle cap, right? Is that all I need to do? Is there a code word or something?"

"He can hear you, you know."

I shot a quick glance through the glass wall.

"Not Dane," Jacey said. "Daxx. Daxx can hear you. Probably not very well, since you've got him crammed in your pocket."

Oh! I quickly pulled the bottlecap from my jeans. Within its center, the tiny wolfish image seemed to look expectantly at me.

"Sorry, Daxx," I whispered into my palm. Talking to an inanimate object seemed silly, but in response to my whisper, a soft purr vibrated like a feather boa around my neck. The ghostly contact was startling.

Jacey smirked.

"He'll know if things start to go sour during your trip. Just keep him accessible. Do you still have your waist bag?"

Waist bag...did I still have it? Yes, I remembered seeing it in Dane's room, along with my armored jacket.

"Yes."

"Good. Keep Daxx close and only use him if Dane ends up in a fight he can't handle. I don't want him to find out about this unless it's absolutely necessary. Do you understand?" His expression was intense and demanding.

"Yes," I whispered. As if in response, the warm feathery vibrations moved down my arm, circled my wrist, and vanished at my palm. I tucked the bottle cap back into my pocket.

"How is he?" Dane asked. CieCie had already taken Jacey his bowl of curry and was setting four places at the table.

"He seems okay," I replied stiffly.

Dane shot me a concerned sideways glance. Hastily, I pointed to my ear and then to the glass box above our heads. He nodded in understanding and took a place beside CieCie at the table. Moments later, Gilroy emerged from the far corner of the warehouse.

"S'that dinner I smell?" His nose twitched like the snout of a bloodhound. CieCie giggled and waved for him to join us.

Tomorrow was going to be another long day so I was grateful when talk of our trip was kept to a minimum. Instead, I sipped velvety curry from my bowl, listening to Gilroy and Dane share stories.

"Mom was wicked with a flip flop!" Dane was saying. "I'm serious, man! I remember back in LA when I refused to finish my dinner, she'd chase me all around the house with the damn thing. Needless to say, I learned to clean my plate."

CieCie and I giggled in unison.

"So, a good 'ol whack in the ass? That's the secret, eh?" Gilroy mused, scratching his stubble mischievously.

"Try me, old man!" Dane taunted.

An idea crossed my mind. Lifting my leg, I stealthily shot it behind Dane and kicked him square in the seat of his black jeans. He jumped in surprise, whirling around to find his attacker, but my foot had resumed its inconspicuous position under the table. Gilroy shot me a knowing smile.

"What the hell was that for?" Dane asked, looking at CieCie.

Her eyes grew wide. "What was what for?" she gasped.

Gilroy nodded another sly smile in my direction. I lifted my leg and swiftly kicked Dane again, sending him stumbling forward. This time, he turned his betrayed emerald eyes to me.

I smiled innocently. "You didn't finish your dinner," I pointed out with a nod toward his half-empty bowl.

The kitchen erupted with laughter.

"Think that's funny, do you?" Dane's eyes melted into their playful predatory gaze. My heart raced.

Oh, I liked this game. And I *really* liked the way Dane was looking at me. I smoothed my hair in a sweet gesture that I hoped would provoke a reaction from this beautiful boy. It worked.

He lunged, sending my feet scrambling as I raced across the warehouse. Stupid giddy laughter escaped me as I felt his presence grow nearer. The ground thumped loudly behind me as he gave chase. CieCie was cheering, "Get her! Get her! Get her!" from the table. I rounded the corner of the couch and turned.

Dane was on the other side, matching my movements with his arms open and waiting. "Might as well give up, Vivian. I'm going to get you." The threat was thick and honey-sweet, dripping from his eager lips.

Maybe I wanted him to catch me. *No, not yet.*

He darted to the left. In response, I fled to the right. "You were saying?" I purred.

His eyes grew wide with childish wonder. Then he lunged forward. His foot sank threateningly into the creaky cushion before rocketing over the back of the couch. I had no time to react, the distance between us gone. He bent low, swiftly scooping me up with a forearm under my knees.

"Hey!" I screamed. He was cradling me in his arms like a baby. "Put me down!"

CieCie and Gilroy were still laughing across the warehouse. From their point of view, it must have looked like a game. But as Dane looked into my eyes, the breath was stolen from my lungs.

"I caught you," he whispered victoriously.

His arms were solid under the weight of my body. I couldn't speak. My heart thudded against my ribcage.

"Now what am I going to do with you?"

His gaze narrowed into emerald slits that devoured my frantic emotions. *Was he going to kiss me?* Surely, not here. Not in front of Gilroy and CieCie! I squirmed under the expectant hunger of his gaze. He blinked, snapped from his trance.

"I wonder if you're ticklish," he taunted before dropping me over the back of the couch. I landed with a smack onto the leather as Dane loomed over me, his fingers jutting and poking into my ribs. It felt like my jaw had come unhinged. I let out the most unflattering caw of laughter, flailing my arms to push him away.

"Stop! Stop! Stop!" I squealed. His hands were unrelenting, digging into my ribs and under my arms. I sucked in broken gasps, trying to desperately wiggle free from his assault. His hands made their way down my stomach, where my shirt had risen, exposing my bare skin. *Oh.* His fingers were warm. *Oh, no.* I wasn't used to contact like this.

Clangs from the kitchen called my attention for a moment that lasted just long enough for him to take advantage of my vulnerable skin. CieCie and Gilroy had moved to the sink out of sight. And Dane's hands were suddenly there, sprawled wide and still over my stomach. A wave of heat radiated through my core.

Our game turned into something else entirely. Breathing heavily, he bent his head low and planted his warm lips into the exposed divot of my hip. Fire raced through my limbs. My body was locked in place. I would have burned alive, willingly incinerated right there on the spot, but Dane suddenly pulled away at the sound of a cork popping somewhere behind us.

With a triumphant grin, he smoothed my white shirt back over my stomach and stood as if nothing had happened.

The room was spinning. He was spinning. My world was spinning.

"I smell alcohol. Let's go see what Gilroy is concocting," he said, offering his hand.

What was this boy doing to me?

"You're going to give me a heart attack." I took his hand with a heady gasp, and he pulled me to my feet in a swift fluid movement.

"Why's that?"

His cocky grin was criminal.

"You know why."

"Do I?"

This game he was playing was criminal.

"I think you know exactly why."

"Do you want me to stop, Vivian?"

And I enjoyed the role of victim.

"No."

His arm snaked around my hips, tugging me toward the kitchen where CieCie and Gilroy were setting out tiny clear glasses. How was I expected to act normal around him? Everything was changing. My inner wiring was being reprogrammed, coded with a new collection of vivid and confusing emotions that consumed every inch of me.

"Did you win?" CieCie called playfully. As she spoke, she placed a handful of opalescent dice on the table, along with an unmarked bottle of caramel-colored liquor and a stack of colorful cups.

"I always win," Dane smiled, tugging my belt loop inconspicuously.

Not wanting CieCie and Gilroy to wise up to his mischief, I pulled away and met CieCie at the table. *Time to sober up from the Dane-intoxication.*

"Wow, these are really pretty," I murmured, picking up one of the six sided dice. Light danced within its frosty opal center, reflecting out in pastel shades of blue, purple, pink, and orange.

"We're playing Liar's Dice," CieCie announced, filling one of four shot glasses that Gilroy placed on the table. "Do you want to play?"

"I've never heard of that one," I admitted.

"Don't worry. We'll go easy on you," Dane winked, snaking up beside me.

CieCie placed her hands on her hips. "No, sir, Dane. You know the rules. Get on your side of the table. You cheat."

Dane crossed his eyes like a child and stuck his tongue out but did as he was told. I sat across from Gilroy. CieCie stood closest to the kitchen counter, and Dane stood opposite of her to my right.

"Alright kids, errybody grab a cup. One fer dice, one fer

drinkin'. And if ya'll need one for pukin', well...trash can is in the corner."

We each grabbed our cups from the center of the table, as well as a shot glass of liquor. Dane took a green cup, CieCie took pink, Gilroy took blue, and I grabbed red. Inside was a set of five opalescent dice. Gilroy motioned for us to turn our cups upside down on the table as he explained the rules.

"Liar's Dice is a game of my youth. The objective is to bet on what you think each player's got hidden under their cup. Fer example, I might place a bet that Dane's got four threes hidden under his cup. We move clockwise 'round the table. So Viv'an, with you bein' next in line, you can either challenge my bet or increase the bet. If you don't agree with my bet that Dane's got four threes, you can challenge. Or you can increase the bet by sayin' he's got five threes. We'll all go 'round the table til somebody's ready to challenge a bet.

"Once there's a challenge, Dane shows us his dice. If the challenge's right, that person wins an takes a die from Dane. If the challenge's wrong, Dane wins an takes a die from the one that challenged. Person that loses a die takes a shot. Lose all yer dice, yer out. Last person left wins."

Oh god. This was confusing.

"Don't worry," Dane smiled. "We'll help you."

"Why 'on't we do a quick practice round," Gilroy suggested.

It took several rounds for me to fully understand the rules of the game, but once I did, I was on fire. Over the course of an hour, Dane lost 3 dice to incorrect challenges, and for each die lost, he took a shot. CieCie lost one die, which was a blessing because she nearly spit her shot across the table the moment it touched her tongue. By the end of our game, Gilroy and I were left with full hands and full shot glasses.

"Well, ain't that jus the pits. Bein' good at this game ain't no fun for a thirsty dog."

Dane leaned heavily against the table, eyeing the remnants of the caramel liquor bottle. "May's well drink it up, Gilroy," he slurred. "Me thinks I'm done. Pretty sure. Vivian, you pretty sure? Pretty? Vivian?" His eyelashes fluttered lazily. Drunk Dane was certainly amusing. And ridiculously cute.

"Yeah, I'm done," I smiled, sliding my full shot glass across the table. Whatever they were drinking was stronger than anything I'd ever had on Earth. And I had a history of dramatically bad hangovers. "Have at it, Gilroy."

"Y'all sure now?"

"Yeah, I'm sure. If we're going out tomorrow, I want to stay sharp."

Gilroy glanced at Dane, who was stacking his dice into a tiny pyramid.

"Least that makes one of ya thinkin' ahead," he mused. He tipped back his shot and slammed the empty glass against the table. Dane's tiny pyramid vibrated apart.

"Aw. You broked it," he whined.

"Y'all get this mess cleaned up 'er else I'm gonna break you," Gilroy threatened, tipping back my shot and *again* slamming the empty glass against the table.

While CieCie and Dane cleared the mess, I decided to make another quick visit to Jacey. It was hard to have fun knowing that he was stuck in his room alone. You'd think an advanced society would at least have TVs or something to pass the time. But before I reached the doorway to his glass-walled cubby, a long breathy snore filled the air. He was asleep. That was probably for the best. He needed time to recover.

I leaned over the railing to check on CieCie and Dane. They were rinsing glasses in the sink below. CieCie giggled as Dane shook a dishrag over her head. *Good.* I had time to escape to the bathroom.

The long fluorescent bulbs flickered to life as I flipped the switch, illuminating the dirty tile and single oxidized sink. The sight of the shower stall in the far left corner made my skin itch.

Oh, a shower. It had been too long. My black jeans were still stained with dark blood spatters, and my hair was heavy with grease. *How attractive.*

I inspected the showerhead and taps. It seemed like a normal shower. Cautiously, I cranked the tap. The spout sputtered to life, running orange with rust before transitioning to clear hot water. My body itched feverishly, longing for the heat. I needed to ask Dane for a towel. Reluctantly, I twisted the tap again, and the water ceased.

"Anxiousss, are vee?" a voice hissed in my ear. I gasped, stumbling forward into the wall of the shower stall.

"Daxx?" I whispered. I looked frantically around the bathroom, half expecting to find my black-cloaked manifestation of insanity. But I was alone.

"I know you're here," I whispered. Every muscle in my body was tense and alert, but I collected my wits and stepped back out of the shower. "Daxx, where are you?" I quickly pulled the bottle cap from my pocket.

As I opened my fingers, a thin gray mist flowed from my palm. My heart pounded as the ribbonlike cloud circled my legs, then my torso, and then rested weightlessly around my shoulders. From the soft translucent shadow, a long mouth parted, revealing rows of glistening white teeth.

"You ssseem...unsssettled," Daxx's bodiless mouth hissed.

A shiver like centipede legs scampered down my spine. *Would I ever get used to this?*

"Unsettled is definitely a word for it," I admitted. There was no use in hiding my emotions if Daxx could feel them. "I'm nervous about tomorrow."

A long pink tongue lolled from the brim of the hovering

toothy jaws.

"No?" Daxx rasped, "This year isss deeper than that."

"What do you mean?" I fired an anxious glance at the mirror but instantly wished I hadn't.

Draped from my neck, Daxx looked like a grotesque fur stole. His body reflected fully and far too large for my small frame to hold. My gaze darted to my shoulder where his mouth hovered, but outside of the two-dimensional plane of the mirror, he was nothing but smoke and teeth.

"Much deeper than thaaaat," he snickered.

My frustration blistered. "Of course, I'm fearful," I retorted, looking back to the mirror. Two milky eyes watched inquisitively from the glass. "Jacey is injured. Dane and I have to go back...back out *there* tomorrow. I'm dimensions away from home with no idea how or when I'll be able to get back. I have every reason to be fearful."

A long crooked smile curled across Daxx's lips. "You don't vant to go back," he hissed.

Frustration morphed to fury. "Yes, actually, I do," I growled.

And then, there she was again—the image of my mother, digging desperately through my dresser drawers and kitchen cabinets as tears rolled down her swollen cheeks. I'd left no trace for her. No miracles that would lead her to my captor's hideaway. She would search for me to the ends of the earth, and even there, she would find nothing but the ghost of my existence.

The length of this absence, of this torment, of this void—it all rested on Dane, Jacey, Gilroy, and CieCie. Until we discovered the extent of Mr. Rivera's sinister scheme, *home* wasn't safe. Until I was absolutely certain that my return wouldn't put my mother at risk, this strange cube-shaped void in reality was the closest thing to home that I had.

17

TRUTH LIKE GOSPEL

"**C**heck it out, Vivian!"

CieCie held a twisted copper wire in one hand and a palmful of tiny colored bulbs in the other. Her large pair of brown goggles dangled from her neck. I smiled curiously, not understanding what I was seeing.

"They're lights!" she laughed. "I picked through our junk bins and plucked a few from old scrap Central Connect devices. Gilroy and I are going to wire them together for the tree party!"

"That's very crafty of you."

She glowed at the compliment. "Oh, thank you, Vivian! We're going to have so much fun!"

With a little bunny hop, she bounced to the kitchen table where Gilroy waited with an assortment of tools. In perfect synchrony, they pulled their goggles over their eyes and began poking and picking at the collection of bulbs and wires.

As I turned away from the table, a pair of long muscular arms looped my waist.

"Where'd you get off to," Dane whispered.

His voice was still oiled with intoxication. I dropped my hands to my pocket, tempting his fingers away from the small circular indentation. A mysterious bottle cap could lead to unwanted questions. To my relief, he eagerly complied, and our fingers snaked together. Though my body was snared in his iron grasp, my mind was eons away, still consumed by the hushed whispers of a wolfish monster.

"Jacey was asleep so I made a quick trip to the bathroom. Speaking of which, do you mind if I grab a quick shower? I'm beginning to look like a crime scene." I nodded down to my blood-spattered jeans.

It wasn't a lie. I truly did need a shower. But I also needed an escape. The joy I'd experienced earlier had since been drained from my body, and I was left alone in my mind, fighting with the very darkest of my buzzing bees. Daxx had agitated the hive. *What made him think that I didn't want to go home? Was it because I'd flirted with Dane? Could Daxx hear us even now?*

Dane's neck craned over my shoulder, and as it did, my body shivered uncomfortably.

"I could join you," he whispered into the small of my collar bone.

The proposition was seductive, deliciously sweet—and startlingly dreadful. He dragged his lips across my neck and up toward my ear. The bees screamed in protest. *Too soon! He's drunk! If you allow this to start, where will it end?*

"No," I said, gently pulling away.

His face contorted, and a look of hurt crossed his drunken heavy eyes.

I instantly craved the need to rectify. "Dane, I'm like... really gross. Grosser than I've ever been. Let me get cleaned up, and then we can hang out for a while. I'll have a lot more fun after I've scrubbed this grime off. And the blood."

Relief flooded over me as Dane's lips slipped back into their usual playful smile.

"Towels aaaare...in the locker. Yeah. Locker. S'next to the bathroom door."

"Thank you," I smiled and headed upstairs.

I stole a navy tee shirt and a pair of striped blue and white boxers from Dane's room and pulled a sandpapery towel from the nearly-hidden locker beside the bathroom. When the bathroom door closed behind me, I impulsively locked it. No unexpected drunk guests. Maybe another time. Not tonight. I needed to be alone.

Taking a deep breath, I stepped into the steamy water. The showerhead had a bullet sharp pressure that melted away the tension I'd carried for three long days. My body relaxed, and I surrendered to the sensation. Under the flow of hot water, the bees fell into a slumber that allowed me to articulate my own thoughts.

Like my body, my emotions were stripped naked. There was no hiding from my own truth. No matter how hard I tried to outrun it, the nagging tug persisted. I was falling for Dane. Falling harder and faster than I'd ever fallen before. And this frightened me.

Why? What was I afraid of? He was perfect. Not the type of perfect that I'd used to classify Ryan. Dane was far from *perfect*—but he was perfect *for me*. He was kind, protective, understanding, young, and free-spirited. And he accepted me for who I was. He was the kind of perfect that I'd needed all along.

But—which was the bitter word that seemed to place limitations on everything good that ever happened to me— Dane and I were destined to be worlds apart.

Someday soon, I'd have to part ways with him, and anything we'd built would crumble to ruins. The image was painful, and I knew that the closer I let him grow to me, the more my departure would decimate us both. What was the right choice? Cut the budding emotions now before our three days evolved into a lifetime of painful memories? Or listen to my instincts and surrender to the wild tendrils that entrapped my heart?

Someone knocked softly on the door.

"Vivian? Are you in the bathroom?"

It was CieCie.

"Yes, I'm in here!" I called out over the hiss of the shower.

"Vivian, I'm so sorry to bother you, but we found something. Something important. You may want to hurry."

Her voice was tight with urgency. I cranked the water off and reached for the towel that hung from the corner of the stall.

"I'm coming!" I called.

The shadow of her feet lingered under the door for a moment, almost as if she wanted to say more, then they were gone. I dried myself as quickly as I could, pulled on Dane's clothes, and sprinted across the catwalk with my hair bundled in a towel. I could see them before I'd even made it down the stairs.

Gilroy stood with his arms crossed, facing the leather couch where CieCie and Dane sat close together. Of the three, Dane seemed the most distraught. His elbows were propped on his knees, and his face buried in his palms.

My feet gathered speed, causing the towel to slip from my wet hair and fall to my shoulders. I made no move to adjust it. I only wanted to get to Dane. At the creak of my descent down the stairs, his head shot up, and I was met with hollow green eyes.

"What's going on?" I demanded. Dane looked weakly in Gilroy's direction.

"We er...well, Viv'yan, we just got a message," Gilroy stuttered.

"A message from who?"

Everyone in the room held a haunted look as if they'd all just witnessed a ghost. Gilroy was the only one who seemed able to speak.

"We don't know right now."

"Well, what did it say?"

"It, uh...well, Viv'yan, don't be feelin' scared or nothin', alright? Yer safe 'ere with us, y'all know that."

"Just tell me, Gilroy!" I demanded. It was strange to be so assertive with him, but it was more unsettling to see him rendered uneasy.

He looked down at his boots, eyes hidden under the brim of his tattered brown hat.

"It jus' said, 'Yer times runnin' out.' An it came through Dane's Central Connect, which means somebody's likely keen on our livin' arrangements."

Dane closed his eyes, and I understood. This could only be Mr. Rivera. He must have figured out where I was hiding and who I was with. Sending a message to Dane's Central Connect would ensure that I received it. But how did he know I was with Dane? There must be an informant. Someone from The Channel clued him in. But who? Dane and I hadn't been seen together by anyone except—

"Rhett told Mr. Rivera that I'm here," I stated flatly. The answer was so clear. *How hadn't I seen it before?*

My skin pricked as everyone looked up at once. "In the fiber," I explained, "when Rhett found Jacey and I, he'd asked me where my boyfriend was—the boyfriend, of course, being Dane. I played along because I knew it was the only way I'd be able to convince him to send help. But right before he left, he called me by name."

"You never told him your name," Dane hissed. His expression was tight, swimming with memories of our first encounter with Rhett.

"No, I didn't. Which means someone must have told him. I could sense that he knew more than he was letting on."

This was the only explanation that made sense. Rhett must have contacted Mr. Rivera after our first encounter and told him who I was staying with. And if he contacted Mr. Rivera again after our second encounter in the fiber, he'd know Jacey was injured. This made us vulnerable.

Fear ripped through me. For the first time in days, the black-cloaked figure surfaced in my mind, and a familiar paranoia prickled the back of my neck.

"Does Rhett know where the warehouse is?" My voice quivered.

Gilroy opened his mouth to speak but quickly closed it, shooting an anxious glance at the warehouse door behind us. A heartbeat later, CieCie was there, clicking the lock. Her face was linen white, starkly contrasting the panicked blue eyes that were now sunk unnaturally far in her face.

This was getting serious. With another potential player in the game, we were losing traction in our quest for answers. First Ryan and Mr. Rivera and now Rhett.

"Y'all don't be saying a damn thing to Jacey 'bout this, ya hear? Not 'til we learn more." Gilroy's words were stern and controlled, but the creases on his forehead deceived him.

I was suddenly very aware that Daxx was still in the bathroom, tucked in the pocket of my discarded jeans. *Keep in your pocket!* Without him, I was vulnerable. We all were. And for reasons that I couldn't explain, my chest seemed empty without his lingering presence.

"I'm going to go dry my hair," I announced, pulling the towel from my shoulders. Without looking back, I escaped up the stairs. When I reached the bathroom, I closed the door behind me and grabbed my pile of clothes.

"Things are getting bad, Daxx." I hadn't removed the bottle

cap from my pocket, but I was certain that he could still hear me.

After a moment, a muffled hiss caressed my ear. "Bad indeeeed."

I left the bathroom in a shuffle, peering into Jacey's room as I passed. It was dark and quiet. He needed time for his body to recover yet here we were, faced with yet another obstacle, another danger that threatened the lives of my new companions. The last thing Jacey needed was more stress.

A pang of guilt overtook me as the torments of my mental hive intensified. *This is all your fault. If you hadn't been so naive back on Earth, you would have never gotten yourself into this mess.*

Dane was sprawled out in bed when I stepped into his room with my bundle of clothes still pressed tightly against my chest. A familiar song played from a small speaker in the corner, and I realized it was the one he'd been dancing to in the kitchen on my first night on The Channel.

"What's wrong?" he asked when I didn't move from the doorway.

The heavy drag of his voice cleared slightly. I felt relieved that he was sobering up.

"Everything," I admitted. Carefully, I placed my bundle against the wall near Dane's clothing rack, tucking my jeans at the very bottom. When I looked up, Dane was smiling weakly.

"You're wearing my clothes."

"Sorry," I flushed. "I didn't want to bother CieCie."

"Don't be. They look better on you anyway."

His gaze was warm and appraising. Heat blossomed on my cheeks, and I lowered my eyes as I walked to the bed and sat at the edge. Accepting compliments had always been difficult for me, but with Dane, it was even harder. With my stomach still flip-flopping like a fish out of water, I changed the subject.

"What's this song?"

A bright glimmer crawled into Dane's eyes. "It's 'Evolution Once Again' by Big Data."

"I recognized it from my first night here," I laughed. "You were dancing around the kitchen to it just before Jacey told me about the psycho assassination attempt."

It shouldn't have been funny—up until this point, I'd felt nauseous even thinking about my first night on The Channel— but Dane's grin multiplied at the memory, and we were both giggling like children.

Spending time with him was becoming so easy, so natural. As our laughter simmered down, the room grew quiet, and I took in the lyrics to the song. An unexpected heatwave raced down my spine like wildfire. That wildfire blazed into an absolute inferno when I realized Dane was still sprawled out, smiling, and watching me as if I was the only thing left in the room. I fumbled for a question that would take my mind off the heat that was building between us.

"So, you guys listen to Earth music here?"

"You seem to forget, Vivian. I'm from Earth."

"Oh, that's right," I blushed.

Dane shook his head, and I was surprised to catch a touch of red on his own cheeks as well.

Oh, my.

Before I had time to ask more burning questions about music from other dimensions, Dane locked me back into his two-hundred-and-ten degree gaze.

"So," he nudged my back with his bare foot. "Rhett thinks I'm your boyfriend?"

Shit! I didn't know how to respond to that. The encounter in the fiber was one I wouldn't soon forget, but it also wasn't one I wanted to actively dwell on.

"I guess so." I couldn't keep the sudden indifference from seeping into my voice.

Dane's foot pulled away, and he sat up, propped on his forearms. I glanced up in time to catch a fleeting trace of inexplicable frustration on his face. His lips slowly split into a smile that was so beautiful, I had to look away at risk of soaring straight into the sun.

The drastic shift was confusing. I wondered if I'd offended him, or maybe I'd misunderstood his reaction. Before I could decide, he spoke again with molten honey dripping from every word.

"Lay with me?"

The wildfire that had grown into an inferno was now a full blown nuclear meltdown. I hesitated a moment too long. Without warning, his arms were around me, dragging my body to the head of the bed like a rag doll. My muscles tensed at once, protesting against the unexpected contact. But he was so warm, and his arms were tight and needy, causing one corner of my consciousness to cry out in distress and the other to sing out in euphoria.

But I hadn't had the chance to decide.

It was all happening so fast.

What if this wasn't the right choice?

"I've waited all day for you." His voice lingered like smoke in the stagnant air, tangling with the lyrics to a song I had already grown to associate with this beautiful boy. Then his lips were on mine, and my muscles resigned of their own accord.

With my white flag raised high again, I relinquished control and put my faith in the urgency of his unyielding tongue. My inexperience mingled with his proficiency, sending us both into a nosedive of heady groans and hungry hands. I tangled my fingers into the tawny tufts of his hair, keeping a starved grip on him and the slow burn he ignited within me.

This is wrong.
This is right.
This is too much.
This isn't enough.
How did this start?
How would it end?

The music cascaded into its final violent notes, striking through my arching spine as his hands traced my side, over my stomach, across my hips. A shock wave riveted through my body. I shot my hands to where his fingers began to tug down the elastic of my waistband.

"No," I whispered just as the final piano notes of the song faded out.

"No?" The question was temptingly wicked on his breathy voice, ripping through the silence like a challenge.

I had to reel myself back in. I was caught in the snare, and if I didn't escape now, the fire in my heart could very well be the fire that would incinerate us both.

"No." As I said the word, I pulled his hands away from the danger zone.

His eyes were puzzled, and I watched as the green flames snuffed out one by one. I knew that I shouldn't feel guilty, but I did.

"I don't understand."

"Dane," I said after a moment. "This is moving too fast. We barely know each other."

"I'm trying to know you," he whispered, and as he did, he closed his eyes and leaned forward.

I caught him with a single outstretched finger over his pursed lips. His eyes shot open.

"And I'd like to know you, too. Just...not like this. Not yet, at least."

For a moment, he remained motionless, with his still-wet

lips curled up under the pressure of my index finger. He smiled against my skin and pulled away.

"You're really bad at this, you know." His voice was calm, but something about the cold indifference buried within was familiar, flickering my intuition to life.

Yes, I vividly remembered this unsettling coldness—this voice, riddled with a strange nonchalance that masked a one-hundred meter tiger pit underneath. It was the same tone Ryan used when I told him that I didn't want to move in with him on the night I decided not to "complicate things"—the night that complicated *everything*. It was also the precise moment that I'd decided to continue dragging things along at an unbearably dry pace, never progressing, never growing, never warming enough to develop anything *real*.

If I'd said yes to Ryan that night, would I even be here right now?

Had I failed a test?

And if so, was I failing another?

"You're important to me."

The fearful whisper was all I knew to say. I was doing it again. I was falling back into the same pattern, denying myself of what I truly wanted for fear of complicating a good thing. Dane was what I wanted, I was certain of that. How could I ever want anything more?

Dane's expression softened. His arms gripped me tight to his chest. "I don't know what you're thinking but stop thinking it. I'm not upset with you. I mean, I want you—but I've wanted you since the moment I laid eyes on you." He brushed a tendril of hair from my cheek. "We've had a long day, and we'll have an even longer day tomorrow. You should probably get some sleep."

The buzzing pressure in my skull was unrelenting, but Dane didn't allow me to stray far enough to fall into the dark void of my thoughts. Warm against his chest, my mind grew hollow and dim, and all my fear and confusion liquified as we both drifted.

The morning passed quietly. When Dane left to start breakfast, I dressed in my dirty armored clothing and visited CieCie's room where she knit my hair into a long fishbone braid. Then I visited Jacey's room, and he reminded me—*again*—to keep Daxx in my waist bag during our trip. He was beginning to sound more like his bossy self.

As soon as Dane and I returned, I'd give Daxx back to Jacey, and hopefully, he'd mellow out. The idea of leaving him vulnerable was maddening. But he'd told me that the trip to dimension one's fiber wouldn't take long and that there was no reason to worry. His words did nothing to restore my sanity. Jacey was still unaware that Rhett was somehow involved, and I cursed Gilroy for not allowing me to be honest with him.

After breakfast, I cranked the buckle of my waist bag around my hips, laced my boots, and hugged CieCie goodbye. Then Dane and I were off, heading south toward the Edge Station that would lead us to Quadrant Four. The walk was significantly shorter than our previous trip to Quadrant Two. As we walked, Dane explained the lay of the land, and for once, The Channel was beginning to make more sense.

"So, if you envision The Channel as a Rubik's cube, each of the building tops would make up the individual square's of the cube's surface," he explained.

"And we're traveling between the cracks?"

"Exactly."

"And fibers to the other twenty-six dimensions plug into the rooftops?"

"Now you're getting it!" he beamed. "Gilroy's place is its own little square block on the fifth side of The Channel. So the warehouse's geographical coordinate would be North M-5 because the entrance to the warehouse faces the north alley."

"And where are we going now? What square on the cube?"

"Right now? We're heading to the Edge Station at South M-5. Then we'll take the Edge Station staircase, which will spit us out on Quadrant Four. From there, our fiber will be right beside the Edge Station. Q-4, I believe it is. You'll know it when you see it."

"Because it's dark?"

He smiled as if he'd thought of something funny. "Yes," he said coyly, "it's very, very dark."

Our journey to the Edge Station only took a few minutes. It was identical to the one I'd traveled through with Jacey two days ago. A dark stairwell dipped into the ground, its mouth illuminated by the flicker of a blue neon sign: "To Quad Station 4"

"Ladies first," Dane smiled, gesturing for me to lead the way. My stomach churned.

"I don't know if that's a good idea," I said, remembering my constant collisions with Jacey's back during our first Quad Station trip.

Dane's eyebrows shot up curiously. "You're not afraid, are you?"

"No. Well, yes, but no. Not of the dark. I wasn't blessed at birth with flawless coordination."

"Ah," he nodded, "the vertigo. That's normal for first-timers. I promise you'll get used to it. Didn't Jacey warn you?"

"No. I'm realizing that everything is 'leap before you look' with Jacey."

"Yeah, I remember those days," he said, and his voice held a trace of something I couldn't recognize.

I wondered briefly if he was thinking about their mission to dimension twenty-seven. The thought caused me to linger on Dane's beautiful face longer than what one might consider normal.

Was this really the same man who had carried the body of a dead child across dimensions? He'd risked his life for CieCie's little sister, just to bring her body to safety. I could hardly believe that Dane, *my Dane*, had done something so selfless. He was a hero. A true hero.

The desire to touch him was too much to bear. I reached out and took his hand in mine. His face lit up, unaware of the dark mental projections that raced violently through my mind. I had my own questions for him about the dimension twenty-seven mission, but I decided to save them for a quieter time.

"Well, Viv, you're in luck. Because, unlike Jacey, I'm an excellent tour guide."

He tugged my hand, and we both stepped into the darkness of the stairwell.

I was relieved to find that my second trip through the Edge Station was much easier than my first. We giggled like children as the stairs shifted from down to up, and I even backtracked a few paces just to experience the alien sensation again. If I didn't know better, I would have assumed there was magic at play.

"I see light ahead. We're close to the exit," Dane announced.

I was busy thinking about something that hadn't occurred to me until that exact moment. "How the hell did Gilroy get a big ass wagon through this stairwell when he brought Jacey and I back from the Mercantile fiber?"

Dane turned to me, puzzled. The light ahead cast a soft line of blue that outlined the sharp contours of his face and reflected from the moisture of his bottom lip. His profile was so breathtaking that I had to remind my ears to listen.

"He didn't take the wagon through the stairwell, silly Viv. He took the cargo transport station. These tunnels are only intended for foot traffic. Vehicles have to use designated cargo transport areas of the Edge Station."

Silly me. Of course, the magical flippy floppy tunnels had designated vehicle lanes. I rolled my eyes, pushing past Dane, and walked toward the light.

He quickly caught up to me, still grinning like a carefree child, and together we stepped into the blue curtain of glow that bathed the ascending staircase. I blinked, adjusting to the brightness. But Dane wrapped his fingers around my wrist and tugged me back into the dark.

Was this his idea of flirting? I opened my mouth to protest, but he clasped his fingers over my lips.

"Rhett is up there!" he hissed.

My blood ran cold, sending the hair on my arms awry. "You saw him? You're sure?" my voice muffled under his fingers.

"Yes!" he whispered, releasing my face. "He's sitting on his tetra."

"His what?"

"His tetra. His bike," he said hastily, dropping into a low crouch and edging up the stairs. I followed his lead, kneeling a stair below him.

From our dark cubby, I spotted a man in a long brown coat sitting on the saddle of a large bike. Its tires were circles of solid aqua light, bathing the wet pavement in an ominous glow. An orange flicker sent a flare of contrasting color across Rhett's face as he lit the end of a cigarette and puffed. The light ceased with the click of metal, and Rhett swiftly tucked the lighter into his coat pocket.

"What's he doing here?" We were so close that I could smell the hash burn of tobacco.

"Don't know. But he likely won't come down here if he's got his bike. He'll have to take the cargo transport station."

Dane's voice was relieved, but alarm bells still rang sharply in my mind.

"Where does Rhett live?" I asked anxiously.

"I don't know. Quadrant Three, I think. Why's it matter?"

"Don't you find it suspicious that he's lingering so close to Quadrant Five? What if he goes to Gilroy's place? He knows that Jacey is hurt."

We remained silent, crouching in the shadows with our eyes glued to Rhett. He took a long drag from his cigarette, tipped his head back, and exhaled a wispy stream of smoke. It captured the blue light from the bike, glowing in soft suspension before dissipating. He flicked the glowing nub from his fingers, sending its orange tip flitting through the air.

Dane and I ducked in unison as Rhett's head tilted toward the tiny orange trail of light. The cigarette butt hit the ground in front of the stairwell with a spark and bounced down the stairs, narrowly avoiding my boot. I held my breath. Dane reached out to steady me. All was quiet for several excruciating seconds.

The abrupt roar of an engine ripped through the silence. The sound was deafening, echoing through the tunnel in three distinct revs. I clasped my hands over my ears. Dane remained alert, raising his body slightly as the sound grew dimmer.

"He's leaving," Dane announced.

We both stood and watched the back tire of Rhett's bike speed through the darkness until it vanished. I was relieved to see that he was going in the opposite direction of Gilroy's place.

"Guess that answers your question," Dane mused.

I followed him to the street, and we paused together where Rhett's bike had just been.

"Wonder what he was doing," Dane said. He cocked his head. Something on the ground caught his eye. *A clue?* It looked like a small shred of folded paper. "What do we have here?" He picked up the paper and as he unfolded it, my throat constricted into a knot. Scrawled on the center of the white scrap was a familiar black wolfish design.

Dane handed the picture to me. It seemed to be hand-drawn in dark pencil or charcoal, but I was certain that this was the same image inscribed within Daxx's bottle cap.

"Looks like Rhett has taken up art. Wouldn't have been my first choice of hobbies for him. He seems like more of a chess club guy."

I feigned a smile, betraying my instinct to drop on the pavement hyperventilating.

What did this mean? Did Rhett know about Daxx? Is this why he was working for Mr. Rivera?

A million violent buzzes radiated through my skull. All this conspiracy—could it all have been caused by Jacey? He'd said Daxx was a weapon, and I'd seen firsthand just how dangerous Daxx was. Could Mr. Rivera be trying to steal him?

"What's wrong, Viv? You look like you're gonna get sick or something."

I folded the paper and tucked it in my pocket. The ground under my feet was swaying from side to side. I needed to talk to Jacey. *Damn it, why hadn't I just told him about Rhett?*

"I'm fine," I lied. "Can we get moving? I want to get back to the warehouse."

Dane took my hand and squeezed it. My palms were moist and clammy, and they squished uncomfortably in his grasp. I wished I could just tell him the truth. But I'd made a promise to

Jacey. And if Dane knew about Daxx, it might put him in more danger.

Staying calm was the best option. Rhett obviously wasn't going to Quadrant Five, which gave Dane and I the time we needed to get the ink and return home. Then, regardless of what Gilroy advised, I'd tell Jacey what was going on, and we'd find a solution together.

"We're already here, Viv." Concern creased Dane's face. I hadn't realized that he'd been looking at me. "You sure you're okay?"

"Yes," I said bitterly.

He frowned. "Viv, relax. Rhett wouldn't break into Gilroy's place. And even if he did, Gilroy would kick his ass from one side of The Channel to the other. They're a tough group, even CieCie. They can hold their own."

I despised the wave of guilt that crashed over me. The truth danced on my tongue, daring my lips to part and release like gospel. I hated keeping secrets from Dane. But even more than that, I hated being in a position where keeping secrets from Dane was necessary.

As if reading my turmoils, Dane clasped my face in his hands. He paused, holding my mind and my heart captive within the depths of his eyes. He tilted his head to the side and kissed life back into me. My lips yielded under the pressure. Like a dose of the most addictive of drugs, I was subdued by the sweet taste of his venom.

His eyes smoldered as he pulled away, and I held his forearms to steady myself. This didn't help to sober me, though. The way his tight corded muscles flexed under the rough texture of his navy sleeves kept my thoughts scattering into the most wicked corners of my consciousness. A flawless white smile parted across his kiss-swollen lips, which shone wet under the pink glow of the nearby buildings.

"You think I don't see what I do to you?" My breathing hitched. "I see everything, Vivian. The way you sway when you walk in front of me. The way you watch my lips like you want to own them for yourself. Why do you keep trying to fight this?"

"Do you want the honest answer?" I whispered.

"The honest answer is the only one I'd ever want." His gaze was piercing, ripping through the walls I'd built around my heart.

I couldn't be honest about everything, but I could be honest about this. The words fell from my lips in a jumble.

"I've never been this close to anyone before. And I'm afraid that if I get close to you—or if I tell you how I really feel—you'll think it's stupid or push me away. It really is stupid, though. I barely know you, and I know it sounds absolutely absurd. I promise to not get upset if you think it's silly—because I have a history of overthinking and messing up good things—"

"Vivian," he stopped me with a finger to my lips. I froze. "Just tell me," he demanded in a voice that was as smooth and sweet as honey, and I couldn't fight him any longer.

"I think I'm falling for you."

His long exhale danced on my cheek like butterfly wings. I watched myself, reflected back within the glisten of his wide eyes. Then he crushed my body against his chest, and unexpected tears burned down my cheeks.

I cursed myself for acting this way. For being so weak, sniveling and crying when I should be focusing on more pressing matters. But Dane's arms gripped me tighter and for once, I considered the possibility that maybe he needed this just as much as I needed him. That maybe, I wasn't crazy. Maybe I wasn't falling too fast. Maybe I was falling at just the right speed, neck-and-neck in a downward spiral with this beautiful carefree boy.

"We should probably get going," he whispered, but he didn't let me go. We stood together, basking in the afterglow of my confession for just a few more silent moments.

When he pulled away, his eyes were pink around the edges. *Had he been crying?* I wasn't sure how to acknowledge it nor did I know if he'd want me to, so I didn't. Instead, I took his hand, and he led me across the street.

"This is the place," he said, raising a finger in the direction of another large roll-top door. It was identical to the door Jacey and I had taken to Mercantile dimension's fiber. But that would mean...

I looked up. There was no sign of a glowing, translucent tube.

"Where's the fiber?"

"Blacked out, remember?"

"I still thought I'd be able to see it." There was nothing there at all. The sky above was an uninterrupted grid, set over a backdrop of crimson sky.

"Not until we're up there," he said.

I followed him through the familiar roll-top door, but everything beyond its mouth was eerily different. The long hall leading to the elevator was the same distance as the first I'd traveled through, but this one was cast in darkness. Silhouetted against the light of The Channel alley, our bodies cast long ghostly shadows across the tiled floor.

"Let's go."

His voice dropped to a whisper that matched the atmosphere of this sinister forgotten place. I encouraged my feet to move forward, but they were heavy and unwilling, so I let Dane lead.

"Spooky, eh?"

"That's an understatement," I whispered just as my foot caught the lip of a broken tile, and I fell forward onto my palms.

"Damn it, Vivian," Dane whispered. "Be careful! Are you okay?"

The bite of his voice was startling. Embarrassed, I took his hand, and he pulled me to my feet where I was met with his concerned eyes.

"I'm sorry," he said, and he bent to brush the dust from my knees. "I guess I'm a little spooked, too."

We continued, more slowly this time, until we reached the ominous elevator doors. On cue, they opened, and we were blinded momentarily by a bright white light. The inside of the elevator was immaculate. Dane shrugged in surprise.

"I guess it can't get dirty if it seldom opens. Well, you know what to do, Vivian. Leap before you look."

Together, we stepped inside, and the doors closed behind us. The overhead light sputtered with an audible succession of plinking bursts before flickering into absolute blackness.

18
THE BLACKEST FIBER

The floor pushed up on our boots, rocking me back against the wall of the elevator. Limited by the depths of the dark, my senses took charge, making up for the vision I'd lost. The taut groan of the elevator shaft, the adrenaline that pumped Dane's heart heavy and fast, and the rip of my erratic breathing as I braced myself for the unexpected. A bell sounded brightly, and the elevator door sighed as it slid open.

"Take my hand," Dane ordered.

I fumbled my fingers into the darkness, feeling around for his familiar warmth. When I found his steady hand, I gripped it tight and pulled my body as close to him as I could. Our arms were in full contact, bracing each other as we navigated our way out of the pitch-black elevator.

"Didn't you bring a flashlight or something?" I whispered. Even at the lowest volume I could pitch, my voice was a crack of thunder that shattered the silence.

"No," Dane answered, warily testing his own volume. After taking gauge, he adjusted so his words were barely audible. "You can't bring external light in here. These plants we're hunting are sensitive. Even the slightest bit of light could scorch them." He paused. "You have your waist bag, right?"

I dropped a nervous hand to the leather band around my hips. "Yes."

"Good," he whispered. "We'll use it to transport the plants safely. We're looking for a blue mushroom. They're called putocrypes. This is the only place in all of the known dimensions where they grow."

I was barely listening. Something else snared my attention. A new complication had churned. If we filled the bag with mushrooms, I wouldn't be able to open it without destroying them once we left the dark of the fiber. And that meant Daxx wouldn't be able to protect us if something happened. Rhett was still out there somewhere, lurching around like a slimy leech. I needed to keep Daxx accessible.

Thinking quickly, I gracelessly asked, "How do we turn the mushrooms into ink?"

"We don't." Dane was perplexed and wary from our blind stake, but he continued.

It was shameful to manipulate him in this way, but I needed to keep him occupied.

"The arms dealer is the one who will make the ink. He'll pick through them—"

As Dane rambled on, I kept one hand buried in his fingers while the other tugged on the zipper of my waist bag. Deliberately slow, I used my palm to muffle the sound of the zipper gliding against metal teeth.

"—and after he finds the very best ones, he'll grind them into a sort of poultice—"

I sifted through the bag, searching for the cool smooth texture of the bottle cap.

"—because it's not like a tattoo gun. He actually has to cut the skin in order to lay the Central Connect wires—"

I caught the sharp edge between my middle and index

fingers. Carefully, I tucked the cap into my palm and extracted it from the bag.

"—then he rubs the glowing ink into the incisions. And fuck, does it hurt! When I had my first cybernetic tattoos, I nearly—"

But before I could push the cap safely into my pocket, a humid chill passed through my palm, and feather-soft fur raced up my arm. *Oh no!*

"Dangerrrr. Vorboding, ah yesss. I tassste it."

I gasped and released Dane's hand at once.

"What's wrong?" he whispered, but his voice wasn't filled with the horror of someone who just heard the demonic hiss of a monster. "Vivian? Are you okay?"

A deep breathy chuckle vibrated across my shoulders.

"Sorry," I choked, "I thought I heard something."

"I didn't hear anything," Dane said after a moment.

His warm fingers snaked between mine again. Nausea twisted my stomach.

"Do not vrett, Viviaaan," the breathy hiss taunted, somehow only audible to me. "I am the ssspace between shadowsss, exisssting within vibersss of your mortal planesss."

From the corner of my eye, I caught a glimpse of a soft blue glow. My saving grace.

"There!" I said, much too loud. Dane's hand jerked at the sudden volume. "Sorry," I amended. "The mushrooms. I see them."

"Good eye!" Dane said brightly.

A frisson like the dragging edge of a blade scraped over the soft tendon of my neck. "Thisss one causes you much...uneasssse."

My heart leaped into my throat. This was getting dangerous. I needed to get Dane away from Daxx.

"Dane, I'm scared," I said, ripping the buckle on my

waistband open. "Here," I shoved the bag in his direction. He was standing closer than I thought, and the bag collided hard against his chest.

"What the—"

I interrupted him. "Take the bag and go fill it. I'll wait here."

"Are you sure?" His voice was louder, disbelieving.

Damn you, Daxx! No wonder Jacey said the beast was *a part of him.* They acted just alike.

"No. I'd like to stay here. This place freaks me out," I insisted. *Jacey better pray he's still asleep when we get home.* Dane hadn't moved.

The maddening scrape against my neck persisted. "At your bidding, hisss bonesss, ssso easy to sssnap. His sssskin, so easssily torn awaaaay."

"Damn it, Dane! I have to pee!" I shouted, grasping onto any shred of hope that I could lead him away long enough to subdue this stupid freakshow of an animal.

I heard Dane fumble forward. The zipper of the waist bag wailed as he stumbled noisily toward the light. "Sorry, Vivian. For fuck's sake, just say something next time. We could have stopped somewhere..." he continued grumbling as he walked.

The moment I was positive he'd moved a safe distance, I pulled the bottle cap back out of my pocket. "Daxx, get in your cap," I demanded, my voice no more than a breath. There was no response. "Damn it, Daxx! Get in your *fucking* cap!"

Inches from my face, a light spread menacingly slowly into the cut of a wicked Cheshire grin. Snared between Daxx's teeth were several gooey mushroom chunks. The span of his mouth lit up as if a glow stick had been emptied between his jaws, and his tongue lolled lazily out. A long glowing purple drip of ooze hung suspended in the air.

"You're disgusting!"

"I caaan only be as disssgusting as the massster who beckonsss," he hissed smoothly.

Livid beyond my limit, I reached out and snatched his glowing jaw from the air. It was light and solid in my hand—like a helium balloon begging to be released—and I easily pulled it to my face. The purple glow dripped between the barbs of grotesque teeth.

Vivian from a few days ago would have died on the spot, convulsing from the heart attack this demonic sight would have caused. But today's version of Vivian was done with Daxx's bullshit, immune to the sticky purple saliva that seeped over my hand.

"Get. In. Your. Cap."

His lips curled in morbid amusement. "As you vish, Viviaaaan."

In his parting gesture, my entire face was met with the sticky texture of Daxx's feverishly hot tongue. Then he was gone.

Furiously defeated and covered in a layer of disgusting goo, I shoved the bottle cap into my pocket and turned in the direction that Dane had gone. I could faintly make out the dark silhouette of his body in the distance, occasionally obstructing the glow as he skirted the line of mushrooms. I decided that I'd better help. The sooner we were back home, the sooner I could shower away this slime.

"What happened to you?" His face was faintly visible in the glowing light as he turned.

My face, hair, and jacket were doused in a glowing purple sludge. *Damn it, Daxx!*

"I, uh...couldn't hold it anymore," I lied. "I tried to find a place to use the bathroom...but I fell down...into a bunch of glowing goo."

"On your face?" he asked, amused. This was humiliating.

"Yes," I growled.

Dane snorted as he tried to suppress a snicker. I wasn't above adding him to my growing shit list.

"Well, while you were...doing that," he stuttered, clearly making an effort to preserve some of my dignity, "I was able to collect a pretty good batch of putocrypes. Not sure if it'll be enough, though. Honestly, these are some of the puniest little mushies I've ever seen." He bent low, plucking a little blue toadstool from the ground.

"Is there anywhere else we can look?"

Dane flicked the tiny mushroom into the darkness. It bounced three times across the ground and landed a few feet away, rolling on its top like a dreidel.

"I'm sure there are more. We'll have to walk a little deeper into the fiber, though." He held up the leather bag, its contents gleaming in the darkness and illuminating the underside of his jaw. He looked like a camper, poised to share a cheesy ghost story. "At least we'll have light this time."

Holding out my waist bag like a lantern, we plodded farther into the depths of the dimension one fiber. Every so often, a new splash of glowing color would appear—a red-spotted flower with a scent like burning plastic, a strange turquoise vine with tendrils like fingers that tickled our boots as we passed. But no mushrooms. We'd traveled far enough that the sterile cold stillness set in.

This must be what dimension one was like. A chill ghost of a planet, floating in the eternal void of a failed solar system. At least life found a way to continue on, here in this place that was untouched by light, sound, or even the faintest whispering breeze.

"Did you ever get to see dimension one? Before the fiber was severed, I mean?"

Dane seemed startled by my question. He paused briefly,

collecting his bearings. "No," he answered. "Dimension one was severed while Jacey and I were still in training. It was a big shit show, though, I'll tell you that. The Five would only allow so many refugees into The Channel and only the ones who had value."

"Value?" I echoed.

"Yeah. Like, a skill or strength. A utility."

"But why?"

"Use your imagination, Viv. We couldn't possibly keep all those people here. Dimension one was unified, but they weren't even aware of our existence until the final days and only because we were nice enough to offer aid. The Five were only willing to bring in people who could provide a decent ROI."

Return on investment. I knew the term from my days at Premier. But if that were the case...

"They sold them?" I gasped.

Dane stopped and gave me a *so-what* look. My mouth dropped open.

"Do you know how much money it takes to feed that many people? We don't have organic growth on The Channel. Everything has to be imported. And the people we sold barely covered the expense of housing them for the few months they took refuge. Jumpers were basically living on scraps because it was apparently the 'noble thing' for a soldier to do."

He kicked a glowing red flower with the tip of his boot, sending it sailing through the blackness. I couldn't believe what I was hearing.

"You wonder why we have so many rivalries among Jumpers?" he growled. "It all started when we took in refugees from dimension one, and the entire lot of Jumpers nearly starved to death. We were fighting to survive. After the refugees were sold and split off into other dimensions, the Jumpers just kept on fighting. It became a part of our culture.

"Especially those of us who were still trainees when the whole damn thing happened. It's like it was bred into us or something. In the most influential stage of our training, back when we should have been learning control, we had to fight for even the smallest scraps of food. So yeah. Sorry but fuck dimension one. The whole lot of them."

The words hung heavy in the air, filling the space between us with a dark tension that I'd never experienced around Dane. He started walking again, not checking to see if I'd followed. After a few moments, the blue glow of the waist bag grew distant. With a reluctant sigh, I followed after him.

"What's wrong?" His voice had lost the comfort I'd felt before.

What *was* wrong? Was I right to judge him? This was his world, not mine. I had no idea what he'd gone through or the struggles he'd survived. But surely he couldn't agree with...*with selling people.*

Every time I opened my mouth, the words fell back down my throat, retreating and leaving me in cold solitude. Dane had been through so much, this I knew. But his views on dimension one were so out of tune with his character. I bit my lip, transfixed by the vision of Dane rushing through the ruins of a totaled city, cradling the body of a bruised and bloody child. I couldn't swallow the thought fast enough.

"What about dimension twenty-seven?"

He froze in icy rigor.

Shit.

"What *about* dimension twenty-seven?" His voice was calm and slow, but the words were heavy.

"Fuck refugees, right?" I shrugged, holding the high ground. "That's what you said. So what about CieCie? She was from dimension twenty-seven, which would make her a refugee."

He pivoted on his heels in a militant gesture, and for the first time, I saw the long-buried soldier who he'd tried so hard to suppress. Stone sharp and deathly still, his eyes dared me to say more.

With a creak in my voice, I dared. "And what about Mia?"

At the sound of her name, he snapped. The bag of mushrooms hit the ground, sending several blue streaks bouncing through the dark. His hands were tight around my forearms.

"You don't know a fucking thing about Mia," he whispered through bared teeth.

Our noses were only an inch apart, but I wasn't afraid. Not of Dane. Not of *my* Dane.

"I know that you saved her," I said evenly.

His eyes narrowed into the sharpest of green slits, faintly illuminated by the mushrooms that were scattered around our feet.

"If I'd saved her, she'd fucking be here." The pain in his voice simmered like a pot on the boiler.

I wanted nothing more than to ease this tension, this hurt that he was carrying. "You did everything you could," I whispered.

His hands released their grip on my forearms. I was surprised by the lingering soreness left behind.

"Yeah," he whispered. "I did. I did everything. Even after she was gone and in the ground, I did *every-god-damned-fucking thing*."

"Dane, it's okay. Look, I'm sorr—" I reached to touch him, but he whirled away from my hand.

"Vivian, stop. Just stop. You have no idea what you're even talking about."

"Then explain it to me!" I pleaded.

His head hung low, and his fingers snaked painfully in the tangles of his tawny hair. I watched as his knuckles tightened in the dim glow, gripping hard into his scalp. Then he relaxed his grip. Slowly, he turned back to me with a gaze that was cloudy and tired.

"Explain it to me," I repeated, more quietly. My body trembled, fighting tears that threatened to spill over.

He closed his eyes. "I did everything I could," he whispered. "And every single day, I'm forced to live in the shadow of my mistake. Jacey would have saved CieCie, whether I was there or not. None of it mattered. Mia was already dead. I didn't need to be there. I wasn't supposed to be there."

"But you brought her body back...for CieCie," I said softly.

He shook his head hard and fast. "No, Vivian. CieCie would have been fine either way. What I did...what I *truly did* was fuck myself. I fucked myself out of a life. And ever since that day, I've had to stand back and watch Mr. Perfect play the role of perpetual hero."

"Jacey?" I asked. What did he have to do with this?

"Vivian, did he not tell you what happened after we returned from dimension twenty-seven?"

"No," I whispered.

He laughed a humorless chuckle. "Mr. Hero," he uttered bitterly to himself. "Of course he didn't tell you what happened after we got back...because he wasn't fucking there to see it."

What? I shifted uncomfortably.

Dane must have sensed my confusion. He spread his arms theatrically wide and took a step toward me.

"Oh yeah, Vivian. I hate to be the one to burst your bubble, but Mr. Perfect isn't so perfect. The moment we got back to Gilroy's place, he was out of there. Gone. Fucking poof. He packed his shit and vanished. And do you know who took care of CieCie?"

I swallowed the lump that was building in my throat.

"That's right. I did," he spat. "And do you know who took the blame when The Five realized we'd violated protocol by bringing a civilian to The Channel? Again, me."

My heart pounded furiously, filling the quiet space between us with its erratic rhythm. "What happened?" I dared to ask but quickly wished I hadn't.

His face became feral, each shadow-filled cavern filled with a million words that he'd likely never uttered to anyone. "I was fired."

"I thought you said you quit," I objected.

"Damn it, Vivian! I lied! I've lied over and over again, convincing myself that it'd be better to take the fault and save Jacey the dishonor. But he did us wrong. All of us. He abandoned us. I lost everything...and all the while, Gilroy and I were left caring for a traumatized, broken girl. It's like, my whole world was crumbling around me—and I couldn't even deal with it because I was too busy dealing with the mess he left behind."

"So wait," I said, holding back my swarm as they buzzed about the agitated hive. "Where did Jacey go? Did he tell you?"

"Fuck if I know!" Dane shrugged. "He just packed up all pissy in his usual Jacey-fashion and bailed. He was gone for two months. Then he comes back all hero-homecoming style, wooing CieCie with gifts and smiles like nothing happened. And suddenly, they were best friends. Like, fuck me, right? I may not have been the one to carry her out of twenty-seven, but fuck, I was the one who slept beside her bed because her nightmares were so bad that she'd wake up screaming. I was the one who cooked for her every night, while Gilroy taught her how to wire Central Connect units. Jacey didn't do shit."

"You're not...mad at CieCie are you?" I muttered.

His expression grew sharp again. "What? No! Of course not. I'd never blame her for...for, I don't know...wanting to be close to him, I guess? I get that he saved her. It just...it hurts, you know?" And as he said the words, his expression melted, and he looked vulnerable, ripping away the bandage to expose an open wound.

Why had Jacey lied to me? Or—I guess he hadn't truly lied —but he'd definitely withheld the full story. And something occurred to me, slithering restlessly in the back of my mind. "When did all this happen?"

"Two years ago," he replied sullenly.

*Two years...*That's when Jacey said he was tasked with Daxx's extermination. I remembered his words. *Anger, anxiety, aggression...Daxx feeds on those negative emotions.* Could all these negative emotions stem directly from the incident at dimension twenty-seven?

I didn't have time to put the pieces together now. We needed to finish our mission and get back home. Rhett was still lurking around somewhere—and I had more than a few choice words for Jacey concerning Daxx who, somehow, Rhett also knew about.

"I told you there was something going on with him." Dane's hushed voice broke the silence. "I told you he's been acting strange. Something happened to him while he was out on his own."

Yes. Daxx happened. I was certain. But I couldn't tell Dane that.

"Viv?" There was something there, swimming within his eyes that I couldn't begin to identify. "When you and Jacey were out alone, did he say anything?"

"He said a lot of things." My voice was clipped. Being the terrible liar that I was, I couldn't risk talking about this with

Dane. We needed to get home where I could confront Jacey first.

Dane was clearly unsatisfied with my answer. "Yes, I'm sure he did. But did he mention anything strange? Did he slip at all, or say anything that might..." He trailed off.

"That might what?"

He bent to pick up the discarded waist bag. "Look, never mind, okay? Either way, it's over. Me wallowing around being pissed about it isn't going to change anything. I'm not a Jumper anymore. I've come to terms with that. Life was really dark for me for a while, but I'm getting over it. In fact, life was dark until..." He paused, kneeling to scoop the scattered mushrooms back into the bag.

"Until?" I prompted, crouching beside him to pick up a mushroom.

He took it from my hand, lifting his gaze to mine. Like magic, the electric current was there once more, ripping violently through my veins.

"Until you arrived."

Oh.

"Vivian, I feel like I'm falling in love with you or something."

OH.

The "or something" didn't dilute the words at all. I rocked back on my heels, completely and utterly at a loss. Was I supposed to say it back?

"Dane...I..."

The set of his mouth changed ever so slightly. "You what?"

It was happening again—my inability to commit to my feelings, regardless of how real they were. It was like I was trying to speak another language that I knew by ear, but my own lips didn't know how to form the words. I was aware of how stupid I must look, crouched down with my mouth open, and the look of a rabbit caught dead in the emerald eyes of a fox.

He exhaled a long breath from his nose and dropped his gaze. "Let me guess." His tone was raw as he began placing mushrooms back in the bag. "You can't love me back. Because you have to go home."

I flinched mentally. There were a million things I wanted to say, but only three words would form on my lips. "Yes. I do."

"You don't, though," he challenged.

We'd placed the last of the mushrooms in the bag, and he stood, leaving me alone on the ground. I was too shocked to move. The vision of my mom was there again. She was watching the flatscreen that sat on my dresser, her legs draped over the edge of my bed, and one of my old tatty souvenir tee shirts clasped in her hands. Her eyes were glassy as she wept into the shirt, watching the news station with unblinking fatigue.

"Yes. I do." I repeated the words, but this time, my tone was a brick wall of intention. No love could replace the love I held for her. I wouldn't leave her to wonder for the rest of her days what happened to her only daughter who vanished without a trace.

The light was fading. Dane had already started to walk in the opposite direction that we'd been heading.

"Where are you going?"

"We have enough. The place had been plucked clean. I'm ready to go home."

The swallowing darkness was no longer the biggest of my fears as we sauntered toward the elevator. Dane was deathly silent. The scene was so familiar, I could almost smell the leather interior of Ryan's Mercedes. A mental storm was spinning in my head, and there was certainly one spinning in Dane's as well. It was like the black-cloaked figure and my beehive joined forces, crashing down in an assault on my sanity.

Underfoot, the ground was leveling out. Blue light from the waist bag reflected from a smooth surface ahead.

"There's the elevator," Dane mumbled absently.

That tone. It cut through me like a hot blade. The words held no significance, but they carried a cold wind with them that left me shivering.

I tried to bridge the distance between us, craving his touch. But the faster I stepped, the longer strides he took. After a few attempts, I began to understand his unspoken message. He was pissed. And because it was the first time I'd ever seen him this way, the pain in my chest was unbearable.

Every voice in my head demanded that I reach for him. Take his hand. Pull him to my lips. Kiss away the conflict and make him forget that it ever happened. But fear of rejection overpowered my desire so I stayed stagnant, awaiting some cue that would tell me that we'd be okay.

The elevator was closed when we arrived. Blue light from our bag was amplified in the reflection of the brushed metal doors, exposing the fear that stained my face. Dane's brow was constructed of hard lines and dark angles that shouted louder than his voice ever could. I gripped my arms tightly around myself, causing my leather sleeves to creak like rubber. Dane glanced up for a moment, clearly assessing my demeanor, then dropped his gaze to the bag. The light vanished as he pulled the zipper shut.

"Here." He pressed the bag against my chest.

I unhinged my arms just long enough to take it and snap the buckle around my hips. My chest was an empty void that craved to be made whole. *How had things changed so fast?*

My conscience was quick to point blame at Dane's sudden

mercurialness, yet somewhere deep down, a more logical corner of my brain cried out to be recognized.

Ryan, Jacey, Dane—all these men displayed similar mood swings, despite being very different in character. The common denominator, the thing that always seemed to trigger the fuse that detonated every good situation, was *me*. My anxieties and doubts always wiggled their way from the deepest recesses of my mind, projecting outward and onto the people I cared most about. My grip around my torso tightened, and I repressed the ambush of emotion that swelled in the corners of my eyes.

"The door is open," Dane muttered.

I took a deep, cleansing breath and reached out until my fingers found the cold frame of the dark elevator and stepped inside. Dane followed. I heard the click of a button and the slide of the doors sealing shut. The fluorescent light decided to flicker back to life as the elevator made its descent.

My eyeballs were shocked, blindly fluttering as they adjusted. Dane's silhouette was fuzzy, but I could faintly make out his arms furiously rubbing his eyes. Everything came into focus just as the doors began to open. Through the widening slit, I noticed the dark figure of a man waiting on the other side.

Time moved in disjointed fragments. My body fell against the wall of the elevator just as Dane shot forward in a flash. I was alone as the brushed metal doors slid shut again. A clatter of metal and an ominous thump sounded from outside.

I briefly considered staying inside where it was safe, but I cursed myself for even thinking about it and plunged my hand between the closing split of metal. *Dane was in danger!* The doors retracted like theater curtains.

I exhaled in relief. Behind them, Dane stood a few paces away with his arms at his side. But as I stepped out of the elevator, the air between us fizzled and snapped, and fear gripped me as my gaze plunged to the source.

A strange double-sided weapon was clung at waist level to Dane's hand. From each end, a cruel curved blade licked the air with green electric tendrils. He stood, defensively angled, evaluating me with a dangerous sideways glance that sent the hair on my arms standing like goose skin. My focus dropped to the dark heap that lay motionless at his feet and the red pool that was rapidly crawling across the white tile between us.

19

TREE PARTY

"Dane?" My voice was frail and unfamiliar.

Cautiously, I took another step forward. Dane's brow fell slightly, but his eyes did not stray from mine. I made a conscious decision to ignore the man that lay between us, stagnant in a way that only death could inflict.

I swallowed hard, collecting myself, and asked in an even voice, "Who is this?" Still fixed on Dane, I pointed a trembling finger toward the body.

The rise and fall of Dane's chest slowed to calm, but I was unnerved by the angle in which he still gripped his blade.

"I don't know," he whispered. His voice was deceptively controlled as if he were answering a question about something trivial.

I took another wary step forward.

"Why do you still have that out?" I shifted my inquiring finger from the body to the curved blade that clung to Dane's palm.

His fingers clenched around its hilt. "I don't know."

Time seemed to catch up all at once, like a wire pulled tight on a spindle. I rolled my shoulders, snapping away a few irrational thoughts, and stepped briskly forward to examine the body. The man had landed on his front, with his head tilted awkwardly toward the wall.

I'd never seen a dead person before. Not outside of a funeral home, at least. It was different from those I'd witnessed in caskets, who were painted to look like angelic sleeping statues. This man was still warm with his plump skin full of placid blood.

Heavyset, he was round at the middle and had a crown of brown hair that wisped around a shiny bald dome. He wore a black collared shirt and plain gray pants. Scrawled across his right arm was a faded tattoo. It reminded me of a circuit board, covered in parallel lines that angled off and joined together in several small diodes. The design was different from the Jumper's Central Connect tattoos I'd seen.

When I looked back to Dane, he hadn't moved at all—but his eyes were different. He seemed to be gauging my reaction. My gaze drifted to the double-ended blade, still clasped tight to his palm. The same as Jacey's polearm, the center hilt of the weapon was connected to the fleshy tight sinew of his wrist. One of the tapered ends was stained red, dripping its own tiny offering to the growing puddle that pooled around Dane's boots.

"So, what happened? Did he attack you, or..." I didn't know what option two could be, but I left the question open for interpretation.

Dane's frown returned. "It...it happened so fast. I saw him reach for something. I just snapped." His eyes grew wide. "Vivian, we have to go. We can't be seen here with a body."

In a flicker of dancing green light, Dane extended his blade out in front of him. It fizzled and snapped, spitting a protest of sparks as it was consumed into the flesh of his wrist. My hand clasped over my mouth as I watched the weapon vanish. Then he leaned over the body toward me, hastily grabbing my wrist and tugging me forward. Our feet smacked noisily down the long hall as sticky blood clung to the hard textured soles of our boots, leaving a fading red trail behind us.

Together, we fled from the scene, checking every dark corner before stepping onto the neon city street. A buttery thick haze appeared, capturing the colorful light within haunting clouds and masking our escape.

I remained silent the whole way through the Edge Station. Dane kept his eyes forward, sterile but alert. I concluded that he must be in shock and decided it was best to save questions for later. It didn't stop the questions from buzzing inside my own mind, though.

As usual, my hive hummed a furious stream of disorganized protests and theories, and as usual, none of them made sense. *Who was that man? Had he attacked Dane, or had Dane acted out of impulse?*

Seeing Jacey fight had been shocking, but at least, in my own mind, I'd seen the encounter as fair and just. The man from the fiber had been trying to kill me. He'd injured Jacey and likely would have finished him, if not for Daxx.

But this man...he didn't appear to have a weapon. He just looked like a normal guy who'd been waiting outside the elevator, maybe to collect his own batch of glowing mushrooms. He wore no armor. He didn't have tattoos like a Jumper. And now, he was dead, left face down in a puddle of his own blood.

Were the dead avenged here? Did The Channel have its own team of crime scene investigators? It didn't seem likely, as dangerous as Dane and Jacey described it to be. No, this man would likely remain in that long black hallway, stiffening with rigor until another unlucky street goer stumbled across him.

We'd stepped through the threshold of Quadrant Five, and Dane turned to face me. His arms hung limp at his sides, and his face was sallow.

"Dane," I whispered. He avoided my gaze, but I persisted. "What happened back there?"

"I..."

"You what?" I demanded.

He flinched. "I thought...I thought he was going to hurt you."

"What made you think that? Dane, I looked right at him when the elevator doors opened. He was just standing there. What did you—"

His arms were around me, crushing my body tight to his chest. He dropped his cheek to my shoulder, and a long, unfamiliar sound muffled through my hair. He was sobbing. My neck quickly became hot and saturated. A swell of sympathy washed over me.

"Dane, hey. It's okay."

"No, it's not!" he sobbed. His breathing became erratic against my skin, the way mine often did during a panic attack.

Lifting my arms, I gripped him tight. He reminded me of a child who'd just scraped a knee. There was no attempt at control. His nose sniffled and snorted, and his breathing came in sharp gasps, which only made me squeeze him tighter.

"We'll get through this," I whispered into his ear, and I pressed my cheek against his feverishly hot skin. *My Dane. My poor, stupid Dane.*

After a few moments of being cradled in my arms, his breathing gained some semblance of a rhythm. The sputter of his chest calmed, and his sniffles grew fewer. I pressed my lips into the tufts of his hair, feeling the heat radiate from his scalp.

At the sound of my kiss, he tilted his chin just enough so that I could see his face, now blotchy and moist. The skin under his eyes had swollen into fragile pillows, and his emerald irises glistened in crisp contrast.

Gently, I leaned and kissed each of his puffy lids. Then I kissed his lips, and his body melted like honey in my arms. Leading our dance, I deepened the kiss, experimenting with his reaction. He followed my rhythm with whisper-soft skin and a gracious mouth that parted eagerly under my silent command.

I don't know what drove me to kiss him in this way, as if my lips could fix whatever snapped apart inside of him tonight. But as we stood, bathed in the flickering glow of the fluorescent Edge Station sign, I decided that I no longer needed to look for answers or solutions. I just needed Dane. And more than that, I needed Dane to *know* that I needed him.

We returned to the warehouse, hand in hand. Dane requested that we not mention the incident to Gilroy, Jacey, and especially CieCie. I agreed. With all the new complications that emerged just since we'd set out today, our hands were more than full enough. So naturally, we made the decision to keep the man from Quadrant Four a secret. Dane assured me that he wouldn't be missed. Murder on The Channel was common, and fibers were moral dead zones.

Granted, we weren't in the fiber when the incident took place, but we were right outside of one. Dane was confident that the deed would go unnoticed. His steady voice was reassuring, yet the image of the blood-soaked body remained vivid in my uneasy head. I repeatedly pushed the thought back into the deepest recesses of my mind. If I was this traumatized, I couldn't imagine what poor Dane must be going through.

"The door is locked." The handle was unyielding in Dane's hand when we arrived at the warehouse door. He cranked it left, then right but was only met with the sound of shimmying metal.

"Try knocking," I suggested.

With Rhett still creeping about, Gilroy had likely taken extra care to keep the place locked up tight. I smiled humorlessly at the thought of Rhett somehow breaking in. He'd looked plenty tough but not tough enough to win in a fight against Jacey, Gilroy, Daxx, and Dane.

Another image surfaced, this time of Dane poised with his blood-spattered blade drawn. *Was I a psychopath for thinking that he looked dangerously attractive in that horrific image?* I shook the thought away. It couldn't be healthy to romanticize a moment that had likely scarred us both for life. *And yet...*

"Got'damnit! Would y'all just holt yer dang horses?"

Dane was beating on the metal door with the ball of his palm. The handle clicked, and the door parted open. Gilroy's face slid cautiously from the crack. His whiskers twitched like a cat with a whiff of tuna, but a look of relief was painted across his leathery face.

"We don't want none," he shouted, slamming the door.

Dane looked at me and rolled his eyes dramatically before lifting his hand to knock again.

The door slowly eased opened, and Gilroy's face peeked back through the crack. His cheeks were split into a huge smile. "Didn't ya hear? I said we don't want none."

I felt bad for Gilroy. He was clearly in a good mood that I knew Dane wouldn't reciprocate. When Gilroy's playful gaze landed on me, I bit my lip in a deliberate way, trying to silently communicate that the day had not gone smoothly. Gilroy seemed to understand. He nodded at me and opened the door, standing aside so Dane and I could pass.

I kept my focus forward, avoiding any more silent

communication that might give too much away. Gilroy had a knack for reading body language.

It wasn't until we reached the brown leather couch that I realized the reason behind Gilroy's lighthearted mood. The warehouse had been transformed into a colorful junkyard of light and paper decorations. Hundreds of tiny bulbs blinked in alternating patterns, illuminating the branches of Mia's trees and setting the leaves awash with color. From the catwalk hung a line of different shaped paper snowflakes, each dangling from silvery shimmering wires.

"O-M-G! You guys aren't supposed to be here yet!" CieCie's voice squealed. She was waddling from the kitchen with a huge bowl of popcorn held out in her arms. "Gilroy, why'd you unlock the door?"

"Well, dangit, CieCie. I tried to tell 'em we didn't want none. But they was persistent as stray cats." He winked at me, and I feigned a smile.

Dane was standing at my side, but his posture was rigid. I placed a supportive hand on his lower back.

"Why don't you go clean up," I whispered, and as I did, I kicked his blood-stained boot.

He looked down with an expression that slowly transformed from annoyance to panic. The blood hadn't made it to the leather of my own boots, and the red that had stained my soles was worn away. But Dane's toes were completely saturated.

"CieCie, you did a wonderful job," he announced, and his voice was so bright and warm that I had to force my jaw from falling to the floor. "I'm going to go shower. Then, if you'd like, I can cook dinner for your party."

She beamed at him, placing the bowl of popcorn on the coffee table and nodding as fast as a hummingbird.

I was completely astounded by his calm disposition. The

sly fox was back, unruffled and carefully composed. It was so easy for him. I wished it was easy for me, too. Deep down, I knew the distraught boy was still in there, somewhere, waiting to be set free. It pained me—but I was grateful to have been able to get a glimpse of the face underneath the carefully composed mask.

Maybe tonight, I could allow him to crawl under my mask as well. The thought sent a quiver down my spine and a rush of heat to my cheeks.

Dane started toward the catwalk when another familiar voice sounded above. "Back so soon?"

Like a magnet pulled toward its opposite pole, my gaze shot to the catwalk. And there, leaning casually over the rail was Jacey. His jaw was deeply shadowed in a thick stubble, and his raven hair was messy and unkempt, but he looked well. *Better than well.* The feverish sheen had gone from his face, replaced by his usual wide and wolfish grin. I fought the urge to run to him for fear that I'd either hug him or hit him—or both.

Dane flashed up the stairs and brushed dismissively past Jacey in a way that no one could ignore. I bit my lip, waiting for confrontation, but none came. Instead, Jacey shrugged and made his way, a bit wobbly, I noted, down the steps. When he reached the bottom, his blue eyes captured mine, almost as if he'd been waiting to see me. A smile still played on the edge of his lips.

"What's wrong with tall, lanky, and loathsome?" he asked, nodding toward Dane's room.

I shook my head and bugged my eyes, but Jacey wasn't as keen on my silent communication as Gilroy was. He stared at me like a confused puppy who didn't understand why they'd just been bopped on the nose with a newspaper.

Frustrated, I jabbed a sharp finger at Dane's cubicle, then

placed it over my lips in a *shhh* motion. He seemed to understand.

"Later?" he asked, hopeful.

I nodded, though I knew I wouldn't be able to tell him everything that had happened. Not that I didn't have plenty of my own to tell.

The bottle cap in my pocket was practically burning a hole through the denim. I wanted to hand it back to Jacey right then, but I quickly realized that he wasn't wearing his usual black jeans. They'd been replaced by baggy gray sweatpants and a white tee shirt that clung to his muscles like saran wrap. No pockets and definitely nowhere to hide the bottle cap inconspicuously. I could see everything—and I made a conscious effort not to look at the "everything" he had out on display.

What mattered was that he was alive and looking more like himself. Everything about him seemed calmer and healthier, even with his forearm still bound in a tight bandage. That reminded me—

"I have the mushrooms," I twisted to Gilroy, who had replaced Dane behind the couch.

The wolfish grin reappeared on Jacey's lips as I unbuckled the bag from my hip. "See? Good investment, right?"

"Yes, actually," I admitted. The bag had definitely made the trip much easier. We may have never found our way out of the blackened fiber without it. I handed the bag to Gilroy, and as I did, I hoped like hell that I'd get it back. It was beginning to grow on me.

"Thank ya, Viv'yan. I couldn't get ahold of my arms dealer, but I'm gonna call 'em again here in a few. He's a good buddy 'o mine. Names Bill Rowe. Good man, Bill is. But he can get 'imself lost in a bottle erry now an then. I remember this one time..."

Gilroy droned on, but I was no longer listening to his story. My mind drifted back to its newest landing pad—the body, still out there, lying face down and unnaturally still.

Maybe it was just morbid curiosity, but I wondered what would happen to him. Where did The Channel dispose of bodies? Did he have a family? Would someone miss him tonight? As hard as I tried, I couldn't get the thought of the man —now nothing more than a cold corpse—out of my head. My stomach burned with the pressure of a lead weight. Up until now, I'd handled everything so well. Too well, maybe.

Gilroy cackled. It sounded like he'd just concluded the punch line of his story so I compiled my face and laughed with him. *See, I could be a sly fox, too.* Sly enough for Gilroy, at least.

When I looked at Jacey, his head was low, closely analyzing my expression. His hypnotic eyes probed below my skin, digging and poking and rooting under my mask. *Shit.* I was the pack mule of secrets, and none of them were mine to tell. I needed to do something else. Something that would keep my mind off the elevator man.

"Let me help!" I called out to CieCie. She was seated on the couch with a long spool of silver wire and the massive bowl of popcorn.

Her face lit up. "Yay! We'll get done twice as fast if we both start on opposite ends. Then you can help me hang them." She picked up a piece of popcorn and stabbed it with the sharp end of the wire, sliding the kernel to the middle of the unspooled spindle.

I smiled as I watched her, but from my peripheral vision, I could see Jacey was still staring. He knew something was up. And he wasn't going to be as easy to shake as CieCie. My best bet was to keep talking about other things until Dane returned.

"I used to make popcorn garland with my mother," I

explained, walking to the couch and starting on my end of the spool.

CieCie asked a million and one questions about Christmas on Earth, and I was grateful. She didn't allow for a single moment of silent tension. From mistletoes to gingerbread houses, I covered all the basics. CieCie was especially interested in the big red man who broke into everyone's house once a year. The concept had never come off as strange to me until I explained it out loud.

"And he doesn't take anything?"

"No, he only leaves things. Gifts. For good children."

"And what about bad children?"

"The bad kids get coal in their stockings."

"Stockings? Like pantyhose?"

"Um...no. More like socks."

"And he puts...coal in them? To ruin them?"

"No," I laughed. "For the children to find in the morning."

"But what are they supposed to do with the coal? Burn it?"

"I think it's more of a symbolic thing. The children look in their stockings expecting to find toys, and instead they only find coal."

"That sounds kind of mean."

"I don't think anyone actually gets coal in their stockings. It's just something that parents tell their children to make them behave."

"Oh. That makes sense. So what about the cookies? I did the math this morning, and something isn't adding up, Vivian. There are an estimated 500 million houses on Earth. If he only ate one cookie per house and only the houses with children, he would still be eating 396 million cookies. How does he eat all of them?"

By the time our long wire was completely beaded with popcorn kernels, Dane had returned in a fresh set of clothes. I'd expected to see him in something more casual, but he was dressed in black jeans, boots, and an armored black jacket with a fur-lined hood that rested on his back. I caught myself digging my teeth into my bottom lip as he strolled down the metal stairs. Hell, he looked good, even if he was way overdressed for the party.

"I put a fresh set of clothes on my bed for you," he winked once he reached the warehouse floor. "I know how you like to steal my clothes."

His eyes shot to Jacey, and his brow furrowed for only a fraction of a second before he started toward the kitchen. There was clearly some one-sided pissing contest taking place in Dane's head, and I wished that he would knock it off.

I understood that he was still sore at Jacey for leaving after the dimension twenty-seven mission and today surely resurrected a few harrowing memories. But the sour-puss attitude hadn't started until he'd kissed me. *This couldn't possibly be jealousy, could it?* Even if it was, being pissy to Jacey wasn't going to make anyone's life easier.

I thought about going to the kitchen to reassure him. Maybe I could sneak a kiss, and he'd lighten up. But first, I needed to change. My clothes hung heavy on my body, and my gray armored jacket was beginning to make me sweat. How did they wash clothes on The Channel? This would be my second day wearing this outfit. I'd have to ask Dane later.

Jacey volunteered to help CieCie hang the popcorn garland so I could take a shower. I gathered the clothes Dane set out for me—a baggy black V neck and navy boxers—and retrieved a towel from the locker beside the bathroom.

As I undressed, I realized that Daxx was still in the pocket of my jeans, along with the tiny shred of paper that Rhett dropped. "I'm just showering. Don't come out until I give you back to Jacey," I whispered as I removed them. A hushed purr vibrated through my hand, then stopped. He must have heard me.

I placed the cap and paper on top of my dirty socks, deciding that it would be easier to just put them back on and tuck Daxx and the paper inside, rather than trying to hide them in my waistband. Especially since Dane had a tendency to put his fingers in that general area.

The thought was so intriguing that it followed me into the shower, and it caused me to do things I wouldn't normally think to do. I stole a razer from the ledge—not caring which one of the boys it belonged to—and shaved my legs twice. I even bent and shaved the single irritating hair that grew from each of my big toes. *Did men look down here?* I wasn't willing to risk it.

My body wash choices were limited to a near-empty bottle of "Cotton Candy Dreams" and one that was just called "Oak." The smell reminded me of a used car dealership, but I didn't want to use up CieCie's cotton candy soap so I lathered my hands and dealershipped every inch of my body. At least I was clean. That was the important part. Not that I was hoping anything would happen tonight...but if it did, I'd rather be prepared.

I quickly rinsed, dried, dressed, and brushed my fingers through my damp hair. Hastily, I pulled on my socks and tucked Daxx and the drawing in the band. I'd need to return Daxx to Jacey before Dane and I went to bed. *Dane and I.* I liked the way that sounded.

Once I was satisfied with myself, I skipped downstairs. Cleaning away the crud dramatically lifted my mood, and I no longer thought about the man from the elevator. Instead, I met Dane just as he was setting the table and caught him from behind with my arms around his hips. He stiffened for a moment but relaxed as soon as he realized it was me.

"I was wondering what was taking you so long." He looked me up and down, clearly pleased.

"Thanks for the clothes. You're right. They do look better on me," I teased with a twirl.

"No need to thank me. I enjoy seeing you in them."

I was relieved to see him behaving more like himself. He took a quick glance around and planted a kiss on my forehead. Yes, much more like himself. Things were finally feeling normal again.

"Did you use my body wash?" he asked as he pulled away.

Ooops. Guilty. I batted my eyelashes innocently. No wonder the smell was so familiar. It was the scent that clung to his jacket on the night I'd arrived at The Channel. Somehow, that night seemed so far away.

"I think I used your razer, too," I confessed.

A flicker of amusement lightened his face. "Use anything you need while you're here, Viv." The words carried more intensity than the sentence warranted. His voice made my skin crawl in bizarre ways.

"Maybe I will," I called over my shoulder as I sashayed out of the kitchen, totally aware of the green eyes that escorted me out. *This was fun.*

Jacey and CieCie finished hanging the popcorn garland and moved on to gingerbread decorating. Only there were no real gingerbread men to decorate so CieCie cut out several people-shaped cardboard cookies. She and Jacey spread them across the makeshift coffee table along with tons of colorful wire clippings, cloth scraps, and buttons. Jacey carefully glued a wire mouth to his gingerbread cutout, while CieCie created an intricate pink fabric skirt.

"Jacey! Your ginger-man is frowny!" she cried. Jacey eyed his creation with confusion. "Ginger-men can't be frowny!

They must be happy!" She twisted to me. "Tell him, Vivian! You're the Christmas expert."

"She's right, Jacey," I teased. "You're going to have to turn that frown upside down."

I sat beside him to examine his work. The little man had lopsided button eyes and a sad curved wire for a mouth. "Here," I said, leaning over Jacey's knees and tilting the corners of the mouth up. "Now he's happy."

Jacey watched me with an unfathomable expression. I picked up his gingerbread man and held it beside his head. Their faces were like a pair of Greek theater masks. I couldn't help but laugh at Jacey's frown. This seemed to confuse him even more.

"Smile, damn it!" I laughed, punching him playfully in the shoulder of his unbound arm. After a moment, he let out a few amused nose exhales, which was enough for me.

"Dinner is ready," Dane called.

His smile was the one I was most eager to see. But as I turned, I realized with disappointment that his heavy brows had returned, and he scowled at Jacey from across the warehouse. *This childish attitude had to stop.*

I was grateful when Gilroy came to the table, full of stories about his youth. Apparently, he'd been born on Mercantile dimension but moved to The Channel after The Five noticed his proficient technology skills. He told us stories about the food his Mammy used to cook—beans and capperloin with roast fisswert and stolen casks of fozzockle.

Every now and then, I'd exchange glances with Dane. He smiled briskly, but he was always the first to release the gaze. I was also aware of Jacey's burning stare, which alternated between Dane and I. Our strange behavior clearly hadn't gone unnoticed. Which is why I wasn't surprised when Jacey asked me to meet him in his room as Dane and CieCie cleared the dinner dishes. Dane's shoulder's stiffened to his ears, but I ignored him and followed Jacey anyway. When we stepped into his room, he closed the door behind him.

"You still have my boy?"

"If you mean your *voul beast*," I enunciated the words mockingly, "then yes. I do. And before I give him to you, you should be aware that he was a holy terror."

Jacey looked surprised by this news. I pulled the bottle cap from my sock.

"Your *boy* decided to come out right when Dane and I got into the dimension one fiber."

"Did he..."

"No. He didn't. It was pitch black, thankfully. I was able to get away from Dane long enough to get him back into his cap, but it was a close call," I added and dropped the cap into Jacey's palm.

The moment the metal made contact with his skin, a chill passed down my spine. It was like a hairline crack had formed in the dam of my consciousness. A few seeping buzzes whispered threats into my ears. At the forefront of their grievances, the image of Dane returned. This time, it wasn't his attractive green eyes that my memories were drawn to. It was the way he stood when I stepped out of the elevator. He'd looked like he was waiting for someone else to appear.

"You feel it, too."

"What?" I asked frantically. *Had Jacey somehow seen into my thoughts?*

"When Daxx transfers power. I can always sense when he's close."

Relief rolled through me. "Yeah, I guess now that you mention it, I do. No wonder you were all piss and vinegar when we got back today. And here I thought you were just happy to see us."

"I was happy to see you," he argued. He looked mad and that reminded me of something else important.

"Did Gilroy tell you about Rhett?"

"Yeah," Jacey sighed. "I'm sorry about that, Vivian. Rhett's a weirdo, but I don't think he'd try to attack any of us. Honestly, I think Gilroy is wrong. There's definitely an informant, I'm certain of that. But I don't think it's Rhett."

"That's impossible," I protested. "How else would Mr. Rivera know where I'm staying?"

His face crumpled. "I'm not sure," he admitted. "But we should be careful. I suspect that someone is spying for Mr. Corporate Big-Wig."

"Well, there's more you should know."

This piqued his interest.

"Dane and I saw Rhett today on his bike, over on Quadrant Four. When he sped away, he dropped something. A piece of paper."

I bent down again, pulled the shred from my sock, and handed it to Jacey. His hardened expression gave nothing away as he stared at the wolf-shaped sketch. There was something he wasn't saying. I could tell by the stiff set of his jaw.

Just before I was about to question him further, Dane appeared at the door. He didn't have to knock for us to sense his arrival. Fury radiated from his eyes like bullets.

"I have more to talk to you about. Later," I whispered. I turned and exited the room.

Dane stood aside to let me pass. I stopped in my tracks when I didn't hear his footsteps following behind me. He stood frozen, locked on Jacey who tossed the silver bottle cap like a coin. Thankfully, Jacey didn't seem to notice him.

"Dane," I called, "come on. CieCie will be waiting."

He hesitated for a moment, watching Jacey with predatory eyes before he turned and followed me down the catwalk. My blood boiled the entire way to the warehouse floor. I quickly surveyed the area—no CieCie, no Gilroy. I whirled on Dane.

"Will you cool your fucking attitude?"

"Excuse me?" he said, astounded.

"You heard me, Dane! Stop acting like...like an adolescent boy."

His expression became guarded. "What did he want you up there for?"

"He wanted to know what was wrong with *you!*" I shouted. "If you don't want to tell everyone the truth about what happened today, maybe you should at least try to act normal. Jacey knows that something is up. So, please stop putting me in a situation where I'm forced to continuously lie. If you haven't noticed, I'm not very good at it."

The tension in his shoulders released. "I'm sorry. I guess I'm just on edge."

Before I could respond, CieCie's shrill voice echoed through the warehouse. "Storytime! Everyone meet at the trees!"

It was clear that CieCie and Gilroy were the only ones still excited about the Christmas party. We all sat cross-legged around the brightly decorated tree, and I did my best to play along. Especially since Jacey and Dane wouldn't stop exchanging scornful glances. *Were all boys this difficult?* I'd never had brothers so I couldn't be sure.

"Vivian, why don't you start!" CieCie suggested. I hadn't been listening.

"Start what?"

"Storytime, of course!" she chided. "Gilroy shared his childhood over dinner. Tell us something fun from when you were a kid. Bonus points if it's a Christmas story!"

I didn't like this activity. None of my stories were fun and exciting. I didn't come from a dimension with interesting creatures or freakishly advanced technology. After a moment of thinking, I decided on something that was at least happy, even if it wasn't particularly entertaining.

"Okay, here's one. When I was around ten years old, my mother had the brilliant idea that we'd make handmade Christmas gifts for all our friends and family. I wanted to make clay bowls, and since my mom worked for a craft store at the time, she had everything I needed to make them.

"That night, I spent hours sculpting all these different bowls and vases. Mom said we could paint them after they baked solid in the kiln so I stayed up extra late to see the finished creations...but when she opened the oven door, they'd all melted, completely flat."

The memory made me laugh. "My poor mom. She looked more mortified than I'd ever seen her. We ended up painting the flat clay disks anyway, and we told everyone that they were platters. No one knew any different. It was a secret joke between Mom and I." A single tear rushed hot down my cheek. *Damnit. Not now.*

I brushed it away quickly but not quick enough. Jacey was watching. He reached from somewhere behind him and pulled out his black scarf. It smelled of fresh linen. I took it graciously and blotted my eyes.

"Dane's turn!" CieCie announced. He straightened next to me.

"Eh, I'm not really in the mood tonight, CieCie. Next time, okay?"

I nudged his shoulder hard, and he shot me an angry glance. "Don't be a party pooper," I whispered. It was a command. CieCie deserved more than his sour-puss mood.

He sighed heavily, composing a smile that didn't meet his eyes. "Okay," he conceded. "Well, you all know I'm originally from Earth dimension. And my dad—man, was he a hardass after Mom died."

This was the first I'd heard about Dane's mother, aside from his flip-flop story yesterday. Pity swelled in me, but Dane didn't linger on the topic.

"When I was a kid, I use to fuck around, just to get under his skin. You know. Girls sneaking through my window. Coming home drunk. The works. My drunk of an older brother used to rat me out, and I hated him for it." His face split into a huge toothy grin.

I tried to picture it—Dane as a rebellious teen. It wasn't hard to imagine.

"So one time when I was seventeen, Dad had to go off on this business trip. I figured he'd be gone a while, and my brother was off at college or something. Fuck if I know. Anyway, I decided to throw a house party while they were gone. Usually, when Dad left, he'd be gone for weeks at a time so I figured I'd have everything cleaned before he got back.

"That morning, my buddies and I talked some homeless guy into buying us a bunch of bottles in exchange for a pack of cigarettes. We invited everyone we knew, and apparently, they all invited people, too. Long story short, the house was packed —and Dad's a wealthy guy so our place was huge and full of expensive shit. Everyone was packed in like sardines. People started getting drunk, and shit started breaking. The TV, whiskey glasses, plates, pictures on the walls—they ripped the place apart."

His eyes grew intense. "Then Dad shows up out of nowhere. His flight had been rescheduled. He walks in and starts yelling, and all these kids are climbing over each other like rats. They poured out of every door and window of the house so damn fast. I blinked, and everyone was gone. Just me and Dad."

Everyone held their breaths, waiting for the funny part of the story to come.

Dane put his head down, and his hair fell in a dark curtain over his forehead. "Dad sent me off to join the military after that. My brother moved on to be his little prodigy. I guess every family has their bad kid."

No one spoke. I stared at Dane, completely dumbfounded. Way to kill the buzz. He clearly didn't listen to the rules of storytime. Even Gilroy seemed lost for words as he looked around the room aimlessly.

CieCie cleared her throat after a moment. "Okay! Thanks, Dane...for sharing. Um...Jacey, how about you next?"

Jacey seemed just as irked as I was. His incredulous eyes lingered on Dane for a moment longer before he broke away and started his own story. As he did, Dane shot me a quick smile before directing his focus to his bootstrings. He mindlessly fumbled with them as Jacey began.

"Well, you guys already know that I don't have a lot of childhood memories. Gilroy took me in pretty young. I've got a lot of stories about him," he and Gilroy exchanged a quick knowing smile, "but he'd probably kick my ass if I told any of those."

"You bet'cher ass I would."

Everyone laughed in unison, aside from Dane who was still playing with his boot strings. I nudged him on the shoulder. He nudged me back. *What did that mean?*

"So, instead of a childhood story, I'll share one of CieCie's favorites."

Her face lit up.

"Several months ago, I got sent to Earth dimension for a quick eval. Nothing big. I just needed to take a sample from the Atlantic Ocean to compare with the samples that another Jumper brought back from the Pacific. Anyway, that part isn't important." He winked at CieCie, and she giggled, clearly familiar with the plot of the tale.

"While I was there, I picked up a few stuffed animals for CieCie. And stupid me, I forgot to bring a bag. So there I was, walking through the Earth dimension fiber—I shit you not, one of the most dangerous fibers you could cross through—with a rainbow unicorn, a pink cat, and a fucking penguin in my arms."

No wonder Jacey was so adamant about me carrying a bag. I laughed out loud, picturing the scene in my head. CieCie and Gilroy joined in. Dane stayed quiet. I nudged him again. He nudged back. *What was his problem?*

"So, this guy—a real badass looking dude—comes walking up to me with his weapon drawn. It was this toothpicky rapier-looking thing. He tells me to hand over the unicorn. I thought he was joking at first, but he points his little twig at me—and that, of course, sets me off. I end up kicking this fucker's ass with my polearm in one hand and an armful of toys in the other."

"And I love you for it!" CieCie erupted into giggles.

He smiled at her with a heart-melting big-brother grin that I envied. I'd always wanted a brother as a kid. And Jacey was as sweet as a brother could be.

"That was right around the time that you got back, right?"

Our shocked eyes all shot to Dane. His voice was smug, and his jaw was tight.

Where was he going with this? I gave him another nudge, much harder this time. He ignored me.

"You know," he snarled. "After you abandoned us?"

Jacey shot to his feet. His chest puffed wide as he loomed over Dane. No one else dared to move. Dane's expression was indifferent, gazing at Jacey with calm composure.

I wanted to intervene, but no words would come out. *Why*

was he doing this?

Jacey's shadow enveloped Dane's entire body. "If you have something to fucking say to me, you better stand the fuck up and say it like a man."

Even with his arm bound in gauze, Jacey was terrifying. I was quite certain he could snap Dane in half, even without his good arm.

I willed Dane not to react, but to my disgust, he stood with a slow casualness that caused my blood to run cold. He leveled his gaze with Jacey's, and the faint trace of a smile formed at the corners of his lips.

Were they going to fight? I looked desperately to Gilroy, but he seemed as much at a loss as I was.

"Well?" Jacey hissed.

I held my breath.

Dane folded his arms over his chest in an arrogant manner. He clearly didn't think Jacey would hit him. I wasn't so sure.

"You think you're invincible," Dane said evenly, threateningly.

In response, Jacey held up his bound arm. "Clearly, I'm not."

Dane shook his head. His grin widened. "No, Jacey, see— you always just assume you can get away with anything. You can bail on us, and I'll clean up the mess. You can bring another civilian to The Channel—" He shot a quick glance at me. "— and I'll clean up that mess, too. Then you go and actually get yourself hurt—and look. Here I am cleaning up your mess *again.*"

Jacey leaned heavily on one hip. Annoyance tinged his brows.

"And now—now I've found something that makes me happy, and you're trying to take that, too."

The frown vanished from Jacey's face in an instant. "You

can't be serious. Is this about Vivian?"

He spoke my name as if it were a bad word. As if I weren't sitting less than three feet away. Dane let out a breathy chuckle but didn't respond.

"Un-fucking-believable," Jacey shouted. "Dane? Hey buddy? Newsflash—but Vivian doesn't belong to you. She has a home and a family. She's leaving as soon as we make sure she'll be safe."

Dane scowled, but Jacey continued.

"I don't know what the hell is going on in your hormone-filled little pea-brain, but just because there's a pretty girl in the house, it doesn't mean you get to just...lay claim on her."

The warehouse fell into silence. I wanted to jump off the roof. But Jacey's words were sobering, and maybe sobriety is what we all needed.

I would be leaving soon, and Dane would be nothing more than a bittersweet memory. This was something I could live with, even though it hurt—but it wouldn't destroy me entirely. I could move forward. I would be okay. Dane, on the other hand, I wasn't sure. He was made of flags in every shade of crimson red, and this rapid attachment he'd formed to me was becoming dangerous.

CieCie jumped between them, tears streaming down her face. "No fighting! No more fighting!" she cried. "This was supposed to be fun! You're ruining it. Both of you." She turned on her heel and darted to the couch, where she buried her face in the cushion. Poor CieCie. She didn't deserve this.

The boys broke off after CieCie's intervention. Gilroy and I sat with her on the couch, allowing her to share the story she'd been saving until it was her turn. Tears dared to brim my eyes, and I found myself burying my nose into Jacey's scarf every few minutes. This wasn't fair.

After her story was over, Gilroy walked across the warehouse to a small record player that he'd set up for the party. He placed the needle onto the spinning black vinyl, and Elvis's voice sang about a blue Christmas. This gave me an idea.

I took CieCie's tiny hands into mine and pulled her to the center of the warehouse. Gracelessly, I started dancing. I wiggled my hips, jumped from foot to foot, shimmied left, then shimmied right. Her eyes were wide and confused, but she quickly understood the game and began following my improvisational moves. Gilroy turned the music up, and a smile curled up under his peppered mustache.

The track switched to a faster beat—"Santa Claus is Comin' to Town." I switched my moves to match the faster tempo, and we both giggled hysterically as we jumped, swayed, and bumped into each other. The previous stress of the night had been washed away. CieCie was smiling and laughing like an overjoyed child and in that moment, nothing else mattered.

I grabbed her hands and pulled them up, down, and all around. Her arms were loose noodles in my hands, following my lead. By the time the song ended, both of us were breathless. I put my hands on my knees, sucking in deep breaths with a splitting smile still on my face. The night may not have been all good, but this made up for all the tension.

As I stood straight again, I felt a hand on my shoulder.

"Dane," I gasped, whirling around. "You scared me. What are you—"

Silently, he took my hand and snaked his arm around my waist. He pulled me close as the opening notes of "Evolution Once Again" started to play from his small portable speaker that sat beside the record player.

There was a fluid grace to his movement that surprised me. He wasn't improvising. This was a dance—a real dance. With every step, he tugged and manipulated my body with ease, and I followed along with his tender grasp, trusting in his sure footing. With a silent finesse, he dipped me low, nearly to the ground, then lifted me back into his arms, where he snared me in his emerald gaze. His expression was heavy and tired, but he smiled in a way that made my chest sore.

"I know I can't keep you." His voice was like silk against my cheek. He twirled me out in a long and graceful arc that left me gasping. When he reigned my body back into his arms, his eyes were closed. "But your presence here is all that I am, for however long that you stay."

My body tipped back once more. I let myself fall back against his sturdy forearm as the words radiated through my heart. It wasn't fair that every word for love had already been sculpted. I needed a new word. One that hadn't yet been uttered in any dimension where the fingers of humanity touched.

Dane knew pain the way that I knew pain. And he knew love the way I dreamed of knowing love. But no amount of love was enough to make me forget the home I'd left behind, and I was trapped with an inferno of indescribable emotions that terrified me more than anything ever had.

Dane's neck craned, and he placed his lips softly on mine. A swirl of panicked thoughts cycloned through my head, but when my gaze shot to where CieCie and Gilroy had been, only the record player and tiny speaker remained. I refocused on Dane. He hadn't moved, lips maintaining feather-soft contact but never advancing into the flow of a kiss.

He murmured a bittersweet vow against the pink petals of my skin. "Just for now is long enough."

20

THE BAD KID

The warehouse was quiet, and the lights were dimmed low. I sat on one of the leather couches, tucked warm under the comfortable weight of Dane's arm, while we watched the alternating flicker of the light splashed trees. For the time being, I was content in the mutual understanding that our days were limited, and I was determined to enjoy each moment. *Just for now is long enough.*

I nuzzled my head into Dane's shoulder, and he kissed the top of my head.

After a few moments, Jacey sauntered down the stairs.

"CieCie is asleep," he reported, plopping hard on the couch opposite of us.

I adjusted myself, but Dane dug his fingers into my shoulder and held me in place. Jacey seemed unphased by the sight of us together so I settled back into his arms—which was coincidentally exactly where I wanted to be. We were only human. At least we could enjoy the time while we had it. *Just for now.*

"Some night," Jacey remarked.

Dane nodded. "Yep."

"At least CieCie seemed to enjoy herself. For the most part," Jacey added.

Dane's muscles tightened under me. I poked his thigh hard with my index finger. *Knock it off. He's just making small talk.*

Jacey tipped his head back and took a deep breath. For several moments, the room was peacefully quiet. The ambiance made my own eyelids grow heavy. It had been quite a day. Too long for my liking.

Jacey sat back up slowly. As he did, I realized his spine stiffened just slightly, and there was a change in the arch of his eyebrows. He seemed troubled with something, though nothing had happened in the last few minutes to cause it.

"Gilroy said that Bill didn't pick up his call today."

"Yeah, he said that already," Dane answered curtly.

Jacey ran his fingers through his raven hair. "He tried again a few minutes ago. No answer at Bill's place."

"Maybe he's out," Dane suggested.

"Yeah, that's what I said, too," Jacey replied, his face shaded with confusion. "Which is why Gilroy called Larry. He said he hasn't heard back from Bill all day. It kind of puts a damper on our plans of getting my CC inked this week."

I nestled my head into Dane's arm again. More time together. Not something either of us would object to. But even with the news, Dane's body remained tight under my weight. I wished he would lighten up. This wasn't bad news for either of us, even if it was bad news for Jacey.

"I think I'm going to pop over there tomorrow, if Bill hasn't turned up by then," Jacey continued. "He's a drunk, for sure, but it's not like him to ignore calls from Larry."

My head fell against the couch cushion as Dane sat up and pulled his arm from my shoulder. He straightened his spine and met Jacey's confused gaze.

"That's really stupid, Jace." His voice was even but deathly firm. "You're injured. You need to stay here."

"I'll be fine."

I collapsed, startled into the hollow space on the couch beside me as Dane jumped to his feet. *Don't fight. Not again.*

"See, there you fucking go. Poking your nose where it doesn't belong. Is it so hard for you to just keep yourself out of trouble?" There was an accusing ring to Dane's voice.

Even Jacey was visibly confused by the switch, leaning forward to the edge of his seat. "Dane, it's just over at West L-5. I need to get the putocrypes over there before they dry out. Larry can at least begin processing them until Bill—"

Dane's hand slammed against the metal table. The sound echoed through the warehouse like a crack of thunder.

"Dane!" I gasped.

He ignored me. "Fuck you, Jacey."

Our jaws fell in unison, but Dane wasn't finished. "Do what you want, as usual. I don't give a fuck anymore." He turned on his heels and raced noisily up the stairs.

Jacey looked like he had just been slapped. "What the hell is his problem?" he gasped, glaring at me, as if I was in on the secret.

"I have no idea," I answered, and this time it was true. Dane's sudden anger was popping like a breaker box. But if anyone could calm him down, I knew it was me. "I'll go talk to him."

When I reached Dane's room, he was shoving clothes into a bag. Cautiously, I stepped through the door with lead-heavy heels.

"What are you doing?" I whispered. My chest pounded, and my bees swarmed in a hysterical frenzy.

He zipped his bag loudly shut without looking at me. "Leaving."

"Why?" I didn't recognize my voice. It was cut off, deprived of oxygen.

Dane turned, slinging the bag over his shoulders, and captured me in a cold stare. "I just need to go."

Every syllable was a needle in my chest. After everything that happened today, he was leaving? *No.* I had to stop this. Words fell from my mouth in no particular grace.

"Dane...I'm sorry. I mean, for tonight. I'm sorry you're hurting. I know this is hard. It's hard for me, too! I've never felt anything...I mean, I don't know how to handle it all. I just know that...I really do love you. Dane. Please."

I stacked the sentences like a barricade. I didn't need any of them to make sense. I just needed one of the estranged combinations to stop his feet. We could talk this through. Whatever was going on with him, I was willing to help him through it. I was willing to do anything, just to keep him here with me.

For a moment that passed with the friction of an eon, he stared blindly, straight through my body with painfully torn emerald eyes that grew glassier and glassier. *Please, Dane.*

His voice was no more than a strained whisper. "Let me go, Vivian."

Those four words split the ground under my feet and swallowed me up. Dane brushed past without even sparing a glance in my direction, and I watched helplessly as he stalked down the stairs.

At the bottom, Jacey waited for him with balled fists. "Man, what's your deal!" he demanded.

Dane pushed past with a dismissive snort.

"Hey!" Jacey shouted. "I'm talking to you!"

The warehouse door creaked open, then slammed shut. Dane was gone.

The room cycloned in violent circles. My hive had been

hit, dead impact with a baseball bat. It bounced around my skull, unleashing a flood of darkness.

Why?

Why was he like this?

Where was he going?

When would he be back?

Damn it!

We'd been okay—better than okay! We danced and smiled. He said "for now" was long enough, and now he was running? *Running from who? Me?*

My knees hit metal, and I crumpled to the floor like a paper flower. *Was this all my fault? Had I ruined the possibility of "us?"* I heard a sound like a slow roar of thunder, and the catwalk buzzed against my face.

"Come here." Jacey wrapped a single arm around my torso and used his entire body to lift me from the floor before I could protest.

"Hold onto my arm. Come on, I've got you."

I closed my eyes, and in a flash, I was in Jacey's room. He dropped me clumsily onto the bed, and I rolled into his unfamiliar blankets. They were rough and scratchy against my cheek. Not like Dane's sheets, which held his warm oaky scent. But they did smell like something...

"Why does your bed smell like cotton candy?" I murmured, mindlessly focusing on anything that might ground me.

Jacey was pulling Daxx's bottle cap from his pocket. "Uhhh...it's probably from my body wash. Why?"

I snorted. So, Jacey was the Cotton Candy Dreamer. That figured.

"No reason," I breathed and closed my eyes again. My white flag was in the air. I didn't want to exist anymore. None of Jacey's movements phased me as he bumbled noisily around the room. He could have been shooting heroin, and I wouldn't have lifted my head.

Just as I began to drift, a weight pressed on my back. *Hell no!* I opened my mouth, ready to call Jacey every dirty word for pervert that I knew, when I realized that it wasn't him who crawled into bed with me.

"Should haaave allowed meee to vinish him offfff."

"Shoosh," I murmured. Daxx settled like an oversized house cat on my back. The pressure was nice, like my weighted blanket back home.

Drowsily, I opened my eyes. Jacey was on the floor beside the bed, his arms folded on the mattress, and his chin rested on his uninjured forearm. His heavy gaze was locked intently on me.

"If you're expecting me to do a backflip, you're going to be severely disappointed," I grumbled.

The wolfish grin reappeared, and he slowly blinked.

"What are you smiling about?" I whispered. "Don't tell me you've fallen in love with me, too."

Jacey snorted loudly and buried his face into his arms. "Not a chance," he said gruffly.

I believed him.

Calm waves washed over me. The sensation brought me back to the beach—the way the water laps your toes when you stand at the shore. The world was falling away around me, replacing the scene with a white serenity that controlled my breathing into a perfectly synchronized rhythm. I couldn't remember why I'd been upset before. Everything here was quiet and perfect, just the way an addict might describe the perfect high.

"See why I need him?" Jacey whispered dreamily.

"Hmmm?" I opened my eyes and found a clean white space, wiped of all fear and anxiety. Jacey was there, glassy eyes dressed in the finest satin blue. Daxx purred heavily on my back.

"Daxx," Jacey whispered. Dark lashes splayed out like curtains as his eyes closed softly. "He takes me here. When the world is falling around me, I always have a place to fall. You're like me." The words shimmered in the soft white light of the void.

Clarity. We were the same, Jacey and I. Two souls torn from the same tattered cloth and left to cope with our own mental hive.

I reached out and placed a hand on his wrist, but he didn't open his eyes. This was a high that he knew how to fully submit himself to. He was here, yet so far away and at peace with the world. A dream-void sailor lost in the sea of his mind. I wanted to learn how to let go, too.

"Where did Daxx come from?" I whispered.

"I stole him."

The swift answer didn't surprise me, but that may have just been Daxx's influence on my emotions. Or maybe it was because somewhere deep within my consciousness, I already knew. I smiled, though I wasn't sure why.

"From Rhett?"

"Yes."

Daxx purred harder. I gripped my sobriety just enough to keep my thoughts orderly.

"You were right then. Rhett isn't the informant."

"No."

"Does he know you stole Daxx?"

"He's speculated. But no."

A cold nose touched my ear. This didn't startle me either. For some inexplicable reason, I expected it. "I am content heeeere," Daxx hissed smoothly, and his response sent me nuzzling into the blanket.

A subtle buzz released from Jacey's nose. I opened my eyes to find his lips puffed out with each even breath, and his eyelids draped like lavender petals, peaceful in this void. The intoxicating calm was too much as the heat of his breath whispered against my skin. I closed my eyes, fully submitting to the tranquility and allowed Daxx to take hold of my mind along with everything that swam within it.

That night, I didn't dream of a dark-cloaked figure. Instead, the walls of my consciousness were clean and white, bathed in a warm light that reminded me of the way the early morning sun danced on my bedroom wall back home.

I woke to the sound of clicking metal. Clicking, clicking, clicking. Groggily, I opened my eyes, determined to find the annoying sound. Jacey was tightening a belt around his hips. Clicking, clicking, clicking as he cranked the metal buckle tight. He twisted abruptly at the sound of my yawn.

"Sorry."

"For what?" I asked, sitting up on my elbows.

"Waking you. I need to get over to Bill's place. His partner still hasn't heard from him, and everyone's getting worried."

"Can I come?" I didn't want him to go off on his own. And I definitely didn't want to sit around all day, replaying the events of last night through my head.

He shrugged. "If you want. CieCie washed your clothes this morning. They're on Dane's bed."

His expression darkened. I could tell that he immediately regretted saying the name, but I pretended not to notice as I started for the door.

"Thanks. I'll be down in just a few. Wait for me?"

He nodded and kneeled to lace his boots.

THE CHANNEL   333

When I reached Dane's room, I forced my gaze away from his empty clothing rack. *He'd be back.* I had to believe that he would. My clothes were stacked in a neat pile at the foot of the bed. There was something unfamiliar on top—a red hair tie. Sweet CieCie thought of everything. With my pile in hand, I passed Jacey on my way to the bathroom.

"I know this is kind of a shitty thing to bring up," he said, stopping me with a hand, "but Dane is the cook of the house. We're gonna have to grab something on the street."

"Sounds fine to me," I murmured, then brisked into the bathroom. There was no time for a shower so I settled for a few quick splashes of cold water on my face. I dressed in my white kevlar, black moto jeans, and gray jacket, and pulled my hair into a messy bun.

Dane's discarded clothes still lay in a heap on the floor. I decided to leave them there. I didn't want to look at them anymore. A lone little bee buzzed in my ear.

He's not coming back.

I shooed it away.

Jacey was waiting on the couch for me when I made my way downstairs. CieCie sat on the opposite couch with her bug-eyed goggles strapped to her face. She was tinkering with a black palm-sized rectangle that looked a lot like a phone.

"Hi, Vivian!" she called.

"Hey, CieCie. What are you working on?"

Jacey answered for her. "It's Dane's Central Connect. Dumbass took off last night and left it here, which means he'll be back. CieCie is going to see if he sent any messages before he left. I'm hoping we can figure out where he went."

Intrigued, I sat beside Jacey and studied CieCie's hands as they worked. She tugged a wire from the back of the device and connected it to another.

"I assume it isn't as easy as just turning the thing on?"

Jacey chuckled. "No, definitely not. It has a retinal scanner on the front. CieCie's gonna have to hotwire the thing to bypass the security system. It'll probably be an all-day thing, though. We should just go."

"CieCie," I said, and she looked up from her work. "I could stay here with you. If you want me to."

"No!" she squealed at once. The shrill sound made me jump. "Jacey shouldn't even be going off on his own. You have to watch out for him, Vivian."

Jacey smiled warmly. "She isn't at all happy that I'm going, but I promised you'd protect me." He winked.

"Don't worry, CieCie. I'll take good care of the big dumb-dumb."

She looked like a little toothy bug as she smiled. "Thank you, Vivian. I'll message you if I find anything."

A rumble ricocheted through my stomach as Jacey and I stopped in front of one of the many rolltop doors on our way to West L-5. It was a short walk, and I was grateful when Jacey had informed me that there was a curry bar only a few minutes away, located on North L-5. A stocky man with a blue mohawk stood at the counter. His face was grease-smudged, and his many scars collected dirt and grime like gutters. The sight of him caused my stomach to curl up and hide.

"Jacey!" he boomed. His voice was just as greasy.

"Hey, Ed. How goes it?"

"Eh, you know. It's going. What'll it be?"

We left the roadside bar with two paper cups of orange curry. I admitted to myself, quite bitterly, that this curry was nowhere near as good as Dane's. *The little prick.* But it was warm and mostly edible. I tipped back the cup and finished it off in a quick swig. We tossed our cups in an overflowing roadside scrap bin without slowing our pace.

"A quick warning about Larry," Jacey cautioned.

We turned south down the L-5 alley, and I saw in the distance a red flickering sign shaped like an arm. *I loved a good pun.*

Jacey continued as we approached the arms dealer's building. "Apparently, he sounded pretty torn up when Gilroy talked to him this morning. He and Bill have been together for over thirty years. It isn't like Bill to just run off like this so Larry is likely to be a mess."

The weight of the word *together* sunk in. Poor Larry. I didn't know who Bill was, but I cursed him for not coming home last night. Hopefully, Larry would find him soon.

Jacey knocked hard on the metal door and waited under the veil of red light. His features were eerie under the crimson glow, which left deep shadows dancing in the depths of his many scars. The monster was in his element. Even with his injured arm, I couldn't help feeling untouchable beside him. He knocked again, louder this time. Still no answer.

"He must be working," Jacey muttered.

"Try opening the door," I offered.

He twisted the knob, and it creaked open. With a shrug, Jacey cautiously stepped inside. I followed, closing the door behind me with a click.

The long fluorescent bulbs above our heads flickered like strobes, flashing short glimpses of the room. It was cluttered with workbenches, toolboxes, and strange humming machines. No wonder Larry couldn't hear us knock. I surveyed the space, looking for any sign of movement.

"There!" I said, pointing to the distinct pattern of a plaid shirt that peeked from behind the workbench.

It looked like Larry was tinkering with something on the

floor. Jacey smiled at once, stepping over boxes and wires as he hurried over to the bench. I followed close behind but stumbled over the curled lip of a rug and caught myself on Jacey's shoulder.

"Sorry, Jacey. I—"

The words were stolen from me, cut free from my vocal cords. Jacey was frozen ramrod straight, blocking my body. With my hands still clenched around his shoulder, I peered around him to see what caused him to go stiff. I quickly wished I hadn't.

There on the ground lay the body of a man. He appeared and vanished, over and over with each flicker of light. Around his face pooled a black reservoir of blood. I had no time to register the scene or catalog my emotions.

The acidic burn of bile raced into my throat. I turned to the nearest scrap bin and vomited my breakfast in a painful heave. Jacey placed a hand on my back, but his eyes were still glued behind the workbench.

My chest constricted, and my stomach twisted with another sharp convulsion. *Was it the blood? The curry? The last thread of my sanity finally snapping away?* Everything came up at once, projectiling from my gut like a geyser.

Bleary-eyed and wary, I scanned the room, looking anywhere but the body. I couldn't handle another bloody corpse. It was too much. My focus bounced from machine to machine, then from box to box. I balanced my frantic mind between the objects in the room, trying to keep myself from vomiting more.

As my gaze drifted, I caught a glimpse of a framed photo on Larry's workbench. Two men were standing in suits, hand in hand. The acid returned. I heaved again before looking back at the photo, determined to understand its significance to me.

Larry was standing to the left of the portrait. And to the right, another face I recognized...

"Oh, no."

"What?" Jacey demanded.

Dread crept over me with cold claws that claimed every nerve in my body. Jacey's eyes were wide with alarm, but I couldn't speak the abominable words that I knew to be true.

A beam of light sliced the room as the door behind us opened and closed again. I braced myself against the metal scrap bin, not needing to lift my head to know who had just entered the room. Jacey's breathing increased to a rapid deathly tempo.

"What are you doing here?" he demanded.

A sharp crackle filled the air, and green light sputtered across the room. Reluctantly, I lifted my eyes—and just as I'd expected, Dane stood between us and the door.

"Vivian."

The way his teeth bit into his lip as he mouthed my name sent another convulsion through my body, but there was nothing left in my stomach. My gut painfully contracted and coiled. When I looked back to Dane, his eyes were narrowed with sharp lines of concern.

"Come here. Come stand with me."

Every syllable pounded the air from my lungs. I was frozen, deathly still, with Jacey's hand still rested on my back. His eyes were locked on Dane's weapon as it spit green bolts into the air around each blade.

"Dane," he said evenly, as one might speak to a child. "Go home. Whatever is going on with you, we can figure it out. Okay?"

"Vivian," Dane called to me again, ignoring Jacey entirely as he crooked a brow and extended his arm to me. "I'm asking you to please come here."

"Don't move, Vivian," Jacey commanded.

I couldn't move, even if I'd wanted to. Death himself was here, counting my heartbeats one by one.

Jacey held out a steadying hand. "Dane, I need you to talk to me. Tell me what's going on." He was deceptively calm, but I could see from the corner of my eye that one of his hands was drifting toward his pocket.

It was too late. Dane's watchful eyes caught the movement, blazing like the strike of a match. He thrust his blade forward in warning, sending a flash of sparks sizzling across the concrete.

"Drop that hand, Levetin. Don't think I don't see you."

Jacey obeyed, stepping forward so that his leg touched mine. "Sorry," he said, holding his hands up, and as he did, he softly kicked my boot. A silver glimmer danced somewhere below. He was trying to tell me something.

I looked down swiftly, and there at the brim of his pocket was the bottlecap, barely contained behind the denim of his jeans. *How could I grab it without Dane seeing?* I looked back up, just as another wave of vicious nausea slithered around my stomach.

"I'm sorry," Dane whispered. "Look, I'm really sorry. But this is the only way to fix everything. The only way to set the clock right. Vivian, I don't want to hurt you. I've never, ever wanted to hurt you."

I had no time to react. The convulsion passed through my spine so powerfully that I crumbled to my knees. My hands planted on the cold stone floor, and my spine retched in another dry heave as Dane continued.

"When I got that call," he whispered in his honey soft voice, "I knew my time had come. To show them I could be something more than just... just the bad kid."

The bad kid. I heard these words last night.

"Let me pick her up," Jacey interrupted.

Dane's muscles flared furiously as Jacey wrapped his arm around my torso and hauled my body to my feet. He stumbled with an intentional clumsiness, and as he did, I plucked the bottlecap from his pocket.

"Always getting in my way," Dane growled.

Now that the bottle cap was in my hand, Jacey puffed into a defensive flair. "Dane, when will you get it through your head? I'm not trying to take Vivian from you!"

"Of course not," Dane agreed. "You've taken everything else from me. Yet every time I try to take something in return, you slip out of my grasp. But you fucked up the Earth eval. This should have ended days ago."

He took a menacing step forward. The bottlecap was pressed so tight in my palm that the teeth bit into my skin.

"And ever since then, I've been pulling the strings, trying to drag you where they wanted you, but you always seem to slip away. They keep failing. They aren't good enough to finish this. But I am."

Every word collapsed my lungs, each syllable falling in domino succession. My hands trembled as I took a step toward Dane. Jacey reached to stop me, but I shrugged him away. The cards were falling into place, one by one.

"This whole time," the words trembled in midair as they left my lips, "it's been you. You were Mr. Rivera's informant."

Even after I said it, the accusation sounded absurd. Dane couldn't be the reason behind it all. My eyes were pleading, begging his expression to change. To deny these appalling allegations. But he remained fixed and steady, devouring me where I stood.

"Goddamn, Dane," Jacey shouted.

Dane's eyes ripped from mine in a malevolent snap.

"Is this because I left? You wanted to murder me...because you lost your fucking job?"

"Goddamn YOU for leaving when I needed you!" The scream was so loud, so deafeningly painful that it stole the air from my lungs. "I lost everything!" Dane's face contorted into a rabid snarl, and the ledge of his eyelid glistened red.

There was a fragment of my soul that begged me to run to him, but the tethers of fear that bound my feet were stronger. And all the while, the bees whispered in their ominous chant, *my Dane, my Dane, my Dane.*

"No," Jacey's growl was low and even. "You lost your job, Dane. It was a job. A job you didn't even want. You said it yourself. You're only here because your dad pushed you to join the military, and Channel recruiters snatched you up."

A venomous sneer crawled across Dane's face as he pulled the black hood of his jacket over his head. The action caused my chest to detonate. My heart pounded, rocketing from my chest and vibrating through my ears. Through the shadow of the hood, I watched the malice return to Dane's lips, the same lips I'd kissed just last night.

Then they parted as he whispered, "Who the fuck do you think ordered me to kill you, Jacey?"

21

CLARITY

Jacey pulled my body protectively behind his. My nightmares had spawned to life, lashing out in a terrifying illustration I'd painted so many times. The lights above flickered fiercely, casting us in blind flashes of darkness as Dane lurched forward. Cowled under the shadow of his hood, my dark cloaked figure twirled his execution device in a violent display of glowing green streaks.

"You don't want to do this!" Jacey threatened, but a heartbeat later, Dane lunged across the room with an agonizing wail.

I cinched my eyes and waited for impact. There were many ways to die here, and I'd already come close several times. Splattered in a dysfunctional elevator, stabbed by a rogue traveller, crushed by a speeding tetra, devoured by a demonic wolfish creature. If death was as sure tonight as the sky was crimson and if I were to have the power to choose my fate, I supposed that a quick death by the one I loved would certainly be a tempting option.

There was no time to file and catalog my emotions nor was there time to build answers or conclusions that might give me some semblance of closure. In a few moments, I'd be dead, afterall. And everything that lay in between that void and this moment, I wanted to fill with the one thing I was sure of—I loved Dane. Even through all these chilling revelations, I would graciously look into his swollen emerald eyes, even knowing that once mine closed, they would not reopen.

Just as I took what I'd assumed would be my final breath, a force like a wrecking ball crashed against my chest, tumbling me across the floor. Pain seared through my tangled limbs, but it wasn't the pain of a twisted blade. No, it was the pain of being thrown across the room like a sack of potatoes.

My skull throbbed, and the scene in front of me split in two, drifting in a tectonic motion until it aligned again. From my position in the corner of the room, I realized that Dane had his weapon raised above his head. Terror rushed through me as I watched it fall in a green blur that was angled directly toward Jacey's face. "No!"

The sharp clang of metal on metal echoed through the room. Orange sparks rained down in a curtain that surrounded Jacey. Above his head, his hands grasped a metal pipe that caught the sputtering blade in midair. But I could see that his weak arm was trembling under the force of Dane's weight. Still too weak to draw his own weapon, Jacey didn't stand a chance. I couldn't let this go on. With no regard for my own safety, I shot across the room.

"Get off of him!"

My voice tore Dane's attention away just long enough. Jacey thrust the pipe forward, catching Dane off balance, and clearing the way for his steel-hard leg to plant itself right into Dane's exposed ribs. The crack of the impact made me certain the fight was over.

Dane stumbled to the side, writhing in pain, and I couldn't halt the sickening pang of pity that rolled through my gut. He didn't look like a monster, not to me. At that moment, he looked like home, my safe place. A deceptive fox, dressed in the whitest of wools. And I hated the desire that willed me to run to him as he stood, doubled over and heaving in agony.

"You had enough?" Jacey's voice was a gasping bellow that thundered across the room. He was visibly exhausted, leaning against the pipe that he now held vertically to the floor.

Dane heaved a few painful breaths, vanishing then appearing over and over again with each flicker of the lights. A single red trickle trailed down his jaw, and his eyes were fixed to his boots. "I have," he hissed painfully.

In a flash of green light, he ripped forward in a furious assault. His blade moved so quickly that I could no longer make out its exact location. It existed in a blur, spitting a curtain of sparks in its wake. Caught off guard, Jacey dodged clumsily out of the path of the blades downward strike, causing Dane's weapon to collide with the concrete floor in an earsplitting clang.

"Yes, I've had enough—enough of your lies," Dane spat, pivoting again.

Jacey was already across the room. He kicked a box out of his path, creating himself a defendable piece of ground. But he was backed into a corner. I gripped the bottlecap in my palm, torn between the elaborate mask I knew and the deceitful stranger underneath.

"Enough of your patronizing." Dane side-stepped so his body was perfectly aligned with Jacey's. "And I've had enough of you."

He rushed in, twirling his blade in a wide arch before ripping a horizontal line through the darkness. If Jacey had been just an inch closer, the weapon would have found its home in his torso.

My fingers crept open, reluctant to free the manifestation of hate, anxiety, fear, loathing. Daxx was the physical embodiment of every emotion he consumed, and his time with me over the last few days was bountiful. Releasing him meant death. For any future with Dane and I. For what had been and what could be. For who I was and who I'd become. It would mark me as a murderer, a monster. And I knew that I'd never forgive myself, even if there was no other way that I'd make it out of this place alive.

My gaze shot to Jacey, begging for the right answer. I couldn't bear the weight of this decision. Not alone. In a fragment of an icy second, where his eyes were struck with more emotions than I could recognize, we connected with the force of two magnets bound by opposing poles.

The room fell away in shards, plummeting like a broken mirror to reveal a serene white space. The clean walls, the brilliant light, free of torment. In that familiar plane between the fibers of reality, we stood across from each other, equal parts torn in two.

I closed my eyes and baptized my soul, cleansing away every constraining bee in my hive. Breath like glacial winds rocketed through my lungs, clearing the tight claws that gripped my heart. When I opened my eyes, Jacey was there, too. His face was serene, and his eyes were a bottomless blue that spoke a million silent words. He nodded. A decision had been made. *Clarity.*

In a deafening roar, a raging black storm erupted from my palm. The room vanished in a cloud that seemed familiar to me yet so foreign. My hair whipped in wild tendrils, and black clouds raced around my body like a hurricane.

Between their buffering current, I could see Dane's twisted expression, stripped of the boyish charm that I loved. Beneath the mask, I could finally see the ugliness that he'd tried to hide. The sly fox in our flock, guided by the hands of Mr. Rivera's puppeteering.

Behind me, I could sense the manifestation accumulating like the belly of a swollen cloud. Gluttoned through every torment that he'd devoured from my core, it towered over me—a black shadow of a nightmare, solidifying into a long Cheshire grin that hovered just above my shoulder.

"What is that?" Dane cried out. The light in his eyes grew dimmer like a flame snuffed out in the night.

A low breathy chuckle vibrated against my jaw. This was the epicenter of it all. The mask that twisted and turned me, puppeteered by a force we'd yet to uncover. And all the same, a crime that could not go unpunished.

Daxx's milky eyes leveled with my face, starving for release.

"Vivian!" Dane pleaded through the hiss of the storm. "Vivian, I never wanted to hurt you! I wouldn't have! Damn it, Vivian! I love you!" The words rocketed into my heart, hitting their mark one by one.

Daxx hissed an anxious whisper. "The indecisssion in you. I tassssste it."

"Damn it, Viv, listen to me! With Jacey gone, we can move forward! You said it yourself, you'll never be able to go home with my dad chasing you. He's going to find you eventually, Viv. Project Katharízo didn't specify that anyone else had to die. It's Jacey he wants, not you."

I held his gaze firmly, turning his words over like a coin.

"We can go home, back to Earth. We can have a chance. You can work for Premier—the real Premier. Viv, the technology we're building, you wouldn't believe it. We're going to change Channel transportation forever! And everything can go back to normal. Better than normal because you'll have me. And your mom! Viv, you can see her again!"

My heart stilled. *Mom?* The longing in my face threatened

to betray me. Dane's eyes shone glossy and bright, tears swelling in the corners as he extended his hand to me.

"We could go tonight," he added. His voice was becoming excited, and a smile played on his lips. "Viv, just step outside for a minute. Just a minute. That's all I need."

My feet inched forward. I hadn't given them permission, but they moved by some invisible force that called to the deepest crevice of my soul. This could all be over. I could jump into Mom's arms tonight and play it all off as a bad dream.

"You're sure?" I whispered through my quivering lips. "We can go tonight?"

"Yes!" Dane smiled the honey-sweet grin that I'd grown to love. His face was open and inviting, holding the gates of freedom ajar for me. "Tonight. Right after we leave. We can be at her house in an hour. Go outside and wait. I'll only be a moment."

I placed another unsteady foot forward, and as I did, Jacey folded his arms over his chest. His eyes were narrow but calm with acceptance.

"Viviaaaan," Daxx hissed venomously, "on your vord."

I quieted him with my hand. *What was right?*

By the end of the night, I could be back in my apartment. Back with my beloved comforts. My familiar routines, my paperback books, my warm weighted blanket—and my mom. I could hold my mom in my arms and whisper away all the fear she'd surely endured over the last few nights. Dane and I could be together, and I could work for Mr. Rivera's company, doing whatever it was that they actually did. The visions called my feet forward another step.

"That's it, Viv. Go on outside. It'll all be okay."

A smile creased my lips. "I always thought you were wearing a mask," I whispered.

He smiled warmly in return, lowering his blade to his side as I continued.

"And I tried so hard to look underneath."

"Viv, I'm so sorry. I had to. Dad completely disowned me after the fiasco on dimension twenty-seven. This was the only way to—"

I silenced him with an outstretched palm, dropping my gaze to the floor. "But I realized today," I continued, "it isn't a mask at all." When I lifted my eyes, both of our smiles faded. "It's a mirror. And there's only one face reflecting out. It's always only ever been that...One. Single. Face."

"Vivian. Damn it, I'm not like him. Not Dad or Ryan. The work they are doing is important. More important than the life of one Jumper. With Jacey gone, my brother can take his place, Dad can finally make amends with The Five, and we can get off this god-forsaken cube and...and start living."

The words were fire on my spine, but I kept my expression indifferent. Ryan wasn't just Dane's brother. He was also trying to become a Jumper.

"Viviaaaaaaaan," Daxx rasped impatiently. I shook away the new information and smiled curtly.

"I think I'm ready to start living," I admitted.

The boyish smile returned to Dane's face, and his body relaxed. From behind him, I could see Jacey's arms fall to his sides. It was there on his face, as clear as the revealing light of clarity that pulled so many secrets from the dark. His face was void of anger or frustration or guilt or shame. He stood, watching me. Accepting me. Accepting my decision without question.

My whisper was an icy calm that plummeted the temperature of the room. "What you're offering me isn't a life that I'm willing to live."

I looked at Jacey, avoiding Dane's incredulous eyes. He

would have to do it. I couldn't be the one. "At your word," I mouthed. Jacey nodded in agreement.

"Christ, Vivian! Take the easy way out! Take the dog outside and wait for me!"

Dane's frantic scream sent a black fog shooting across the room. It twisted and contorted, filling the entire space and contracted into a solid black mass that solidified in front of him.

"I've been called demon," Daxx snarled, and as he did, his mouth split completely apart, held together only by a few fleshy shreds of sinew. "Devil. Monster. Voule beast, yesss."

My gaze didn't stray. I watched, unblinking as Daxx snaked around Dane's body in black successions, feasting on the fear that radiated from him.

"But dog? Only once before."

"What are you doing?" Dane screamed.

I knew he was feeling it. The pain Daxx had consumed from me, all plummeting down at once. Numb with my sober reality, I uttered quietly to myself the words that I finally understood. "Feeding my nightmare."

"Daxx," Jacey ordered, and as he did, the black swirl froze in place. The grotesque creature and Dane were eye-to-milky-white-eye, locked in the seductive dance of predator and prey. Silence permeated between us all, and the breath I held in my chest burned with searing precision that scorched my throat dry.

"You've always been my brother," Jacey whispered at last, his voice rusted with anguish. "Even when I left, I always cared for you as if you were my own blood."

Face stained in simmering hatred, Dane looked over his shoulder to where Jacey stood. "Fuck you, Jacey."

The tendrils on Daxx's hackles bristled with anticipation.

Jacey closed his eyes, and the room frosted over with doubt. *Maybe he wouldn't,* I began to tell myself.

Then those haunting blue eyes crept open, and all emotion, all brotherly love they'd once radiated was gone.

"Break him."

One by one, the lights over our heads exploded. A storm of glass rained across the room, shattering around our feet in a deafening roar. In the dying moments between light and dark, my eyes locked onto Dane's. Green, endless, bitter, cold.

I wanted to stop time for just those few fragile seconds, I wanted to stop the clock and rewind until I reached a notch in the timeline where I could put everything back as it should be. But as the final bulb shattered overhead and the emerald glisten of Dane's eyes vanished, I knew with undisputable certainty that this was the true epicenter. At this very moment —*everything had changed.*

Dane's sudden scream ripped through my spine, slicing my heart like a rusted blade. There was a revolting snap. And then, there was silence.

My vision was blurry, and my skin was cold. Jacey supported my weight as we stumbled back to Gilroy's place. Where once a lead weight rested in my chest, there was now a deep indentation, sputtering with each breath. My heart was too small to accommodate the blackhole it housed.

Daxx offered to take the disorienting grief away. I rejected the offer. I'd made this decision. Right or wrong, I wasn't sure. But I made it, nonetheless, and I needed to reconcile with the conviction.

Jacey was quiet, too. The lines in his face were deep, the circles under his eyes painted in shades of violet desolation. Neither of us made an effort to fill the silence. We allowed it to surround us as our heavy feet scraped forward, caught in the riptide that dared to pull us under. Even if we could somehow live with this choice, how would we tell Gilroy and CieCie?

A hot tear burned down my cheek. The swell started, and I refused to let it overflow. *Not yet.*

Jacey's fingers dug into my shoulder, but I could barely feel him there. My heart beat painfully slow, but I could barely feel that either. And an image—familiar and agonizing—floated through the black like a photograph caught in the breeze, beckoning my attention with all its might. And I did my very best to ignore that, too. But every few steps, it returned, mocking me from under the shadows of a black hood.

Our return to M-5 was slow. Neither Jacey nor I were in a hurry to get back home. When we did, we'd be faced with questions that we wouldn't easily be able to answer, and I'd be faced with a name that I wasn't sure I could handle hearing. *His* room would still be there—a sterile apparition of memories I'd need to forget if I ever wanted to live.

My legs grew heavier with every step closer, threatening to crumble underneath me. But Jacey's grip around my body was unrelenting. The quiver in his chest and the weight of his boots pulsed through me as we moved along. He was suffering. Like me, he was ripped in two tattered fragments. The night would be impossible to endure on our own, but with each other, maybe we could survive. I held onto that hope with both hands.

"Smoke."

The pitch of Jacey's voice was strange to me. I blinked, not understanding the meaning. His pace quickened, and I was dragged along, while forcing a glassy focus on the building ahead.

He was right. There was smoke. A lot of smoke. Cold realization crept over me.

"It's coming from Gilroy's! Run!"

No measure of speed would have carried us fast enough.

My mind was completely blank, watching unblinking as the warehouse burned from the inside. Flames lapped from the window ledges, feeding greedily on the home I'd made here. I couldn't move. I couldn't breath, not even as Jacey ripped at the handles of each of the rolltop doors or when the red hot metal sent him wheeling backward.

"Damn it!" he screamed. "Gilroy! CieCie!"

"Jacey! Got'damn it, Jacey," Gilroy's voice called out. He emerged from the corner of the warehouse with a face covered in soot.

"I can't find 'er! I can't find CieCie!"

The scene existed in a tunnel, my feet glued to the pavement. This was it. This was how it ended. I'd made my decision today, and I'd been warned of what would happen. This was my punishment. I'd chosen wrong.

From the corner of my eye, a sudden movement tore my attention away from the flames. A shimmering circle of light rippled through the dark at the opposite end of the warehouse. It shimmered like a disk, floating vertically in place but not quite solid.

A tall silhouette with golden hair strided forward from the dark alley, stopping to observe us, before stepping up to the circle. The man lifted a leg and stepped inside, as easily as if it were a door. *Was it...some sort of portal?*

"Come back here!" Jacey screamed. He took off at full speed, barreling toward the strange anomaly. As he lunged to grab its shimmering frame, the circle sputtered away, like an analog TV being turned off. In its place, an object lay glowing on the pavement.

"What is it?" I called weakly.

He picked up the item and turned it over in his hand, but his face fell at once.

"Damn it," Gilroy screamed. "Spit it out, boy!"

Jacey returned to us with his head low and held out the item—a glowing screen, with wires splayed from the back like severed veins.

"That's Dane's CC Unit!" Gilroy cried. The name sent a violent wave of pain through my spine. Gilroy ripped the device from his hand and tapped the screen. A message appeared.

To: Daniel Caufelt Rivera
From: James Caufelt Rivera
Subject: Time's up

Daniel,

Your brother has taken care of everything. Be out of the warehouse by 10 a.m. Detonation will occur at noon. Stand by for further instruction.

James C. Rivera
CEO | Advanced Transportation Technology
Earth Dimension Six | 38.5801° N—121.4960° W

Gilroy crumbled to his knees, and like the final support beam of the house I'd built around my heart, I crumbled, too. Time slowed to a somber crawl, suffocating my mind and claiming the final strands of my sanity. The flames above lapped in a muffled roar, having no wind to carry their touch. We were left frozen, damned to watch them consume the sacred place where life once blossomed.

Embers streaked across the grid-lined sky, dancing as their edges burned and leaving glowing amber trails in their wake. I watched as they cascaded, one by one, like snowflakes from a swollen cloud. But I knew better. Snowflakes were beautiful and innocent things. Their kisses were chill and playful—not like the embers that bit my tear-soaked cheeks, laying waste to the life I'd grown so fond of.

I'd been warned.

I didn't listen.

"She's gone. She's gone. She's gone." Gilroy muttered the words into the dark billow of smoke that rose from the brick shell.

Where did we go from here? How could we ever continue on? Mr. Rivera would be looking for us, and with Dane gone, I was positive that this terrible nightmare was far from over.

I looked over my shoulder, pleading for Jacey to give me the answers that I knew he could never give. Pleading for something, for anything to make this nightmare feel bearable. Because if this was all real, I had nothing left to hope for. But to my disbelief, the space behind me was empty, dotted only by the drifting flakes of falling ash.

"Jacey?" I whispered.

Gilroy lifted his head for a moment but quickly dropped it again and began to sob the tears of a man who had lost everything.

He didn't have to say a word.

I already knew—could already sense it.

Jacey had left us.

I SURVIVED BOOK ONE

Vivian's adventure
continues in...

DIATOMIC

Hungry for more?
Enjoy this exclusive sneak
preview from book two of
The Channel series.

TEXTS FROM YOUR EX

I don't imagine that death itself could have looked much bleaker or much crueler than this. An all encompassing white space seeped through my cortex, flooding my senses and removing all traces of anything tangible. Like paint to plaster, I soaked in the void, relishing in the feeling of complete oblivion until I could barely grasp a sense of self.

Nothing is what I wanted to feel.

Nothing is what I had.

Nothing was my life.

"Thisss isss not what clarity isss for," a breathy inhuman voice hissed into my ear.

"Shoosh-it, you."

"Viviaaaan, I mussst intervene."

"Daxx, I said shoosh," I snapped, grasping the small black screen in my trembling hands.

If this was my first time, maybe he wouldn't have been so anxious. Not that I really cared what my smoggy Xanax-pet had to say about anything. Even if I had cared, it wasn't enough to stop me from activating the tiny black screen in my hands as I sat cross-legged in the bottomless plane of nothingness and settled into my daily ritual.

In a burst of green light, the screen sputtered to life, and my finger glided to the "Messages" button.

"Thisss issn't healthyyy," Daxx rasped under his breath, but I didn't acknowledge his whining this time.

What could a creature made entirely of bad juju know about health?

With a slow exhale, I opened the long thread of familiar Central Connect messages and began.

To: Daniel Caufelt Rivera
From: James Caufelt Rivera
Subject: A proposition

Daniel,

I hope this message finds you well. It has come to my attention that your brother has thrown a wrench in our plans. Scratch that. *Wrench* doesn't even begin to describe what he's done. Long story short, I've placed him on temporary leave. If he messages you, please don't indulge in his delusions.

Our doe is on route to the meeting place and should arrive soon. I just want to confirm that the buck has left The Channel and is also on route. Let me know when you can.

James C. Rivera
CEO | Advanced Transportation Technology
Earth Dimension Six | 38.5801° N - 121.4960° W

To: James Caufelt Rivera
From: Daniel Caufelt Rivera
Subject: Re: A proposition

For fucks sake, Dad. Chill with the formalities. I'm your son.
Not an employee. Christ.

Anyway—yes, Daddy dear. Jacey left this morning. He seemed
convinced, but IDK. I'd prefer to not do this again, just sayin'.
Hacking a CC unit isn't exactly in my job description, and the
old man has a nose like a bloodhound.

Soooo...You gonna tell me what Ryan did? :D

Daney Boy
CEO | Naps and Booze
Nowhere Dimension | 666° N - 666° W

To: Daniel Caufelt Rivera
From: James Caufelt Rivera
Subject: Re: A proposition

Daniel,

You are, as always, a tick in my asscrack. We have code names
for a reason. Use them. And no. You can ask him yourself.

James C. Rivera
CEO | Advanced Transportation Technology
Earth Dimension Six | 38.5801° N - 121.4960° W

To: James Caufelt Rivera
From: Daniel Caufelt Rivera
Subject: Re: A proposition

Dearest Jamethy Caufelton Rivereton the Third,

Fucking gross. Don't talk about your asscrack again. Like...ever.

Thanks, Daddy.

Sweet Baby Boy
CEO | My Bedroom Enterprise
Nowhere Dimension | 666° N - 666° W

To: Ryan Race Rivera
From: Daniel Caufelt Rivera
Subject: SACK TAP!

Dad says I'm the favorite again.

Wtf did you do?

Dane the Fav
CEO | Bestest Bro-Bro Ever
Nowhere Dimension | 666° N - 666° W

To: Daniel Caufelt Rivera
From: Ryan Race Rivera
Subject: Re: SACK TAP!

It's not what I did, so much as what I keep trying to do.

This girl isn't the one. We should have picked someone else.

I'm losing my mind over here.

Ryan R. Rivera
COO | Advanced Transportation Technology
Earth Dimension Six | 38.5801° N - 121.4960° W

To: Ryan Race Rivera
From: Daniel Caufelt Rivera
Subject: Sack tap retracted

Christ man, you good?

Dane the Fav
CEO | Bestest Bro-Bro Ever
Nowhere Dimension | 666° N - 666° W

To: Daniel Caufelt Rivera
From: Ryan Race Rivera
Subject: Re: Sack tap retracted

No. I'm not. But it's done, and I really don't want to talk
about it.

Ryan R. Rivera
COO | Advanced Transportation Technology
Earth Dimension Six | 38.5801° N - 121.4960° W

To: Ryan Race Rivera
From: Daniel Caufelt Rivera
Subject: Re: Sack tap retracted

Well, you know where I'm at, if you change your mind.

I care about you, even if you are only the 2nd favorite child.

Dane the Fav
CEO | Honorary Favorite Child INC.
Nowhere Dimension | 666° N - 666° W

To: Ryan Race Rivera
From: Daniel Caufelt Rivera
Subject: FUUUUUCK

Broooo, bad news. The girl bumped into Jacey, and he saw the fucking rheotron! He's tailing her now. Said she took a cab to a bar. I haven't told Dad yet. WTF do we do?

Dane the Fav
CEO | Naps and Booze
Nowhere Dimension | 666° N - 666° W

To: Daniel Caufelt Rivera
From: Ryan Race Rivera
Subject: Re: FUUUUUCK

Son of a bitch. I'm calling her now. I'll let you know.

Ryan R. Rivera
COO | Advanced Transportation Technology
Earth Dimension Six | 38.5801° N - 121.4960° W

To: Ryan Race Rivera
From: Daniel Caufelt Rivera
Subject: Re: FUUUUUCK

DO NOT LET HER GIVE HIM THAT RHEOTRON!!

Mr. Losing-His-Cool
CEO | Naps and Booze
Nowhere Dimension | 666° N - 666° W

To: Daniel Caufelt Rivera
From: Ryan Race Rivera
Subject: Re: FUUUUUCK

Big problem. Your fuck-head roomie took the phone from her, screamed something totally unintelligible, then the line went dead. Pretty sure he knows.

Contact him immediately.

Ryan R. Rivera
COO | Advanced Transportation Technology
Earth Dimension Six | 38.5801° N - 121.4960° W

To: Ryan Race Rivera
From: Daniel Caufelt Rivera
Subject: Re: FUUUUUCK

I didn't have to. He called me.

Apparently, he rheotronned back home and wants me to meet him at J-5. He didn't say anything about the girl.

Mr. Losing-His-Cool
CEO | Naps and Booze
Nowhere Dimension | 666° N - 666° W

To: Daniel Caufelt Rivera
From: Ryan Race Rivera
Subject: Re: FUUUUUCK

Message me the moment you're with him.

I'm not saying anything to Dad until I hear from you.

Ryan R. Rivera
COO | Advanced Transportation Technology
Earth Dimension Six | 38.5801° N - 121.4960° W

To: Daniel Caufelt Rivera
From: Ryan Race Rivera
Subject: Re: FUUUUUCK

Hello??? It's been over an hour. Where the hell are you?

Ryan R. Rivera
COO | Advanced Transportation Technology
Earth Dimension Six | 38.5801° N - 121.4960° W

To: Daniel Caufelt Rivera
From: Ryan Race Rivera
Subject: Getting pissed

Dane, I swear to god, if you don't message me in the next 30 minutes, I'm portalling there.

Ryan R. Rivera
COO | Advanced Transportation Technology
Earth Dimension Six | 38.5801° N - 121.4960° W

To: Ryan Race Rivera
From: Daniel Caufelt Rivera
Subject: Re: Getting pissed

Bro, chill. I'm fine.

So is your girl btw. *Real fine.*

She told me everything. You're a dumbass.

Mr. Back-To-Cool
CEO | Definitely the favorite child
Nowhere Dimension | 666° N - 666° W

"Viv'yan? Got'damnit, are ya'll on that CC unit again?"

In the blink of an eye, the white paint oozed and dripped away into complete and total blackness. My quiet place was gone, replaced with a familiar yet much-less-comforting scene. Dim light from a patch of plutocrypes glinted from Gilroy's goggles as he stood over my still-dazed shell of a body.

Crap. Busted.

"Yeah," I fumbled, suddenly sobered with the shame of being found like this—yet again. "Sorry, I was just doing more research."

"Viv'yan, I know what yer doin," he huffed with the exasperation of a concerned father. "And I get it, I do. Ain't a day goes by that I ain't thinkin' about CieCie and Jacey—" He choked off the name as if it physically pained him to say it out loud, then shook his head dismissively before continuing. "But this...this ain't research. This here is obsession. We both been through them messages multiple times now, and there ain't nothin' in em that we 'on't already know."

With a reluctant sigh, I hopped to my feet and dusted my knees. As much as I hated to admit it, Gilroy was right. We had work to do. Sitting around stewing over past events certainly wouldn't change the horrific truth that led us here.

We had taken refuge in the blackened dimension one fiber two weeks ago, after the warehouse burned and after Jacey had...

Panic seized my chest.

Not again.

I couldn't bring myself to think of that day. Life had pummeled me in steady, violent successions ever since I'd left Earth—ever since I was ripped away from my home and my mother and everything I'd ever known or loved. The last month of my life had just been one heart-shattering tragedy after another. But Jacey leaving? No, not leaving but *abandoning* us. That hit differently.

And since that day, that dreadful, sickening day when I looked over my shoulder for comfort and only found the void of the man I'd put my faith into, an echo reverberated through every chasm of my soul.

Goddamn you for leaving when I needed you! I lost everything!

That voice.

I would give anything to forget that voice, and the way it cradled my name on honey-sweet currents that flowed through my dreams. I would give anything to forget *him*—to will him from existing in a place within my memories. And on some days, with Daxx's help, I could push him out of the forefront of my conscious awareness. I could convince myself that he wasn't important—that he never had been.

But then, there were days that I found myself crawling on my hands and knees, toward the elevator shaft where I first caught a glimpse of the demon that lived within him. As if I could rewind and say something—anything—that would change the course of events that led us here. But even now, when I passed through the threshold between the elevator doors, I only saw that creeping puddle of sticky blood.

I'd been damned. Eternally damned to skim through his conversations with Ryan, with Mr. Rivera, just hoping for a clue or an answer to the question that had replaced all the others and stood a threatening pike with my heart skewered right through its point.

"C'mon, Viv'yan," Gilroy called from a few feet ahead. Though he spoke at a normal volume, the sound thundered through the dark fiber like a sonic boom. The quiet was going to drive me mad.

"Coming!"

"And bring that dog," he added wistfully. The chill of feathery fur immediately tightened around my neck in response.

"I've been called demon—" Daxx's raspy voice began, but I cut him off at once.

"Devil, monster, anger-eating Roomba...I've heard this all before, Daxx. Save us the dramatics, will you please? I'm *soooo* not in the mood today."

His body tensed, bristling like a cactus. At one time, that response would have stifled a reaction from me. But I'd become so used to Daxx over the past few weeks that he was more like a talking feather boa than the epitome of dread.

"There are timesss, Viviaaan," he hissed, "that you truuuly pusssssh me."

I shrugged with enough force to leave him skittering for balance on my shoulders. "Right back at you, Cujo." I doubt he understood the reference, but it quieted him up, nonetheless.

On most days, I was grateful for his company, in spite of our constant jeers and bickers. If he'd truly bugged me that much, I could have kept him locked in his bottle cap like Jacey did, which was probably for the best, at the time. After Jacey bailed, telling Gilroy was necessary. How else could I have explained what happened to...

No.

Tears pooled over the brims of my eyes, and a fury of shredding claws raked through my heart.

No! Damn it, not now!

I lifted a trembling finger to my mouth and bit down hard onto my knuckle, sucking in long breaths through my teeth.

I'd been fine. Everything had been fine. Why now?

Daxx wrapped himself a little tighter around my neck but remained silent. The panic attacks were getting worse. I'd always had an anxious brain—my hive of endless voices—but the inferno that raged inside my head had reached new volumes as it burned the very last strings of my sanity, leaving behind a dusting of grief that I fought to wade through with every ounce of my dwindling strength.

I'd give anything to simply and passionately *hate him*. Hate wasn't an emotion I'd ever acquainted myself with until I arrived at The Channel, but now I latched onto it with both hands. Try as I might, his face was the stone that always evaded the river of rage, parting the current and leaving me with only the memories that I knew would destroy me if I lingered on them too long.

"You sure ya'll are gonna be alright?" Gilroy had stopped outside the elevator doors. His face strained with fatherly concern, which only upset me more.

I didn't want him to worry about me. But I also knew the way my face contorted when we approached this elevator and my breathing hitched when we reached the bottom. My best hope was to keep myself talking.

"I'll be okay," I said, pulling the silver bottle cap from my pocket and fighting the urge to run headfirst back into the blackened fiber. "Daxx, time to go."

Icy chills surged in fast spirals down the length of my arm as Daxx retreated to his summoning device. I hated locking him away, but today was the day. Any confrontation from street goers would only make this trip more unbearable.

As if that were possible.

"You ready, kid?" Gilroy asked.

"As I'll ever be." And in an ominous response, the elevator door slid open.

CAN'T GET ENOUGH?

Spend some quality time with the Author and enter exclusive merch GIVEAWAYS in the OFFICIAL Channel-Jumpers Facebook Group.

www.facebook.com/groups/channeljumpers

Listen to Charcter Playlists and Shop The Channel Merch Store!

www.explorethechannel.com

ACKNOWLEDGMENTS

I owe eternal thanks to my Granny, who left me a goodbye note before her passing in 2020 that lead me to write this insane story. Our memories of handmade ornaments and Elvis at Christmas time will live on in my heart forever.

Next, I owe many thanks to my wonderful educators. Of those, Michelle Carn, Abby Williams, Megan Sullivan, and Tim Elliot, who still follow me on Facebook to this day...for some reason.

An eons worth of gratitude to everyone who helped me make this story possible, including my beta readers, Amber and Cody. You shaped the groundworks and caught the ugliest of my mistakes before my editors ever had to deal with them.

Speaking of which, where the hell would I be without Michelle Badger of FourEyed Books and my developmental editor, Amber Morant? Thank you for editing this mess of words and helping me to turn it into a book. I'm pretty sure Michelle knows my characters even better than I do by now, and she officially holds the world record for "most consecutive read-throughs" of *The Channel*.

Lastly, I thank my wonderful family, who will likely be the only ones to read all the way through my acknowledgements. To my mom Gail, who never doubts me when I tell her about my next mountain of a goal. If I was stuck in another dimension, you bet your ass that I'd do anything and everything just to get back home for you. To my dad Steve, who was the first person to ever read the silly short stories I wrote in middle school—and actually enjoyed them! I hope this one raises the bar. To my stepdad, Jim, who actually made me do my homework as a kid and challenged me to read books that were way above my reading level. I don't know if this book would have been possible without that inspiration.

To my in-laws, Tina and Mark, who helped to keep my kiddo out of the house and occupied during many much-needed writing sessions. In a weird way, you're just as responsible for this book as I am. To my grandma Susie. I'm not sure if you'll ever read this, but I hope you do, and I hope you know how much I love you. To all of my wonderful friends, who have been impatiently awaiting the release of this book for over a year. Especially Jessica, who was the first person to ever buy merch from The Channel's webstore. I hope you cherish it just as much as CieCie cherishes her Bubba's Car Wash tee.

To my daughter, Taylor. You're too young to read this book, but I hope when you're old enough, it makes you laugh, cry, and understand why I locked myself in my office for so many nights when you were nine.

Lastly and most importantly, to my husband Marc. You've been my rock throughout this whole process. If not for your ability to come up with funny insults and crazy science fiction politics, the book would have been far less interesting. You've given me the time, strength, and courage to write the insane story that has lingered in my heart for over a year. Even if no one reads this book, I was happy to put in the time knowing that Jacey and Gilroy made you laugh out loud on multiple occasions.

And sure, maybe it's cheesy. But thank YOU. Yes, you. The reader, who picked up a strange book with a weird cover, self-published by a first time author. I hope you'll join me for the next chapter of Vivian's adventure.

ABOUT THE AUTHOR

 Starla Moore is a business coach, YouTuber, and lover of all things fantasy. After the passing of her grandmother in 2020, she put pen to paper and started writing as a way to cope. Within 12 months, she had finished her first book (*The Channel*) and immediately began planning the expansion of the series.

Aside from writing, Starla also enjoys reading #BookTok recommended YA and NA novels. In 2021, she started the *Crave the Book* podcast with her co-host Amber Marie, which explores the Crave vampire series by Tracy Wolff.

Starla lives in Ohio with her husband Marc and her daughter Taylor. She has two very fat cats named Bubbers and Toots, as well as a senior Chihuahua named Itty and a Shiba Inu named Ammy.

facebook.com/explorethechannel

instagram.com/explorethechannel

tiktok.com/@starlakmoore

CPSIA information can be obtained
at www.ICGtesting.com
Printed in the USA
LVHW040829180122
708608LV00019B/1028/J

9 798985 159516